BETRAYAL

OF

JUSTICE

MARK M. BELLO

A Zachary Blake Legal Thriller

Published by 8Grand Publications
West Bloomfield, MI 48322

Printed in the United States of America

ISBN: 978-1732447189

This book is dedicated to America, land of the free, home of the brave.

Chapter One

"My fellow Americans: I am very humbled yet emboldened by your vote to elect me as your president. I thank you for your support. I've earned your vote, and I will now embark on the task of securing your continued trust. I intend to do that by delivering on the promises I made during my very contentious campaign with Secretary Goodman. To accomplish these promises, we, the people, have to be vigilant and bold. We have to take this country in a new direction.

"This new direction starts with securing our borders. Under our current immigration system, our borders are porous, wide open for drug dealers, rapists, murderers, and terrorists to enter our country unchecked, able to move about freely to do all kinds of terrible things to law-abiding citizens. Other countries are not sending the best and brightest to our country. They are dumping 'human toxic waste,' and it is my job to clean up the mess.

"Furthermore, my ineffective predecessor has enacted recent unconstitutional restrictions on our citizens' right to bear arms through a series of illegal and unethical executive orders. These restrictions have left our citizens virtually defenseless against deadly, terrorist threats.

"My first order of business as your president will be to rescind these executive orders, restore full Second Amendment rights to our people, and encourage all of our law-abiding citizens to purchase weapons to defend against the scourge caused by our current, extremely ineffective, immigration system.

"My second order of business will be to secure our borders. No longer will drug dealers, pimps, pushers, rapists, murderers, or terrorists be able to freely enter our country through our southern border. I will build a second-to-none border defense system across our southern border, impenetrable border walls, and I will make Mexico and South America share the cost. I will do the same along our northern border. Canada will pay for our northern border defense system and help police it. If either or both refuse, we have ways of convincing them to ante up. These countries, indeed, all countries in the free and not so free world, rely on trade with the United States. We are their largest customers and trade partners. Let's see if they prefer tariffs on all goods entering the United States of America. We also provide serious aid and military support to many of these countries, and they will soon begin paying for that support or it will be terminated. There will be no free rides from the John administration.

"The third order of business will be to beef up law enforcement in this great country of ours. We will increase border security and immigration and naturalization enforcement. We will create a new federal police force within the Department of Homeland Security answerable only to its secretary and to me. This force will be the finest of its kind and will be tasked with protecting our citizens from foreign interests seeking to destroy our country and our citizens.

"We will make America beautiful again. We will modernize our airports. We have the worst airports. Third world countries have better airports than we do. We will make our country's airports the biggest, brightest, most technologically advanced, and beautiful airports in the world. We will repair and replace our crumbling roads and bridges. Our crumbling infrastructure will be replaced using state-of-the-art equipment manufactured right here in the good ole USA.

"We will put America back to work again, as these tasks will be performed by American-born workers. Advanced technology systems will require workers with twenty-first-century advanced technological skills. In with the new, out with the old, I say. Our natural resources will once again take center stage in the global economy. No more political correctness in energy production. We will put people back to work in Pennsylvania and West Virginia and produce energy for our people at a fraction of the current cost. How will we do this? By producing energy right here in America and curtailing our dependence upon foreign sources, especially those sources that sponsor terror. We will focus on price and American pride rather than the junk science and political correctness, which has driven up the cost of our energy and ignores resources we can mine for-profit and supply to all corners of the globe. It is high time for America to assume its rightful role as a global energy leader.

"Finally, we will round up and deport all of those who have entered into and remain in this great country illegally—round them up and toss them out. I have no use for criminals, and these illegal immigrants are a huge part of the criminal element that makes all of us law-abiding citizens less safe in this country.

"We will combat terrorism and the global terrorist threat by taking the war to the shores of the terrorists and by banning all current and future immigration from any country I deem to be a sponsor of terrorists and terrorist activity. And, we will create jobs by assembling and training the best and the brightest national immigration and deportation force in the world. We will beef up federal, state, and local law enforcement departments, which will create more law enforcement jobs, manpower necessary to tackle the problems of local, state, national, and international crime. It is time to prioritize safety in this country. We will be the law and order capital of the world.

"We will make America safe again. We will make America strong again. We will put America first again. We will make America secure again. We will make America prosperous again. We will make America *pure* again. With your help and God's will, we will succeed in making America a shining city on a hill once again. Thank you . . ."

Chapter Two

". . . God bless you, and God Bless the United States of America."

Arya Khan watched the Ronald John acceptance speech again and again on her laptop. Who was he talking to? She had been glued to the national television news stations for months, watching every report she could. She was fixated on social media and reviewed real news, false news, or *any* news she could find that would help her understand the issues and calm her fears that this man could actually become the President of the United States.

She tried to provide reasonable commentary when an article permitted comment. She engaged her friends and fellow students in thoughtful conversation. The polls seemed to favor Secretary Goodman, a decent, inclusive politician whose campaign slogan was "We are one America." The polls, as Arya had feared, were dead wrong.

The campaign battle was waged along racial and ethnic battle lines. John seemed to be the candidate of white Christians who, he claimed, were being shoved aside by politically correct politicians seeking to promote the rights of minority interests. The 'minority interest' that bore the brunt of the new president's rage was the Muslim population. Throughout the campaign, he referred to terrorism as "Islamic." He vowed to stop the flow of Muslims into the country and to "weed out" those Muslim criminals who were already here.

But whom was he talking about? Not Arya and her family? She was born in the United States. She was an American citizen. Her parents were naturalized citizens and as loyal to the United States as any Christian person. Weren't they all endowed by the Constitution with the same rights and privileges as Ronald John? Didn't she have the right to life, liberty, and the pursuit of happiness? Could this evil man make good on these promises?

Arya *was* an American citizen, born in Dearborn, Michigan, the daughter of devoted parents who fled war-torn Yemen in the mid-1960s for a better way of life in America. Arya's parents worked hard to establish roots in the multi-cultural Dearborn community. They owned and operated a popular local fruit market, purchased and built from the ground up with the sparse remnants of family money earned in the old country.

Arya's ancestors fled Northern Yemen at a time when the small Middle Eastern country was involved in a series of conflicts with Egypt and then-President Gamal Abdel-Nasser. Nasser sought regime change in Yemen as far back as 1957. In 1962, he offered the Free Yemen Movement financial support, office space, and airtime on the radio in an effort to bring about the change he sought. Nasser's prestige took a severe hit as the result of his falling out with Syria and the dissolution of his UAR (United Arab Republic). He sent expedition forces into Yemen, concluding a quick victory might assist him in regaining a leadership role in the region.

A quick victory was not achieved, and the country became embroiled in a war waged on multiple fronts, involving several governments, and political and geographic interests. By the middle of 1965, approximately 15,000 Egyptian men and 40,000 Yemenis were dead, and Egypt was facing a financial crisis.

Despite billions in foreign debt, Nasser implemented his "long-breath strategy." He planned to reduce troop size from 70,000 to 40,000, withdraw from the east and the north where his positions were more exposed, and concentrate on two particular border areas. The United States threatened to revoke some or all of a multi-million-dollar food and infrastructure aid package, and, still, Nasser refused to pull his troops out of Yemen. He vowed to stay in Yemen for twenty years if he had to. The twenty years never happened. Significant economic and political pressure prompted Nasser to negotiate a treaty in 1967 and Nasser withdrew his troops.

In 1966, multiple gas bombings were reported, along with numerous injuries and fatalities. The most significant attack occurred in their own village, Kitaf, where gas attacks caused 270 casualties and 140 deaths. Arya's family was safely in America by then, embarking on a new life in the land of the free.

The family settled in Dearborn, home to the largest population of Arabs in the United States. The city's Arab community has been growing for at least a century, a growth that accelerated simultaneously with the Detroit area automobile industry.

Henry Ford, in the early and mid-twentieth century, recruited thousands of Middle Easterners to Dearborn to work at Ford's mammoth River Rouge plant. Contrary to the stereotype, many of those who fled the Middle East for a better life in the United States were not Arab, they were Iraqi Christians, Chaldeans, fleeing Muslim persecution. Dearborn, however, seems to be one place where Muslims and Christians have been able to live and thrive in harmony, peace, and prosperity.

The community has certainly not been without conflict and controversy. Orville Hubbard was Dearborn's most famous and longest-serving mayor. He served from the early 1940s to the late 1970s and embraced segregation. In 1985, a man named Michael Guido won the mayoral election in Dearborn after mailing pamphlets to constituents promising to address the city's 'Arab problem.'

A few decades before, the introduction of bilingual education was controversial, as were halal options in school cafeterias and the sight of traditional headscarves on Muslim women. Not so today, however, as the city, informally known as the Arab and Muslim capital of the United States, has elected its first Arab-American city council president and added its first Arab-American chief of police. Dearborn is the home of the largest mosque in the country, and a third of its population is of Arabic descent. Its crime statistics and its average annual citizen income figures are slightly less than the state median.

In the midst of all of this local peace and harmony, a man named Ronald John was now the President-elect of the United States. He campaigned on a platform that promised to "rid America of the Muslim scourge." *What does this mean?* Arya pondered. *Does this man seriously intend to engage in the process of deporting all Muslims, whether here legally or illegally, whether citizens or non-citizens? Isn't that unconstitutional?* Arya Khan was inspirited and . . . terrified.

Chapter Three

". . . God bless you, and God bless the United States of America."

Keith Blackwell and some bigoted friends were assembled at a local pool hall listening to the new president's acceptance speech. Keith hung on every word. He was pumped, tired of writing hate blogs, and ready for action. When the address was over, Blackwell stood at attention, saluted, and shouted aloud at the television. "God bless you, Mr. President!" The John victory was a victory for all white nationalists. "Make America pure again? Hell yeah!" he and his friends cheered.

Keith remembered election night. He and most of his buddies were gathered at the same pool hall for an election night party. Contrary to popular belief, Keith was convinced Ronald John was going to shock the world and win the election. The men drank heavily, shot some pool, and talked about how great the country would be if a like-minded white patriot became president of the United States.

"The Republican Party needs a fuckin' wake-up call. They're a bunch of pussies," Keith addressed no one in particular.

"Shit, man—there's no Republican Party anymore. Until RonJohn, the Party was just a more moderate wing of the Democratic socialists," cried one of Keith's buddies.

"Fuck yeah, man," Keith bellowed. "When RonJohn wins, *we* will be the face of the Republican Party. How cool will that be? Those so-called conservatives in Washington will owe *us,* big time."

"Blood and soil, baby! Blood and soil," shouted another, guzzling a brew.

"All these politically correct left-wing shitheads tell us this is a great country because of its diversity. This country was great before black and brown people arrived. The mistake was bringing them here in the first place.

"We built this fuckin' country, and they pollute it with their in-breeding and white hate. Make America Pure Again? Hell yeah," Keith shrieked. His buddies held out their beer bottles, pumped their fists, and chanted 'hell yeah,' several times.

"Remember watching television with your parents? Little House on the Prairie, Beaver Cleaver, Father Knows Best, Brady Bunch, Happy Days, fine white family shows with white Christian morals. You know what I mean? Today, Jews own the media and show shit on TV that's against God—races mixing, inbreeding, faggots raising kids, Jew comedy, a bunch of crap. You can't watch television anymore. I want to see a white, civil society, where white rights count, and there's none of this garbage polluting my children's minds."

Keith belched loudly. He leaned into the pool table and declared, "eight ball in the corner." He pointed with his stick and calmly sunk the shot. He held out his hand, and a long hair scraggly dude begrudgingly slapped a twenty into his palm.

"Double or nothing." Scraggly Dude demanded.

"Rack'em," Keith pointed at the table, one eye glancing at the huge flat-screen television screen over the bar. "Fuck, yes!" He cried. "RonJohn just won Michigan!"

"Holy shit!" shouted Scraggly Dude. "I never thought it was possible!"

"Oh, ye of little faith. Ronald John is going to shake up the world, and we will too! America is fed up living all mixed together—hasn't worked out too fucking well, has it? Black Lives Matter march in the streets while the camel jockeys declare jihad. Nips build nukes and ship us poisoned goods. Kikes control the media and lie to fucking everyone. Let them all go back where they came from.

"What they promote will lead to the disappearance of our people. This is *our* country. White Christian people built it, we made it great, and we're taking the fucker back!" Keith cried, tears rolling down his cheeks. Everyone cheered and toasted again.

Scraggly dude shot the white ball into the rack. He wanted his money back.

"All John needs is Pennsylvania, and he wins! This is getting serious," shouted the like-minded bartender. "I can't believe this shit."

"Another doubter," Keith scowled, shaking his head from side to side. "I should have bet the election with you dickheads. I would have won a fucking fortune," he declared. "White power, baby! When this is over, instead of all this politically correct diversity bullshit, we are going to reclaim this country's white identity! Make America pure again! White is might!"

The group cheered and raised glasses. "Quiet—sssssshhhhh." Keith suddenly and frantically began to wave his hands. He put a finger to his lips and pointed at the television. "They're about to call Pennsylvania."

The Fox News reporter stared into the camera. "We have a projection in Pennsylvania, folks. I hope you're sitting down. Ronald John has won Pennsylvania! According to my electoral vote calculations, Ronald John will soon be declared the next president of the United States, woo-hoo!" The reporter pumped his fist up and down

The bar broke out in raucous joy. Keith Blackwell climbed up on a barstool, steadied himself, and stood at attention before the large-screen television. He saluted and shouted. "God bless you, Mr. President!" He began to wave his arms, orchestra style, and led all bar patrons in an off-key, drunken rendition of "God Bless America." The television they were watching was a Samsung, manufactured in South Korea by people these men often referred to as "short, dangerous, yellow nips," a fact which escaped their narrow minds.

Keith Blackwell was born in Howell, Michigan. He was the grandson of a former Ku Klux Klansman who preached white supremacy to his family until it became the family creed. Young Keith was taught, early and often, to hate those who caused "impurity" in the white race. His mother abused drugs at an early age and struggled with various forms of addiction throughout Keith's entire life. In fact, she was abusing drugs while she was pregnant with Keith. She and Keith's dad were huge bigots. She hated blacks, Jews, Asians, Muslims, Hispanics, and anybody else who wasn't white and Christian. She spent her free time getting high and stepping out on her husband at all hours of the day and night. Why the two of them stayed married all of those years was a mystery to Keith.

Keith was a rambunctious little boy. His parents were not churchgoers, but Keith found comfort in the Bible and attended church, most often on his own. He attended Bible school, posed many questions, and was often dissatisfied with the minister's answers. *If there is no Christ in your life, your life isn't worth living. You can't embrace others or "love thy neighbor" if thy neighbor does not accept Christ as their savior.*

He was much worse than a simple bigot. He believed in white Christian supremacy and became increasingly disenchanted with a church that preached love and tolerance of other races and creeds. *Today's church is bullshit—there are other ways to worship, other ways to live.*

Eventually, Keith joined a white supremacist cult, a faction of the Neo-Nazis, a group he would soon fully embrace. This was his calling. He received a message from God to 'terminate impurity' in the world, and he embraced this mandate. He needed a base of operations, a place to develop his termination skills.

At age 18, Keith was caught shoplifting high-end electronics at the local Wal-Mart store. He was taken down to police headquarters, processed, fingerprinted, and charged with larceny over $1,000, a felony. His court-appointed attorney negotiated a plea deal. Keith could face felony charges, or he could enlist in the US armed forces division of his choosing. If he did so, the charges would be reduced to a misdemeanor, and his service to his country would serve as his probationary period.

Keith wanted the charges dropped or, in the alternative, wanted a complete expunging of his record at some point in the future. The local prosecutor would not budge off the original offer. Keith was guilty and had little choice but to accept the deal. Besides, he expected nothing good from a corrupt criminal justice system. The charge would stay on his record, and his fingerprints and DNA would remain in the criminal database. *If I keep my nose clean, what do I have to worry about?*

Keith enlisted in the United States Army and spent significant time in Southeast Asia. This was his first exposure to Asians who, he decided and later wrote, were "vastly inferior to white people." As such, "they should not be immigrating to the United States and impregnating our women."

During Operation Desert Storm, his unit was stationed in Bagdad, where he had his first encounter with Muslim Arabs. Keith questioned the United States' role in the Middle East, was determined to survive the war, and start a movement to undermine American involvement in Middle Eastern affairs. Using the pen name Nomo Islam, he wrote a blistering anti-Muslim manifesto entitled "Why Does America Assist Terrorist Countries?"

After receiving his honorable discharge, he returned home to Howell a hero. He sought, but could not obtain, suitable employment. Minorities or, as Blackwell so rudely called them: Niggers, Spics, Kikes, Camel Jockeys, Chinks, and Nips, snatched up all of the good jobs whites used to do. One day, after applying for and being denied a job at a Dearborn assembly plant, Keith wandered into the local office of The Conservative Council, or TCC, as it was known. He showed its leaders his manifesto, and his white supremacist future was cemented. He moved to Dearborn, developed a website called "USA 1Pure," and posted his manifesto as its initial blog posting.

The post went viral, and Keith became a household name in the local supremacist movement. He publicly advocated for the destruction of Holocaust memorials worldwide and suggested replacing them with Hitler monuments. He argued blacks are, by nature, violent people, and could never live in harmony with white people. He suggested blacks should embrace slavery and return to their roots as a subservient society. He also continued his blistering attack on the Muslim community.

President Ronald John's call for the mass deportation of Muslims was music to Keith's ears, and Keith immediately embraced and supported the John campaign. He raised hundreds of thousands of dollars in campaign funds and was thrilled to discover the money was accepted by the campaign and put to good use. He became an ardent John supporter. He attended John rallies, carried Make America Pure Again signs, clashed with liberal demonstrators, and wrote article after article attacking Secretary Goodman as a "kike" whose broad agenda for America would cost real Americans jobs by the thousands.

"It is high time for real Americans to take back this country."

When John won his first primary, Blackwell wrote: "Ronald John is the man! He will be the Republican nominee, mark my words. When he receives the Republican nomination, he will, almost certainly, beat the liberal Jew, because white people everywhere will finally be able to vote for someone who represents our issues and interests."

John was certainly not a traditional candidate. RonJohn, as his closest friends and supporters liked to refer to him, degraded women. He nicknamed his opponent "Frail Allison" because she once became ill on the campaign trail and "lacked the balls" to be president. He denounced Muslims as "terrorists," proposed barring Muslim immigration, surveillance of mosques, and suggested a database to keep track of all Muslims living in the United States. He referred to blacks as "hopeless people with nothing to lose by voting Republican for a change." To John, Mexicans were "pimps, pushers, rapists, and murderers." He promised to build a huge barrier along the southern border to prevent these "sullied elements" from entering our great country. Keith Blackwell cheered at every one of these statements.

Unlike most elections, where words matter and are used against a candidate who preaches bigotry and hatred, none of this horrible rhetoric stuck to John, at least not in a negative way. He narrowly won the Electoral College contest despite losing the popular vote to Secretary Goodman. Blackwell sang in praise of John's many bigoted statements and promised undying support to "our exalted, supreme leader." Keith was pumped, tired of writing, and ready for action.

Chapter Four

". . . God bless you, and God bless the United States of America."

Zachary Blake and Jennifer Tracey watched the president-elect's acceptance speech with appropriate trepidation. Zack was Jewish, and Jennifer was Catholic. They met when Zack handled her case against the priest who sexually abused her two young sons, Kenny and Jake Tracey. The legal battle against the priest, the church, and the clandestine organization that tried to cover up the priest's current and previous predatory activity was legendary in Detroit area legal circles.

The case made Zack famous and quite wealthy. His law practice was booming, and he was in constant demand as a television "talking head" on all things legal. Life was good. But, the best part of the good life he found for himself was his relationship with Jennifer and her two boys. Zack and Jennifer were now a couple, and he had a solid, almost father-son relationship with her two boys. He was in love, hopefully, for the last time in his life. Soon, the couple would be husband and wife.

When he agreed to represent Jennifer and her sons, Blake was teetering on alcoholism, bankruptcy, and disbarment. He was handling two-bit court assignments and traffic tickets and screwing them up. Jennifer's telephone call, visit to his office, and retention of his services to handle her case began a career renaissance. When Jennifer inexplicably stuck with him after he tried to sell her out, he returned to his former glory as a highly successful trial lawyer and became the family's champion. Love soon followed.

The multi-state investigation, the discovery of a vast church conspiracy to cover up the crimes of predator priests, and the eventual multi-million-dollar verdict and settlement changed all of their lives. Zack found success and love after a series of personal and career failures, most of which were self-induced. Jennifer found love and reestablished faith after her husband died in a tragic accident, and the church she relied on for comfort and support betrayed her boys in a vile manner. The boys were referred to a caring psychiatrist who helped them heal. The success of the case provided them with the vindication they needed to move forward as young men. The prospect of a second 'father,' Zachary Blake, was the icing on the cake.

Zack's professional success provided him with certain freedoms. He could hire the finest secretaries, paralegals, and lawyers money could buy. He could travel the world while others did the grunt work. He could handle the cases he wanted, the cream of the crop. He could participate in social justice causes, those near and dear to his heart. He was free to handle pro-bono cases where impoverished people needed superior legal services but couldn't afford to pay for them.

He contributed large sums of money to charities, especially those that promoted justice for the less fortunate, the injured, the disabled, and the downtrodden. He donated his time and money to state and local justice associations. His favorite was the Michigan Association for Justice, which fought against multiple Michigan legislators seeking to curtail rights guaranteed by the 7th Amendment of the United States Constitution.

Zack contributed to local, state, and national political campaigns, but only if the candidate cared about 'his people' and about justice and equality. Jennifer, after her litigation experience with the church, was fully supportive of Zack's David vs. Goliath battle with powerful anti-justice forces. They were a team when it came to contributions to those who promoted justice for all.

Both Zack and Jennifer contributed considerable money and time to the Allison Goodman campaign for President. They hosted fundraisers, attended events and rallies, lobbied friends, family, colleagues, and anyone else who would listen. Goodman's loss to someone they considered to be an anti-justice bigot felt like a gut punch to both of them. They were sick to their stomachs. They sat together on the couch in the great room of Zack's beautiful Bloomfield Hills home, watching polls declaring Goodman ahead, early votes trickling in that supported those polls and later election results that turned a promising night into a nail-biting horror show. When it was over, Goodman won the popular vote, but John won the decisive Electoral College and the presidency. Gerrymandering played a prominent role in the shocking result.

As John finished his speech, Zack couldn't help but wonder how a country that had been served by a brilliant and inclusive president for eight years now chose to elect a narcissistic, xenophobic, homophobic, Islamophobic, anti-Semitic racist with no experience in government. He vowed to keep an open mind, to judge Ronald John on his deeds in office rather than the offensive words he'd uttered amid a hard-fought, bitter campaign. But he would be watching this president. Rumored cabinet appointees were white men of dubious character and large pockets. The ages of individual Supreme Court Justices were of significant concern to Zack, as were the nominations President John would make if these elderly Supreme Court Justices retired or passed away.

Zack smiled to himself and wished the justices good health and long life. He would fight this president with all of his resources and skills if Ronald John conducted the country's affairs as distastefully as he did his recent campaign. RonJohn be forewarned: Zachary Blake, kick-ass attorney at law, was watching him.

Chapter Five

The Mosque of America in Dearborn was the largest mosque in the United States. Its Imam, Baqir Ghaffari, was a recognized authority on Islamic theology and law. He was preparing to deliver the traditional Friday sermon, the *Khutbah,* to his worshipers. He was concerned. Ramadan, the ninth holy month of the Islamic calendar, was near, and Ghaffari feared some type of attack was imminent. President Ronald John was sworn in two months earlier and began to deliver on his campaign pledge to purge America of people who were, in his view, Islamic terrorist influences. To Ghaffari, this pledge was code for the unconstitutional stereotyping of all things Muslim.

Ghaffari was sure President John and his followers wanted to isolate, round up, oppress, and ultimately rid—deport—all Muslims from the American continent. Furthermore, whether the new president was serious or not, many of his followers believed in this cause. If the president did not follow through on this oft-delivered campaign pledge, his alt-right followers might attempt to illegally deliver it in his stead.

Ghaffari stood and gazed at his congregation. The atmosphere was tense, and a feeling of impending danger rose in him. He was positive those in attendance sensed the hostile atmosphere surrounding their community. There was not much he or anyone could do other than to devote themselves to higher callings, to be messengers of peace and understanding for all. He rose and began to address his followers.

"My friends, the American Muslim community is in turmoil. The 'land of the free' does not seem to apply to Muslims these days. We begin to question our leaders; indeed, we begin to question ourselves. What does it mean to be Muslim in America in the twenty-first century? So today, we ask: Why are we Muslim, and how do we achieve freedom?

"The answer, of course, is all praise is due to Allah. He guides us. We seek protection and assistance from him. If we need forgiveness, we ask it of him. If we are guilty of bad deeds

or victims of our own evil, if we are otherwise led astray, we
seek refuge in him. There is no god but Allah, and Muhammad is
his messenger, his servant. He who accepts them as his guide has
earned the victory in all he tries to accomplish.

"Are you Muslim simply because you were born into a
Muslim family? Are things that simple? This may be true; this
may be your truth. But being Muslim is more than that, is it not?
There should be *pride* in being a Muslim. We should *want* it and
want it *badly*. If we were not born into a Muslim family, would
we still be Muslim? Would we *want* to be?

"Islam recognizes freedom of choice. We choose to be
Muslim. We choose to worship and love Allah. Islam, as a matter
of fact, means we voluntarily submit to or accept his will. We are
a peaceful lot. Islam derives from the word *Salam*, which means
'peace.' Those who perform acts of peace are *Mu-salaam* or the
short version, 'Muslims.' Allah and only Allah will hold us
accountable in the next life for our actions and choices made in
this one. He has proven this to us by sending us his messengers,
men like Adam and Ibrahim, Noah, Moses, Jesus, and lastly, and
most importantly, Muhammad. All have preached the same
message, and this is the accepted Muslim position: There is only
one true god worthy of worship, Allah.

"Islam recognizes the body has a limited time on this earth.
While the body originates from the earth, the soul emanates from
Allah. It does not die. We must nurture a healthy soul. We must
worship, obey, and remember the greatness of Allah. We must
honor him through our thoughts, our prayers, and our good
deeds. Only then do we find *Salam*.

"And what of life's purpose? Why are we here? Where are
we to go from here? Can Islam answer these age-old questions? I
strongly believe it can. We have all sought answers to these
questions. We have different goals in life, different solutions. But
whose answers are correct?

"Many believe the accumulation of wealth is life's purpose.
But what would life's purpose be *after* wealth is accumulated?
What if we are *born* into wealth? Would that mean life had no
meaning? The definition of wealth is different for different
people. It is different for different age groups. To a child, it

might be a favorite toy. To a teenager, it might be a fancy sports car. To an adult, it might be a nice home or prestige in his community. To a senior citizen, it might mean good health or long life, for who among us would trade good health or long life for money? Again, we turn to Islam, to our faith, for the answer.

"Islam teaches us the meaning of life, its purpose, is *Ibadah*, the worship of the one true god, Allah. In Islam, life is a temporary vessel in which an individual displays his worthiness for a wonderful afterlife. Life and death are accepted as a mere beginning, not as the end. There shall be a day of judgment, and each and every one of us will be rewarded or punished, as the case may be, by their faith, deeds, efforts, and accomplishments during our short stays on this earth. Life is a test, a final exam, and the dedicated and faithful pass the exam, while the wicked and aimless fail. Death is merely a waiting place until the day of Allah's holy judgment. Reward or punishment is Allah's decision alone. Our own actions on this earth will dictate our fate in the afterlife; will the afterlife be spent in splendor or purgatory?

"We must remember we are created by Allah *Ad Dunyah,* to spend limited time in this world. We all know if we live, we must eventually die and be buried. We also know our time in the grave can be painful or pleasing, depending upon the life we lived on earth and the positive or negative choices we made. We know we will be resurrected on the Day of Judgment by Allah, and acquiring power or wealth or engaging in the depravity of sex, alcohol, drugs, or gambling will not benefit us one iota on that day or in the afterlife.

"Where we go after we die is up to Allah, in His infinite wisdom. But it is also up to us how we honor him, worship him, and commit ourselves to his holy word. Where are we going? What will happen? No one knows for sure, but we can find comfort and assurance in obedience to Allah. The meaning of life, indeed, our very salvation in the afterlife is tied, absolutely, to that obedience.

"Now, I wish to say a few words about current affairs. I do not, typically, discuss politics or world affairs in my *Khutbah*. However, these are challenging times for us all. Certain forces, led by our newly elected President, have declared war on Islam. This declaration is based on the misguided notion all Muslims are the same, and all Muslims are dangerous. Nothing could be further from the truth. The truth is there are peace-loving Muslims all over the world who live in fear of jihadists and, because of these jihadists, must also live in fear of their non-Muslim brothers and sisters. Why? It is because all Muslims are stereotyped as jihadists. Sadly, many of our non-Muslim brothers and sisters have responded to the rhetoric of Ronald John.

"Peace-loving Muslims must make their presence known, despite the risks to themselves. They must speak out against terrorism, against jihad, against oppression, bigotry, and isolation. They must forge relationships with peace-loving non-Muslims and form a new community dedicated to peace, harmony, and brotherhood. We must learn to live together, to celebrate our ethnic and religious differences. Freedom to worship is an essential cornerstone of our democracy, the grand experiment that is America.

"An important factor that has made this the place where immigrants desire to settle is the freedom to be who we are, while others are free to be who they are, without persecution, in this wonderful melting pot, this community of diversity we call America. If America fails to be that place one day, I do not want that failure to be on the shoulders of the American Muslim community. I want us to rise above hatred and bigotry. I want us to seek out brothers and sisters from other cultures, creeds, and religions and find common ground, despite our differences. If someone treats us violently, we must treat him with fellowship, love, and peace. If those worthy efforts fail, if the great American experiment fails, it will be because others, not Muslims, did not want it badly enough. It will be because they did not understand their own creed that all men are created equal; all men are entitled to peace, love, and the pursuit of happiness.

"America does not need to be made 'pure' again, at least, not in the context President John invokes. America's purity exists not in the isolation of its diverse people, but in the embracing of all people as one, dedicated to the proposition, as the Declaration of Independence states, that all are created equal. This is why I am a member of the Interfaith Council here in the Detroit area. The council works to forge bonds, to promote mutual understanding and respect for people of various faiths. I have established lasting friendships with religious leaders of different faiths, seeking to appreciate all we hold sacred, while at the same time extending hospitality and providing wise leadership as we try to tackle the pressing issues that threaten our democracy.

"America is already pure. We do not need Ronald John or his followers to make it so. Almost 50 years following his death, the words of Martin Luther King Jr. are as appropriate today as they were then and are as fitting to us as to Christians.

"I know we, as a people, will get to the Promised Land. And so, I am happy tonight. I'm not worried about anything. I do not fear any man! Mine eyes have seen the glory of the coming of Allah. *As-salamu Alaykum.*"

Two days after delivering this *Khutbah*, these beautiful words of peace and salvation, a Muslim girl, a member of the mosque, had her hijab, the traditional headscarf, set afire by a man who, witnesses described, was a white man in his late 30s with an athletic build, tall, unkempt, with a swastika tattooed on his forearm. The young woman was victimized because she refused to remove her hijab as ordered by her attacker. Immediately after the attack, the man escaped into an alley hidden by the darkness.

The woman was spared serious injury because of the heroic efforts of some young neighborhood men who witnessed the incident and smothered the fire before significant damage could be done. The 'lucky' young lady suffered some singed hair and minor scalp burns. She was treated and released at Oakwood Hospital.

Dearborn police promised an investigation, but the Dearborn Muslim community was dubious. Many members of the Dearborn Police Department supported the new president, who promised to be a 'law and order' president. President John promised a criminal roundup of people from countries that were principal sponsors of terror, which was music to the ears of the predominately white police force. A community spokesman called the incident a hate crime and called on the police and the

FBI to conduct a vigorous investigation. But few in the Muslim community expected law enforcement to do so, especially since the woman was not seriously injured.

One week later, a 19-year-old Muslim woman was accosted while seated on a bench outside the Fairlane Town Center Mall. The victim was on a meal break from her evening shift job and was seeking to enjoy her dinner in a quiet setting. She was wearing a burqa.

As she stood to return to work, a man in his late 30s approached her and shouted: "If you are going to live in America, dress like an American!" He grabbed the bottom of the burqa and attempted to rip it off of her. She resisted and tried to pull away. He pulled her toward him, and as she whirled around, the young woman took a punch to the face. Infuriated and terrified, she began hitting the man and scratching at his face. He was wearing a long-sleeved sweatshirt, but she thought she saw the end of a tattoo on his wrist.

The frustrated perpetrator, after checking his face for blood, called the young woman an Isis sympathizer, reached into his pocket, and snarled, "I'm going to kill you, bitch."

At that moment, the mall doors opened. Several shoppers heard a commotion and poured out to see what was going on. The man fled, on foot, into the night. The shaken 19-year-old observed a lighter in the man's shirt pocket. Police officers arrived on the scene, as did reporters who received a tip from a witness. After questioning the terrified teenager and other shoppers, the only statement made by police to reporters was, "This guy was trying to scare her—we don't think he intended to hurt her." According to press reports, the police were 'investigating.'

The following week, the mosque was firebombed. Someone threw a Molotov cocktail through a sanctuary window while people were praying inside. The fire spread rapidly, and people scattered in terror, trampling upon others while racing for the exits to safety. The mosque suffered significant damage. A few worshippers were seriously injured during the stampede, but none had life-threatening injuries. Many people were treated for injuries related to being stepped on as worshippers rushed to

escape the inferno. Others were treated for minor burns and
smoke inhalation. Witnesses observed a white male, mid-30s,
with tattoos on his arms and a scratch on his face, running from
the scene.

Again, the Dearborn Police promised to investigate. The
Bureau of Alcohol, Tobacco, Firearms and Explosives (ATF)
became involved, and the community allowed itself to dream
justice might prevail. Would city and federal officials finally take
these incidents seriously?

Arya Khan followed the three events and promised herself
she would carefully monitor the so-called investigations. Arya
did not hold out much hope any of the incidents would be taken
seriously or investigated vigorously. In reviewing the accounts of
the events, she wondered whether the police were considering
the possibility the same suspect was involved in all of them. She
focused her attention on the eyewitness accounts: In the hijab
incident, a well-built white male in his late 30s, with a tattooed
swastika on his arm, was seen running to and disappearing into a
dark alley. In the mall incident, a man, identified as white and
late 30s, attacked another young Muslim woman because of the
outfit she wore. The man may have had a tattoo and was
scratched in the face by the victim. In the mosque firebombing,
witnesses saw a white male in his mid-30s with tattoos on his
arms and a scratch on his face running from the scene.

Arya was confident the same man committed all three
crimes. All involved a mid to late 30s white man with a tattooed
arm or arms. All involved fire and, in all cases, the man escaped
on foot into the night. These factors were too similar to be
ignored. Were the police considering them? Would they consider
them if the victims were Caucasian, not Muslim? "How many
late 30s white men with arm tattoos and facial scratches live in
this area?" she wondered aloud.

*These are hate crimes. This man is a terrorist. Am I the only
one seeing this? Why is it, when the Muslim community is
targeted, the perpetrators are not called terrorists, but when a
Muslim perpetrates a similar offense against a white citizen, he
or she is branded a terrorist? Isn't this a distinction without a
difference? Why the double standard?*

Arya was raised to be a responsible citizen. Her parents believed and taught her a person deserved respect from his or her fellow citizens regardless of race, creed, color, or religion. They preached respect for the law and respect for law enforcement officers. But they also encouraged her to stand up for herself and her fellow Muslims, to be a strong, independent, Muslim-American woman. They encouraged Arya to be outspoken on behalf of her community and vigilant in protecting it. They admired Allison Goodman, and often repeated a line from one of her speeches:

"If you see something, say something. If something seems out of whack, it probably is out of whack."

Arya had serious doubts about the police. Would they take the crimes and the investigation into them seriously? She decided to let things play out and see whether the perpetrator would be brought to justice. She studied criminal justice in school. If the police chose to do nothing, perhaps she would spearhead or conduct her own investigation. The Dearborn Muslim community needed to be free of this terrorist. The sacred mosque was severely damaged, and two young Muslim women were victims of terrorist attacks. Arya had an obligation to her community.

Chapter Six

Keith Blackwell arrived home relatively unscathed. He parked his 2013 Chevy Silverado truck in the driveway. The large vehicle was in desperate need of a wash, covered in soot. He stepped into his modest house, removed his mud-stained boots, walked through the living room and into the bathroom, and studied himself in the mirror. He noticed his blue, checkered lumberjack wool shirt was torn, and a piece of material was missing, but he thought nothing of it. He checked a large burn mark on his arm and re-checked the facial scratches he'd suffered from the previous assault.

He removed his filthy clothes, walked to the shower, and turned on the water, feeling the cascading water with his right hand until it turned to a comfortable level of hot. He stepped in and stood under the relaxing warmth of the shower water. He winced as hot water hit the burn mark and scratch on his face.

No big deal, he thought. *Delivering a strong message is worth a little pain.* He was quite proud of his recent accomplishments. Many talked the talk of white supremacy, but few had the guts to walk the walk. Keith was unique—he walked the walk. He was now being talked about. *These foreign invaders will think twice about flaunting these ridiculous costumes on our American streets.*

Keith considered himself a disciple of David Lane, a 1980s white supremacist and member of a terrorist group known as *The Order*. Lane coined a slogan that became known as the *14 Words*:

"We must secure the existence of our people and a future for white children."

These fourteen words embody what may be the most popular white supremacist catchphrase in the country. Many, including Keith, wear a '14' tattoo, prominently placed on their bodies. Never mind Lane was tried, convicted, and sentenced to 190 years in prison for racketeering, conspiracy, and violating the civil rights of a Jewish talk radio host, murdered in 1984. Lane spent the rest of his life in an Indiana prison and died there in 2007.

Keith believed, as did Lane, the white race was doomed to extinction if it continued on its present path. He believed other races craved white women, and those non-whites were spreading their seed and destroying the purity of the white race. Television aggrandized equality of the races and depicted mixed-race relationships as acceptable, even preferred. Keith no longer watched traditional cable or broadcast television for that reason.

White women did not appreciate the sacrifices white men have made on their behalf. They were willing to give themselves to anyone. Who could blame them? It wasn't their fault. It was the white man's fault for permitting integration, changing laws to improve race relations (whatever that meant), and for opening the doors of white society, the precious borders of this country, to minority and foreign interests.

The time to stop the nonsense came when the towers fell at the hands of the camel jockeys. It was time to stand up or face white extinction in the white homeland that we fought so hard to settle. America needed to rebuild the homeland and fight to defend its borders. American men needed to shape up and maintain healthy lifestyles; stop drinking beer and smoking grass. They needed to stop doing drugs and join the fight to save our society from the infiltrators. Whites needed to stop marrying out of their race and stop being out-procreated by other races, creeds, and religions. Birth rate trends favoring non-whites had to be reversed.

Keith and like-minded citizens supported and were energized by the campaign and election of Ronald John. He and they determined the country must rid itself of Muslims, blacks, Jews, and other non-pure races and religions. These supporters often carried 'We Don't Need Them' signs, and this simple slogan became their consistent campaign war cry. Keith and his ilk believed it was imperative for America to embrace a pure society, the heritage of the white, Christian, Euro-American, and assimilate to its own culture.

The recent presidential election was a call to action for Keith Blackwell. Three strikes in two weeks was a good start. Keith stepped out of the shower, dried himself with the nearest towel, and stood, again, peering at his naked physique in the mirror, flexing a bit as he studied himself. *This is just the beginning. They haven't seen anything yet!*

***

Ronald John made many promises on the campaign trail. What he became most identified with was his promise to "rid America of the Muslim terrorist scourge." Less than three months into his presidency, he issued a series of executive orders banning all immigration from certain Middle Eastern countries.

One of the listed countries was Yemen. Now, the new president was implementing a process of systematic, likely unconstitutional, deportation of Muslims who were already here legally. He didn't intend to discriminate. Whether a Muslim was in the country legally or illegally, whether they were citizens or not, John believed the Constitution permitted the expulsion of enemy combatants to the United States, and the President of the United States had the constitutional power to label someone an enemy combatant. His rhetoric and policies were reminiscent of the 1950s, Senator Joseph McCarthy, and his House Un-American Activities Committee. Anti-John protesters were already making vivid comparisons between McCarthy and the new president.

To Ronald John, comparisons to or parallels with McCarthy were misguided, a diversionary tactic to stall his post-election mission. This was a real crisis. Muslim extremists threatened our American way of life. Anti-American Islamic terrorism was on the rise, and the president promised all pure Americans he would put an abrupt end to terror. There was no room in our great country for anyone even suspected of being an Islamic terrorist. The president's closest advisors tried to convince him he needed a stated reason to deport someone. Being Muslim would not be enough, they warned. John promised to take their advice under advisement.

Chapter Seven

Jack Dylan was a grizzled veteran of the Dearborn Police Department. He was born in Detroit, but his family moved to Dearborn Heights after 1967 and Detroit's well-publicized, summertime riots. The city landscape changed drastically after that summer. White people fled the city for the suburbs in droves.

Jack attended Catholic school and went to high school at Dearborn Divine Child High School. His parents were not wealthy. Jack worked his way through high school and began taking and paying for college-level courses at Wayne State University in Detroit. He enrolled in an entry-level criminal justice course at Wayne and loved the class, deciding, then and there, to major in criminal justice. Despite his parents' objections and concern for his safety, Jack chose to study to become a police officer.

While still in the criminal justice program at Wayne State, Jack applied for and was awarded a paid internship at a large detective agency. He excelled in the program and was the only intern at the agency to be offered part-time work and tuition assistance.

After two years at Wayne State, he transferred to the University of Michigan–Dearborn and completed his degree in Criminal Justice. He continued to work his way up the ladder at the detective agency and was offered full-time employment, but he was passionate about public service.

He discussed the issue with his boss, told him how he felt, and thanked him for all he did for him. The boss, a veteran private detective and former cop who worked with many police departments in the city, told him to follow his dreams and fulfill his destiny. He told Jack how proud he was to have worked with him and to have mentored him. The agency's investment in Jack would be repaid by Jack's success in the public sector. Jack promised not to be a stranger and, wherever he landed, to be of service to the agency, if at all possible.

Jack entered the Wayne County Regional Police Training Academy and graduated with the highest marks in its history. He rapidly advanced in the department, going from patrolman to detective to chief of detectives in record time. He became the youngest chief of detectives in Dearborn police history, answerable only to the chief of police.

He was assigned to investigate the recent rash of criminal activity against the Dearborn Muslim community. His first moves were to assemble a task force of dependable Dearborn detectives of different skills and ethnicity and to call a press conference. In his initial statements to the small assembly of local reporters, Jack hit all the right notes:

"In response to recent attacks upon Dearborn residents, we want to assure all of our citizens we intend to protect you, and we will do all we can to deter those who would threaten harm or do harm to any of our people. We will aggressively investigate and bring to justice anyone who threatens violence or perpetrates harm in our city, regardless of what neighborhoods they come from. The Dearborn Police has worked diligently to develop and maintain a positive relationship with and respect for our diverse community. We will not tolerate violent behavior of any kind or from any source. We condemn, in the strongest possible terms, acts of terrorism, and that is how we view these recent attacks. They are acts of terrorism, pure and simple. We condemn such acts from wherever they originate, and we will bring the full force of the law down upon anyone who is proven to participate in terrorist activities of any kind.

"Over the years, there have been similar crimes across the country. These have not been limited to the Muslim community. Churches and synagogues have been vandalized, torched, sometimes destroyed. Citizens have been attacked for a variety of reasons, not necessarily limited to their ethnicity. When these incidents have involved white Christian churches, community reaction has been shock and outrage. Community members would ask or comment:

'How can someone do this to a church, a place of worship?' or, 'I feel like someone came into my home and violated my own place.' So, why is there less concern when these cowardly incidents are perpetrated against Dearborn's Muslim community? Where is the sense of outrage for our Muslim neighbors, Dearborn citizens all? Should we not feel the same sense of violation and shock even though these worshipers pray to a different version of God than we do?

"I have been a cop for a lot of years, and I have encountered many despicable people and horrifying acts. I have learned, for instance, crime and destruction know no religious or ethnic boundaries. Recently, especially in our town, these crimes have been directed at people of the Muslim faith, but these crimes are not much different than those perpetrated at other times in other places.

"When I visited the mosque and surveyed the damage, I thought of those other places, those other circumstances, and other times. A building is damaged, but a church, synagogue, or mosque is more than just a building. It is a place of worship. It is more than mere brick, mortar, drywall, glass, wood, steel, fixtures, and other building materials.

The congregation is still intact, even though the building suffered damage. It is a faith-based community, much like yours and mine, regardless of ethnic or religious persuasion. It is a collection of believers, like-minded people who come together to worship and pray. My message to the person or persons who did this: You can burn buildings, even destroy them. You can attack people who are, perhaps, weaker than you. But you cannot destroy faith. You cannot destroy resolve.

"This community of faith, with the assistance of the inter-faith community of Dearborn and the greater Detroit Metropolitan community, will rebuild this beloved house of worship. I call upon all communities of faith to lend their assistance. On behalf of the Dearborn Police Department, I am announcing the formation of a special task force that will stop at nothing to bring the person or persons behind these attacks to justice.

"Behind me are some of the finest officers in the Dearborn Police Department. To my right is Asher Granger, one of the finest forensic criminologists in our department, indeed, in our country. Next to him is Noah Thompson, a world-class expert in

cybercrimes. To my left is Shaheed Ali, our expert on Muslim
affairs, customs, and religious or cultural matters. Detective
Lieutenant Ali will act as a cultural liaison between the Dearborn
Police and the local and extended tri-county Muslim community.

"I make this pledge, here and now. These fine officers,
together with the entire Dearborn Police community, will solve
these crimes. I call on all citizens, all members of the law
enforcement community, state, federal, and local, to help us hunt
down the perpetrator or perpetrators. Together our citizens, our
religious leaders, our police officers, and our public officials will
bring them to justice. We will gather evidence, find them, arrest
them, prosecute them, and lock them up. I will now take
questions."

"Yes," came a female voice from the crowd. Dylan scanned
the room for a raised hand and found Nancy Strauss from the
Detroit Free Press.

"Ms. Strauss?" Dylan called.

"Have you developed any leads to any suspects in any of the
incidents that have occurred since the election?" Strauss
inquired.

"No," Jack admitted. "It is very early in the investigation. We
don't know whether these are the actions of one individual, a
small number of individuals, or many. We are asking for the
public's help. If you know anything, please come forward. If you
see something or hear anything about these heinous acts, please
contact . . ."

Keith Blackwell sat in a reclining chair in his living room
with a beer snuggled in his hand, his arm resting on the arm of
the chair and his feet up on the recliner. He was physically fit
and usually quite disciplined when it came to nutrition, but he
believed he earned *this* celebratory beer. He took a large swig,
savored it, belched, and snickered as he watched the press
conference.

While some criminals may be uncomfortable with their
actions, Blackwell was quite proud of his. He was well aware
that criminals, when suspected and questioned by the police
about the crimes for which they are accused, often display signs
of nervousness. They fidget or fuss, bite their nails, or look the

other way when questioned. Keith Blackwell would do none of those things.

If Keith were brought in for questioning, one of two things would happen. He would deny any involvement without hesitation or thought and make use of the many alibi witnesses he had at his disposal, believers in the cause, all. Or, he would proudly admit his crime, do time, and pass the torch on to the next willing soldier in the battle for white supremacy. Quietly, as he watched Dylan promise to "come for him," he decided on a course of defiance. He would outsmart any interrogator, best any investigator, and thwart any attempt to stop him from defeating his sworn enemy.

Arya Khan also watched the press conference, with skepticism. Typically, the FBI investigated hate-crimes, those motivated by racial, religious, gender, sexual orientation, or other prejudice. She couldn't count on a branch of the federal government whose leader considered deporting people despite their status as law-abiding US citizens. In Arya's view, the newly elected president was himself engaged in systemic hate crimes against Muslim Americans. His Muslim deportation program, especially as it applied to American Citizens, was illegal and unethical. She hoped the Constitution and the court system would combine to stop these illegal and deplorable policies.

When she found out Dylan was appointed lead investigator in the recent incidents involving the Muslim community, she searched his pedigree online. She discovered he had a ninety percent solve rate and was a highly decorated detective in the Dearborn Police Department. She was impressed to read he was the youngest person ever appointed chief of detectives. Watching his demeanor and listening to his words of warning to the perpetrator, part of her conscience experienced a moment of buoyancy, cautious optimism justice would prevail, and the perpetrator would be apprehended.

She was also pleased that one of the task force members was Muslim and would act as a liaison between her and her community. She was counting on open dialogue and exchange of information with his office. However, Arya's more stoic side doubted Dylan, Ali, or anyone else in the Dearborn law enforcement community would seriously investigate crimes against the East Dearborn Muslim population. She considered the possibility this was simply one more Dearborn cop giving lip service to and pacifying the oft-terrorized constituency of Dearborn Muslim citizens.

If the shoe were on the other foot, if a Muslim were terrorizing an Anglo citizen, Dylan would stop at nothing to locate and punish the perpetrator. But did guys like Dylan care about her people? Or did he believe, like many others, the victims had it coming? Arya compared the situation to a rape accusation by someone who was sexually promiscuous. *She was asking for it, wasn't she?* In this case, *Muslims were asking for it, weren't they?* The more she listened and thought about justice for her people, the more she felt she needed to take justice into her own hands.

Chapter Eight

While Jack Dylan was unaware of Arya Khan and her opinion of the Dearborn Police Department, he was quite aware of anti-police sentiment in the Dearborn Muslim community. *No, he thought, I am being unfair. They are not anti-police. They are suspicious we are biased against Muslims when it comes to crimes and controversies between Muslims and white citizens.* He was determined to get to the bottom of the recent attacks and bring the perpetrator to justice. The chief gave him a long leash and permitted him to assemble a task force of three very experienced detectives to investigate.

Asher Granger was a former ATF investigator. He was the only member of the task force who was not born and raised in the metropolitan Detroit area or in Dearborn. Granger was born in Virginia to wealthy parents. He attended private schools through high school and rarely interacted with anyone who wasn't rich, white, or Christian. He did very well in school, and upon graduating high school with honors, applied to and was accepted by Yale University. Asher entered Yale's criminal justice program, intending to eventually go to law school. But, law school was not in the cards.

Quite accidentally, Asher took a course in criminology and quickly became infatuated with the *science* of crime. He followed that class with a forensic science class, and the die was cast. Asher discovered criminal justice was directly associated with law enforcement, crime detection, detention of criminals, prosecution, and punishment. A criminologist, on the other hand, studied the anatomy of a crime, its causes, costs, and consequences. The criminologist studied behaviors and backgrounds of criminals, as well as their sociological trends and tendencies.

While there are many components to this specialty, Asher was fascinated by and focused his studies on crime scene investigation, criminal profiling, evidence collection, autopsies, and interrogation techniques. Psychological behavior patterns, socioeconomic indicators, and environmental factors that lead to criminal activity were of particular interest to him. He was highly intelligent, dedicated to learning, and had an excellent aptitude for mathematics and statistics, essential attributes for anyone seeking a career in criminology.

Asher was too inquisitive to stop at a mere bachelor's degree. He entered a master's program in forensic science at Yale's graduate school, where he studied and developed techniques in crime scene processing, anatomy, organic chemistry, pathophysiology, physical evidence gathering and evaluation, genetics, biochemistry, physics, toxicology, and body fluid/DNA analysis. He received his master's degree in forensic science and completed his doctorate in crime scene processing, specifically related to arson and fire science.

Upon graduation, he applied for an internship with the Department of Justice at the Virginia regional office of the ATF. He took the 27-week basic training program and breezed through with flying colors. He impressed everyone in power at Virginia regional, and its director offered him a position as a senior agent as soon as he completed the training course. Asher was the only person to ever be offered a senior agency position directly out of basic training.

Asher Granger found his calling as a fire investigator and was a rising star at the ATF. He especially enjoyed crime scene investigation and forensics and was able to analyze the most complex situations and solve crimes with the minutia of evidence. His work with toxicology and DNA was legendary at the bureau. His favorite part of the job was done alone in the lab, outside of the public eye. Asher was dedicated, analytical, and deeply devoted to the science of evaluating forensic evidence.

Granger preferred to be called "Ash" because, as he often remarked, with a sly smile, it was a terrific name for a fire investigator. Due to his enjoyment of high-profile cases and his relaxed, charming manner, Granger was tapped as the agent in charge of public relations and media correspondence. Perhaps he was too comfortable and too charming.

The first chink in his armor was an extramarital affair with an assistant. An ensuing scandal and bitter divorce followed. The

final derailment of his once-promising ATF career was a
mysterious 'spat' with a superior officer. That matter was closed,
under seal, but was serious enough to lead to his ouster, by
resignation.

Eager to get away from Virginia, Ash saw a job posting for a
fire investigator at the Dearborn Police Department. It was quite
a comedown in rank and salary, but at least he was still an expert
fire investigator. Despite Granger's status as the new guy, Jack
Dylan decided to put the newbie in charge of the forensic
investigation of the mosque firebombing. Apparently, Jack was
extremely impressed with Granger's resume and work ethic.

Noah Thompson looked and behaved like a teenage nerd. He
had long, unkempt hair and the makings of the beard of someone
who barely started shaving. In other words, Noah couldn't grow
anything but peach fuzz. Nonetheless, he chose not to shave. He
was thin as a rail. Any mother would want to cook him a good
meal. Noah looked like he was 14, maybe 15 years old, but looks
were deceiving. He was not a teenager. He recently celebrated
his 29th birthday and was the youngest senior detective in
Dearborn police history. Cybercrimes was a new department in
Dearborn, and Noah was its chief. While it was unusual someone
so young would become a department chief, it was unheard of
that a former criminal was awarded the position.

Eleven years earlier, shortly after his 18th birthday, Noah
was found guilty of hacking into the local cable company
website and stealing cable television. His theft included all
premium, pay-per-view, and pornographic sites on the system.
He confided—bragged is more like it—to a friend that he was
enjoying free cable services, and the friend demanded that he get
hooked up to free service as well. Failure to do so, warned this
friend, would result in an anonymous call to the cable company
or the authorities. Young Noah seriously misjudged the level of
friendship and resolve in this individual and refused to do the
hack. Hacking cable for your own benefit was one thing. Doing
it for others had a detrimental effect on commerce and the
livelihood of those who owned, managed, and worked in the
cable television industry. Noah was a cyber-crook with scruples
and a conscience. To Noah's surprise, the friend turned him in.

One day, acting upon a tip and with search and seizure warrants in tow, local officials blasted into Noah's house and confiscated his black box cable theft device. Noah was tried, convicted, and sentenced to 18 months in the county jail. He thought his young life was ruined because of a minor lapse in judgment and a turncoat of a friend. But a visit from Jack Dylan changed his life. Dylan heard about the crime and understood the expertise necessary for such a feat.

Thus, Jack came away very impressed with Noah's talent. The only questions Dylan needed answered were the likelihood of Noah becoming a repeat offender and his potential interest in using his remarkable skills for the public good rather than petty crime. Jack decided to offer Noah probation, the opportunity of an early release, a subsidized police academy education, a commutation of sentence, and, over time, a total expunging of his record, in exchange for Noah utilizing his superior cyber talent for the public good.

As young and immature as Noah was, he was not stupid. He viewed cable theft, indeed, cybercrime in general, as a victimless crime. He stole online services he couldn't afford. Who did that hurt? With an education and a career, he didn't need to steal these things. He could afford to pay for them, yes? This was a no-brainer decision. He accepted Jack's offer and never looked back. Now, 11 years later, Noah set up the cybercrime division, solved numerous crimes, saved Dearborn companies millions of dollars in hack preventions, sent numerous hackers to jail, and became the youngest division chief in Dearborn history.

Appointing Noah to the task force investigating the recent attacks on Muslim citizens was an easy decision for Jack Dylan. Dylan was rather confident, given the description of the suspect and the nature of the crime, the perpetrator was someone who would brag about his exploits online, especially on the dark web. Thompson was the best at flushing out websites, postings, comments, or statements made on the dark web between the various hate groups and individual champions of hate. If anything related to these crimes hit the Internet, Noah Thompson would see it and flush out those responsible.

Shaheed Ali was Jack's specialist in all things Muslim. Shaheed was born in East Dearborn and was a lifelong Dearborn resident. He was 35 years old and the director of Muslim citizen relations for the Dearborn Police Department. His parents immigrated to the United States from Yemen, five years apart, in the late 1970s and early 1980s.

His mother came to the country first, with no money and no belongings. Distant relatives in the community housed her and attempted to assist her husband, Shaheed's father, in immigrating to the United States, as well. Shaheed's mother worked in a distant cousin's fruit market. She worked very hard for very little money and managed to impress her employer. In gratitude and as a reward for her loyalty and dedication, he used his own money to help expedite the entry of Shaheed's father into the United States. When the couple was finally reunited, Shaheed was the result, exactly nine months later.

Shaheed went to public school, and, as he grew up, he experienced incidents of anti-Muslim prejudice from classmates and other Dearborn citizens. He excelled in school, despite the prejudice of some ignorant fools, and made friends with fellow Muslims and many white Christians as well. His favorite subject was American history. Shaheed loved his country and learning how it became the multi-cultural melting pot it is today. He especially enjoyed reading about the Civil War, Abraham Lincoln, the abolishment of slavery, the civil rights movement, the Supreme Court's brave rulings that ended double standards in America, Martin Luther King Jr., JFK, LBJ, and The Civil Rights Act of 1964.

He understood the struggle to get to a place where all men are created equal. He could not understand why, in the twenty-first century, Muslims were reliving many of the experiences of early African Americans in the south. He decided to make a difference in his own community. When Shaheed graduated from high school, he chose to attend the University of Michigan–Dearborn. Like Jack Dylan, he majored in Criminal Justice and graduated with honors.

Jack Dylan knew budding talent when he saw it. Because of a growing Muslim population and some stubborn anti-Muslim

sentiment in Dearborn's white communities, Jack decided the
department needed someone to act as a liaison between the
Muslim community, the white, predominately Christian
community, and the extended black community—a small number
in Dearborn—but a considerable part of the Metropolitan Detroit
community.

Shaheed applied for a job with the Dearborn Police
Department directly after he graduated from college. Jack
ignored his inexperience and tapped him to head the new
Department of Muslim Affairs. While there were some
rumblings amongst the more veteran officers, especially some of
the Muslim officers, Shaheed, as he had all of his life, won them
over with his magnetic personality, wit, intelligence, and
excellent communication, organizational, and management skills.
Within a few short years, everyone forgot how young and
inexperienced he was and realized Shaheed Ali was born for this
position. Jack, with his appointments of Shaheed and Noah to
their respective positions as department heads and as members of
the newly formed task force, was thought of as somewhat of a
talent-finding genius in Dearborn police circles.

In appointing Shaheed to the task force, Jack was sensitive to
the anti-Muslim bias accusation the Dearborn Police Department
often had to deal with. Shaheed was his bridge to that community
and his poster child for the falsehood of those accusations. Still,
he and the department had a long way to go to earn the trust and
cooperation of the East Dearborn Muslim community. That
cooperation and trust were vital components of this investigation.
While he was concerned about the negative view Muslims had of
the Dearborn Police, Jack was required to do his job and follow
his instincts, regardless of whose feelings might be hurt or who
might wrongly determine Jack to be an anti-Muslim bigot.

With his instincts intact, Jack determined he could not rule
out, despite the description of the suspect, the bombing was
planned and carried out by someone within the community who
had an ax to grind with the Imam or other mosque or Muslim
officials. Conversely, also true to those sharp instincts, Jack
reasoned Shaheed's knowledge of and ties to the Muslim
community could be used to flush out whether anyone fitting the

description of the suspect had a previous disagreement, words, or encounter of any kind with any member of the mosque or the Muslim community at large.

Chapter Nine

The day after he was appointed to the task force, Ash Granger arrived at the mosque, which was surrounded by yellow crime scene tape and guarded 24/7 by at least one member of the Dearborn Police Department. *A case of too little, too late,* thought Ash. Soon, he and his fellow crime scene investigators were examining every square inch of the mosque, sifting through the rubble, with a particular focus at and near the site of the explosion.

Ash focused on the fact the firebombing was one of three recent crimes against East Dearborn Muslims. He was looking for a pattern of criminal activity. What day of the week were the crimes committed? What hour of the day? Was there any consistency at all? He made a mental note to discuss the days and hours of the other two crimes with his fellow task force members. He knew an attack would come, but he did not expect one this early in the year.

It is difficult to start and sustain a fire in an open sanctuary. As Asher closely observed a colleague sifting through the rubble, he noticed several prayer books and small pieces of wood were piled up in an area hidden from view, near an emergency exit toward the front of the mosque. This was obviously the most severely damaged section of the mosque and the area where the firebomb had entered through the window. Apparently, the perpetrator previously broke in and stacked these items in an area where they would not be too noticeable. This guy knew what he was doing. He did not wish to start the fire when the building was empty. He didn't care whether the building burned down or not. He was not after the building; he wanted to terrorize the people inside and, perhaps, set a few of them on fire. This was clearly a hate crime.

By concentrating combustible material in a single location, he could generate more flame and increased heat intensity. When fire, heat, and smoke combine, the generated smoke becomes "super-heated." It rises, then banks down and builds up.

Experienced investigators compare this phenomenon to filling a swimming pool upside down. The various combustibles inside the mosque are different temperatures when set afire. Relatively quickly, all become ignitable and, over time, become the same temperature as the intense heat and smoke engulf them. This helps to sustain an intense burn. The perpetrator was hopeful the fire would trap at least one person, and, hopefully, many people.

Ash peered out a blown-out window facing the main street. A black pickup drove by. Had he seen this vehicle before? *Didn't this same truck pass by a few minutes ago? What was it? A Ranger? A Silverado?* He tried to remember the nuances of the vehicle. Did he notice a manufacturer's logo? *Yes! What was it?* He closed his eyes and pictured the passing vehicle in his mind. In a moment of intense concentration, a Chevrolet logo came into view. The car was a black Chevrolet Silverado with a red pinstripe along the passenger side. Again, he made a mental note to discuss this vehicle with his fellow task force members. This vehicle and the various witness descriptions of the suspect were the first real clues in the new investigation. The reports were somewhat consistent. The truck was a new development and probably meaningless.

As various members of his team carefully sifted through the rubble, leaving no stone unturned, Ash exited the building through the front entrance, followed by a small group of exterior evidence collectors. They wandered around the perimeter of the structure along the west wall, moving from the front of the mosque to the back, along the sidewall on the left side of the mosque if one is facing the front of the building. They came to the spot where the window was broken by the firebomb. The mosque property was beautifully landscaped with a lush lawn and colorful shrubbery. Ash noticed an area where the shrubs were slightly trampled and moved the subject shrub aside. There in the surrounding topsoil, he observed a deep print. It looked like a footprint of some sort, a boot about size 9 or 10.

Ash was piqued. Footwear impressions were new and convincing evidence tools. The science of comparing these impressions with the footwear of a suspect was now used to solve many cases at ATF. Appropriate techniques of crime scene preservation and chain of custody were crucial in obtaining the necessary impressions. Ash called over his best crime scene process guru, Eric Burns, another great name for a fire investigator, and told him what he found. Eric wasn't an expert at securing boot impressions, but Ash was. He stayed on the scene, gently and professionally providing detailed instruction as Eric engaged in the delicate task of securing the impression.

The science and scope have two main components, recovery, which includes the preservation of the prints, and identification, the science of matching the recovered impression to a suspect's footwear. Ash and Eric were now engaged in the first component. A successful matching process would hopefully take place at a later time.

The fact the suspect may have left a footwear impression was exciting for another reason. Where there was a footwear impression, there might be other forensic evidence. Ash and Eric were not content with merely securing the impression. They knew wherever the suspect stepped, he might have unconsciously deposited other evidence as well. Hair or clothing fibers might be present. He might have cut himself and left blood on the broken glass or left scratch marks on the side of the building. All of these were as good as eyewitness testimony, better, in fact, because physical evidence does not get confused, make mistakes in identification, forget names or faces, or give perjured testimony. The only possible attack against this type of evidence is in how it is collected and whether there was human error in its collection or interpretation. Thus, Ash and Eric handled the scene with precision and care. If they could collect, preserve, and match this foot impression to a suspect's footwear, they could prove the suspect was likely to have stood at the spot where the impression was collected. That plus other pieces of evidence could be the key to a conviction.

"Every contact leaves its trace," recalled Ash out loud from his forensic science classes at Yale. *Who said that?* He tried to remember and was surprised he couldn't. *I'm getting old. Perhaps it will come to me.*

The theory, coined by Edmond Locard at the beginning of the twentieth century, is still used effectively in evaluating physical evidence. Criminals have to begin and end their crime scene journey somewhere. They cannot fly, so there should be some trace of footwear, somewhere. Today's criminal is much more informed, much more cunning than yesterday's criminal was. Television shows like *CSI* have seen to that. Thus, criminals might wear masks to avoid witness identification or gloves to avoid leaving fingerprints. It is almost as easy to conceal footwear impressions as it is to conceal fingerprints, but few criminals think to do so.

The most recurring event that leads to the destruction or inaccuracy of footwear impression evidence is improper securing of the evidence or a contaminated crime scene. Conversely, if the evidence is properly collected and preserved by a skilled crime scene investigator, and that evidence is professionally matched to a suspect's footwear, it can become a valuable tool leading to the arrest, trial, and conviction of a suspect.

Luckily, the only person to travel over to the spot where the impression was found was Asher Granger. As the first officer on the scene, it was his job to determine how wide an area to secure for the investigation, and whether there was any site contamination. He and his fellow techs could find no evidence of anyone else having stood upon, entered or exited at that precise location. Further, there were no weather issues. It hadn't rained in a while, and the print was quite obvious and undisturbed. The person who left the impression made no apparent attempt to cover his tracks.

The only questions remaining were whether the impression could be successfully collected, photographed, cast into a court-admissible impression, and matched to a particular shoe and specific suspect and whether there was any other physical evidence linking a potential suspect to the crime. If collected and preserved correctly, footwear evidence might provide shoe or boot type, make, and size, as well as wear pattern and direction of travel of the suspect.

Ash and his team marked off an additional perimeter with yellow crime scene tape. He made sure the perimeter was wide enough to include any and all impressions that may have been made leading to or from the area where the boot impression was found in the shrubbery near the broken window. The crime scene tape meant no one but the appropriate crime scene investigators were permitted to enter, and no one did.

This was an extraordinary step since the entire Mosque was already taped off following the incident, but Ash was taking no chances. He decided he and Eric would be the only investigators allowed to collect and process evidence in and around the location of the footprint. Both of them were careful not to leave their own footwear impressions anywhere in and around the secured area. However, if they did leave an impression, the protocol required them to note it and eliminate it as their own through the evidence collection process. They also charted a restricted, focused route to minimize that possibility. Utilizing that route, they began, in tandem, to search, survey, process, document, and photograph the entire scene.

Eric spotted and processed a piece of flannel that looked to have come from a shirt of some type. A rust-colored substance, probably blood, was soaked into the material. He retrieved the piece and deposited it into a small plastic bag that was then placed into an envelope and sealed for submission to the lab. Eric was hoping for a blood match in the national DNA database. He further hoped after a suspect was identified and the police obtained and executed a search warrant of the suspect's residence, the rest of the garment could be found, and fibers collected and compared to result in a positive match, further incriminating that suspect.

Eric and Ash searched the area very carefully. They tagged and bagged glass fragments they hoped would yield DNA or partial prints. They located another boot print that looked to be a counterpart to the one found near the shrubbery and marked its spot as they had the other. They now had right and left boots. Eric photographed both impressions numerous times from multiple angles and distances. He then proceeded to cast them.

A cast is a three-dimensional structure that essentially reproduces the footwear. The purpose of the cast is to secure the impression in case inclement weather or some other circumstance destroys the evidence. Notes and photographs were used to document the position of the markings and the area surrounding their location. This is important in determining the suspect's direction of travel. An interior search might produce similar corroborating evidence. In the past, plaster of Paris was the material of choice in casting footprints. Modern crime scene techs now used dental stone, which has proven to be much stronger, more durable, and harder than plaster of Paris. It can also be cleaned with appropriate cleaning solutions and suffer no loss of surface erosion.

Casting is crucial because it provides a pseudo-duplicate mold of the original impression and duplicates the actual size. It also captures the characteristics of the shoe or boot's sole, which cannot be reproduced in a mere photograph. Eric carefully followed appropriate guidelines for mixing and pouring the dental stone solution. After completing the procedure, he left the cast to set for at least a half-hour and repeated the process on the second impression. When he finished his work on the second one, the first was ready to lift.

He placed a knife along the perimeter of the cast and stuck it directly into the ground and under the cast while gently prying in an upward motion. Soon, the cast began to break free, and he was able to remove it from the surface. He had previously prepared packaging to transport the cast and carefully placed the cast into the package for transport. Again, he repeated the procedure for the second impression to prevent breakage during transport.

The ultimate objective was to produce two casts that were usable and admissible in court. Both Eric and Asher were considered to be experts in crime scene investigation and had been previously qualified by their education, personal experience, and testimonial ability. They would have no problem qualifying as expert witnesses in this case, when and if the time came for them to testify as to the procedures used to secure and preserve the evidence.

On the inside of the mosque, evidence technicians found a charred rag doused in some type of ignitable fluid. They carefully tagged and bagged the item, hoping the lab could use fingerprint powder and lifting tape to secure fingerprints or other evidence from its surface. They repeated the procedure over and over on broken glass, debris, and other paraphernalia in the hope of lifting fingerprints or DNA from the various surfaces. One team concentrated exclusively upon the area where wood material and books were stacked up to improve combustion. The different teams worked for hours into the night until all possible physical evidence had been collected. It was a productive day. They were several steps closer to finding the dangerous criminal who committed these heinous acts.

As Asher walked to his city vehicle, a large black truck rounded the corner and passed him by as he entered his vehicle. It was a Silverado, but was it *the same* Silverado? There was no moon and little illumination from evening city lights in the area, but he thought he could make out a red pinstripe running along the side of the vehicle. He could not see the driver. As the car flew by, he concentrated on the back license plate, clearly a Michigan vanity plate. At least half of the numbers or letters were concealed by mud, but he could make out the first two characters. They were the letters *US*. Ash made a mental note to contact the DMV and run Silverado plates bearing those two letters in combination. It was a long, fulfilling day, a day where several clues were recovered and would soon be in the process of hopefully leading to the identification of a suspect. Ash got into his car, started it, and began to drive away from the curb. His mind wandered to the large, black Silverado. *This is our guy.*

Chapter Ten

Noah Thompson sat in front of his sophisticated Mac-based computer setup. The screens were blank. Noah was trying to devise a plan of attack in his cyberspace pursuit of the mosque bomber. *If he is anti-Muslim*, Noah reasoned, *then he is probably an anti-Semite and a racist, too. What sites would he migrate to online?* Noah logged in and opened Safari. He entered "anti-Semite, racist, anti-Muslim" on the search line and clicked 'return.' He was surprised to see how much animosity and bigotry there was in the world. Before his eyes was a smorgasbord of hate. His screen displayed multiple listings of organizations, groups, and individuals who preached hatred and bigotry in one way or another.

Noah scrolled the list and randomly clicked on several anti-Semitic, racist, and Islamophobic rants. The more he searched and clicked, the more depressed he became about the state of religious and ethnic freedom in the self-proclaimed land of the free. "What is wrong with these people?" he exclaimed out loud. *And they put **me** in jail?*

Noah, now fully engaged, continued to scroll and click through lunch and into the late afternoon. He took careful notes, trying to establish a pattern of thinking or behavior consistent with the mosque bombing. He attempted to identify and concentrate on local sites, those within a 100-mile radius of the Detroit metropolitan area. After a while, the places and rants began to run together. He was finding the true meaning of "they all look alike." He was about to call it a day when he came across a pro-white, anti-Islamic rant authored by a white supremacist. It was penned as an announcement of religious movement and events and was written by someone named Nomo Islam:

"We offer our hardy congratulation to our country's savior, Ronald John, our exalted and supreme leader, who will make America pure again.

"To date, we have chosen to act randomly. We have wreaked havoc on a synagogue here, disrupted a religious event there. We have targeted individual towelheads with fire and brimstone. Perhaps they should wear these ridiculous costume headdresses tightly around their necks, noose-like, rather than upon their filthy, lice-ridden heads. We no longer wonder how flammable the fabric is. We no longer wonder how hot their houses of gutter propaganda must become before they burst into flame. We are having an impact. Satan is confused and backpedaling rapidly. But it is not enough. Our hit-and-run tactics have been successful, but we must do more.

"Soon, the people of this country will experience an event like no other event they have ever experienced. Our organization, USA 1 Pure, will host 'Freedom to be White Day,' encouraging all of our supporters to educate Americans about the Muslim threat to our freedom, jobs, and our right to assemble and to worship. This day will feature educational events throughout the country. There is only one pure nationalist society. That society is the white Christian society, and only the white Christian society is worthy of salvation and freedom of speech. All other groups are offspring of the devil and, as such, are enemies of God Almighty and his chosen people.

"Who are the chosen people? They are not the Jews. *White Christians* are God's favorite, God's chosen. In the name of Jesus Christ, it is the white Christian who shall claim the Promised Land. It is the white Christian who shall liberate the biblical land of the Middle East from all of the others who present false claims. Once we rid the world of its Muslim and Jewish scum, one at a time, group by group, congregation by congregation, we will assume our rightful place as the chosen people of God in our biblical land, Palestine.

"We must expose the 2,000-year-old lie that Jews are the chosen ones and tear it down, never to rear its ugly head again. Worse than a power-hungry Jewish Israel, however, is the barbaric Middle Eastern Islamic terrorist. These scumsuckers have infiltrated the government of previous administrations, and it is up to us to convince our beloved leader, the honorable and exalted Ronald John, that terrorists are living among us. The fox has entered the henhouse.

"Your fearlessness in challenging these agents of terror, head-on, is to be applauded and honored. We stand with you and will fight with you as you tackle the issues of jihad and Islamic terror. We stand with you and will fight with you as you halt immigration from areas that support jihadists and deport those who are a threat to our safety, indeed, to our very right to exist as a country. We stand with you and will fight with you when you call for extreme vetting of those who seek to enter our once great country. We must fight, with all our might, those who seek to introduce Sharia law and Islamic propaganda to our American shores. Repel the infidels, my fellow Christians, by any and all means necessary!"

Nomo Islam signed the rambling manifesto. Noah entered the name into the Safari search engine block. A Facebook page dedicated to Nomo popped up. The page was created by someone named Keith Blackwell and called for the same type of actions as Nomo Islam. This was a racist blog site, a forum where racists, anti-Semites, and anti-Islamic bigots are lauded. Noah, ever the technical guru, had a sweet setup, with multiple screens and search engines. He placed the Facebook page and the manifesto side by side on two screens. The more he scrolled and read, the more consistencies he saw. Personal attacks were encouraged, as well as group attacks. The rant mentioned the use of fire against Muslim scarves and Muslim 'houses of propaganda.' It suggested using a Muslim headscarf as a noose. Noah clicked his phone and requested a background check on Nomo Islam and Keith Blackwell.

***

At a different location in the same building where Noah Thompson was reading the Nomo Islam, Asher Granger strolled into his office carrying an extra-large cup of Tim Horton's hazelnut coffee. It was 8:00 a.m. He sat down and brought the coffee cup to his nose. He sniffed the sweet hazelnut smell, then chugged down a gulp and called down to the crime lab. He was told all of the collected evidence had been received, cataloged, and processed. Lab techs were beginning the process of evaluating and testing the various samples. The first results would be available in a few hours.

He sat down at his desk, pulled out his iPhone, and scanned his contacts list. He found his contact at the DMV and clicked on his name. The number appeared and was automatically dialed. Andy Toler answered the phone on the fourth ring.

"DMV, Toler speaking, may I help you?"

"Andy, it's me, Ash Granger. How ya doing?"

"I'm fine, Ash, up to my eyeballs in work. What's up?"

"I need you to run a partial Michigan plate for me. I've got a vehicle type, and I know the color. I know it's a late model, but I don't know what year it is. Can you work your magic?"

"I'll do the best I can. Whaddaya got?"

"It's a black, late-model Chevy Silverado truck. The first two characters are the letters *U* and *S*."

"I've had some success with less information than that. Give me a couple of hours, and I'll give you a call as soon as I know something. Warning, warning"—he mimicked the robot in *Lost in Space*—"the list might be a long one."

"That's my problem, not yours. Please, just get me whatever you can get me as soon as possible."

"What's the deal? What's this all about?" Andy wondered.

"The mosque bombing," Ash advised, all business.

"Shit!" Andy exclaimed. "I should have known you'd be involved in that case. I'll get this for you ASAP. Got a suspect?"

"Yeah, if you get me the information I ask for, maybe I do," Ash snapped, harsher than he intended.

"Okay, okay, sorry. I'll get right on it," Andy apologized.

"No, Andy, my bad. There's lots of pressure to resolve this one quickly. Sorry I snapped at you."

"No problem, Ash. I'll get back to you even though you were an asshole."

Ash laughed. "Thanks, Andy. I appreciate it."

"No problem. Peace out."

"Have a great day. And Andy?"

"Yeah, Ash?"

"Sorry, I was an asshole," he snickered.

Ash hung up the phone, chugged down more hazelnut, and contemplated his next move. He was confident he would get a solid lead from the lab, Andy, or both. *Nothing to do but wait.*

Chapter Eleven

At four o'clock on the following day, the task force met to discuss the day's developments. Ash reported DNA testing was performed as a 'rush job' request. Because of the high-profile nature of the case and the fact the lab had almost nothing else going on at the precise moment the request was made, the results were made available in a little more than a day. While the task force members appreciated the quick results, they were even more psyched by the fact that DNA testing on the small flannel segment and some glass shards produced hits.

The blood belonged to a man named Keith Blackwell, whose DNA was in the system because of a felony shoplifting charge with a plea reduction and misdemeanor conviction that occurred several years prior. DNA testing on the sample taken from the fingernails of the female Muslim attack victim was also a match to Blackwell. Granger also reported his encounters with the black Silverado and his capture of the first two characters of the vanity plate.

"My source at the DMV ran the two letters U and S and came up with multiple matches. When the DNA results came back with a match, I returned to the DMV list and cross-checked Blackwell's name with the names on the list, and guess what?"

"Blackwell is on the list," Dylan surmised.

"You bet he is," Granger reported.

"Wait, there's more!" Noah Thompson exclaimed. "I found the website and Facebook page for a guy named Nomo Islam. He writes all sorts of outrageous rants about Jews, blacks, and Muslims. He talks about strangling Muslim women with or burning their hijabs. There is a veiled call to burn houses of worship. And get this: His Facebook page is registered to a guy named . . ."

"Keith Blackwell," Dylan interrupted, now piqued. "Do we have an address on this guy?"

"DMV shows his address as 6127 Orchard Avenue, Dearborn," Ash advised.

"How do you want to play it?" Shaheed chimed in.

"Establish surveillance on this guy, see if he is acting alone or in concert with others," Jack suggested. "I'm thinking of letting him wander around town might be too dangerous."

"Not if our teams never let him out of their sight," Ash offered.

"What do you guys think?" Ash looked over to Shaheed and Noah.

"I like the idea," Noah conceded, always the conspiracy theorist. "This guy has to be a part of some Nazi or neo-Nazi white supremacy group. He's organizing a Freedom to Be White Day rally for a group called USA 1 Pure. I haven't looked at this group yet. It could be a lot of people, a few, or just him. I'd follow him for a while and see who it leads to."

"I doubt he works with others. He's probably a lone wolf," Ash predicted. "Shaheed?"

"In my experience with these fanatics, there are rarely 'groups of one.'" He made quotation marks with his hands. "Follow him for a while. If he starts something or tries to make an aggressive move, arrest him and bring him in for questioning."

"He probably has visible burns and scratches, so I would include a forensic photographer on the surveillance team," added Ash.

"Great idea," Jack agreed. "I'll update the chief and set it up. Thanks, guys. Damn good work! I never expected these kinds of results this quickly," he praised.

***

At nine the following morning, Keith Blackwell strolled down the stairs of 6127 Orchard Avenue. A surveillance team monitored his every move. A photographer flashed numerous pictures, and a telephoto lens captured every exposed mark on his body. There were indeed several scratches and burns on his face and exposed arms.

Blackwell pushed a button on his key fob. Lights flashed, and an alarm beeped on a black Chevrolet Silverado truck parked in front of the modest home. The photographer focused on and snapped a photo of the vanity license plate 'USA 1 ST.' Blackwell climbed into the driver's seat and took off. They followed a safe distance behind as he slowly passed the site of the mosque bombing, apparently to check out—as he had the night Ash observed the black Silverado with the red pinstripe— what police investigators were doing at the site.

There was no activity, but there was enough armed police presence to deter any attempt to inflict more damage. He drove on and stopped at a local Ace Hardware store. A casually dressed member of the surveillance team followed him in and observed him purchasing some rags, 10W-40, and lighter fluid. He took out his camera phone and took the risk of snapping a photo of Blackwell with the items before they were bagged up. Luckily, his activity was not detected.

Blackwell did not shoplift. He paid for the items and exited the store. He climbed back into the Silverado and drove a few miles to a storefront on Schaefer Avenue, in a rather surly part of town. The photographer attached a telephoto lens and snapped Blackwell entering the storefront through a door with faded lettering on the building itself, covered by a new, makeshift sign that read USA 1 PURE. The team could not determine how many people were inside the building.

The team leader made an immediate decision to break the surveillance group into two. When Blackwell exited the store, one team would remain to see who else walked in and out of the building, and the other team would maintain surveillance on Blackwell. The leader called Jack to fill him in about the storefront and questioned whether they had enough evidence for a wiretap of the building. Jack promised to discuss the matter with the FBI, ATF, and local and federal prosecutors. They had not decided yet whether to formally bring the feds in or prosecute the case as a state hate crime.

About an hour later, Blackwell exited the building without the package of materials he purchased at Ace Hardware. Was someone else now in possession of those materials? One team would remain on site while the other would continue to tail the suspect.

Blackwell re-entered the Silverado. It started with a loud roar. He gently inched it away from the curb, then drove slowly as if he was watching everything and everybody around him. This forced the team to stay far behind him, creating a problematic surveillance situation. They didn't lose him, but they also couldn't see what he was doing. He again drifted past the mosque, almost obsessed with the building and the goings-on in and around it. Was he planning another attack? Hopefully, Jack would decide enough evidence was gathered to make an arrest and achieve a conviction before anything like that happened. Blackwell returned to the Orchard Avenue address, parked the vehicle, got out and strolled into the house, where he stayed put for the rest of the day.

Back at the Schaefer storefront, the surveillance team observed some activity. A gang of motorcycle riders drove past the surveillance team and pulled up in front of the store. All of the men were stereotypical, elderly, gang members. Several had shaved heads—skinheads, some would say. Others had long, unkempt hair that cascaded out when those who wore helmets removed them. All of them wore leather jackets, and all of the jackets displayed a swastika in the front and the letters TCC across the back in a logo that linked the letters.

One older man with long, messy, grey hair took charge of the rest, barking orders the surveillance team could not hear, and all of the men entered the store. The photographer snapped several pictures and a close-up of this leader. Hopefully, they could get a facial recognition match and find out who this guy was. What they couldn't figure out was why Blackwell was not among them. Who was he to them? Was he management or a peon? Was he a key member or a drudge? Did they like him? Trust him? Were they supportive of his actions, or would they turn on him if ordered to?

The surveillance team remained vigilant, watching and waiting, cursing that they didn't have a man on the inside or some sort of listening device to pick up the conversation. They needed a warrant for that. Hopefully, Dylan would come through. About three hours after the men entered the store, they exited. All mounted their respective bikes and took off in different directions. There was a meeting of sorts. What was discussed? Were these the leaders of USA 1 Pure? What was this organization about? What were they planning? These were questions that needed answers at some point. A call was made to Dylan with a suggestion that four teams of two maintain 24-hour surveillance on the storefront until Jack called it off.

Chapter Twelve

Arya Khan strolled into police headquarters at approximately eleven the following morning. She approached the desk sergeant and requested Shaheed Ali. When asked if she had an appointment, slightly embarrassed, she mumbled, "No." She hadn't thought of that simple courtesy. *This case, this country* . . . Ronald John and his ilk were getting to her.

The sergeant invited her to have a seat and indicated he would see if Detective Ali was available. He picked up the phone and dialed a number, mumbling something Arya could not hear. After replacing the handle back on the phone, the sergeant looked at Arya and advised, "He's on the phone or in a meeting. He'll be with you in a few."

What does that mean? A few what? Minutes? Hours? Is he on the phone or in a meeting? Which is it? Is he avoiding me? Isn't he the person who reaches out to the Muslim community? Arya was so distrustful she got herself all worked up.

As she became increasingly convinced he was avoiding her or wouldn't see her, Shaheed Ali came through an atrium door and into the large lobby area. He walked up to Arya with a broad smile and pleasant demeanor.

"Ms. Khan? I'm Detective Ali, Shaheed, if you please. What can I do for you today?"

Arya was taken aback by his politeness and genuine warmth. Plus, he was *quite* handsome. She stuttered, "W-well . . . th-thank you for seeing me, Detective Ali . . . uh . . . Shaheed. If you have a few minutes, I'd like to talk to you about the mosque bombing. I won't take up too much of your time . . ."

She was trying to regain her composure. Still, he was a very handsome man with an endearing smile.

"No trouble at all, Ms. Khan."

"My name is Arya. Please call me Arya."

"Arya then. Can we speak out here, or would you like some privacy?" he inquired.

"Actually, if you don't mind, I would like to talk privately," she decided.

"Okay, please follow me." He motioned her to go in the direction of the atrium he came through. He opened the door, stepped aside, and held it until she was through the door. *Chivalry is not dead.* She smiled, nodded a thank you in his direction, and followed him through a bit of a maze of hallways and offices. Shaheed stopped at a modest, all-glass office he identified as his own. He invited her to have a seat and offered her something to drink. She declined.

"Now, Arya, what can I do for you?"

"As a member of the East Dearborn Muslim community, I was wondering what was being done to find the man responsible for the mosque bombing." She was polite but demanding.

"We are working around the clock, leaving no stone unturned. We have identified potential suspects and are following up on several leads. We hope to make an arrest very shortly." He was a tad too mechanical for Arya's taste.

"What does 'identified potential suspects' mean?" she pressed. "Do you have anyone in mind? Can you provide any names?"

"Not at this time, Arya. We are not ready to reveal the names of suspects, bring anyone in for questioning, or make an arrest. But we are getting closer and closer every day." He flashed a broad smile with perfect teeth.

"But, Detective Ali, surely you have . . . what do you call it . . . like that TV show . . . a person of interest?"

"Please call me Shaheed, Arya," he chirped. "Not yet, we don't. We will advise the community as soon as we zero in on a particular 'person of interest,' as you call him." He chuckled as he uttered 'person of interest,' then picked up a file on his desk and began reviewing its pages.

The phone rang, startling both of them. They shared a chuckle, as Ali picked up the receiver and pressed it to his ear.

"Detective Ali."

He listened briefly before responding to the caller.

"I'll be right there," he muttered. Turning to Arya, he was dismissive, "Are we done here, Arya, or do you have more questions?"

"I have a few more questions if you don't mind," polite but steadfast.

He didn't mind. "Wait here, then. Make yourself comfortable. I'll be right back."

He flashed that smile again. Arya found herself tingling. He left the room, and Arya was alone in his office. For a short time, she sat and considered the questions she wanted to ask. After a while, she rose and walked around his office, studying plaques and awards he hung on walls or placed on desks. *He is quite the decorated officer.* She moved to the right of his desk to walk to the back wall and view an award. As she started toward the back wall, she noticed Shaheed left a file sitting open on the desk.

She looked out the glass walls and door and saw no one around. Walking around to the other side of the desk, the face of what looked to be a teenager was staring back at her, an old mug shot. Beneath the picture was a name, Keith Blackwell. *Is this the suspect?* She looked at the page opposite and saw the words USA 1 Pure and two addresses.

She again scanned her surroundings to see if anyone was coming or even paying her attention. Satisfied no one was monitoring her, she reached into her purse, pulled out a notepad and pen, and copied the two addresses. She calmly walked back around the desk and sat down in the same chair she occupied previously. Less than 30 seconds later, Shaheed returned. Arya looked flushed.

"Everything okay?" Shaheed wondered.

"Fine," Arya huffed. She rose. She was now in a rush to leave.

Shaheed looked confused. "You had more questions?"

"I changed my mind," she blurted, rushing to the door. "Will you let me know if anything develops? My community is in dire straits and needs some answers as soon as possible." She tried to remain calm.

"It is my community, too, Arya. We're doing all we can. We are receiving new tips and developing new leads every day. I'm certain we will see some real progress very soon."

"Well then, Shaheed, thank you for taking some time to see me and talk to me. I appreciate it. Have a wonderful day," she gushed.

"No problem at all." Shaheed hesitated. Her demeanor changed. She was anxious to leave and transparently phony. "Are you sure everything is okay?"

"It's fine; I just forgot about an appointment, and now I'm late," she lied with a straight face. "Thanks again for your time."

"No problem; goodbye." There was that smile again. "Can you find your way to the lobby?"

"Yes, thank you, very thoughtful of you. I know you're busy. I can find my own way out. Thanks again." She bowed twice, turned, and rushed down the hall. Shaheed watched her as she went.

"Is this lovely lady going to be a pain in my ass?" He wondered aloud. The phone rang, and he answered. His busy day was consuming him once again. Soon, he forgot all about his conversation with Arya Khan.

Chapter Thirteen

Rabbi Joseph Norman, 'Rabbi Joey' to his congregants, looked out at the beautiful setting in the backyard of Zachary Blake's Bloomfield Hills mansion. He smiled and signaled for all to be seated. When the guest settled down, he proceeded.

"Welcome, family and friends. Jennifer and Zachary are so happy to have all of you here today to share the celebration of their wedding day. You are here because you are the ones who mean the most to this very happy couple. I welcome and bless you with these words: Blessed be you who have come here in dedication to all that is loving, good, and sacred. We welcome you in joy."

A sole violinist began to play a beautiful melody, and Kenny and Jake Tracey walked down the aisle together, smiling at various guests as they strolled toward the rabbi and their priest, Father William Stern, who stood under a beautiful flowered canopy, known in Jewish tradition as a *chuppah*, a symbol of the new home being consummated. The boys arrived at the canopy and took their places on opposite sides of the clergymen. After Kenny and Jake, Jennifer's sister, Lynne, and her family walked happily down the aisle. An elated Zachary Blake came next, smiled broadly at family members and friends as he ventured toward the *chuppah*. His thoughts briefly went to the first time he did this. His first wife, Tobey, and their daughters were not in attendance today, a reminder of the mess he made of life before Jennifer.

The music stopped briefly. The crowd turned to the back of the yard, and the violinist began to play a bridal melody. Jennifer Tracey appeared at the back. She paused and stood at attention, as previously instructed by the wedding planner. She didn't like being the center of attention, but she loved Zachary Blake and was happy and proud to be his bride. Zack looked back at Jennifer with a tearful smile. *Is there a more beautiful person in this world? How did I get so lucky?*

The planner motioned Jennifer forward. She slowly glided down the aisle, tears in her eyes, until she reached Zack's side. The two looked at each other and joined hands. Rabbi Joey recited the *Shehecheyanu*, a traditional Jewish prayer thanking God for giving us life, sustaining us and bringing us together for this joyous occasion.

"Out of two different and distinct traditions, Jennifer and Zachary have come together to learn the best of what each has to offer, appreciating their differences, and confirming that being together is far better than permitting religious differences to keep them apart. As we bless this marriage under the *chuppah*, we will also light a unity candle, the Christian symbol of two people becoming one in marriage," Rabbi Joey preached. "Father Bill?" Joey invited Father William Stern to continue the ceremony.

"Blessed are you who come here in the name of the Lord. Serve Him with joy—come into his presence with song. Most awesome, glorious, and blessed God, please grant your holy blessings to this bride and this groom." Father Bill glanced at Jennifer and her sons and smiled, acknowledging the long and painful road they took to arrive at this happy moment.

Rabbi Joey retrieved a cup of wine and held it up to the happy couple. "Two thoughts come to mind as I hold this cup of wine. The first is that wine is a symbol of the sweetness we wish for your life together. There will be times when you drink from other cups, bitter ones, but life offers an opportunity to savor the sweetness. We toast to wish you a life filled with goodness. My second thought is that wine is a symbol of sharing. May you enjoy a long life together, grow in love, and share happy moments like this one, the one that unites you. As you continue to share in each other's life, you will, as a symbol of this enduring cooperation, share this cup of wine." The rabbi recited the blessing over the wine and offered each a sip from the cup.

Father Bill recited from I Corinthians: "Love is always patient and kind. It is never jealous or selfish. It does not take offense and is not resentful. Love takes no pleasure in other people's sins but delights in the truth. It is always ready to excuse, to trust, and to endure whatever comes. Love does not end. There are in the end three things that last: Faith, Hope, and

Love, and the greatest of these is Love." Zack and Jennifer turned to each other and smiled.

Father Bill turned to the happy couple. "It is time now for the main event, the moment you've all been waiting for," he quipped.

"Jennifer, Zachary, have you come before Rabbi Joey and I freely and without reservations to give yourselves to each other in marriage?"

"We have," they pledged in unison.

"Now that we have established your intentions, please join hands and repeat after me:

"In the name of God, I, Zack take you, Jennifer . . ." Zack repeated this phrase and the following phrases when prompted by Father Bill:

" . . . to be my wife, to have and to hold from this day forward, for better for worse, for richer or for poorer, in sickness and in health, to love and to cherish, until death do us part. This is my solemn vow." The priest took Jennifer through the same process.

Rabbi Joey stepped forward. This ceremony was a true inter-faith event, swaying back and forth between the two clergymen. Joey would now preside over the exchange of rings. He motioned for Kenny and Jake to present the rings. The two boys pulled rings from their pockets and proudly handed him to the rabbi. They turned and smiled at their mother and returned to their places. Rabbi Joey turned and faced the couple.

"These rings in their unbroken wholeness are token of the continuity of your love. May their shining substance be a symbol of the enduring trust and affection you bring to one another. Zachary, as you place the ring on Jennifer's finger, please repeat after me: "I am my beloved's, and my beloved is mine.""

"I am my beloved's, and my beloved is mine," Zack repeated.

"With the ring, I thee wed."

"With this ring, I thee wed," Zack repeated.

As before, Joey had Jennifer repeat the same process.

Father Bill stepped forward, and Zack rolled his eyes ever so slightly. He was impatient. He wanted to be married to this beautiful woman, the love of his life. Bill's task was to preside over the lighting of the unity candle.

"In the wedding liturgy, candlelight symbolizes the commitment of love these two people are declaring today. Before you are three special candles. The two smaller ones symbolize the lives of the bride and groom. Until today, both have shined as individuals in their respective communities. Today, they publicly proclaim their love in the new union of marriage.

"They do not lose their individuality, but, in marriage, are united in so close a bond, they become one. Following the profession of their marriage vows, they will light the large center candle from the smaller candles to symbolize this new reality. Henceforth, their light will shine together, for each other, for their families, and for the community.

"From every human being, there rises a light that reaches straight to heaven. When two souls are destined to find one another, their two streams of light flow together and a single brighter light goes forth from their united being."

Rabbi Joey stepped in and recited the Seven Wedding Blessings as Jennifer circled her intended seven times, symbolizing their mutual protective care. "We rejoice in your happiness and pray this day is the first of many blessings the two of you will share together in the days and year ahead. You have spoken the words and performed the rites that unite your lives in accordance with two traditions. Because of the power of your love and the commitment you have made to each other this day, I declare your marriage to be valid and binding, and I pronounce you husband and wife."

The two clergymen approached the couple and held their hands over their heads. The recited the benediction, alternately:

"May the Lord bless you and keep you.

"May the Lord shine his countenance upon you and be gracious unto you.

"May the Lord look upon you with favor and grant you peace."

Rabbi Joey brought forward a cloth napkin, which contained the traditional Jewish wedding wine glass. "We conclude this joyous ceremony with the traditional breaking of the glass. The fragility of this glass suggests the frailty of human relationships. The glass is broken to protect this marriage with prayer . . . May your bond of love be as difficult to break as it would be to put together the pieces of this glass."

The rabbi set the cloth on the floor, and Zack stomped on it, breaking it into tiny pieces. Everyone shouted, "*Mazel Tov*," the traditional Jewish expression of congratulations.

Jennifer and Zack turned to each other, beaming with joy. They embraced in a long, passionate kiss.

"Ewww," Jake shouted. "Get a room!"

"Ditto," cried a happy Kenny. "Welcome to the family, Zack."

"Likewise," Zack managed, tearfully grateful. "Let's party!"

And they did, all through the night.

Chapter Fourteen

Imam Baqir Ghaffari sat in a makeshift office provided for him in a small office building owned by a member of his community. He was writing the Friday evening *Khutbah*. There was a knock on the door, and three men walked in. One man wore a cleric's collar; another wore a suit and the third a suit and yarmulke. Ghaffari recognized each man. He greeted them warmly with handshakes and hugs, then invited them to sit in the bridge chairs that sat near the small desk he was using. He was surprised to see his friends from the Interfaith Leadership Council of Metropolitan Detroit.

"Oh, my friends. I am so glad to see you!" Ghaffari exclaimed. "To what do I owe this pleasure? How did you find me here?" He was genuinely puzzled.

Rabbi Joseph Norman spoke first. "The Lord works in mysterious ways, Baqir. He led us to you." He sounded completely serious.

Bishop William Stern of the Detroit Archdiocese and pastor of Our Lady of the Lakes in Farmington Hills spoke next. "We are so sorry about your misfortune, Baqir. We wanted you to know the Interfaith Leadership Council will do everything in its power to help you through these difficult times."

Lutheran Pastor Louis Michael offered his own condolences. Afterward, he pledged, "Baqir, I am certain I can speak for my brothers"—acknowledging the men who were with him—"when I say an attack on one of us is an attack on all. We condemn, in the strongest possible words, the attacks upon members of your community and upon your mosque, your holy house of worship and fellowship. We want to offer you and your community sanctuary. Please, Baqir, please, we want you to consider utilizing our buildings, any or all of them, for your services and your community events. If you desire privacy, we will provide temporary barriers to separate our services and events from yours. We will also coordinate schedules to limit the number of conflicts in our services and programs. We not only speak for the three of us, but we speak for all members of the Interfaith Leadership Council."

Baqir Ghaffari was stunned speechless. He stared at the three men with a bewildered look on his face. He began to tremble slightly—tears formed in his eyes and began to trickle down his cheeks. The three men rose, walked behind him, and placed their hands on his back, offering comfort. He looked up at them and smiled through his tears. Finally, he composed himself and spoke.

"Oh, my dear friends. What a generous, heartfelt offer! Just when I begin to think the world has gone mad, and everyone is against my people, three men and a wonderful organization redeem my faith. You give me hope for the future. Thank you! Thank you! I am beyond grateful for your generosity and compassion. I am sure you had to get approval from your congregation, which is an amazing accomplishment. Please let all of your clergy, staff, officers, and congregants know how appreciative we are of this offer.

"We have partnered with neighborhood mosques to share events and services when possible, and the Muslim community has really pulled together over the bombing and the other terrible assaults on our citizens. But there are scheduling conflicts, and it is good to know there are other places for us to carry on our important work. Thank you again, my friends. All glory to Allah. I thank him for bringing you to me."

"It is our pleasure, Baqir," Rabbi Norman assured. "There but for the grace of Allah go I," he smiled.

Ghaffari began to tear up again and tilted his head downward. "You three and the entire Interfaith Council have been such good friends," he gushed. "Again, thank you, from the bottom of my heart."

"It is the least we can do, Baqir," Bishop Stern retorted. "Let us know if there is anything else you need."

"Prayer," Ghaffari suggested. "Allah, God, Jesus . . . the intent is the same. You three are shining examples, touched by the light of Allah. I shall never forget this gesture of brotherhood and peace."

The three men rose, embraced the Imam again, and bid farewell. After they were gone, Ghaffari sat alone, gazing out the window. He walked to the side of his desk, where a Muslim prayer rug, a *Sajjāda,* adorned the floor. He kneeled down on the rug and began to pray.

"Thank you, Allah, for bringing my brothers of faith here today. Please bless them as I do by thanking them for their thoughtfulness, kindness, and generosity. The Prophet Muhammad, peace be upon him, once declared: 'He who does not express gratitude to those who do you a favor, does not express gratitude to you, Allah. Whoever does you a favor, reciprocate, and if you can't reciprocate, pray for him until you think you have reciprocated.' I pray for my dear friends now. I pray for all of my brothers and sisters of the Interfaith Council. Thank you, Allah, for their brotherhood and their extraordinary offer to our community."

As he prayed, he bowed, over and over. And, as he bowed, the tears returned, slowly dropping on the prayer rug. Finally, he stopped bowing and praying and remained face down on the carpet, prostrate, completely submissive, mildly convulsive, soaking the *Sajjāda* with tears.

Chapter Fifteen

Arya Khan returned home from her meeting with Shaheed Ali. She was mildly perturbed he didn't share information about this teenager, Keith Blackwell. *Was this the suspect?* She removed her shoes and her hijab, walked to the den, and sat down in front of her computer.

She clicked on a button, and a password request appeared. She typed in 'Glory2Allah,' and her Yahoo screen appeared. She typed the words *USA 1 Pure* in the search engine box and hit 'Enter.' Nomo Islam's manifesto filled the screen, and she began to read its disturbing contents. It was absolutely horrible, and she shook with fright.

Who are these people? Her eyes scrolled the rant. *What have American Muslims ever done to them? We love peace and tranquility. We are a prayerful people. Perhaps we don't pray the same as our Christian brothers and sisters do, but many men and women of God believe, regardless of our religion or our religious differences, we all pray to the same God. I have never read such evil thoughts. How does someone who writes such hateful words have the unmitigated gall to call himself a Christian?*

She scanned the article and website, looking for the name behind the pseudonym, Nomo Islam. Under different circumstances, she may have thought the pseudonym clever, even funny. But this guy, this group, wanted to kill her and her fellow Muslims. They wanted to cleanse the United States of all non-white, non-Christian people. This was not the least bit funny.

She continued to search until she came across a link to a Facebook page. She clicked on the link and a bald man, late 30s maybe, wearing a leather jacket bearing a swastika on the front, dominated the screen. The words *USA 1 Pure* appeared under the picture, as did the words *Nomo Islam, AKA Keith Blackwell*. She studied the image, then tried to recover the memory of the teenager she saw in Shaheed's office. She tried to picture the teenager without any hair. *Could it be the same guy? Was the picture over 20 years old?* She could not remember seeing a date on the photograph. She wished she had been able to spend more time with the file. As it was, Shaheed almost caught her with the file as he returned to his office. This Keith Blackwell certainly matched the description of the person eyewitnesses indicated they saw at each terrorist attack on Muslim citizens and the mosque. *Is this the guy?*

Arya reviewed the Facebook page. There was a link to the USA 1 Pure rant and to other white supremacist websites and social media pages. Apparently, USA 1 Pure had a Twitter page and tweeted often. There was a LinkedIn page and a Snapchat page in addition to the Facebook page and website.

Arya typed the two addresses, the Orchard Avenue address first, into the search engine box. Other than the fact that the address was located in a blue-collar residential section of Dearborn, there was no additional information available in the search. But when she typed in the Schaefer Avenue address, the office of USA 1 Pure appeared on the screen. There was no additional information, but Arya was confident this was the headquarters where Keith Blackwell penned his manifesto of hate and where he plotted his successful bombing of the Mosque of America.

Yes, this is the guy, this Keith Blackwell. He is the despicable anti-Muslim bigot and racist suspect everyone is looking for. And, aside from the police and his hateful cult, she was the only other person in the world who knew who he was. Arya Khan was determined to do whatever was necessary to bring him to justice.

Chapter Sixteen

The Supreme Leader of the hate group tagged with the benign name The Conservative Council, or TCC for short, was an 85-year-old man by the name of Benjamin Blaine. He looked and acted 20 years younger, and was a hard-core white supremacist with the proverbial record as long as an arm. Blaine liked to tell his soldiers: "I was lynching niggers in the South before any of you were sucking milk from your mommy's titties." Blaine was born in Mississippi in the 1930s. His father was a member of the Klan, as was his grandfather before him. His grandfather owned a plantation in Jackson, where he owned and mistreated many slaves. He also made a nice chunk of change running a slaving operation, bringing them in from Africa and selling them to nearby plantation owners.

"Granddaddy," as Blaine called him, was quite the cruel overseer. All of his slaves were branded so other plantation owners and townsfolk would know to whom they belonged. If a slave under-performed or tried to flee, he or she would experience the whip, and many had permanent lash marks to show for it. Blaine's father had numerous mixed-breed half-brothers and sisters from Granddaddy's legendary escapades with his female slaves. Rumor had it one slave tried to escape, and when he was caught and returned, Granddaddy chopped his right leg off at the shin so he couldn't run away anymore. He couldn't hide, either, because his wooden leg made so much noise, everybody knew where he was at all times.

Blaine loved to hear his father and grandfather's stories about life in the Deep South in the nineteenth and early twentieth centuries. As a slave owner's grandson and the son of a man who longed for the "good ole days of slavery," it was not a surprise Benjamin was a cruel racist. But, he was more than that. The Conservative Council was dedicated to the proposition that the U.S. Constitution got it right in the early years of our once great country—all men were *not* created equal. In fact, some men were not men at all, not entitled to the full constitutional rights our white Christian founders enjoyed. The fact that subsequent, gutless leaders like Lincoln, Kennedy, and Johnson thought otherwise mattered little to him. The Constitution was sacred. The only sensible Amendments were the 1st and 2nd. The 1st allowed the Klan the right to free speech and assembly. And the 2nd allowed Klan members to purchase weapons and shoot any bastard that got in its way. Some non-white, impure people were equal, alright. They were equal to each other, equal in their inferiority to white Christians, and equal in the sense he hated the fuck out of all of them equally.

Today's tolerant, politically correct society made him sick to his stomach. The kikes had all the money, and the spics, nips, chinks, and niggers were taking all the jobs. Worse than those people, though, were the camel jockeys. The stinking Muslims were killing white people on American soil, and they had to be eradicated. Blaine was buoyed by the rhetoric and promise of Ronald John. He'd campaigned hard for this great man, and he was pleased to see he was not only a man of words but a man of action as well. But President John could not rid the country of the Muslim scourge all by himself. He needed foot soldiers on the front lines. TCC was dedicated to the cause of ridding the country of as many non-whites as possible in as many ways possible.

Keith Blackwell was in the process of proving himself to Blaine. He was not yet a member, and not all members were aware of him. Even some on the executive board were unfamiliar with Blackwell. He was trying hard to impress, but his lone-wolf behavior in attacking two Muslim women and bombing a mosque in the middle of town broke two cardinal rules of Council doctrine: 1. Never act alone. He violated this by creating USA 1 Pure and by committing three acts of terror without TCC involvement. 2. Always follow orders. The firebombing of the Dearborn mosque was a thing of beauty, and Blaine marveled at the balls it took to do what he did. However, neither Blaine nor any of his deputies authorized the bombing, and Blackwell was careless to boot. According to Blaine's well-placed source at Dearborn PD, Blackwell was a suspect, about to be arrested. Apparently, Blackwell left DNA, fingerprints, and boot prints at the scene, and the police spotted his vehicle cruising around the mosque. *What an idiot!*

Blaine assembled his deputies for a 'what to do about Blackwell' meeting. "I call this emergency meeting of the executive committee of The Conservative Council to order. The only issue here today is to discuss the Dearborn mosque firebombing and a recruit named Keith Blackwell's unauthorized, unplanned execution of this incident outside of the auspices of the TCC executive board. We can be thankful he acted under the banner USA 1 Pure, and not TCC.

"My source at Dearborn PD advises Blackwell has been identified as the perpetrator. They have DNA, fingerprints, and more. He will be arrested, indicted, questioned, and probably tried and convicted. He might take a plea. He has been a good soldier and may keep his mouth shut, but who knows what might happen if he faces maximum jail time. Besides, he's a fuckin' rookie! He acted alone, without authority, and we have a chain of command and a planning committee for a reason. Before I decide his fate, I wanted to hear from you guys. Does anyone have anything to say?" Blaine spoke as if this were the executive board meeting of a Fortune 500 corporation and not an emergency gathering of a bunch of stone-cold racist killers.

"What's the timetable for the cops? Have they brought him in for questioning?" One member wondered.

"Not yet, but my source says an arrest is right around the corner. 'Imminent' was the word he used," Blaine warned.

"He seems like a good soldier," another offered. "I know he's a rookie, trying to impress, but he's got a lot of guts. All on his own, he wreaked havoc on the enemy and put his own money where his mouth is. Unlike a lot of guys in this movement I come across, he walks the walk. He doesn't just talk the talk."

"He knows technology. He set up that terrific website with that rambling manifesto. Did you guys see that thing? It was fucking beautiful, man! His own picture is featured. He put himself front and center on the thing. We've been responsible for a lot of mayhem in this town, but none of us have made our views public like this guy. Nobody has taken credit like he has, not even you, Ben." The member was almost awestruck.

"That's kind of the point, young man. I don't necessarily agree high-profile shit is a good thing. I've spent my whole life staying under the radar if you get my drift," Blaine reasoned.

At executive board meetings, board members could speak without fear of reprisal. That was important to an open exchange of ideas and thoughts.

"That's why I called for this meeting, I'm having a lot of trouble with this. But he went off half-cocked, created a rogue, boastful website, and he may have put our organization and all of us in jeopardy. We can't have that. If he gets arrested and he mentions us to save his own ass, it is over for us. These politically correct, melting pot pussies will come after us hard. Do we sacrifice one for the greater good of all?"

"I don't think we have any choice. We can't take the risk of Blackwell opening his trap or trying to tie this 'USA 1 Pure' or whatever the fuck it is with the Council. If we get to him before they do, that risk is eliminated," a member argued.

"Couldn't we confront him with the problem and get him to lay low or leave town for a while, or some damn thing like that?" another suggested.

"My source says they have 24-hour surveillance on him," Blaine advised. "Had we acted quicker, maybe that would have been an option. But Elvis has left the building on that one."

"I don't see much choice here," one member determined.

"Neither do I," another agreed.

"Ready to vote, then?" Blaine scanned the men, returning to his Fortune 500 demeanor.

"Ready!" The men shouted in unison.

"All in favor of silencing Blackwell, say 'aye.'"

Nine men chimed 'aye' in unison, including Blaine.

"All those opposed?"

"Aye," one timid voice evoked.

"The aye's have it; Blackwell is history," Blaine concluded. "Let's talk logistics."

Chapter Seventeen

Over the next few days, there was absolutely no activity at the Schaefer storefront and very little activity at the Orchard residence. Jack was forced to terminate surveillance at Schaefer and was authorized to continue more limited surveillance on Blackwell. The money just wasn't there for the long haul. *What's the price of safety?*

Jack approached the prosecutor with the laboratory, computer, and DMV evidence. They had a solid suspect. Was it enough for search and arrest warrants? The prosecutor promised to take it to a judge. He was waiting for the right one. When Jack received the green light, the decision was made to execute the search warrant whether or not Blackwell was home. If he wasn't home, officers would be stationed in a subtle radius around the house, and wait to arrest him when he arrived.

A team of officers dispatched to 6127 Orchard Avenue, Dearborn. No one was at home; at least, no one answered the door. So, they broke down the door and barged in. A search of the house produced a pair of muddy boots with tread that appeared to be a match for the cast Asher and Eric took at the crime scene. They also removed a shitload of white supremacist material, some bomb-making manuals, and other racist garbage. Searchers also found a plethora of lighters, lighter fluid, rags, and rocks. Asher and an assistant searched an office/den and found a map of Dearborn with locations marked off in yellow highlighter pen. A quick telephone call determined all of the sites were Muslim mosques, meeting centers, and businesses. Apparently, Keith Blackwell had more mayhem planned for the Muslim population of Dearborn.

After a thorough search, seizure, and cataloging of the seized items, following a strict chain of custody police procedures, the officers left the house. If and when Blackwell returned, he might think a tornado visited 6127 Orchard Avenue.

***

As fate would have it, Jack Dylan called off surveillance at the Schaefer address a day too soon. The executive board of The Conservative Council hate group had, ironically, used the same storefront rented by Keith Blackwell for advocating USA 1 Pure to plot the demise of Keith Blackwell, the man who founded the organization. Their TCC council meeting had just adjourned, and several men departed the Schaefer location in late model cars and motorcycles. The group decided to shutter this location and devised a simple strategy to shut Blackwell up for good. Blaine would follow Blackwell and determine the appropriate time and place for the final deed. He decided to carry out this mission alone. The involvement of too many people meant too many ways to screw up the mission. In truth, Benjamin Blaine trusted no one, including his own comrades.

Meanwhile, Arya Khan had two addresses to check out. She decided to visit Schaefer first. When Arya arrived, she observed a large, black Silverado parked in front of the storefront address. She parked her car across the street and waited for a sign of activity inside the store. There was no movement and no lights on in the store. Suddenly, the door to the storefront opened, and a man she recognized as Blackwell stepped out. Arya was so startled by his appearance she jumped, banging her head on the roof of her small Ford Focus.

Blackwell pressed his key fob, and the Silverado chirped and flashed lights. He entered from the driver's side, started the truck, and drove off. Arya waited, breathless, allowed him to travel a short distance, then began to follow him. Arya maintained a safe distance and even let a few cars to get in between them. The Silverado was the largest vehicle in the immediate vicinity, so she could easily see it without its driver noticing her. At least, Arya hoped that was true. She wondered if this was what it was like to be a cop or a private eye. *This is exhilarating!*

Blackwell drove through town, through a commercial section, and then through a residential subdivision. He turned off Michigan Avenue onto Orchard Avenue, a residential street of modest homes. Arya knew where he was going, to the second address she noted, 6127 Orchard. She decided it was safer to hang back a bit.

Blackwell pulled up to his house and saw the condition of the door. The lock was shattered—the door was swaying in the wind. He reached into the glove compartment, pulled out a gun, and exited the vehicle. Cautiously and quietly, he approached the front door, nudged it open with the gun, and quietly slipped in. *What the hell?*

The house was in shambles. Was he the victim of a robbery? *Should I call 9-1-1?* He tiptoed around the house and strolled into the den. He saw his desk was ransacked and looked around to see what was missing. His expensive Ultra 4D curved screen was still hooked up. His watch sat on the desk. Expensive stereo equipment remained intact. The only items missing were items related to his USA 1 Pure activities.

Blackwell suddenly realized this was no burglary. The cops executed a search warrant. *They know who I am!* They came to arrest him. In an instant of revelation, his bravado was gone. He was in a panic. He needed to get out of the house and out of Dearborn, ASAP. He ran to the front door, forgetting he was holding a gun. As he ran through the door, he ran into the blade of a Benchmade 940-1 Osborne, held by none other than Benjamin Blaine. The unkempt TCC leader turned assassin twisted the knife with one hand and grabbed the gun out of Blackwell's hand with the other.

Blackwell was too stunned to resist. His mouth gaped open in horror, and his eyes bore into his killer with a look of recognition, shock, and betrayal. As the life oozed out of him, he pitched forward, leaning into his killer. The man was holding him up as if embracing him, in case the neighbors were watching. Blaine inched Blackwell backward, past the threshold of the door, and gently laid him down in the front hall, leaving the door open. He fled on foot, fluidly for a man of his age, leaving the Benchmade planted in Blackwell's stomach, blood flowing in spurts around his soon to be lifeless body. A motorcycle engine roared to life nearby, probably around the block, and the cycle could be heard riding and fading as it fled the area.

Arya watched these events in horror, in the safety of her Focus, three houses down. She pulled out her cell phone and dialed 9-1-1 to report a stabbing at 6127 Orchard Avenue in Dearborn. After allowing ample time for the murderer to be long gone, she exited the Focus and ran to the home. Blackwell lay on the floor, the top half of his body through the door, the bottom half outside the door. He appeared unconscious, but Arya could see he was still breathing, still alive. She hovered over him and whispered, "Keith, can you hear me?"

She ran into the house and quickly found the kitchen. She opened a few drawers and found some kitchen towels and rags. She went to the sink, turned on the hot water faucet, and waited until the water was lukewarm. Then, she ran back to Blackwell and placed towels around the wound and the knife in an effort to stem the bleeding. The towel became soaked in blood, almost instantly. Arya couldn't think of anything else to do but pray.

"Allah! I have accepted you as the Lord, Muhammad as the prophet, Islam as the religion, the *Qur'an* as the holy book. Please help and comfort this man through these difficult moments. Ease his pain. If the hour of doom is upon him,"—she looked down at Blackwell with a spiritual kindness he did not deserve—"bless him and resurrect him as you would all of those who come to this moment. Pardon his misdeeds on the day of reckoning and assure paradise awaits him.

"There is no god but Allah, the gentle, the kind. There is no god but Allah, the high and the great. All praise be to Allah, the lord of the seven heavens and the lord of the seven earths, and whatever is in them and whatever is between them and whatever is above them and whatever is below them, all praise be to Allah, the lord of the universe."

Suddenly, in a moment of sheer terror for Arya, Keith Blackwell rose into a sitting position, grunted grotesquely, brushed the bloody rags away, and pulled the knife out of his stomach, blood now gushing out of a gaping wound. He dropped the knife to the ground, locked eyes with Arya, and grumbled, "Help me."

The irony an anti-Muslim racist would utter these last words to a Muslim woman during words of prayer and resurrection was lost on Arya as she struggled for control. She felt helpless. *Only Allah can bring him comfort.* Panic was setting in. Arya was dizzy and sick to her stomach. As Keith Blackwell took his last breath, some unknown force compelled Arya Khan to pick up the knife. The last thing she heard before sheer terror overtook her own consciousness was: "Dearborn Police, drop the knife!"

Chapter Eighteen

Arya regained consciousness. She did not know how long she was out. A woman with a jacket that read City of Dearborn, Medical Examiner, was kneeled on the ground in front of Arya and hovered over Blackwell's body. Blood continued to trickle out of his knife wound. Arya tried to rise, but her head was spinning. She waited for the dizziness to subside and tried to reach behind herself to push herself into a standing position. Arya could not do so because her hands were handcuffed behind her. She tried to lift her head a bit. Arya saw men and women walking and searching all over the front lawn. She could hear many more voices and footsteps inside the house. Furniture was being moved aside. Someone ascended or descended a stairway.

A cell phone rang. Arya heard someone say, "Dylan." She tried to listen, but the voices faded as a man walked away from her vicinity. Arya was horrified. *What is going on?* She quietly and tentatively spoke to the lady in the jacket.

"Excuse me?" The lady ignored her. "Excuse me, miss," she repeated, with a bit more volume and control. The woman suddenly realized the suspect had regained consciousness and was addressing her.

"Yes? May I help you?" the woman whispered.

"Who is in charge here?" Arya wondered. Her head was still spinning.

"That would be Detective Lieutenant Jack Dylan. I think he's in the house."

"Will you please summon him?" Arya requested. "There has been some sort of mistake."

"What mistake is that, may I ask?" The woman snarled.

"These handcuffs," she looked behind herself, trying to raise her arms. "Why have I been handcuffed?"

"Well, sweetie, that's not an unusual procedure when you stab someone to death," the woman snapped.

Arya was horrified. *They think **I** did this?*

"What are you talking about?" she protested, agitation creeping into her voice. "I found him like this. I didn't stab anyone! I'm the one who called 9-1-1."

"Save it for the jury, sweetie."

"Jury?" Arya was officially terrified. She tried to regain her composure. She decided to politely address the woman again. "Will you please summon the person in charge, Dylan, I believe his name was?"

"That's the guy," she uttered, annoyed, wanting to return to the body. "I'll 'summon' him for you." She gestured the quotation marks.

The woman stood up and walked away, disappearing into the house. Less than a minute later, she was back, with Jack Dylan directly behind her. Arya recognized him from the televised press conference. She was relieved to see him. *He'll straighten this out. If not, perhaps he'll let me talk to Shaheed.* But Dylan's tone and manner were surprisingly harsh.

"Well, if it isn't Sleeping Beauty, back from the dead. I've never had a killer take a nap at the murder scene before."

"Lieutenant, I did not kill anyone. I did witness the murder, and I would be happy to discuss it with you and give you a full description of the man who did it."

Dylan continued to talk down to her. "Well then, miss, I guess that does it. If you claim the soddit defense, I guess I have to let you go."

"I don't understand." Arya was totally confused. "I don't need a defense—I've done nothing wrong. What is this 'soddit' anyway?"

"Some-other-dude-did-it," laughed Dylan. "Get it?"

Jack Dylan was nasty, much different than he was on TV. Arya did not care for his attitude, but he was her only ticket to freedom, and she had to be respectful to him. Dylan was conflicted. *Should I Mirandize her, or is this discussion an excited utterance?* He wondered if her statements might be considered contemporaneous with the crime or some other exception that excused a failure to issue Miranda warnings.

He decided to give her a bit more rope, hoping she would hang herself with it. He'd Mirandize her shortly, a calculated gamble. He was somewhat ambivalent. After all, this woman saved him a lot of work and the taxpayers a lot of money on a Blackwell trial that would never be. On the other hand, she made apprehending any co-conspirators considerably more difficult.

Arya did not think this was a laughing matter. "These handcuffs are hurting me. I demand you remove them immediately. I have done nothing wrong. I followed Mr. Blackwell from an address on Schaefer to see what he was up to. He drove here, saw the front door wide open, looked around, and went inside. While he was inside, this old biker guy came up, and when Mr. Blackwell came back to the door, this biker animal plunged a knife into his stomach and held it there until Blackwell collapsed in a pool of blood."

"Who is this Blackwell guy to you? How do you know his name?" Dylan sneered.

Arya hesitated. *Is snatching a glimpse of a police file a crime? If it is,* she decided, *it is something far less than murder!*

"My name is Arya Khan. I visited with Detective Shaheed Ali today. The mosque bombing was a horrible crime that affected everyone in my community. I am Muslim, by the way."

"I couldn't have guessed," Jack snickered, focusing on her hijab. "Please continue," He prompted, treading on thin ice with Miranda.

"I wondered if Shaheed had developed any leads or suspects on the bombing, but he advised he hadn't. He got a phone call, excused himself, and left the room. While he was gone, I noticed a file lying open on his desk. I know it was wrong, and I apologize, but I walked around the desk, glanced at the file, and saw Blackwell's picture and two addresses. I wanted to see who this guy was and what he was up to. I wanted to help.

"I went to the Schaefer address first, and there he was! He was just leaving. So, I followed him here, saw him go into the house, and was waiting for him to come out so I could continue to follow. Suddenly, this other guy shows up, the old biker guy. He hoisted himself onto the porch, stood up against the front wall next to the door, and when Blackwell came out, the old biker guy stabbed Blackwell hard, in the stomach. He started bleeding everywhere. It was horrible. And the old guy, he just ran away like killing someone was no big deal!" Tears formed in Arya's eyes.

"I waited to make sure the guy was gone and not coming back. I heard a motorcycle start up and leave. Then, I got out of my car and called 9-1-1. There is probably a record of my call, no? After I called 9-1-1, I ran to the porch to see if I could help or comfort the man in some way."

"You are quite the private eye, young lady. You followed a man who was identified as a dangerous suspect. You watch a lot of cop shows on TV?"

"I don't know . . . I wasn't thinking . . . I wanted to help . . . As I mentioned . . . to see what he was up to." Arya trembled. Tears welled in her eyes. She became distant and looked away.

Jack was fearful she would clam up. He wanted her to keep talking. He decided to lighten up, smiled, and placed a hand on her shoulder. "Please, continue your story," he encouraged. Was he past his Miranda obligation? *She is on a roll. I can't give her the warnings now, can I?*

Arya came back from wherever she had gone. Now her voice was quivering. "He had a serious stab wound . . . I-I thought he was dead. I was terrified! I prayed for him. Suddenly, he sat up straight, pulled the knife out of his gut, and more blood began to shoot out of the wound. It was terrible! He dropped the knife, looked at me, and whispered, "Help me." Then, he lay back down and died.

"I picked up the knife, looked at him, and felt dizzy and nauseous. I remember someone yelling, "Dearborn Police, drop the knife." I must have fainted from the shock at that point. I woke up with these handcuffs on"—Arya held up her arms behind her back—"and that woman was working on the body next to me. That's all I remember."

"How do you know Detective Ali? Obviously, well enough to be on a first-name basis." Dylan couldn't help being cynical.

"I saw him on TV at the press conference. You claimed, at the conference, he was the 'go-to guy' for the Muslim community. I met him today for the first time. The mosque is the centerpiece of our community. It is vital to my family and me.

Many in our community are deeply troubled, deeply hurt, and distrustful of the police. I wanted to know if you had a suspect or how close you were to making an arrest. Shaheed was very kind, not too forthcoming, but he has a gentle manner. He told me to call him Shaheed. I took advantage of him by stealing a look at the file. I am terribly sorry, but I am not a murderer." *Why won't he believe me? I couldn't do something like this!*

"Describe the guy who, you say, stabbed Blackwell." Jack toned it down to give her more rope, looking for a back-and-forth conversation.

"He was older, a rather burly, scruffy, man. He had very long, unruly hair and a flowing beard. He has tattoos and a stud earring in his left ear. He looked like he needed a bath. He wore an old, beat-up black leather jacket with some type of lettered insignia on the back of it and, I think, a swastika. Blackwell had no chance, even though he had a gun. The guy was quick for an older man. Blackwell didn't see him until it was too late. That's all I remember," she gasped.

Jack continued to lighten up on her. He studied her face. She didn't look like a cold-blooded murderer, but, in his experience, looks could be deceiving. Maybe Blackwell surprised her. Perhaps she acted in self-defense. Who knew? Or maybe, just maybe, she was telling the truth. Jack put his hands under her armpits and helped her into a standing position.

"Let's get you down to the station and turn your story into a formal written statement. I'll talk to my boss, and he'll decide what we do with you going forward. I'm not going to lie to you. This looks bad. My officers arrived to find you hunched over a stabbing victim, holding the murder weapon. You look guilty as hell to all of us."

"Why would a murderer call 9-1-1 and report a murder she just committed? Does that make any sense to you? Does it?" she demanded. She was making a good point and doing a half-decent job selling it.

"I've seen a lot of crazy things in this job. Maybe you made the call to make it look like you weren't the killer. Who knows? You had a motive. You have pretty much decided he was the guy who firebombed your mosque, for Christ's sake! You had the means, and you had the opportunity. You were caught holding what is probably the murder weapon. You have blood on your clothing. If you were a cop, what would you think?"

"I can see how it looks to you, Lieutenant, but I swear, I am innocent!"

"You can tell that to the judge, Ms. Khan. I have to take you in. You have the right to remain silent. Anything you say can and will be held against you in a court of law. You have a right to an attorney. If you cannot afford an attorney, one will be appointed for you at no charge. If you decide to answer questions without an attorney present, you have the right to stop the questioning at any time and demand an attorney. Do you understand these rights as I have recited them to you?" Dylan was all about the business of Miranda now.

"Yes, I understand. But wouldn't it have made more sense for you to tell me these things before you questioned me?" She wasn't being a smart-ass—she was genuinely curious.

"Your statements were voluntary, made before you were a suspect or under arrest." Dylan struggled to explain. His failure to Mirandize her might become a future problem.

"But you told me I wasn't under arrest," Arya protested.

"You're not under arrest. We need to get your signed statement, and then the chief and the prosecutor will make a decision on whether to charge you." Jack grumbled, losing his patience.

"If I am not under arrest, why do I need to wear these painful handcuffs?" she whined. She picked up her arms behind her back to show them to him.

"Because I said so! It's protocol," he snapped, losing his temper. "You're a murder suspect, get it?" Arya hung her head and shut her mouth.

Dylan walked her to his black Ford Taurus and opened the rear passenger side door. He helped her in and was careful not to bump her head or let her fall too far, too fast, into the seat. A metal grid separated the front seat from the back seat, giving Arya the feeling she was already incarcerated. They drove in silence to police headquarters.

Chapter Nineteen

Arya and Jack arrived at police headquarters, where she was processed, fingerprinted, photographed, and led to a small metal desk. She looked around the busy squad room. There were similar metal desks; men and women jammed all over the place. She looked around and found Dylan talking to a man who seemed to be no more than 18 years old. Shaheed walked up to the two men. They conversed a while, and Shaheed looked over to her as they spoke. They made eye contact for a second. Shaheed smiled, nodded his head, and returned to the conversation. The three men chatted a while longer. The meeting broke up, and Shaheed walked toward her. The other two went off in different directions.

"Hello, Arya." Shaheed greeted her as he approached the desk. "You've been a busy lady, I hear. Can't leave you alone for a second, can I? What were you thinking, following a dangerous guy like that? You could have been hurt, killed." Shaheed displayed genuine concern. Was this 'good cop, bad cop' like she had seen on TV? Did his comments about her being hurt or killed mean he believed her story?

"I don't know what I was thinking, Shaheed," she gasped. "I guess I wasn't . . . thinking. But I didn't kill that guy. I couldn't do something like that, even to the guy who tried to destroy our mosque."

"I understand, Arya. Tell me what happened, please," he encouraged.

"I told your buddy over there everything I know and everything I saw." She nodded toward an office a few feet away from where Jack Dylan was seated, feet up on the desk, yelling at someone on the telephone.

"I know you did, Arya, but would you mind going over it again? I need to take a formal statement."

"I want to talk to my parents. I want to see an attorney immediately. I don't want to talk anymore. Your friend, Mr. Dylan over there, was very unkind to me. He treated me like a criminal when I assured him I was only trying to help. Mr. Blackwell was stabbed! He was dying! What was I supposed to do? Sit in my car and do nothing? What would you have done, Shaheed?" Arya cried.

"He didn't mean anything, Arya. We are all under a lot of pressure to solve this thing and bring those responsible to justice. I want to help you, but I can't do that unless you cooperate fully," Shaheed reasoned.

"I did give a full statement, and he mocked me, accused me of being a murderer, and then read me my rights. Who gets read their rights *after* their statement is coerced?" Arya persisted.

Shaheed didn't care for that comment. *Hopefully, she doesn't say anything like that to an attorney. Did Jack really coerce a statement from her?* He decided to change the subject. He was mindful of the fact she just requested a lawyer. He wasn't looking for an admissible confession, just a conversation.

"So, you decided to act like Angela Lansbury and solve crimes for the police?"

"Who's Angela Lansbury?" Arya wondered.

Shaheed rolled his eyes. "She's . . . never mind," came the amused reply. "I know you gave a full statement, but in order to put this behind us, we need a formal, written statement. Then, we can cross-check it with all of the evidence we find and process at the scene. Finally, we analyze that evidence and try to determine if your story represents a plausible alternative scenario. Do you understand where I am coming from?"

"Alternate scenario to what? To me being the murderer?" Arya was fatigued, perturbed. She wanted to leave.

"Arya, I promise you I will personally and fully investigate the crime scene evidence. If it points to a different person, I will do everything in my power to prove he's the murderer, not you. But I need to get your statement first."

"I would like these handcuffs removed. They are hurting me, Shaheed." Arya pleaded.

Shaheed opened the desk drawer, took out a key and some type of white powdery substance, and removed the handcuffs. Arya began to rub her wrists. Shaheed unbuttoned her sleeves and poured the powder on her wrists.

"Rub the powder in. It will help."

Arya began to rub the powder into her throbbing wrists. "Thank you, Shaheed. This written statement . . . uh . . . are you sure it is necessary, that it will help me?"

"If you're innocent, it's always better to cooperate with the police."

"But your boss, Lieutenant Dylan, thinks I murdered that guy!"

"We will all keep an open mind, and I, personally, will leave no stone unturned to find the truth. It is what I do, and I am very good at it. Trust me, Arya. I will get to the bottom of this, one way or another."

Arya studied him. He seemed to be a kind, gentle man with a straightforward manner. Under any other circumstances, she could see herself becoming friends with this man. *Today, though, he's a cop, and the cops think I'm a murderer. He could probably get any criminal to confess his or her crime. Should I trust him?*

Arya settled on a middle ground. She decided to write out a statement, as Shaheed requested. Basically, she would repeat, in writing, precisely what she told Jack Dylan because it was the truth. *How can the truth hurt me?* In return, she would demand Shaheed let her call her parents and speak to a lawyer.

"Shaheed," she looked into his eyes for signs of deception. "I will write out this statement you're demanding, but only on one condition. I want to call my parents and let them know I'm okay. After that, I wish to speak with an attorney, right away."

"That's two conditions," Shaheed smiled.

That charming smile again . . . "Two conditions then," Arya shrugged, smiling back at Ali, the first time she'd smiled since this ordeal began.

"Agreed," Shaheed acknowledged. "You write out a statement, sign it, and I'll let you talk to your parents and see an attorney. Deal?"

"Deal."

Shaheed brought a pen and lined paper and left her to write out the statement. He did not go far. He walked into Jack Dylan's office and sat down.

"She agreed to write out a formal statement," Shaheed advised. "She wants to talk to her parents, and she wants a lawyer."

"What do you think about her, Shaheed?" Jack inquired. "What is that famous gut telling you?"

"There are stone-cold killers who couldn't plunge a knife into someone's stomach, then stand there and watch him die. It is a brutal way to kill someone. She strikes me as a gentle soul, not one capable of this brand of brutality. My gut instinct is there's little chance she's guilty of murder. Having said that, let's see where the evidence leads us."

"It's difficult to escape the fact she was standing over the victim, holding the knife, with blood all over her. That's pretty damning stuff, and hard to overcome," reasoned Dylan.

"I know, but her story fits the facts just as well as the scenario she's the killer, maybe even better. I'm sorry, but I just can't picture her lying in wait, stabbing Blackwell, and then attending to him while waiting for the police. She gives a very detailed description of the killer. Fabricating that level of detail is difficult. She saw an old biker guy with tattoos, a motorcycle, a diamond stud, long, grey unkempt hair? This is quite a description, no? And from the description, if we believe her, it is reasonable to assume the killer is a member of some group Blackwell belonged to. Maybe this was a hit. Maybe they wanted to silence him. As it happens, they got lucky and got an even bigger break. Along comes Arya Khan. She picks up the knife, gets caught holding it, and now she is the suspect instead of the guy with the stones to commit the crime, the guy with an equally compelling motive."

"And, there's the 9-1-1 call," Dylan conceded. Was he beginning to believe her story?

"What 9-1-1 call?" Shaheed had been told the main bits of Arya's story, but not the details.

"Someone called 9-1-1 to report a stabbing at Blackwell's residence. The caller was a female. Arya says it was her who made the call."

"That's interesting. If it is true and it was Arya, what killer summons the police to the scene of a murder she committed and waits with the victim until the police arrive?"

"A very cunning one. What if Arya did it on purpose so she could posit the soddit defense? She kills him. She decides to blame it on some old white supremacist biker dude because she did some research on Blackwell's little group of racists. She looks around and decides no one saw her stab Blackwell. She concocts the defense, invents the biker dude, calls 9-1-1, and waits there for the police. It's a nice little end-around to confuse us into thinking she's innocent, no?"

"That's quite a stretch, Jack," Shaheed argued. "What is it about this girl that makes you think she's a killer and a terrific, perhaps pathological, liar?"

"Terrorism goes both ways. When the towers came down, I wanted to kill someone. I wanted to lash out. The mosque bombing was, for Arya, like the towers were for me. That's a powerful motive." Jack sounded like a man who was trying to convince himself Arya Khan was a woman capable of a brutal murder.

"The murder weapon is a Benchmade hunting knife. What are the chances an observant Muslim woman owns or borrowed a hunting knife?" Shaheed wasn't buying Jack's arguments. In fact, he was even more convinced Arya was telling the truth. Jack was his boss and seemed satisfied she was guilty. Shaheed would defer for now.

"We can hold her for 72 hours, book her if we have to. We can always let her go if new evidence comes to light. I don't like the idea of releasing someone who was holding the murder weapon while standing over the victim's dead body. Let's ask the chief. Give him Arya's statement and all of the facts. If he decides to charge her . . ." Jack shrugged.

Jack and Shaheed looked over at Arya, diligently writing her statement. Was she a cold-blooded killer or an innocent patsy in another man's crime? The two men were in vastly different places on the confusing subject of Arya Khan.

Chapter Twenty

As promised, in exchange for her written statement, Arya was permitted to call Hamid and Riah Khan. She had not yet called an attorney, although she was granted permission to do so. She didn't know an attorney and, besides, she hadn't been officially charged with any crime. She was in some type of holding pattern. Shaheed called it a 72-hour hold. She did not understand her own legal status. *Am I under arrest or not?*

When she reached her parents by telephone, they were initially not much comfort. In fact, they were panic-stricken. They did not trust the police or the government in general. They did not know a criminal lawyer but promised to try to find her one. *That* was a comfort, because of all the people she knew in the world, her parents were the people she trusted the most. If there was a good lawyer out there, perfect for her case, her parents would find him or her.

Arya was reluctant to talk in any detail with her parents out of fear the police were listening in or recording the conversation. She could not have been more correct. Arya told them she was innocent of the charges—they knew that already, as this was *Arya*, their sweet daughter—and she was an eyewitness to the murder.

"*Allahu Akbar,* Arya! That must have been horrible!" Riah cried.

"It was horrible, Mother, but I am all right. I'm a lot better than Keith Blackwell," Arya reasoned.

"Who is Keith Blackwell?" Hamid wondered.

"Keith Blackwell is the man who firebombed the mosque, Papa."

"*Allahu Akbar,* Arya. Are you sure?" Her father was beyond shocked.

"Yes, Papa. The police had a warrant for his arrest, and they had just searched his house. When he arrived home, the police were gone, but another man came to his front door and stabbed him," Arya related.

"So, why do they think you did it, sweetheart?" Riah was confused.

"Because when the killer left the house, I called 9-1-1. Then, I ran over to the guy who was stabbed to try to help him. In doing so, I picked up the knife. I don't know why, but I did. When the police arrived, they saw me hovering over the body with the knife in my hand. Now, they think I did it because of the mosque."

"Do they know it was you who called 9-1-1? A murderer wouldn't do that. She certainly wouldn't stay at the scene of the murder, attend to the victim and wait for the police to arrive," Hamid reasoned.

"That's exactly what I argued," Arya, grunted. She grew more despondent by the minute.

"It makes no sense. Surely the cops see that." Hamid growled.

"So far, they don't see that at all. I am trying to persuade them to find and listen to the 9-1-1 call. I want them to run what they call a voice recognition test."

"What is that, Arya? How will it help?" Hamid inquired.

"It is a computer program that helps the police identify someone's voice. If the computer can prove I'm the one who called 9-1-1, it will help prove my innocence. After all, what sense does it make for a murderer to call 9-1-1 and report a murder he or she committed?"

"So, then will they let you go?" Riah prayed. "When?"

"I don't know. Right now, I'm in limbo. I don't know if they are going to charge me with Mr. Blackwell's murder or not. If they charge me, I will probably have to stay here. If they don't, I can probably go home."

"Charge you? *Allahu Akbar,* Arya!" Riah cried.

Shaheed motioned her that the call must end.

"Mama, Papa, I must hang up now." She started to cry while they continued to do so. "Please find me a good lawyer. It appears I'm going to need one."

"Don't say that, Arya. Everything will be okay; Allah watches over you," Riah consoled.

"He wasn't watching over me this time, Mama."

"Please, Arya! Keep your faith. Faith gets you through difficult times."

"You know I have faith, Mama. What I need now is a good lawyer. Please find me one, Mama and Papa. I have to hang up. I love you both very much . . ."

"We love you too, Arya . . ."

The phone beeped twice, and she was gone. Hamid and Riah Khan heard only silence. They looked at each other, burst into tears again, and embraced for several seconds. When they stood apart, both decided to call the Imam. He would know an attorney or, at least how to find one. Hopefully, he knew a *great* attorney because their baby girl was going to need one.

***

Hamid Khan was scrolling the contacts list on his iPhone moments after he heard the two beeps that meant his daughter's call was terminated. He found the number he was looking for and clicked on it. The line rang a couple of times, and Imam Baqir Ghaffari answered on the other end of the call.

"Hello?"

"*Asalaamu Alaikum*, Imam Ghaffari. This is Hamid Khan. Do you have time to talk?" The Imam heard the desperation in Hamid's voice.

"*Alaikum Salam*, Hamid. I am so sorry. I was going to call you. I have heard about Arya. This is terrible and ridiculous, the idea Arya could have hurt much less killed, anyone."

"How did you find out, Baqir?" Hamid was stunned that anyone knew anything. All of this murder stuff was still developing. The events only consumed part of a day. To Hamid, the short time seemed like an eternity once he discovered his precious Arya was sitting, alone and afraid, at police headquarters.

"I have friends at Dearborn PD who alert me when a member of our community is in trouble. What is going on? Do you know anything?"

"No, I don't. They let Arya call me, and that's how I found out she was in trouble. She tells me they think she killed a man. They think it is the man who firebombed the mosque. All of us have hate in our hearts for this man, but Arya? She wouldn't hurt a fly. You know this as well as anyone. Tell your friends at Dearborn PD she could not have done this. She is not capable of killing someone. Please?" His voice was cracking, pleading with the Imam.

"Calm down, Hamid. I know Arya is not capable of murder. I know she did not do this."

"He was *stabbed*, Baqir! Can you imagine Arya sticking a knife into someone's body?" Hamid cried.

"No, no, I can't, Hamid. I will talk to them, but I do not have any power over there. They will not listen to me. They will not release her just because I say so."

"She needs a professional, Baqir. She needs the best lawyer we can find. Money is no object. I will sell my home, sell my store. I will cash in my stocks, bonds, IRA. I don't care. I have to help my precious Arya, my sweet little girl." Hamid sobbed.

"Hamid, you must calm down. You must be strong for Arya. Don't go off selling anything yet. The community will respond. You know that. I will go down to police headquarters and talk with them. I will try to see Arya and make sure she is okay. In the meantime, a few years ago, I met an attorney through a colleague of mine, a rabbi. This rabbi had great things to say about this attorney. He is great in court and fights hard for his clients."

"A Jew? Here in Dearborn? Wouldn't a fellow Muslim understand this better, or, at least, a Christian? I don't know, Baqir. I don't know."

"I didn't say he was Jewish. I don't know whether he is or not. I do know he is highly regarded, and the rabbi thinks the world of him. As for the community, I don't think any of that matters. We need the best of the best to prove Arya didn't do this thing they are accusing her of." Ghaffari argued.

"What's this lawyer's name? Do you have his contact information?"

"No, I don't, Hamid. His name is Zachary something. Zachary . . ." There was silence on the other end of the line as Baqir tried, in vain, to remember the attorney's last name.

"I can't remember," he finally uttered, exasperated. "I'll call the rabbi and get his name and contact information. Please, hang in there, Hamid. We will get Arya the help she needs, and I will pray for her and for your family. Remember, Hamid, Allah rewards those who have been righteous and patient. I will call you back soon."

Hamid Khan was calming some. "*Shokran*, Imam Ghaffari. I appreciate it."

"I will call you as soon as I reach the rabbi and get the name. *Khoda Hafez*, Hamid."

***

The two men terminated the call, and Imam Ghaffari immediately dialed the number of his friend from the Interfaith Council, Rabbi Joseph Norman. Rabbi Norman answered on the first ring.

"Rabbi Joey, may I help you?

"*Shalom*, my friend." Ghaffari used the traditional Hebrew greeting.

"Baqir? How nice to hear from you. *Asalaamu Alaikum.* To what do I owe this pleasure? Is everything okay?"

"I'm afraid not, Joey. A friend from my community is in legal trouble and in need of a good lawyer."

"What kind of lawyer, Baqir?"

"A criminal lawyer, Joey. This person, a beautiful young lady, a kind and gentle soul, has been accused of murder."

"Murder? Oh, my God!"

"Joey, what was the name of that lawyer you introduced me to at the council fundraiser a couple of years ago? You rambled on about how terrific this guy."

"Yes, I did, and he is. I don't know if he does criminal work, though. His name is Zachary Blake. If he does criminal work, he is your man. This guy is a barracuda in court."

"A barracuda?"

"An expression, Baqir. It means he's tough and tenacious."

"I see. Do you have his contact information?"

"Yes, I do, he is in Bloomfield Hills." He scrolled his address list, holding the phone up as close as he could while still able to see the address list. He found the contact he was looking for. "Here it is." Rabbi Norman found Zachary Blake's address on Woodward and his Oakland County 248 area code and phone number and recited it to Baqir Ghaffari. "Please tell Zachary I referred you and say hello for me. I will pray for your young lady."

"Thank you, Joey, I appreciate it."

"Is everything else going okay? Plans for the mosque reconstruction?"

"The insurance company is dragging its feet. We may have to hire a public adjuster. It is sad your own insurance company can't do the right thing, even for a place of worship."

"What's the problem?"

"Truthfully, despite a police investigation that suggests it was a white supremacist, I think the insurance company has been investigating whether our own community torched the mosque."

"That's ridiculous!" Where would they get such an idea?" Rabbi Joey grumbled.

"It's the times, Joey. Muslims are guilty of everything these days, even the destruction of our own place of worship, the center of our community. I cannot explain it, this prejudice and hatred. The jihadists have brought some of this upon us, but non-Muslims are just as guilty when they paint an entire society with such a broad brush. And when I thought it could not get any worse, the voters give us this . . . this . . . Ronald John. Unbelievable!" Rabbi Norman could not recall hearing such frustration and negativity in his friend's tone.

"Cheer up, my friend. The president is not making any friends with his deportation policies or his ban on Muslim travel. People are starting to see him for who he really is. So are the courts and the legislature. We have three branches of government in this country for a reason. He won't get half the stuff he is trying to get through the courts or the Congress."

"Half would be a disaster, Joey, but, hey, we'll get through this, somehow. Moderate forces in the Muslim world will have to be a part of the solution, too, so the jihadists aren't permitted to define who we are as a people."

"Amen to that, brother. Good luck with your friend. I'll talk to you soon. *Asalaamu Alaikum.*" Rabbi Norman smiled.

"*Shalom,* my friend," the Imam sighed.

***

Rabbi Joseph Norman sat back in his chair and looked upward. He thought about the work of the Interfaith Council, his friend, Baqir Ghaffari, and the trouble his people were having all over the world. He thought about prejudice, anti-Semitism, and racism. He thought about Rodney King, the Los Angeles cab driver who was famously beaten by the Los Angeles Police in the early '90s. The vicious beating was caught on videotape, but, despite video evidence of the assault, a Los Angeles jury acquitted all of the officers. The acquittals led to the 1992 Los Angeles riots, during which King made a television appearance, called for calm, and inquired, "Can't we all get along?"

"Can't we all get along?" Rabbi Joey muttered aloud, his brow furrowing.

It would be such a blessing if the relationship between a Muslim imam and a Jewish rabbi became contagious, spreading like wildfire across the land. Peace and community have to begin somewhere, why not across the Southfield Freeway from Dearborn to Southfield and beyond? He breathed a deep sigh and returned to his work.

***

Imam Baqir Ghaffari sat back in the chair in his makeshift office. He thought about his friend, Rabbi Joey. He thought about the Holocaust and the new president. He thought about his fellow Americans and the current political divide. *Was today's Muslim refugee from Syria or Yemen somehow different than a 1930s or 1940s Jew from Poland or Germany? When the Jewish people came to America from Russia to escape pogroms, or Poland to escape the Nazis, would anyone have concluded all those who arrived at Ellis Island were terrorists? How about when the Armenians were fleeing from the Ottoman government in the early 1900s? Or when Chaldeans fled Iraq after America invaded in 2003? Was there American concern? Were they all suspected terrorists?*

Baqir Ghaffari wasn't sure of the answer. He knew these were more complicated, different times. He knew attitudes can and sometimes do change. However, right is right, freedom is freedom, danger is danger, and tyranny is tyranny.

If escaping terror was right before, in all of those cases, how can it not be right now? No people have been terrorized more by the jihadists than Muslim people. Undoubtedly, rational American citizens can see that, no? Moderate Muslims like Imam Baqir Ghaffari must make a difference. *We must make them understand.* This would become his life's work.

Chapter Twenty-One

The intercom buzzed in Zachary Blake's office. Fresh from his honeymoon in the south of France, Zack picked up the receiver. "Yes, Kristen?"

"There is a man on the phone. He is asking for you and only you. Says his name is Hamid Khan. He wants to discuss a new case."

"What kind of case?" Zack inquired.

"A criminal case, I think," Kristen advised.

"Kristen, I don't do criminal work anymore. Give the call to Emma." Emma Pearl was a former judge who left the bench for a lucrative partnership in Zack's busy law firm.

"He will only talk to you, Zack. What should I do?"

"Oh, all right, I'll take it. Thanks, Kristen."

"Putting it through now, boss."

"Please don't call me, boss. I hate that word. We're all family here."

"OK, Zack, here's the call."

"Thanks again."

Kristen clicked off, and the call was automatically sent to Zack. He waited for a short beep. "Zachary Blake, how may I help you?"

"Mr. Blake, thank you for taking my call. My name is Hamid Khan. I was given your number by Imam Baqir Ghaffari from the Mosque of America."

Ghaffari, Ghaffari? Why is that name familiar? Zack pondered.

Khan continued, "He got your name from Rabbi Joseph Norman. He's a friend of yours?"

He dropped the right name. Zack was officially curious.

"Yes. In fact, he is *more* than a friend. You have my attention. What can I do for you?"

"My daughter, my sweet, innocent Arya, is being held at police headquarters while the police investigate a murder. They think she did it."

"A murder? How old is your daughter?"

"Arya is 25. She could not have done this thing they accuse her of."

"What do they say she did?" Zack was intrigued.

"You might recall our mosque was firebombed recently. It was in all the papers and all over the Internet."

*That's where I heard the name, Ghaffari. He was **that** Imam!* Now Khan had his complete attention. "Yes, I remember. It was terrible. Lucky no one was badly hurt. But what does this have to do with your daughter?"

"The police have identified a suspect and Arya, during a visit to police headquarters, found out the identity of the suspect. Mr. Blake—"

"Call me Zachary, please, Mr. Khan," Zachary interrupted him mid-sentence.

"Only if you call me Hamid." *He seems nice, this Zachary Blake.*

"OK, Hamid, please continue."

"Arya has been beside herself over the mosque. This is true for many members of our community. But Arya . . . she took the bombing . . . I don't know . . . personally, do you know what I mean?"

Zack Blake knew what he meant. A few years ago, a priest molested his now stepsons, Kenny and Jake. He took that case very personally and exacted sweet justice from those responsible.

"Yes, Hamid. I know exactly what you mean," he confirmed. "Go on."

"Arya did a very unwise thing. I am not certain what got into her except, as I mentioned, the mosque bombing affected her deeply. One day, the day of the murder, she decided to follow this man, the suspect. She followed him to a store and then to his home. She sat in her car a few houses down while he went into the house. While he was in the house, another man came, an older man in a biker's jacket. He climbed up on the porch, waited there against the wall, and when the guy came out, this older guy stabbed him and killed him. Then, the biker guy ran away and left the other man lying on the porch, bleeding to death." Hamid started to heave.

"Take a moment, Hamid. Take a deep breath. Your daughter saw all this from the car? It must have been terrible for her."

"It was, Mr., uh, Zachary. She was horrified. She didn't know what to do. She called 9-1-1, ran to the porch, and tried to comfort the man and stop the bleeding. She saw the knife, and for some reason, she picked it up. That's when the police arrived. They arrived to see her hovering over the body, holding the knife!" Hamid sobbed.

"Shit," Zack spewed. "Sorry . . . shoot. Hamid, I have to give it to you straight, okay?"

"Yes, Zack?"

"I believe they are going to charge your daughter with murder. To catch someone with the body and holding the murder weapon . . . Arya, is that her name?"

"Yes."

"Arya is in a lot of trouble. That's the straight scoop. Are you sure she didn't do it? As you admitted, she was angry and took what this guy did very personally."

Hamid did not appreciate the question. He wanted an attorney who believed in his daughter's innocence. "I am absolutely certain, Zachary. I would stake my life on it. My daughter is not capable of murder. And to plunge a knife into a man's stomach? It is not possible." His voice shook with frustration.

"OK, Hamid. Where is she being held?"

"Police headquarters in Dearborn."

"That's right; you told me that earlier. Sorry."

"That's okay. Can you help us? I will be forever in your debt."

"This will probably be a first-degree murder case. If it goes to trial and through appeals, it may be costly, you understand that?"

"I can pay you, Zachary, if that's what you mean. And, my community has pledged its support."

"I hate to discuss fees at a time like this, but we might as well put our cards on the table and get the discussion out of the way. I charge $500 per hour, $1,000 per hour for court time. A capital murder case will require a $100,000 retainer. That money will be placed in trust and only withdrawn in increments as I earn it by spending time on the case. I will not waste time or money. I'll return any money we end up not using to pursue the case. I am very good at what I do. I am tenacious, and I will stop at nothing to give your daughter the best possible defense. This will be a tough case, and in tough cases, you need the best. I am the best, Hamid. I am going to go down to police headquarters the minute we finish this telephone call and see what I can find out. How does that sound? Do you want to retain my services?"

Zachary wished to put Hamid at ease. To some, his words would sound boastful, arrogant, or cocky. To Hamid, they were sweet music.

"Yes, I will find a way to raise the retainer, Zachary. A man must be paid appropriate value for his skill and his work. I will find a way. You are hired if you truly want the job and will work hard for my daughter."

"Hamid, I will work harder than any man has ever worked to exonerate your daughter. Do you have an e-mail? I will e-mail you a retainer agreement."

"I do." They exchanged e-mail addresses and were preparing to terminate the conversation.

"Thank you for listening and your kindness, Zachary, Hamid acknowledged. "Oh, I almost forgot, one more thing."

"What is it, Hamid?"

"Today, my wife and I received deportation notices under the new guidelines. Apparently, Arya's criminal situation is playing a role. We now stand accused of raising a murderer. Because we are from Yemen, we are on the list. Arya was born here, so I don't think they can deport her. Of course, if there is a way, this new president will find it."

"Are you an American citizen, Hamid?"

"Yes, we have been citizens for a long time."

"Then I don't think he can deport *you*, either. But, it is not my area of expertise. I will find you the best immigration lawyer in town, and I will include his services in my fee. We will handle the immigration case pro bono. How does that sound?"

"What does this mean, this pro bono, Zachary?"

"It means without additional charge, Hamid."

Hamid was surprised and touched by Zack's generous offer. But, it was not his way. "But that will cost you money out of your pocket, Zachary. I won't allow that, Zachary. I am not a charity case, and we do not know each other as friends. This is business."

"I know a lot of lawyers. Several owe me a lot of favors. It will not cost me a dime," Zack lied. "I will be well compensated for your daughter's case. I cannot stand this president's anti-immigrant policies, but I have hope he will see the light someday. We may be able to get financial assistance from those who oppose his travel ban and anti-Muslim rhetoric. Please, Hamid. Let me do this."

Hamid thought long and hard. *He is very persuasive, this Zachary Blake. I like him. He will do an excellent job for Arya. And he wants to do this. My pride is one thing. My daughter is EVERYTHING . . .*

"Okay, Zachary, you win. But you have to inform me if I owe additional money. If it doesn't go the way you thought it would, you will have to let me pay you. Deal?"

*I like this man. He is honorable. He loves his daughter and his family, and, besides, he probably voted for Goodman. My kind of guy . . ."*Deal, Hamid."

The two men terminated the call. Zachary buzzed his legal assistant, Sandra, and receptionist, Kristen, to let them know he was leaving the office for a few hours. He got into his Beemer and took off south on Woodward Avenue. Soon, he was cruising down the Southfield Freeway at 70-mph in a 55-mph zone, all the way into Dearborn. The vehicle's state of the art navigation system steered him expertly to police headquarters.

Zack parked his car in the public lot and walked up to and into the building. When he reached the reception desk, he read the nametag on the man sitting behind it doing paperwork, ignoring him completely.

"Good afternoon, Sergeant Meltzer. I am an attorney. Here is my bar card and my business card. My name's Zack Blake, and I would like to see whoever is in charge of the Arya Khan investigation."

Meltzer reached out and took the cards with one hand. He continued holding the paperwork in the other. He did not look up at Zack and was borderline robotic.

"And what is your interest in the case, Mr. Blake?" The cop still stared at the paperwork, refusing to make eye contact.

"I have been retained by the family to represent Ms. Khan."

"One second, please."

Meltzer stacked the paper and placed it in a bin on the left side of the long counter. He picked up a headset, turned 90 degrees in his swivel chair, his back to Zack, and began mumbling incoherently into the headset. When he finished the conversation, he turned back and looked at Zack for the first time.

"Someone will be right out, sir. You can wait over there." He pointed to a bank of hard plastic chairs bolted into the floor. Zack shrugged, then he walked over and sat down. As he sat, he reflected on the conversation and chuckled. *What a nice guy . . . Not!*

He waited for about five minutes. A tall, slim man with salt-and-pepper hair came through the inner sanctum and approached him.

"Mr. Blake? I'm Lieutenant Jack Dylan. I'm in charge of the Khan investigation. What can I do for you?"

"I understand you're holding Arya Khan here at police headquarters. Is that true?"

"It is." He was almost as robotic as Meltzer. *At least he looks at me when he talks.*

"What is the charge?"

"She hasn't been charged."

"Then why is she being held?" Zack knew the likely answer but wanted to hear it from Dylan.

"She's on a 72-hour hold for suspicion of murder."

"Whom is she supposed to have murdered?" Again, Zack knew the answer. He was attempting to determine how cooperative Dylan was going to be going forward.

"A white supremacist by the name of Keith Blackwell."

"A white supremacist? Sounds like whoever killed the guy did you guys a favor," Zack smiled.

"Yeah, well, murder is murder. We don't go for vigilante justice around here. You're not from Dearborn, are you, Mr. Blake?"

"No, Bloomfield Hills. Vigilante? Why vigilante? What did this guy do?" Zack continued to test Dylan.

Dylan realized his mistake and appeared to be looking for a way to change the subject. "Bloomfield Hills, huh? How's the weather up there?" He raised his nose up in the air, snobbishly. Bloomfield Hills was only 30 to 40 miles from Dearborn, but it was a more affluent community.

Zack ignored the comment. "Why vigilante, Lieutenant? What did this guy do?" He repeated.

Jack had no choice. He had to answer. "We have solid evidence he was the guy who firebombed the Mosque of America. You familiar with the case?"

"Yeah, I read about it. What does that have to do with Arya Khan?"

"She was a member of the community and attended services at the mosque—very devoted—she was following the suspect on the day of the murder. We have eyewitnesses. The rest is confidential." Dylan was circumspect.

"Eyewitnesses to what, exactly?" Zack toyed with him.

"I can't say, Mr. Blake. Needless to say, we wouldn't be holding her if we didn't have something."

"When will you make a decision on charges?"

"Today or tomorrow, who knows? We are still developing evidence, fingerprints, blood, DNA, footprints. You know the drill."

"Has she been questioned? Did she give a statement? Was she Mirandized? Did she request a lawyer?"

Zack noticed Dylan look away and shift his feet from side to side. These questions made him uncomfortable. *Did he fuck up on the interrogation and forget Miranda?* Zack would have to root out the source of Dylan's discomfort at some point in his investigation. *On the witness stand, maybe?*

Dylan recovered quickly. The average person would not have noticed his momentary discomfort. But Zack Blake was not the average person.

"Yes, she was questioned. She was Mirandized. She was allowed to call her parents and a lawyer. She voluntarily gave a formal statement."

"Without counsel present? She agreed to that?" Zack was incredulous.

"Yes, she voluntarily gave a statement, then wanted to speak with her parents and a lawyer. All questioning was terminated at that time."

"May I see the statement?" The request was more of a demand.

"In discovery," Dylan huffed, with attitude.

"Okay." Zack maintained a pleasant, professional demeanor. "I'd like to see her, please."

"I'll see if she is available."

Zack was trying to be nice, but Dylan wasn't making it easy. *He's starting to piss me off.*

"You admitted she requested an attorney. I'm here. I'm her attorney. She's entitled to counsel. I want to see her. Don't make me demand to see her. Don't make me go over your head. And, for heaven's sake, don't make me go to a judge. It will not be pretty." Zack crossed his arms and prepared for battle.

Dylan capitulated, as he knew he must. "Hang on, Blake, hang on. Don't get your panties all twisted up. I'll take you to her. Follow me."

Zack followed Dylan through a corridor that ended at an elevator. They took the elevator down one floor and arrived at a makeshift series of holding cells. They were all empty except for one with a single occupant, a young, beautiful woman wearing a hijab.

Dylan led Zack to an area to the left of the cells where there was a door. Dylan opened the door and revealed a small office with a small, rectangular table and two chairs on opposite sides. Zack liked the fact there were no windows. These offices often had reflective glass mirrors where the police could eavesdrop on a private attorney-client discussion if they wished to. The room could still be bugged, but Zack didn't see any place to conceal a listening device.

Dylan told him to have a seat, left the room, and a few minutes later, he returned with the beautiful hijab woman. She was handcuffed with her hands in front of her.

"Lieutenant, please remove these handcuffs. They are not necessary."

"Safety is paramount here, sir," Dylan snipped.

"I'll accept full responsibility," Zack offered. "Besides, she is not a criminal—she hasn't been charged with anything."

"Will you sign a waiver?"

"I will."

"I'll be right back," Dylan promised. He left them alone, with the woman still in handcuffs.

"I presume you are Arya Khan?" inquired Zack.

"I am," she hesitated. "W-who are you?"

"My name is Zachary Blake. I'm your new attorney. Your father retained me a couple of hours ago. How are you holding up?"

"Oh, Mr. Blake . . ." Arya Khan gasped, relieved.

"Call me Zack, please." He suggested with a warm smile.

Arya attempted to compose herself. She brought her handcuffed wrists up in front of her and wiped her eyes with her sleeve. "Okay, Zack it is. I am so glad you are here. They won't tell me anything! They won't listen to me. They won't believe me. I told Shaheed everything, and they still won't let me go or tell me what's going on. Maybe you can help."

"Well, I'll do my best. Who's Shaheed?"

"Shaheed Ali. He is a detective here in Dearborn."

"And you told him 'everything?' What does 'everything' mean?"

Before she could answer, Dylan walked back into the room with a document for Zack to sign. Zack scanned it, placed it on the table, looked up at Dylan, and motioned with his hands for a pen, then signed the document. Dylan scooped up the document, walked over to Arya, and removed her handcuffs. "Knock when you're ready," he grumbled to no one in particular. Then, he left the room. Zack and Arya heard an audible *click* as Jack locked the door.

"So, Arya . . . May I call you Arya?"

"Yes, please do."

"Arya then. What do you mean by everything?"

"Shaheed is a very nice man. He is Muslim. He is on my side. I told him everything that happened. I told Dylan, too, but he was not very nice to me. He didn't believe me at all, and he was very sarcastic."

"I'm not surprised. Did either of these gentlemen mention you had a right to remain silent and a right to talk to an attorney?"

"Not right away. Not for a long time. They kept prompting me to tell the story, over and over, and finally, they ordered me to write it all down. I wanted to speak to my parents and to a lawyer. They promised to arrange such a meeting if I would write the statement."

"And did you agree to do that?" Zack was pissed.

"Yes, I did. They allowed me to call my parents, and, apparently, my parents called you, praise Allah." She was very relieved. Tears were again running down her cheeks.

"Arya, this is very important." Zack furrowed his brow and became very serious. "I want you to tell me everything you told Shaheed and Dylan. Don't leave out a single detail. By the way, Shaheed is not your friend. He is a Dearborn cop who, believe me, is trying to put you away for murder. Do you understand? No more statements to anyone but me. Not your friends, not your family, only me. Got it?"

"Got it." She was a quick study.

Zack paused for a moment and studied the young woman. *She is so soft-spoken, respectful, and kind. And, she is beautiful, not a stitch of makeup. Can she possibly be a murderer?*

"Now, I want you to tell me everything you told them."

Arya spent the next half-hour telling Zack the whole story. She left nothing out. Zack listened intently, took a few notes, and when she was finished, leaned his chair back on two legs. He took a deep breath and looked very contemplative.

"Arya, I want you to look me in the eyes and tell me the absolute truth. I don't care if you are innocent or guilty. I will defend you to the best of my ability either way. Did you kill Keith Blackwell?"

She looked him straight in his eyes with her beautiful, hypnotic, blue eyes. "Absolutely not, Mr. Blake."

"Zack, please."

"Absolutely not, Zack."

"Catching you over the body with the murder weapon in your hand is very bad. Coupled with the fact he's the man who bombed your mosque, you discovered his identity by stealing the information from a police officer's desk, and followed him the way you did, I am certain they are going to charge you with first-degree murder. First degree means you planned the murder and carried it out. It was not some spontaneous, sudden event done out of anger. They will say you carefully planned the murder."

"All I did was follow him! I didn't know there would be a murder. I would never hurt—nor have I ever thought of hurting—anyone in my whole life. Why would I call 9-1-1 and wait for the police if I was the murderer?" Arya gasped.

"They will say you did that to draw attention away from the fact that you are, indeed, the murderer. A smokescreen, if you will. Understand?"

"I guess so. It seems like such a strange thing for a murderer to do, don't you think?"

"Yes, I do. But I know cops, and when they zero in on someone, they try to massage the facts to make them fit the scenario they prefer."

"Massage the facts? I don't understand."

"I'm sorry. Let me explain. As you suggested, it doesn't make sense for the murderer to call 9-1-1 and wait around for the police to arrive. But, they think you are guilty. If you were guilty, why would you sit around and wait for the police to arrive? The police need a reason, so they theorize. Do you know what that means?"

"Sit around and figure out reasons," Arya concluded, suddenly illuminated.

"Exactly! In this case, they theorize you called 9-1-1 because you couldn't get away in time and wanted to use the 'why would a murderer call 9-1-1 if she was guilty?' defense."

"That is very cynical, don't you think, Mr. Blake . . . uh . . . Zachary?"

"Yes, but they are cops. You were found with the body, holding the murder weapon. I doubt they will try to dig much deeper. The only way out of this, I'm afraid, is to find out who actually did this, or at least find some alternative suspect or suspects. Considering your description of the victim and the murderer, I would say someone, probably a member of his group or cult, wanted to shut this Blackwell up, permanently. They didn't trust him, so they shut his mouth for him. Get it?"

"I think so," she claimed to understand. "All of that does not sound good for me. Please talk to Shaheed. He seems like a reasonable person."

"I will talk to him and Dylan. I'll see what I can do to get them to either put up or shut up. We need to move this into the legal process so I can get my hands on whatever evidence they have. If they charge you with First Degree, there may be no bail, and you may be here for a while. Not a whole lot I can do about that. We'll have to wait and see. How are you holding up in here?"

"I'm alright. I miss my family."

"I have to go now, Arya. If you remember anything else about that day, even if it doesn't seem important, ask to use a phone and call me. Here is my business card." He smiled, reached across the table, and handed her a card.

"Thank you, Zachary; please thank Papa for me and tell him I love him very much."

Zack rose and knocked on the door to the outside. "I will, Arya. You hang in there, okay?"

"I'll do my best. Thank you for coming."

"No problem at all. Now, remember, not a word about what happened to anybody but me, ever again. Got it?"

"Got it." She smiled and saluted him, like a serviceman saluting her commanding officer. Then, she brushed her finger and thumb across her lips and 'locked' them by twisting her hand at the corner of her mouth.

Zack smiled and mimicked her gestures. "And don't lose your sense of humor," he quipped. "We'll figure this out." A key jingled in the lock. The door opened with Jack Dylan standing just outside the threshold.

"Goodbye, Arya." Zack smiled, holding his index finger to his lips, the classic 'shh.'

Arya returned his smile. "Goodbye, Zack—thanks again." The door closed and locked itself. Arya Khan was, once again, a prisoner in a locked room. And she was alone, very much alone.

Chapter Twenty-Two

Jack Dylan escorted Zachary Blake back to the waiting area where Sergeant Meltzer operated the front desk. Jack spoke first.

"Not sure what's going to happen; my chief will make the call. But, if I had to guess, I think your client is in it for the long haul."

"Look, Jack . . . May I call you, Jack? And I'm Zack."

"Sure, Zack." Dylan lightened up a bit. Zack decided to put his cards on the table.

"Arya says she had long talks with both you and Shaheed, and no one offered her Miranda."

"They were conversations, not interrogations. Before Arya made a formal statement, she was Mirandized. We were not trying to trick her. As a matter of fact, we were trying to find out whether her story was solid or provable. We don't want to charge an innocent woman any more than you do," Jack pledged.

"She's clearly innocent, Jack. I've talked to Arya and her parents at length. They are good people. Does she strike you as someone who could shove a knife into someone's stomach? What type of knife was it, by the way?" Zack inquired.

"She was hovering over the body, holding the murder weapon, which was a hunting knife, to answer your question. Several officers responding to the scene saw the same thing. Her fingerprints were on the knife. The victim's blood and DNA were found on her body and hers on his. Ignoring that kind of evidence is hard. These facts are incontestable."

"I understand, Jack, and while you won't let me see her statement, let me convey to you what I know about her statement. You don't have to confirm or deny what I tell you unless you want to, but I am going to lay it all out anyway," Zack asserted.

"Hit me."

"I am aware of her s-o-d-d-i-t defense. I'm aware she saw the perp and can provide a rather detailed description of him. I'm aware she called 9-1-1. I know you haven't confirmed she placed the call to 9-1-1, but she did, and voice recognition will prove it. I know you're concerned the call to 9-1-1 might have been a smokescreen, and I understand your cynicism, but this is not the type of person who is devious enough to manufacture this detailed alibi within seconds of committing murder. She's also not someone capable of any type of murder, let alone the brutal type of murder you think she committed. Besides, Blackwell is a big, bad dude. And where in hell would a petite, young, religious Muslim lady get a hunting knife? Do you really see this tiny woman, a hundred pounds soaking wet, lying in wait for someone like Blackwell?"

"It's not up to me, Zack. I present the evidence to my chief, and he presents it to the prosecutor. They make the calls here, not me. Or, we might present the evidence to the grand jury, and that would be Wayne County's call."

Zack paused. He was not sure whether the prosecutor would choose to indict and schedule a preliminary examination or present the case to the grand jury. If Arya was charged, Zack could attend a preliminary examination, hear all of the prosecutor's evidence for the first time, and present proof of Arya's innocence.

If the prosecutor decided upon a grand jury, the defense would not be present and would offer no evidence. A grand jury proceeding is not adversarial. Grand jurors are presented only with evidence prosecutors decide to present. The evidence is presented in a light most favorable to the prosecution. It is the proverbial kangaroo court.

Zack also knew, technically, the grand jury is supposed to hear exculpatory evidence or evidence favorable to the defense, but most prosecutors ignore this ethical obligation. The standard of proof before a grand jury is probable cause, a tad more than 50/50 tilted toward guilt. In an actual criminal trial, before a judge or jury, the standard of proof is beyond a reasonable doubt. In the grand jury proceeding, no one on the defense side is present to hold the prosecutor's feet to the fire. And, because of the absence of defense arguments, grand juries almost always return an indictment. When prosecutors bring cases to grand juries, they are looking for a rubber stamp.

Zack much preferred the preliminary exam. He wanted to see as much evidence as he could. Most of the evidence would point to her guilt. However, there might be some evidence to support the presence of a third person, the actual killer. Might there be DNA, footprints, or fingerprints? *Who knows? Anything is possible.*

While the better strategy might be to wait on *presenting* evidence, Zack wanted to hear what evidence the police and the prosecution had. He would get Micah Love, his sterling private investigator, involved at some point. Perhaps Micah's team could track down the real killer.

"Is Shaheed Ali here today? I'd like to talk to him."

"No, he's in the field. I can have him call you."

"That would be great, thanks."

"Anything else, Zack?" Dylan was dismissing him. He was tired of dealing with this lawyer's shit.

"No, that'll do it for now. Here's my card." Jack shot him a "why the fuck would I want your card?" look. "For Ali," Zack explained.

"Got it," Jack understood.

Zack exited the building and walked to his car. He pressed the fob, and the door chirped. He entered, fastened his seatbelt, and took off. Soon, he was cruising north on the Southfield Freeway, back toward his office. Arya *was* in this for the long haul. Hers would be a long, tough case. He wondered which assistant prosecutor would be assigned. He thought about Arya, petite, innocent, beautiful Arya. He thought about the current mood in the country, and the anti-Muslim brushfire POTUS was helping to fan. *We have to find the killer,* Zack decided. *Finding him is Arya's only real chance at freedom.*

Chapter Twenty-Three

The Dearborn chief of police and the Wayne County prosecutor, in conjunction with ATF and FBI officials, decided to take the case to the grand jury and seek an indictment of murder in the first degree against Arya Khan. Under Michigan law, if convicted of the charge, Arya would face life in prison without the possibility of parole.

Grand jury testimony began and ended with eyewitness police officer testimony and the testimony of the DNA tech leader. The chief and the prosecutor decided this testimony was all that was necessary to secure the indictment. Neither Zack nor Arya were permitted to attend or offer contrary evidence of any kind.

Several cops took the witness stand and told the same story to the 18-member criminal grand jury panel. They received a dispatch order to Blackwell's address based on a woman's call to 9-1-1 that there had been a stabbing. When they arrived, they found Arya Khan leaning over the body holding a hunting knife that, later, was confirmed to be the murder weapon. One officer placed Ms. Khan in handcuffs to wait for the officer in charge of the investigation into Blackwell, Lieutenant Jack Dylan. Dylan arrived, and the suspect was taken down to headquarters on a 72-hour hold.

The DNA tech leader was a woman named Anne Nuger. Her official title was a forensic scientist for the Dearborn Police Department. When questioned about what that meant, she explained to the grand jury she analyzed DNA evidence—blood, semen, saliva, skin cells, hair, fingerprints, and footprints— and indicated her job was to offer impartial analysis, write reports, and testify to her findings. She had been doing this for about 11 years, all for the city of Dearborn. She received her Bachelor of Science in Microbiology at Wayne State University, graduating cum laude, and was hired as a junior lab technician for the Dearborn Police Department. She had been promoted three times, leading to her current position with the department.

Finally, she testified she had analyzed and evaluated DNA more than 200 times in her various capacities with the city of Dearborn. She would clearly qualify as an expert witness if and when the time came for her to testify at Arya's trial.

Ms. Nuger testified Arya Khan's clothing was a match for multiple fibers left at the scene. Further, fingerprints and saliva samples were also a match for Khan. The most damning evidence was Arya's fingerprints, found on the handle of the murder weapon. The victim's DNA, blood spatter, and saliva were found all over Khan's clothing.

Shaheed Ali testified he took a formal written statement from Ms. Khan. Ali testified that while Khan did not admit she murdered Keith Blackwell, she did admit she was on the porch with the victim. She acknowledged holding the murder weapon and dropping it when the police arrived and ordered her to do so.

When Ali's testimony was concluded, and as he rose to exit the grand jury room, a juror requested the opportunity to ask questions. The prosecutor, not wanting to alienate a juror or appear to be concealing evidence, permitted the questioning.

"Lieutenant Ali, you mentioned Arya Khan gave a formal statement to the police, is that correct?"

"Correct," Ali confirmed.

"And you indicated Ms. Khan admitted she was there. In fact, she was apprehended there, right?"

"Also correct." Ali glanced at the prosecutor.

"Did she admit to the murder?"

"No, she did not."

"Well, then, why was she there?" the grand juror queried.

Shaheed paused and considered his answer. He wanted to follow the law, honor the investigation, and be respectful to his superiors. However, he could not get past his suspicion they had the wrong person.

"She claimed she discovered the deceased was the person who firebombed the Mosque of America. She discovered who he was by copying his name off of a file I'd left on my desk. She then followed him home and witnessed the murder being committed by someone else. She called 9-1-1, reported the crime, then ran to the victim to comfort him and stop the bleeding.

"According to Ms. Khan, that's how the victim's DNA was deposited on her clothing and hers on his. Just before the police arrived, she picked up the knife. I quizzed her why she would do that, but she had no explanation. The police found her hovering over the body with the murder weapon in her hand. She claimed she picked it up after the victim suddenly pulled it out of his stomach and dropped it on the porch." The more Shaheed repeated Arya's story, the more he believed her version of the truth.

"Did you find Ms. Khan's explanation to be plausible, Detective Ali?"

The prosecutor was helpless. There was no judge or defense attorney present. He could not object to the questions. He nervously awaited Ali's response.

"The more plausible explanation is Ms. Khan is the murderer and was literally caught red-handed." Ali referred to the fact the victim's blood was found all over the suspect's hand. "Is the other explanation conceivable? Possibly, but not beyond a reasonable doubt, in my opinion, and certainly not here where the standard of proof for an indictment is much lower."

"You testified she offered an alternate explanation as to why the victim's DNA was on her clothing and why her fingerprints were on the knife. Let me ask you—did she offer an alternate explanation as to how the murder was committed and who committed it?"

Shaheed was suddenly suspicious of this juror. *Who is this woman, and why is she asking all of these questions? Is she a defense plant?*

"She did," he finally responded.

"And what was her explanation?" the juror probed.

"She claimed she witnessed an older man, possibly a biker, stab the victim and run."

Shaheed continued to wonder where this was going. He didn't expect to be interrogated in this manner. He again glanced at the prosecutor, who shrugged.

"Did you believe her?" The juror inquired.

Shaheed paused and carefully considered the question. In the context, he was not surprised by this one. However, the entire line of questioning was quite unusual for a grand juror.

"As I indicated earlier, I considered her version of the facts possible, not plausible," he posited.

"Yes, but that doesn't answer my question. Let me ask the question a different way. Do you think it is more likely this older man she claims she saw killed Blackwell, or do you think it is more likely Arya Khan committed the murder?"

"You're asking for my gut feeling?"

"Your gut feeling," the juror demanded.

"My gut feeling is, regardless of what really happened, Arya Khan believes she did not kill Keith Blackwell," he conceded. "That doesn't mean she didn't commit the crime. She may have blocked it out and invented this older man to assuage her guilt. I really don't know. All I know is she was literally caught red-handed. Despite this, she remains steadfast that she is innocent of the murder of Keith Blackwell."

"Has any follow-up been done to investigate her story? Have the police been looking for this older man or foreign DNA?" The woman wouldn't let up.

"I don't know about the others, but I have been quietly investigating her story."

"Thank you, Lieutenant. I'm all set."

***

The following day, the grand jury returned an indictment against Arya Khan for the first-degree murder of Keith Blackwell. The vote was 17 to 1. When Shaheed Ali heard the tally, he was convinced the lone holdout was the woman who'd posed all of those questions. If he was suspicious Arya was innocent, why couldn't a lone grand juror be suspicious as well? So, the odds Arya faced in proving her innocence were 17 to 2? He was sitting at his desk, reading the indictment. He tapped the desk and then his temple. Soon, he was rubbing both temples. *Did the crime scene boys check for the presence of another person, or was Arya's guilt a foregone conclusion?*

Shaheed Ali rose and walked out of the squad room, past the sergeant's desk and out into the parking lot. He got into his city-owned Ford Taurus and drove off. Soon, he arrived at Keith Blackwell's house. Crime scene tape surrounded the house, and the damaged front door was boarded up. He exited the car and walked to the city sidewalk adjacent to the private walk up to the house. He bent under the crime scene tape and walked up the private drive to the front porch. As he got to the porch, he looked back to where Arya claimed she parked on the day of the murder. It was a perfect vantage point. If Arya was parked there, she had a clear view of the porch.

He tried to remember her statement. According to Arya, the older biker man came from the right as she faced the house. He stood against the brick wall and waited for Blackwell to exit the house. He mimicked the older guy's actions as Arya described them. He stood up against the house, waited for an imaginary Keith Blackwell to appear on the porch, stabbed at the air that was 'Blackwell,' then turned to his left and Arya's right.

The porch was about five feet long from the steps—three of them—to the front door and eight feet wide side to side. The older man would have had to stab Blackwell, then turn left, run about four feet, and jump from the porch to the ground as he made his escape. The house had a well-tended lawn and plump evergreen bushes planted in the dirt that covered the ground on either side of the porch.

Shaheed did not run and jump, as the mythical older man would have done. Instead, he calmly walked to the edge of the porch and looked down. There in the dirt, to the porch side of the first evergreen bush, was a distinct boot print. Shaheed pulled out his camera phone and took a picture of the impression from his porch location above. Next, he climbed down the stairs, walked across the lawn and stood parallel to the boot print. He took more photos. He pushed a button on his phone, and his contacts list appeared. He scrolled to the *B*'s and located Eric Burns' private telephone number. Shaheed wanted to keep this private for the time being. Eric answered on the first ring.

"This is Eric, may I help you?"

"Eric, this is Shaheed Ali. I need a favor. What are you doing right now?"

"Nothing that can't wait. What's up?"

"I need you to come to a crime scene. Bring your boot print casting supplies. And, Eric?"

"Yes, Shaheed?"

"I'd like this done off the books for now, between you and me, okay?"

Eric paused. *What the hell?* "Shaheed, Jack, and Ash are my bosses, and Ash is the boot print expert. Uh . . . are you . . . uh . . . asking me to do this behind their backs?" Eric stuttered.

"Just for the time being, Eric. I'm testing a theory. If it's viable, I'll disclose it. If it's not, I don't want to waste anyone else's time with it. Needless to say, neither Ash nor Jack share this theory at the present time."

"I don't like doing this behind their backs, Shaheed. I'd rather not." Eric was a by-the-books kind of guy.

"I'll owe you one, big time. If anything happens, I promise I will tell Ash and Jack I ordered you to do it and to keep quiet about it. Please do this for me. You are the only one I can trust with this." Shaheed pleaded.

Eric paused for a more extended time. "Okay, Shaheed, I'll do it. Where am I going?"

"The Blackwell crime scene at 6127 Orchard Avenue," Shaheed reported.

"Wasn't that scene processed?" Eric challenged.

"Yes, but the techs weren't looking for what I am looking for and what I think I just found. Please, get over here with your equipment, ASAP."

"On my way, Shaheed. You owe me, big time," Eric warned.

"And I'll gladly repay you when the time comes, my friend. Now, please, get your ass over here."

"Okay, okay, I'm coming."

***

Eric arrived at the Blackwell crime scene, parked, exited his city lab van, and gathered his equipment. He lifted the crime scene tape and walked on the private walkway leading to the house. Shaheed was standing on the right side of the porch as Eric faced the house. He was looking down over the side, into the bushes.

"Hey, Eric, thanks for coming," Ali smiled.

"I would say no problem, but I'd be lying," Eric groaned.

"Well, I sincerely appreciate it." Charm was the personality trait that enabled Shaheed to get almost anyone to do almost anything.

"So, what's the deal?" Eric glared at the bushes, curious about what he was doing at the house.

"Look, just to the left of the first bush. See the print?"

Eric scanned the spot. "I do!" Eric loved his work and could not get enough of it. He was eager to get another crack at some of the techniques Ash Granger recently demonstrated. Eric was a quick study, but practice makes perfect.

He and Shaheed donned crime tech 'booties' on both sets of feet. Eric carefully extracted his equipment from its case and went to work, taking numerous photos, then prepping and casting the print. Ever careful and cautious, he scanned the area for other evidence, noted the print was leading away from the house, and expertly lifted the impression into a dental stone mold.

After setting it aside to dry, Shaheed thought Eric was finished processing the scene, but he was far from finished. He retrieved an evidence case and removed tweezers, a small shovel, and some clear plastic bags. With the tweezers, he extracted some loose tobacco, probably chewing tobacco, placed it in one of the bags, and marked the bag with a Sharpie.

Shaheed was intrigued. He hadn't thought to look around for more. He was pleased Eric thought to do so, and he was also pleased he was around to witness the find. A two-tech discovery would stand up better in court if this newly discovered evidence was used to exonerate Arya. Shaheed was also gratified that it had not rained since the day of the murder.

Eric began crawling through the bushes, snapping photos of additional places where loose tobacco had fallen. He found two more prints, one heading toward the house and the other away from it. He photographed and cast those prints as well. Shaheed was now on Team Eric, scouting the area ahead of Eric for additional signs of an intruder. They found other partial prints, heading in both directions, and more tobacco in the grass leading to the back of the house. This was going to be a long day.

Their search continued in the backyard kitty-corner to the Blackwell home, with the discovery of more tobacco, a substance that may have been saliva, and additional prints heading in opposite directions. It was clear someone came from the yard to the Blackwell porch or vice versa. The vice versa really didn't make sense, so Shaheed concluded the route was yard to porch and back again. The two men walked, photographed, and gathered evidence all the way to the front of the neighboring home. The search culminated at a spot in the street, directly in front of the house. There in the street, adjacent to the curb, was a fresh oil spot. Eric photographed it and obtained samples.

It was almost dusk when they knocked on the neighbor's door. An elderly man answered and begrudgingly accepted the news the route that Shaheed and Eric traveled from Blackwell's porch through the neighbor's back and front yard was now marked with crime scene tape and could not be disturbed.

Shaheed thanked Eric for a job well done, service above and beyond the call of duty, as Shaheed called it. For his part, Eric told Shaheed he enjoyed working with him; he would process the evidence and let him know what he found. Shaheed reminded him this was temporarily confidential. It was to be kept between the two of them. Eric rolled his eyes at him as if to say: "Do I look like I'm stupid?" Shaheed chuckled. The two men shook hands and left the scene in their respective vehicles.

Chapter Twenty-Four

While Shaheed and Eric combed the Blackwell murder scene, Arya Khan was formally charged with the murder of Keith Blackwell. An arraignment and bail hearing were scheduled for the following morning. Zack was notified in the late afternoon. He called the Khans and told them about the arraignment. He invited them to attend and bring character witnesses.

Zack left his Bloomfield Hills home at 6:30 a.m. and headed south on Woodward Avenue. Woodward wasn't the fastest way into the city, but it was more scenic and direct. Woodward cuts Detroit in half, east side-west side. It was a major avenue into the city before expressways became the preferred mode of travel. Zack decided to take Woodward all the way into the city, mainly to stop at his preferred Dunkin Donuts for coffee on the way.

He was careful not to spill coffee on his custom-made suit. As he drove, he recalled his dog days, after his fall from grace, handling criminal assignments and traffic citation defense. He'd placed a small classified ad offering $99 ticket defense with a guarantee of 'a lesser plea or it's free.' He could barely afford rent, food, and gas. His car was paid for, and he lived case to case. One phone call from Jennifer, now his wife, changed all that. The 'case of a lifetime' returned Zack to his former glory. These days he had a booming practice, a Bloomfield Hills mansion, a beautiful wife, and two great kids.

While the Tracey case caused him to refocus and recharge, success would not have been possible if he wasn't an excellent lawyer in the first place. He got sidetracked, to be sure, but in no way did his temporary slide mean he was not a formidable foe.

He thought about Arya Khan. He was sure of her innocence and hopeful he could convince Wayne County Circuit Judge David Grinder she deserved bail. He scheduled an appointment to see Micah Love in the afternoon. If anyone could find exculpatory evidence and help free Arya Khan, it was Micah. Micah's work was central to Zack's success in the Tracey case.

Hamid Khan paid for and deserved the best possible defense, which required a Micah Love investigation.

Traffic was surprisingly light, and Zack arrived at 2 Woodward Avenue, known to trial lawyers as the City-County Building. His Rolex read 7:20 a.m. He parked the Beemer in the underground parking lot and walked across Jefferson Avenue to the windowed high-rise that housed most of the Wayne County Circuit Court judges.

Zack skipped the metal detector by displaying his bar card and proceeded up to the 14th floor and Judge Grinder's courtroom. He exited the elevator and walked toward the courtroom. Instead of entering through the courtroom door—It was locked, anyway. Non-lawyers are not admitted until 8:30 a.m.—Zack entered through a door that read 'No Admittance.' Once inside the door, a long passageway guided Zack to the chambers of Judge David Grinder.

When he reached the outer office, the judge's court clerk and legal assistant greeted him cheerfully. Also present was Wayne County Assistant Prosecutor Lawrence Bialy, who extended a hand and introduced himself. He would be prosecuting Arya Khan. The clerk advised Zack his client would be brought in shortly and would have a brief opportunity to converse with her lawyer. The hearing would be conducted promptly at 8:45 a.m. Afterward, the attorneys were to meet in chambers to schedule discovery, pre-trial, and trial.

Bialy was a seasoned prosecutor, in his tenth year at Wayne County. He had a reputation as a fair advocate with a passion for justice. He was also very comfortable in front of the cameras, accustomed to high-profile assignments. This was Zack's first case against him. Both men expected this to be a very high-profile proceeding. The government's public assault upon Muslims would make it so. Arya's arrest and prosecution played right into the new president's rhetoric, so Zack expected national press coverage.

Arraignments were not very public. Thus far, Arya Khan's arrest was kept under the radar of the press. Zack was grateful to Jack Dylan, the Dearborn Police, and the Wayne County prosecutor's office for that courtesy. However, there were court watchers present in every courtroom in Wayne Circuit, and soon after a plea was entered in *State of Michigan v. Arya Khan*, the press would most certainly begin non-stop, wall-to-wall coverage of what was expected to be a controversial and sensational trial.

Blake and Bialy were chatting amicably when Arya was brought in, handcuffed, and placed in a conference room. Zack entered the room and prompted the officer to remove Arya's handcuffs. The prisoner's stone face turned to glee when she first caught a glimpse of Zack. She started to speak, but Zack silenced her with his index finger to his lips. The officer removed the handcuffs, and Arya immediately began rubbing her wrists. The officer left the room, closed the door, and stationed himself directly outside.

"Hi, Arya," Zack cheered. "How are you holding up?"

"Oh, Zack, I'm so glad to see you and glad to be out of that cell!" She rubbed her wrists. "And I hate those handcuffs. When will this nightmare be over?" She groaned.

"Well, we have a tough row to hoe. Hopefully, we can proceed with you out of jail rather than inside of it," Zack rallied.

"Oh, please! By the grace of Allah, that would be wonderful," Arya prayed.

"Let's not count our chickens before they hatch. It is very unusual for a judge to grant bail in a first-degree murder case," Zack warned.

"But I am innocent!" Arya pleaded.

"The judge doesn't know that yet. His job is to determine whether you are a threat to society."

"But I'm not—you know I'm not!" She cried.

"I know, Arya, but the judge doesn't. I'll do the best I can to get you bonded out."

"What does that mean?" she puzzled.

"Bail, Arya, bail. Let's see what happens. I called your father last night and advised him to bring a few members of the family and community to provide character testimony. I want to demonstrate you're not a flight risk and have significant ties to the community," Zack explained.

"If you told him to come with people, he'll come with people," Arya assured.

"Okay, Arya, let me try to explain why we're here today, what we hope to accomplish." With pleasantries out of the way, Zack got down to business.

Zack explained the arraignment served several purposes. Initially, the defendant is formally advised of the charges filed against her. In this case, the charge is murder in the first degree. Second, the defendant is advised of the maximum penalty she faces. In this case, that penalty is life in prison without the possibility of parole. Third, the defendant is advised of her constitutional rights. Fourth, the defendant is required to enter a plea. Zack explained she could plead guilty, not guilty, or stand mute—say nothing—in which case a not guilty plea is entered for her. And last, but certainly not least, the most critical part is the issue of bail and conditions of bail if it is granted.

After all of that, the lawyers meet with the judge and the judge's clerk, and they set future dates for discovery exchanges, pre-trial, and trial. Zack wondered if Arya understood how the hearing would go. She nodded in the affirmative. The door opened, and the guard told Zack and Arya the judge was about to take the bench and call the case.

Zack led Arya into the courtroom and to the defense table. The gallery was packed with members of Arya's community. Zack was pleasantly surprised. Hamid came through in a big way. Except for a few court watchers, the place was packed to the gills with Muslims friendly to Arya. And all of them were Wayne County voters.

Arya was not surprised. She was grateful. She went to embrace the adoring crowd, but the court officer stopped her and threatened handcuffs. She saw her parents and acknowledged them with a smile and a tear. They looked ten years older and were wrought with worry. Her smile enlightened their mood a tad.

The judge emerged from a door behind the bench. He scanned the crowd with a look of surprise and dismay. "All rise!" The court officer shouted. The gallery rose, seemingly in unison. "Circuit Court for the County of Wayne is now in session, The Honorable David Grinder presiding!"

The judge assumed the bench and requested, "Please be seated. Calling the case of the *People v. Arya Khan*. Who is appearing for the People?"

"Lawrence Bialy for the People, Your Honor," Bialy stood at the prosecutor's table.

"And for the defense?" the judge inquired.

"Zachary Blake for the defendant, Your Honor," Zack responded.

"Nice to see you, Mr. Blake. It's been a while," Judge Grinder smiled.

"Nice to see you, too, Your Honor. I wish it were under more pleasant circumstances."

"Let's get to work." The judge demanded. "We are here today for an arraignment. I see we have a very large crowd. Welcome to my courtroom, everyone. Please remain quiet and respectful during this proceeding, whether you like what is going on or not. We have our court officer over here." He pointed to the court officer standing to his right, in front of the bench. "His job is to maintain order. If anyone gets out of hand, he or she will be removed. Understood?" The gallery nodded.

The judge continued. "Arya Khan, please step forward."

Arya and Zack, rose, came from behind the defense table, and assumed a position in front of the bench.

"Arya Khan, you are charged with murder in the first degree. The maximum penalty for that offense is life in prison without the possibility of parole." The gallery let out an audible gasp, and the judge pounded his gavel for silence. When the gallery became silent, the judge continued.

"I warned the gallery about making noise. Any further outbursts and I will clear this courtroom," the judge admonished, like a stern parent scolding a child. "Now, let's continue," Grinder commanded.

"It is my understanding the defendant has been provided an Advice of Rights form, has been fully apprised of her rights, and has read the contents thoroughly. She understands her rights and has executed and dated the form. Is this correct?"

"Yes, Your Honor," Zack acknowledged.

"Having been provided with her rights and acknowledging an understanding of those rights, how does the defendant plead?"

"The defendant, Arya Khan, pleads not guilty, Your Honor."

"The plea of not guilty will be entered for the record," Grinder ordered. "We will now hear the People on bail."

Bialy rose and took a position to Zack's right. "The People oppose bail, Your Honor. This first-degree murder charge results from a gruesome stabbing. The evidence suggests the defendant followed the victim for quite some time. She lay in wait for the victim and brutally stabbed him as he left his home. Then, she casually and arrogantly waited for the police to arrive at the scene. We believe she is a danger to the public and request bond be denied."

The gallery stirred noticeably but surprisingly, did not make an audible sound. Grinder decided to let it go. "Mr. Blake? The defense on bail?"

"Your Honor, this defendant has never been charged with a crime in her 25 years of life. She has been an honor student and an upstanding member of her community, a pillar of society. She is a woman of deep faith. The so-called 'evidence' the People have assembled has been targeted at the defendant from the moment the police found her on that porch. What murderer sits with the victim and waits for the police? What murderer calls 9-1-1 to report the murder she just committed?

"Arya Khan has no passport. She has no plans to leave her community. She is innocent of all charges and is fully prepared to fight these charges in court to clear her name, which she cannot do if she flees. And I need her assistance to do so. She is absolutely *not* a danger to the community. She will wear a tether if the court requires that of her. As Your Honor can readily see, there are numerous members of her community in attendance here today willing to vouch for her veracity, community standing, and reputation if this Honorable Court requires such testimony."

"By a show of hands, who in the gallery is willing to vouch for this defendant?" Judge Grinder addressed the gallery.

The entire gallery raised hands. The judge continued.

"Who in the gallery is related in some way to the defendant?"

Nearly a quarter of the gallery raised their hands.

"Your Honor, I object to this query of the gallery. I cannot cross-examine a gallery judicially examined in this manner," Bialy protested. "With all due respect, Your Honor, this gallery examination is highly improper, and I most strenuously object."

"Your strenuous objection is noted for the record, Mr. Bialy. Does either party have anything more on bail?" Judge Grinder inquired. Bialy was visibly miffed at the judge's sarcasm.

"No, Your Honor," the two attorneys responded in unison.

"Bail is set at $1,000,000 cash or bond. The defendant will be fitted with and wear a tether, with the cost of monitoring borne by the defense. If there is nothing further, I will see counsel in my chambers to set dates for discovery, pre-trial, and trial." Grinder pounded his gavel and rose.

"All rise!" The court officer repeated. The gallery rose on command, loudly murmuring, not fully grasping what just occurred. Zack glanced at Hamid and Riah Khan. They looked confused. Arya was handcuffed again and led toward a side door where criminal defendants were placed in holding. Zack approached her and explained bail was granted. However, substantial money was needed to post it. The money would be returned if she did not violate the conditions of bail. Arya advised him to talk to her parents.

Hamid and Riah were panic-stricken as they watched their precious daughter being handcuffed and dragged off through a side door. They waited anxiously as Zack approached them.

"Hamid, Riah, I don't know if you understood what just happened, but this was a terrific turn of events for Arya. Judges rarely grant bail in first- degree murder cases, but this judge granted bail. The problem is you'll have to post 10 percent to a bail bondsman, $100,000, and the cost of monitoring an ankle bracelet to get Arya released," Zack explained.

"And she will be released?" Hamid prayed.

"Yes, Hamid. She will be released until after the trial. If the verdict is guilty, she may continue on bond or be incarcerated again. She will be set free, permanently, if the verdict is not guilty. Understand?"

"Our Imam and the community have already set up a defense fund. So, we have to come up with $200,000, $100,000 for your retainer, and $100,000 for this bond?"

"And the cost of the ankle bracelet and monitoring. Hamid, let's worry about bail. You can pay my retainer as the fund grows. Please try to relax. The bail money is temporary. It is returned after Arya meets the conditions of bail."

"Oh, Zachary Blake, you are a wonderful human being," Riah delighted. "Hamid and I will make certain you are handsomely rewarded for your service to Arya and our family."

"I know you will. Let's go talk to the Imam."

The three of them approached Baqir Ghaffari, and Zack told Ghaffari what was required. Zack was then summoned into chambers. He implored the Imam to commence work on the bail money and excused himself. He rushed into the inner sanctum and into the judge's chambers where Bialy and Judge Grinder were waiting.

"Can she post, Zack?" Grinder queried.

"I believe she can, Your Honor," Zack assured him.

"I went out on quite a limb for your client and her community, Zack. These are difficult times. But I am not going to let national politics dictate how I run my courtroom," Grinder orated. "Don't let me down, Zack."

"I won't, Your Honor. Thank you for your courage. This decision will be criticized in certain political circles. You can be sure of that, sir."

"I know, but it was the right thing to do. It will all blow over unless she violates the conditions."

"That will not happen, Your Honor."

Judge Grinder turned his attention to Bialy. "Don't look at me, Your Honor. This is all you. Did you grant bail in a first-degree case? I hope it all works out." The prosecutor took the opportunity to repay the judge for his previous sarcastic comments made at Bialy's expense.

"Let's set some dates," Grinder grimaced.

The judge set a date for exchanging discovery and for a pre-trial hearing for two weeks afterward. Trial was set four months out, but either side could file a motion to adjourn or extend if additional time was needed. The three men shook hands. Zack eyeballed Bialy and knew he was in for a brawl. This was a significant victory for the defense, and Zack was going to enjoy it while he could. Having Arya available to him while he investigated and mounted a defense was crucial. He did not wish to visit her in jail—thanks to Judge Grinder, he didn't have to.

He exited the judge's chambers the way he came in. Hamid, Riah, and Ghaffari were waiting.

"The money has been arranged," Ghaffari cheered. "I have the account information. We can wire as soon as you wish."

"Great!" Zack exclaimed. "Let's go across the street. There's a bail bondsman over there who owes me a favor."

***

Two hours later, Arya Khan walked out of the City-County Building with an ankle monitor attached to her leg. Zachary Blake and Hamid and Riah Khan accompanied her. The four were unaware that Benjamin watched them from his seat at an outdoor coffee shop.

This is not a positive development, Blaine decided. He'd heard, through police contacts, the girl followed Blackwell on the day of the murder. *When did the girl get to the Blackwell house, and what did she see? Can she identify me? I may have to get rid of her, too. Who cares if one more camel jockey meets her Maker? After all, they're blowing themselves up to go to paradise, anyway.*

He rose, walked over to his motorcycle, started it, and sped off. Arya Khan heard the now familiar noise and glanced in his direction. The rider was a distance away, but Arya could make out the beat-up leather jacket and grey hair spouting out all sides of the man's helmet. A cold chill went through her body. No one else noticed the sound or the man. For no particular reason, she decided to keep this sighting to herself, and continued walking with Zack and her parents. Perhaps later, she'd confide in Zack. *Was this the guy? Is he watching me?*

Chapter Twenty-Five

Because of Judge Grinder's surprise bail decision and the time it took to arrange the money, bond, and ankle bracelet, Zack had to cancel his meeting with Micah Love. The two men rescheduled for the following day. Micah's office was downtown, but Zack had to pick up Arya so he could not follow the same route he'd traveled to yesterday's arraignment. There was no easy, expressway-type method to get first to Dearborn and then to downtown Detroit from Bloomfield Hills. So, Zack decided to drive to Dearborn the way he had when he'd first visited police headquarters.

His navigation system directed him to Arya's address. When he arrived, she was waiting for him outside. She climbed into the luxury car, looked around, impressed, and exchanged greetings with Zack. They drove off, hit I-94 and headed east toward downtown. As he approached downtown Detroit, Zack followed the sign to the Lodge Freeway, M-10, headed south into the downtown area. Micah's office was in the Buhl Building on Griswold, so Zack exited and headed east to Griswold. He parked in a city lot. He and Arya then hoofed it to Micah's office.

One of the amenities of the Buhl building Zack liked best was the elegant old building still had attended elevators. Zack and Arya entered an attended elevator, greeted the operator, and rode to the 14th floor, where the Micah Love Private Detective Agency occupied most of the space. The entrance to his suite of offices was directly across from the open elevator door. They crossed the hall and entered the elegantly decorated office suite. A beautiful receptionist greeted them and offered them drinks, which both declined. Micah was famous for his taste in *human* office décor as well as furnishings.

After a brief wait, a short, stout, aging gentleman with a bad comb-over entered the lobby from the bowels of the suite.

"Zack!" Micah exclaimed. "Welcome home, Mr. Married Man! How was the honeymoon? Lots of fun? Did the lady wear you out?"

Zack's eyes darted to Arya, motioning Micah to maintain a small level of decorum and respect for the young lady.

Micah and Zack were close friends, especially so since completing the case that made both of them multi-millionaires. Micah took a considerable risk by accepting the Tracey investigation on a contingency fee basis. When Zack won a nine-figure verdict, Micah received an eight-figure bonus.

Initially, Micah retired with his windfall. He became bored with inactivity, though, and returned to his office, very selectively accepting new business. Money provides the freedom to choose. While their prior relationship was cordial, Zack and Micah's current relationship was one of mutual respect and accommodation. There was little the two men would not do for each other.

"We had a wonderful time, Micah. I'm not about to share the details with the likes of you. How the hell are you? Everything good? How's Jessica?"

Jessica Klein was a city employee in Berea, Ohio. Back in the day, she helped Micah track down several prior victims of the priest who harmed the Tracey boys. In pure Hollywood fashion, the drab, overweight, forever single guy, Micah, fell head over heels in love with Jessica Klein. More surprisingly, considering Micah's wide girth and grotesque comb-over, Jessica fell for him, too. They now lived together in a mansion-like home in the affluent Palmer Woods neighborhood of Detroit.

"She's great, Zack. She told me to say hello and give you a kiss for her. So, hello . . . I'll skip the kiss."

Arya chuckled. She enjoyed the jovial repartee between the two men.

"How's Jennifer?" Micah inquired.

"She's great. The boys are doing well, too. She says hi, she loves you . . . and I'll skip the kiss, too, if you don't mind."

"Not at all," Micah quipped.

Zack gestured toward Arya and Arya back toward Micah. "Micah, Arya—Arya, Micah. Arya is my client, Micah."

"Pleasure to meet you, Arya," Micah grinned.

Micah walked them through the lobby doors and into the office's inner sanctum. They walked until they encountered a conference room with a long, black lacquer conference table surrounded by several ergonomic desk chairs. Micah invited them to sit down. As Zack settled into the very comfortable chair, he could not help recalling his old one-room office with the broken desk chair that threatened to dump him to the ground every time he sat in it. *Times have certainly changed.*

"Did you get a chance to review what I sent over?" Zack got down to business.

"I did," Micah advised. "It appears the key to the Promised Land is finding this older biker dude. Correct?"

"Correct, Micah. Any ideas?"

"As a matter of fact, I have a plethora of ideas."

"Plethora? A ten-dollar word! Do you know what it means?" Zack kibitzed.

"Funny, smart-ass. May I continue? You're interrupting my cadence."

"Sure. Sorry."

"As I indicated, I have a plethora of ideas." Apparently, he liked saying that word. "You believe the victim bombed the mosque, right?"

"Right," Zack advised, in cadence. He knew when Micah was on a roll; the dialogue had to flow a certain way.

"And, the victim was part of some white supremacist cult or group known as 1 USA Pure, right?"

"Right again, only the name is USA 1 Pure," Zack corrected.

"Whatever, USA 1 Pure, Pure USA, tomato, tomahto, potato, potahto, let's call the whole thing off." Zack interrupted Micah's cadence a second time. Micah was not happy but continued. "Arya's statement, which you haven't seen yet—I'll get my hands on a copy—says the guy she saw kill Blackwell was a long-haired old hippie biker, right?"

"Right."

"So, it stands to reason this guy is also a white supremacist and a member of a similar group or maybe even the same group or cult as Blackwell." Micah was back in cadence.

"Right," Zack marveled. He sat back in the desk chair and clasped both hands behind his head. He enjoyed watching Micah on a roll.

"If that's true, then there has to be a reason why this group wanted to silence Blackwell. Perhaps it is identifying other members of this USA group, or perhaps it is the existence of some other group altogether. If we assume they were all in this together, and Blackwell got careless and easily identifiable, then the group became concerned this Blackwell dude would cave when the cops showed up asking questions. They couldn't have him naming co-conspirators, so they decided to carve the guy up like a Thanksgiving turkey. You with me?"

"I am," Zack winced at the analogy. Thanksgiving would never be the same.

"What's with the snide smile?"

"Nothing, you're cute when you're on a roll. Go on, please," Zack urged. He didn't dare interrupt cadence a second time.

"So, we identify the group. These guys may be USA 1 Pure, some other group, or both. We identify the old hippie, or at least Arya identifies him. We get access to the crime scene and do our own investigation with our own techs. I'm sure the cops focused only on Arya because the idiots figured they'd caught the murderer, literally red-handed. Perhaps there is some physical evidence somewhere at the crime scene that establishes the guy Arya saw was present at the time of the murder. If there is any physical evidence, my guys will find it."

Zack hadn't thought of this. This is why he loved having Micah around when the going got tough. Zack was buoyed with the prospect there might be physical evidence of the guy Arya observed.

"I think he might be following me," revealed Arya. The two men looked at each other, then at Arya, stunned at this revelation.

"What do you mean, following you, Arya? When were you going to tell me this?" Zack fumed.

"Well . . ." she winced. "I just did," she smirked.

"Arya, you need to tell me these things. Micah can arrange protection. This man is extremely dangerous. He's willing to commit murder when he feels threatened," Zack warned. "When, exactly, did you see him?"

"I'm really sorry, Zack. You're right. I should have mentioned it at the time. We were with my parents, and I didn't want to worry them. I saw him as we left the courthouse yesterday."

Micah began talking and thinking simultaneously. "I'll bet there are cameras all over that place. Give me the exact location and a detailed description of the old dude, and I'll follow up on it. This could be the break we are looking for!" Micah had thrown himself full throttle into the investigation. "There is a sketch artist in the building—let me call down there and see if he is available. I'd like Arya to describe this dude to the artist. Maybe we can get a good composite drawing to compare to whomever the cameras captured."

"And you need to put some surveillance on Arya," Zack demanded. "She needs the extra protection. Besides, a surveillance team might surprise the guy and get a good look at him."

"Yeah, that too," Micah agreed. He preferred to devise his own strategy, thank you very much.

"OK, sounds like a plan. Let's get to work," Zack abruptly terminated the meeting.

"Whoa, tiger, first we eat," Micah suggested. "Your treat!"

Chapter Twenty-Six

That evening, a car was dispatched and discreetly placed in a sheltered location near the Khan home. A second vehicle was placed outside the Schaefer location of USA 1 Pure. The following morning, Zack was on the telephone with Larry Bialy asking for access to the crime scene so Micah's crime scene techs could do their due diligence. Bialy resisted, arguing the Dearborn techs had not concluded their work. When Zack threatened to file an emergency motion for access, Bialy wisely acquiesced.

Zack also requested Arya's formal statement, along with all crime scene photographs and forensic scientist and crime scene processing reports and summaries. Zack promised he would provide a formal request no later than that afternoon. Bialy promised to produce the documents as soon as he received the formal request from Zack. He would get the materials ready for delivery in the morning.

Zack would have preferred Bialy accept on faith that Zack would make good on his promise to deliver a formal request, but he couldn't really complain about Bialy's response. So far, the prosecutor was professional and forthright, and more cooperative and pleasant to deal with than Jack Dylan. Zack wondered if anyone from the Dearborn PD had the foresight to even think to look for corroboration of Arya's eyewitness account.

Micah's cyber specialist, his agency's version of Noah Thompson, was a geek by the name of Reed Spencer. Spencer had a history similar to Noah's, only worse. He served seven years of a 10-year sentence for cyber fraud, expertly stealing the identities of wealthy country club types. He was caught when he arrogantly created a password containing his dog's name, "Maggie," followed by the numbers 123. He was convicted in 2007 of hacking into the AmEx black card system and extracting the accounts of high net worth individuals.

The difference between Reed and Noah was that Noah grew up, reformed his ways, and was able to earn the trust of law enforcement officers. Reed, on the other hand, refused to grow up. In fact, he believed growing up was very overrated. Unlike Noah, Reed hated the police. He resented them for catching him over something as stupid as a password. Had he not made it so easy for them, they would never have caught him. His primary motivation when working with Micah was to embarrass the police whenever he was offered the chance. This assignment was one of those opportunities, and he relished it. He was not aware the Dearborn Police had someone as talented as Noah Thompson investigating cyber for the cops.

Reed was ordered to research USA 1 Pure and its related websites. He was to compile a member list for the organization and similar white supremacist organizations. If he came across photos, whether recent or not, he was to duplicate those photos, and, if he could, match one to the composite drawing Micah's sketch artist did from Arya's description of the old hippie biker. Micah scheduled a meeting with his favorite contact at the FBI. The guy owed him a favor, and Micah requested him to run the composite or any photo Reed generated through the Fed's facial recognition software to see if there was a match. This was Reed's idea, another attempt to embarrass the police by investigating something the police showed no interest in investigating.

The following morning, all of the Dearborn Police evidentiary findings were turned over to Zack. Actually, some of the evidence was withheld, because Jack Dylan didn't know it existed. Eric Burns wasn't through processing it and didn't know it was the subject of a formal request. When queried about this failure to produce the evidence later that year, after the case was officially over, Dylan claimed he knew nothing about the evidence because Shaheed and Eric compiled it off the books. Eric insisted he didn't turn it over because he was never requested to do so. The "one hand not knowing what the other was doing" defense was rather comical and became legendary in subsequent police fuck-up discussions.

As Zack and Micah's forensic team, headed by lead tech Mathew Jordan, reviewed the evidence dump, no one was surprised all of the evidence pointed to Arya. However, the police had focused *only* on Arya, while Zack and Micah's team were focused on anyone else in the world. This brought a fresh perspective to the investigation. As such, assuming Arya was being truthful about her soddit defense, her description of the old hippie biker, and his comings and goings, there was a strong chance Micah's team would find physical evidence of the presence of an individual other than Arya and Blackwell. Furthermore, they knew where to look for it, because Arya stated he came through the bushes to the right of the porch and ran back the same way, and through Blackwell's or his next-door neighbor's backyard and, perhaps, to a motorcycle parked on the next street over.

That afternoon, Micah, Matthew, and his crime scene tech team arrived at 6127 Orchard Avenue. Representatives of the Dearborn Police and the Wayne County prosecutor were present only to monitor the techs' activity and report to Bialy.

The techs observed yellow crime scene tape heading off in multiple directions and, to their surprise, noted crime scene tape covering the area they were about to search. Their state of surprise wasn't because they believed Dearborn techs were competent. They knew they were skilled techs. They were surprised because some of the crime scene tape covered areas not listed in the evidence dump. Were they hiding exculpatory evidence? If their focus was Arya Khan, what were they doing in the bushes and behind the house? Micah's techs were puzzled, to say the least, by the extra yellow tape.

This new tape surrounded the centerpiece area of their investigation, the area where Arya's older hippie dude came, stabbed, and made his getaway. If the evidence dump was to be believed, the original crime scene techs had not processed the area in question. This led Micah's team to two possible scenarios: 1. Evidence was withheld from the defense, or, 2. Someone else processed the expanded scene off book. Either scenario represented an interesting development that must be reported to Zachary Blake.

Jordan's crime scene techs worked through dusk, quit for the evening, and returned in the morning. They secured and identified their area of concern with blue crime scene tape. Their mysterious predecessors purged the scene of vital evidence

Jordan's team hoped to be the first to process. Dental stone mold residual was evident. Jordan's techs were pros and wore booties, as Eric and Shaheed had done, so it was relatively easy to distinguish between a suspect's footprint and the techs' prints. Still, the vast majority of prints were previously processed. It would be tough for the team to determine directional patterns, type of footwear, height and weight of the suspect, and whether he was running or walking. In fact, Jordan silently shifted his focus to attempting to find out who processed the scene before his team. He knew crime scene tech people who knew crime scene tech people, and he would make discreet inquiries.

The team had all of the latest tools available. These men were not hamstrung by budget concerns like a government operation was. Thus, prints could be lifted, cast, 3-D scanned and imaged using the latest technology. Jordan's team, as Eric had before them, worked methodically and diligently. Slowly, a pattern began to emerge.

A person traveled one of two ways. He came from the bushes on the front right side of the Blackwell home, traveled through the backyards of Blackwell's house, his next-door neighbor's house, and the house behind his next-door neighbor's house, then back again. Or, he traveled the reverse of this trek. The reverse trek was more logical because it suggested a starting point in the street around the block from Blackwell's house. To buttress this theory, there was gasoline or motor oil residual in the street that was, of course, previously processed, and which suggested a car or motorcycle had parked at the spot.

The height and weight of the person were to be determined, as was his or her gender, although Matthew was relatively confident this was a man, based on the type of footwear the prints suggested. Furthermore, the team found residuals of what they believed to be chewing tobacco, and it was unlikely a woman would use this form of tobacco. The superior equipment was a huge benefit, and Matthew felt better about the scene than he did previously.

***

Reed Spencer sat in front of a computer, staring at the screen. Micah instructed him to research the white supremacist website USA 1 Pure and its related sites. After spending hours trying to correlate this site with that one and that bigot with this one, he reached a conclusion. There was nothing on the World Wide Web connecting the USA 1 Pure site with any other supremacist site or Keith Blackwell with any other supremacist bigot. Reed was very frustrated.

He decided to compile a list of Michigan groups and national groups with Michigan chapters or offices. After hours of research, he sat back and reviewed his "Top Ten Racist Organizations in Michigan" list, paying homage to David Letterman.

- Renaissance America One
- The Free America Party
- Nazi America
- The Aryan American Brothers
- The Conservative Council
- The Ku Klux Klan
- The American Volk
- The White Nationalist Federation
- The LoveWhite Society
- Separatists Unite

The groups had several things in common. All were white nationalists. They were anti-Semitic, Holocaust deniers, anti-multiculturalist, anti-black, anti-gay, anti-Muslim, anti-interracial, and interreligious intercourse. All were alt-right, Christian, and thrilled with the new government's anti-immigration policies.

Unfortunately, Reed was having a difficult time finding a link between any of these groups and Keith Blackwell or USA 1 Pure. Reed searched GoDaddy, Network Solutions, and other prominent website registrants and found www.usa1pure.com was registered to Keith Blackwell. Further technical research demonstrated no one other than Blackwell or Nomo Islam—

Blackwell—contributed content to the site. The site listed no members of the group, and the address on Schaefer was a leasehold, with a lease executed by—Reed guessed the result before he confirmed it—Keith Blackwell. The longer Reed searched, the more he feared Blackwell was a lone wolf. Reed knew this was not helpful to Arya Khan.

Reed also knew Arya provided a composite drawing of the man she saw stab Keith Blackwell. He did not know Zachary received, in the evidence dump provided by Bialy, a photograph of a group of bikers entering the building on Schaefer. Had he known this simple fact, his job would have been made significantly easier. Instead, he decided to research each of the ten groups to see if he could come up with one man or several who matched the description Arya provided. He worked all day. His eyes were strained, his head hurt, and he had a stiff back from hunching over the computer. *I have to get one of those standing treadmill desks.* He put his iMac to sleep, turned off the soft lights that illuminated his home office, and headed off to sleep.

Ironically, Reed and the rest of Micah's men were making the same mistake Dearborn Police were making. Reed was conducting an Internet investigation without knowing or reviewing what was in the evidence dump and without knowing what the Jordan tech guys found, while Eric and Shaheed were conducting a rogue investigation on a man Dylan didn't believe existed. And none of this would bode well for proving Arya Khan was innocent of first-degree murder.

Chapter Twenty-Seven

Eric Burns and Shaheed Ali met in the small conference room at Dearborn Police Headquarters. Eric brought two copies of a report on his findings. Shaheed read the report carefully while Eric waited patiently. After fifteen minutes of silence, Shaheed looked up.

"Interesting. You are certain the prints belong to a man?"

"One hundred percent certain. This would have to be a very overweight woman who stood about six feet tall. She would also be a tobacco chewer and wear Wolverine Floorhand steel-toed work boots. It's a man, Shaheed."

"Steel toes, huh? This lends credence to Arya's version, don't you think?" Shaheed speculated.

"It's not clear when the prints were left. The prints suggest the suspect came and returned from the areas Arya identified. However, I cannot definitively say they were left on the day of the murder. I couldn't testify they were left on that day," Eric surmised.

"What does your gut tell you, Eric?" Shaheed was willing Eric to move closer to where he, Shaheed, was leaning on the evidence.

"Off the record?"

"Sure."

"I think they suggest Arya is telling the truth, but a suggestion of truth does not mean beyond a reasonable doubt," Eric suggested.

"Our burden is to prove *guilt* beyond a reasonable doubt—it is *our* burden, not Arya's. She does not need to prove innocence beyond a reasonable doubt. Let me ask it this way: Between you and me, do you believe these prints create a reasonable doubt of her guilt?"

"It's a close call. I'd say yes, because these prints, the loose tobacco, and the saliva are all consistent with Arya's version of the facts and the existence of this old biker dude," Eric concluded.

"Okay, Eric, let's continue to keep our little side investigation off the record for now," Shaheed decided.

"Why?" Eric was very uncomfortable keeping his investigation and these findings away from his superiors, especially Ash.

"Because I want to see what the defense team comes up with. If and when it is necessary to come clean, I will come clean. And I will take the heat, not you."

"You're the boss," conceded Eric. "Anything else you want me to do?"

"Were you able to run DNA on the saliva?"

"Yes. I called in a favor and got a rush report. Unfortunately, it was negative for a match to anyone in the system."

"Then there is nothing more for you to do. I'll let you know if and when I want you to release the details of our little side adventure."

"You're the boss," Eric chirped, robotically. "You're the boss. You're the boss. You're the boss . . ."

"Cut the shit, Eric!" laughed Shaheed, rolling his eyes. Eric headed for the door.

"You're the boss. You're the boss. That does not compute; you're the boss," Eric the robot repeated this mantra as he went through the door, his voice fading as it closed behind him.

***

The following morning, Reed Spencer sat in front of his computer once again. Today's mission was to find the names of as many white supremacists in Michigan as he could. As Reed worked, he found names. As he found names, he compiled a second top ten list to be crosschecked with the first list of organizations. The new list read like a who's who of Michigan bigots. Reed had no idea there was such a large amount of bigotry in the world, and he was completely blown away by how much of it was living in his own home state. When he reached 20 or so names, he began to whittle down the list into his top ten, which read:

- Edward James
- Duke Davies
- Miles Roberts
- Spence Richards
- Bart Breitner
- Benjamin Blaine
- Kenton McDonald
- Timothy Metzger
- Gregory Bower
- David Mazerra

He placed the two lists side by side and began matching names to groups. Some of the prominent top ten names weren't linked to some of the top ten racist groups in Michigan and vice versa. That eliminated some of the names and some of the groups. He wasn't attempting to *eliminate* any suspects; he was simply narrowing his research starting point. The new list contained six groups and their leaders:

- The Free America Party—Bart Breitner
- Aryan American Brothers—Edward James
- The Conservative Council— Benjamin Blaine
- Love White Society—Gregory Bower
- White Nationalists Federation—David Mazerra
- Separatists Unite, led by Kenton McDonald

Reed was now more optimistic. He whittled his list down methodically and substantially. He excogitated his next move to further constrict his list. He hypothesized the person or groups he was looking for were likely to have publicly espoused radical positions against Muslim and Muslim immigration. He reviewed and re-reviewed websites and biographies of groups and individuals that corresponded to these narrow parameters, including those he previously eliminated. He was circumspect, preferring maintaining individuals or groups if there was any criterion that corresponded to his chosen parameters. His working theory was that those who had not taken a strong combative stand against Muslims and Muslim immigration would be unlikely to firebomb a mosque.

Reviewing the various positions taken by the groups and the individuals, he was able to cross out two organizations and three individuals, without having to restore a name or group previously rejected. By prioritizing names and groups but not completely eliminating them, Reed deleted three organizations corresponding with three individuals that hadn't taken a combative anti-Muslim stance.

He now had a narrow list of three groups and three men:

- The Free America Party—Bart Breitner
- The Conservative Council—Benjamin Blaine
- Separatists Unite—Kenton McDonald

Reed was delighted with the results of this exercise, three promising suspects to share with Micah and the others. He could not find current photographs of the men in question, only photos from a few decades prior. Most of the men were past their prime years. A few would be somewhere between 70 and 90 years old.

He wondered whether Arya's composite drawing would assist them in their search. Neither Reed nor Micah had age progression software. Reed hoped someone with access to this state-of-the-art software would permit him to run the youthful photographs he was able to find depicting his top three. This software, if they were able to get their hands on it, would quickly come up with an enhanced comparison to what each man would look like today. Perhaps his colleagues had additional physical evidence that would help to further refine the list or, optimistically, choose a suspect. With these happy thoughts fresh in his mind, Reed Spencer decided to call it a night.

Chapter Twenty-Eight

Ronald John convened a cabinet-level meeting with his Attorney General, his Secretary of the Interior, and his Secretary of Homeland Security. Interior wasn't actually the correct departmental fit for the meeting's purpose, but because RonJohn had limited knowledge of individual department functions, he invited Secretary of the Interior Gavin Perry. Also present was the newly appointed Attorney General, Geoffrey Parley, and new Homeland Secretary, Kelly W. See.

The topic of conversation was an important trial coming up in Detroit. The president followed the news coverage because the defendant was a Muslim woman accused of murder, two favorable circumstances for the president's crusade to limit or prevent Muslim immigration.

President John was not a politician. He came to Washington as a political outsider, an Internet billionaire who vowed to change Washington, to get things done for people, not politicians. One thing he promised to eliminate was Islamic terrorism—if that meant innocent Muslims might be deported, the end justified the means. Since most of his supporters didn't want them here in the first instance, he considered this a small price to pay.

RonJohn wanted Justice to intervene in the Arya Khan prosecution. He wanted Parley to take over the case—try her and fry her—convict her and put her to death. The case would be a shining example of how the new administration dealt with Muslim scourge in this country. Attorney General Parley, a former senator and prominent racist in pre- and post-civil rights Mississippi, was present at the meeting to brief RonJohn on two issues—the prospect of pre-empting the trial and moving it into the federal system, and the prospect of a conviction in either the state system or the federal system. Which of the two presented a better opportunity for a prosecutorial victory?

Parley would have welcomed an opportunity to please the new POTUS, but this was not that opportunity. John was not knowledgeable about legal issues, but this case was Parley's first lesson in how dumb his new boss actually was. Moving the case was a non-starter, especially at this late stage. It would disrupt and impair the proceeding rather than benefit it or President John's 'tough on Muslims' image. The prospect of a conviction depended upon the evidence. Since this was a local city and county matter, Parley was not privy to the evidence and had no idea what the prospects of a conviction were. He decided to embellish—lie about— his understanding of the evidence to assuage and dazzle the president. Parley was convinced subterfuge was the best mechanism to avert an idiot's ambush.

"Mr. President, the case has progressed too far for us to intervene without having a deleterious effect on the case . . ." he began.

"Deleterious?" the president responded, nonplussed.

"Harmful, Mr. President," Parley snickered.

"I . . . uh . . . *know* what you meant. I meant dele . . . ah . . . harmful in what way?" John blustered.

"Mr. President, a federal prosecutor would have to stop a now mature case and start a new investigation. He or she would have to develop theories for federal preemption, which I do not believe are present in the case. Such a step would be extremely disruptive and would likely diminish rather than assist in securing a conviction."

"Uh . . . well . . . I see. Well . . . let's . . . uh . . . table the idea of pursuing a federal prosecution for the time being. I . . . uh . . . can decide that at a later time. Let's move on to the evidence. How strong is it? Likely to convict this Islamic terrorist?"

"The evidence I have reviewed is solid, sir," Parley lied. "I have been read in on the evidence at all stages of the investigation, and it is compelling. Multiple police officers witnessed the terrorist hovering over the victim and holding the murder weapon. The case is as close to a slam dunk as a Kevin Durant breakaway," Parley quipped. *At least those were the facts reported in the Detroit News and by the Associated Press for anyone, including you, to read, Mr. President.*

"Who's Kevin Durant?" President John inquired.

"Why, sir, he's a basketball player, a good one, sir, and a credit to his race." Parley struggled for self-control.

"Oh, he is . . . one of . . . those?"

"Indeed, sir, he is one of the better ones," Parley advised.

"So, we are on solid ground legally?"

"Absolutely, sir," Parley assured.

RonJohn turned to his Secretary of the Interior.

"Gavin, where does Interior stand on the matter?" President John requested, with all of the authority he could muster.

"Interior has no role here, Mr. President," Perry retorted.

"What do you mean, no role?" the president huffed. "This criminal is an American citizen and committed a crime within the *interior* of our country and against a fellow citizen in our country. How can that not be your role?"

"Mr. President, the Department of the Interior manages our nation's public lands, minerals, and national parks. It handles some of our water resources, our trust responsibilities to Native Americans, conservation, historic preservation, and endangered wildlife species, among other things. It would not involve itself in crimes between two citizens simply because the crime happened within the confines of the USA. This is clearly a matter for the Attorney General, or, perhaps—if terrorism is involved— for Homeland, Mr. President." Perry schooled the president.

"Uh, well . . . I . . . uh . . . understand. As a businessman, non- politician, I'm not completely familiar with everyone's function. I'll be learning on the job and leaning on you all," a rare admission of fallibility from the new president. "That's why I invited both you and Homeland. I thought there might be some overlap."

"No, Mr. President. No overlap. The two departments have two completely different functions."

"I see that now," the president admitted. "Homeland?" He turned to See.

"Mr. President. This murder happened in Dearborn, which happens to have the largest constituency of Muslim citizens in the United States. A white person was the victim. If the Muslim is convicted and sentenced to a lengthy prison sentence, such an outcome will assist your 'Make America Pure Again' efforts and seriously hinder Muslim attempts to assimilate or develop homegrown terrorists.

"Like Gavin, sir, I have been monitoring this situation and its surrounding issues very carefully," he paltered. "Unlike Interior, Homeland *is absolutely* interested and involved when Islamic terrorism rears its ugly head within our borders and against our pure-born citizens. This will not be tolerated while I am the Secretary of Homeland Security," he pontificated.

"That's what I like to hear, See. Keep up the good work," the president blustered. "Gavin, you're excused. Geoffrey, Kelly? I want you to stay on top of this. Coordinate your efforts and your investigations and keep me posted. I want real-time updates on this case, got it?"

"Got it, sir," they acknowledged in unison, glancing at each other and back at the president.

"Dismissed," the president ordered, shooing them away with hand motions.

The three men left the Oval Office befuddled. Was the president really this clueless? They did not dare discuss what they just witnessed because they feared President John's paranoia. There was a distinct possibility there were hidden cameras or listening devices in the Oval Office, indeed, all over the White House. After agreeing to meet for breakfast or lunch in the coming days to discuss things, they shook hands and went off in different directions.

Ronald John sat back in his very comfortable desk chair in the Oval Office. He ran for president on a lark, offending everyone, never expecting to win the election. Alison Goodman was an extremely qualified and experienced candidate, yet he beat the crap out of her, fairly and squarely, with a little help from gerrymandering. Still, she was far more qualified to deal with this Muslim problem than he was, and he knew it. Dealing with the Muslim issue was a centerpiece of his campaign, one of the main reasons he was elected POTUS over Goodman. She was weak on terror while the public perceived him as strong on the subject. He blustered and bragged he was the one to solve it, and now, less than 60 days into his presidency, he wasn't sure what to do. The conviction of Arya Khan would undoubtedly be a step in the right direction.

Chapter Twenty-Nine

Ronald John believed campaign promises were sacrosanct. He connected with voters during the campaign, and he was determined to keep those voters in what he called "Camp John." The best way to do that, he often told his closest advisors, was to keep the promises he made on the campaign trail.

One of his more aggressive campaign promises was to deport Muslims if, during vetting, they proved to be "suspicious" or a "clear and present danger to the public." He wasn't going to let an insignificant document like the United States Constitution get in the way of his promises.

President John recently signed an executive order many politicians, judges, and even his closest advisors told him was unwarranted and unconstitutionally overbroad. RonJohn was not concerned and did not heed their advice. The order essentially halted immigration from a select group of countries in which Muslims represented the majority population. This order was used to begin deportation proceedings against Arya's parents.

Hamid and Riah's deportation hearings were to be conducted in less than a month. They were terrified their daughter was going to prison for murder. They invested the bulk of their life savings on her defense costs. They could not concentrate on their own problems, but it would do Arya no good if they were in Yemen when her trial began. Zachary Blake recommended, and they visited with, an immigration attorney named Marshall Mann.

Mann indicated John's executive order was on shaky constitutional ground—he would not be surprised if the order was rescinded before the hearing ever took place. The Khans loved Mann's confident, brash demeanor. He reminded them of Zachary Blake. However, President John did not rescind the order; he did not back down. If anything, he *doubled down.*

John appeared on national television, in an address to the nation, to announce and explain his most recent executive order, entitled "Protecting Our Nation from Foreign-Born Terrorists."

"By the authority vested in me as president, by the Constitution and laws of the United States of America, including the Immigration and Nationality Act, the INA, and to protect the American people from terrorist attacks by foreign nationals admitted to the United States, it is hereby ordered that no foreign national shall be admitted into the United States if that foreign national is a citizen or resident of Yemen, Iraq, Syria, Iran, Sudan, or Libya.

"Our borders are officially closed to refugees from these countries. I don't care what oppression or national danger they're fleeing from. They will not bring terror to our shores. If their country's leaders are mad at them? Not a problem the USA wants any part of. I am announcing, effective today, all persons seeking to enter this country from those on the list will be indefinitely blocked from entering the United States. I promised the American people our government would engage in a policy of extreme vetting to prevent radical Islamic terrorists from entering our great country. The safety of our people is paramount, and these prospective immigrants represent a clear and present danger to our citizens. This policy shall not apply to Christians or other religions from the regions in question. We will only admit those people who support America, American values, and who deeply love our people and our country.

"In order to protect Americans, the United States must ensure those admitted into this country do not bear hostile attitudes toward our country or its founding principles. The United States cannot and will not admit those who do not support the Constitution or would place violent ideologies ahead of America. We will also not admit those who engage in violent acts of bigotry or hatred against those who might practice a religion different than their own.

"The Secretary of Homeland Security shall immediately review the status of all foreign nationals from these countries, adjudicate any status benefit granted them, and determine whether they are an imminent or potential threat to the security and public safety of our citizens.

"To expedite this process and to reduce the investigative burden on the relevant agencies involved, I hereby suspend all immigration from the subject countries until further notice. Furthermore, to assure the safety of our citizens, previous immigrants, regardless of current status, shall be subject to immediate deportation if there is compelling evidence of non-compliance with responsible citizenship or if said immigrant was admitted into the United States on a fraudulent basis, or who may be a risk to the public safety subsequent to his/her admission. Screening standards and procedures to root out fraud and anti-American behavior or rhetoric shall be rigid, and those government officials shall be granted judgment call authority, in conjunction with rules and regulations established by the Department of Homeland Security.

"I hereby proclaim, pursuant to section 212(f) of the INA, that the entry of nationals from Yemen, Iraq, Syria, Iran, Sudan, and Libya as refugees is detrimental to the interests of the United States and shall be suspended, with retroactive application at the discretion of the Secretary of Homeland Security . . ."

***

Earlier that day, President John met with the Christian Coalition and indicated that minority Christian citizens living in predominately Muslim countries were being persecuted, and under his predecessor's policies, Muslims were flocking into the United States while Christian immigration from the region was nearly impossible. That this statement was a blatant falsehood mattered little to RonJohn. The appearance he was pro-Christian and anti-Muslim was what got him elected and would keep him in office.

The new executive order would remain in effect for 120 days and was subject to multiple renewals "as the crisis continues," to use the president's lingo. Interestingly, countries in the region where John's business interests were located were left off the list, whether previous acts of terror originated in those countries or not.

"We must ensure those admitted do not threaten our welfare and our security," RonJohn huffed.

Almost instantly, human rights organizations and constitutional pundits condemned John's actions, declaring them to be discriminatory, random, and thinly veiled religious persecution disguised as a safety measure. Legal challenges were promised, to which the new president blustered, "Bring 'em on!"

The leader for the Rescue of the Oppressed International Committee declared the order "code for systemic religious persecution and discrimination," and determined that the policies adopted under the order would affect those most vulnerable in these countries—women and children who were seeking safe haven from terrorist regimes. Current and former heads of state in other countries, friendly to the United States, and who were accepting refugees from the affected regions by the tens of thousands, condemned the actions as un-American, extraordinarily cruel and insensitive.

Shortly after the order was implemented, hundreds of people were being prevented from boarding airplanes heading into the country, and others already in the country were being rounded up. The first wave of lawsuits was filed on behalf of citizens from the various listed countries who were being detained in travel locations all across the country. Even legal immigrants, naturalized citizens, and people holding green cards were being barred from flights returning them to a country they lived peacefully in for decades.

The strangest incident, and an unintended consequence of a poorly conceived policy, involved a group of US soldiers stationed in the affected countries and seeking to return to the USA after fighting overseas to keep our country safe. Those men and women and the foreign nationals who assisted the war efforts were now placed in grave danger in the countries they were attempting to exit from.

Unfortunately, preventing immigration from certain countries by certain types of people was not the only item on the president's anti-Muslim agenda. On the afternoon following John's executive order, ICE, the US Immigration and Customs Enforcement agency began an unprecedented one-week sweep of the country, placing 350 people into federal custody and detaining thousands more. This action followed a second presidential order, which mandated a sweep for Muslim immigrants who had prior criminal records or charges pending or were merely suspected of engaging in some type of criminal activity, regardless of severity.

The sweep was conducted under the auspices of ICE's National Fugitive Operations Program, which is tasked with the responsibility of locating at-large criminals and detaining them for deportation. This program was initially instituted to track down immigrants who defied a judge's deportation order. President John was using the program to locate Muslim immigrants who had criminal convictions and were recently released from jail for one reason or another.

ICE agents stopped, detained, and illegally searched a man because he 'looked like a Muslim.' ICE agents found a hand-rolled cigarette they declared was marijuana. The man was released, hours later, when it was determined he was Jewish and ICE's 'hand-rolled drug delivery system' was determined to be a 'tobacco delivery system,' commonly known to billions of people as a cigarette.

Despite many hiccups, an ICE spokesperson called the sweep the most successful weeklong event in history. The spokesperson, speaking on the condition of anonymity, indicated that while crime involving Muslim immigrants in this country was not increasing or at dangerous levels currently—in fact, it was almost non-existent—the president was looking for people who had criminal histories, were Muslim, and potentially deportable. Critics joked it was the most successful one-week sweep of its kind in history because it was the *only* one-week sweep of its kind in history.

Its effect was to terrorize and polarize the American Muslim community. Local jails all over the country were packed to capacity with potential Muslim deportees who were detained by local authorities and held until ICE vans could retrieve them. A jail-crowding crisis was avoided when a federal judge ordered the "prisoners" released because the practice was unconstitutional and illegal.

President John promised a swift and successful appeal. However, before anyone could put pen to paper, hundreds of county officials released the prisoners and stopped honoring detention requests in an orchestrated demonstration of defiance of John's anti-immigrant, anti-Muslim policies. When RonJohn found out about the protest, he threatened to "fire the whole lot of them," until Attorney General Geoffrey Parley advised him he had no authority to terminate the employment of state and local employees.

Another unintended consequence of detaining and deporting immigrants was the displacement of the US-born children, United States citizens in every sense of the word. With no parents at home, the children became wards of the state, and the system became overwhelmed. There was simply no room left to house the surplus after the first wave of children was processed. As a result, the federal government was forced to create "processing centers" and hire part-time, unqualified personnel to watch over them and attend to their needs. Essentially, security guard-level workers were performing the functions of college-educated social workers.

Housing consisted of warehouse-type facilities without adequate plumbing or heating. Cots were set up in columns and rows over several-thousand-square-foot facilities. Children were divided into age groups. Siblings were separated from each other after being suddenly separated from their parents. Facilities were sectioned off by barbed wire or chain-linked fencing. Human beings occupied every square foot of these centers. Because they lacked basic human waste facilities such as showers, food, bedding, and other supplies, the places reeked of body odor and were filthy and disease-ridden. Medical or nursing care was either unavailable or, where it was available, workers were tasked to the limit. "Welcome to America in the Ronald John era," one disgruntled social worker groused. "Is this how we make America pure again?"

Finally, after the death of a 7-year-old girl from exhaustion and dehydration, a federal judge terminated the program, released the parents to their homes, closed the processing centers, and returned children to their parents. Federal Judge Frederick Rosen wrote a scathing 27-page opinion, rebuking the John administration. Rosen opined the order was overbroad. He also determined Federal authorities, acting under the auspices of John's executive order, failed to identify a clear and present danger to the community at large. According to Judge Rosen, the order violated constitutional due process rights of American citizens and failed to guarantee a speedy trial due to a backlog of cases.

This ruling was a tremendous blow to President John's immigration policies. It was also a stark reminder to pro-John forces that he was not a king or dictator; he was president of constitutional democracy. The framers of the Constitution brilliantly created three distinct branches of government to provide appropriate checks and balances for those who abuse power in the United States of America.

Homeland Security Secretary See expressed disappointment with the ruling and announced the department was reviewing the matter with the Department of Justice. Privately, See consulted with Attorney General Parley and the Justice Department, who told him an appeal would be a worthless endeavor. The order violated numerous constitutional protections.

Immigration rights groups and immigration attorneys applauded the federal court ruling. Many stated the decision should extend beyond restoring the previous status quo. Constitutional abuses were so egregious that those affected should be granted immediate and permanent asylum or some other type of special status.

John supporters and anti-immigration groups condemned the ruling, arguing it sends a dangerous message to Muslim immigrants and terrorists that illegal immigration will go unchecked and unpunished in the United States. Terrorists have nothing to fear from the federal judiciary, and a mass influx of Muslim immigrants, including terrorists, into this country was imminent.

Chapter Thirty

In a tense atmosphere where all three branches of government were at war with each other, in a deeply divided America, a deeply divided Michigan and Dearborn-Wayne County, *People v. Arya Khan* wound its way toward trial. There were already stark religious and cultural divides in the region that was home to the country's largest concentration of Muslims. The war between President Ronald John, Muslim nationals, Muslim immigrants, and the federal judiciary was peaking at the wrong time for Arya Khan and Zachary Blake. Picking a jury and conducting *voir dire* would be difficult, if not impossible. The trial was three weeks away, and professionals on both sides were scrambling to make their respective cases.

A meeting between Zachary Blake, Arya Khan, and Micah Love's investigative team was assembled in the conference room of Love Investigations in downtown Detroit. Present were Zack, Arya, Micah, Reed Spencer, Matthew Jordan, and members of the surveillance team shadowing Arya Khan.

The team observed Arya's comings and goings but saw no indication she was followed or monitored in any way.

Matt Jordan went next and reported the crime scene had been processed and, surprisingly, given Dearborn PD's exclusive focus on Arya from the get-go, someone beat them to the idea of pursuing her alibi or alternative theory of the crime. Matt indicated the crime scene people knew what they were doing. He asked Zack whether Bialy had turned over any evidence to support an alternate intruder. Zack indicated Bialy had not. The group concluded Bialy and Dylan were either withholding evidence, or someone processed the scene and conducted a rogue investigation behind Bialy and Dylan's backs.

Matt invited Micah to call whomever he knew at Dearborn PD and find out who processed the crime scene and persuade them to turn over what they found. Matt had struck out with his department contacts. Perhaps motions for discovery violations and prosecutorial misconduct were in order. Zack was extremely

reluctant to disrupt what was, so far, a very cordial and
professional relationship with Larry Bialy.

Next, Matt announced his team's findings. Yes, someone else
had visited the crime scene. This person's footprints and DNA
were found in the bushes next to the porch, Blackwell's front
yard, and the neighbor's front and back yard.

In the street, Matthew and his team found gasoline and motor
oil traced to a large-engine motorcycle. Arya was visibly excited.
Hearing someone processed the scene and verified she was
truthful about an intruder was music to her ears. She understood
it didn't prove this person murdered Blackwell. It also didn't
prove whoever was on site was present the day of the murder,
even though, as the lone eyewitness, she knew it was true.
However, the revelation made her story more believable. There
was some discussion about whether certain things would be
admissible in court, but that discussion was way over her head.

Jordan continued his presentation. He reported the person
was male, approximately six feet tall, and weighed 200 to 210
pounds. He wore Wolverine Floorhand steel-toed work boots.
Based upon his gait, Matthew determined he was an older rather
than a younger man, with a deliberate gait. Matthew pegged him
at 70 or older, but could not be sure. The description and age
were also consistent with Arya's story, and chills ran up her
spine as she heard Matthew's words.

The downside of Matthew's report related to DNA from
chewing tobacco found at the scene. Saliva was processed, but
negative for a match in the system. The man was either not a
criminal or engaged in criminal activity so long ago that his
DNA was not in the system.

Reed Spencer went next. He set up his MacBook, a
whiteboard, and a projector. He pressed some keys on his laptop,
and a PowerPoint presentation appeared on the whiteboard. He
took the meeting participants through his entire process,
demonstrating the steps he took to whittle the suspects down to
three groups and three individual names. He indicated if anyone
had anything to add, he could always add previously eliminated
names or groups to the list. Everyone was impressed with the
work done to compile and narrow such a list.

Zack was intrigued. He suggested they ignore groups and concentrate on the three men, Bart Breitner, Benjamin Blaine, and Kenton McDonald. After all, Arya saw one elderly man, not a group of men. If none of the three turned out to be the guy Arya saw, they could then turn their attention to foot soldiers.

Reed would now deliver the bad news. These were bad dudes, he noted. They were white supremacists, racists, and bigots. He despised anything and everything about them. However, not a single one of these three committed a crime in the post-DNA era, and he and Matthew could find no match to any of them when they ran the crime scene DNA.

They were very discreet bigots and ran their respective groups as shadow individuals. Everyone in law enforcement knew who ran the groups. All white supremacists knew their names, reputations, and which group each was the leader of. However, there were no current pictures of any of these three men. They seemed to exist in reputation only.

He pulled out three photographs and passed them around the table for study. Even Arya, the eyewitness, could not identify any of them as the old biker. She excused herself to use the restroom. Micah pointed to a key hooked to a wood paint mixer with the word "ladies" on it and told Arya where the floor's restrooms were located. Arya tiptoed out of the room as the men engaged in a discussion.

The men resumed their analysis of the photos in her absence. All three men were depicted in black-and-white. Each looked to be in his 20s or 30s. They were clean-shaven, with no identifying characteristics. If they had tattoos, the clothing worn in the photographs covered them. There were no scars, fractures, displacements, moles, or marks, nothing to distinguish these young men from any other young men.

Reed requested the composite drawing of the suspect, as conceived from Arya's memory. Again, the composite and the three photographs were passed around to see if anyone saw what they might consider a match. No one could offer help. They searched through the evidence dump provided by Bialy and found several surveillance photographs of a group of men who were obviously attending a meeting at the Schaefer address of USA 1 Pure.

The men rode motorcycles and were wearing motorcycle jackets with distinctive logos displayed. Reed took the photographs, compared the logo with the logos that appeared in the various websites for the different groups in question, and shouted: "Yes!" Suddenly, everyone's attention focused on Reed Spencer.

"What is it, Reed?" Micah wondered, sharing Reed's excitement and speaking for everyone in the room.

"I have a logo match!" Reed exclaimed, standing and pounding the table.

"With who?" Zack wondered, sharing Reed's excitement. He'd had very little to get excited about with two weeks to go until trial.

"The Conservative Council, TCC for short, Benjamin Blaine, this guy." He re-distributed an old photo of Blaine as a young man. No one saw a resemblance between the young dude in the picture and the old hippie in the recent surveillance photos.

"Are you sure, Reed?" Micah questioned.

"One hundred percent. See for yourself," Reed grinned. He scrolled through some PowerPoint slides until he came across the logo of TCC. He then handed everyone a photo of the group photographed in front of the Schaefer headquarters of USA 1 Pure. There was no mistake. The logos were identical.

"Is there any connection between USA 1 Pure and TCC?" Matt wondered.

"I couldn't find a connection between Blackwell, USA 1 Pure, and any of these groups until I saw this photo," Reed reported. "It's clearly TCC on these jackets, folks."

"It clearly is," echoed Zack, continuing to share Reed's enthusiasm but with a more professional temperament.

"We have our connection," Reed proclaimed.

"It appears we do," Micah agreed. "The question now is: What do we do about it?"

"Aren't we obligated to go to the cops with it?" Matt suggested.

Everyone turned to Zack. "I don't think so," Zack opined. "We have discovered nothing that is new or potential evidence in the case except for the logo, and the Dearborn PD had access to the same information to identify the logo as we did. Furthermore, we have to ask what Dylan or his cronies would do with the evidence if they had it. Would the link to TCC be enough for them to dismiss charges? I don't think so."

At that moment, Arya Khan walked back into the room and picked up the group picture in front of the Schaefer USA 1 Pure location. With one look at the photograph, she shouted with excitement, "That's the guy! That's the guy I saw at Schaefer! That's the guy! Who is he, guys?"

"Arya Khan, meet Benjamin Blaine—white supremacist extraordinaire and the murderer of Keith Blackwell!" Reed announced.

"Allahu Akbar!" Arya shouted. "Let's go to the police right now, Zack!" She eyed Zack, urgently motioning with her head for him to follow as she started for the door.

"Hold on, Arya. Let's think this through, okay?" Zack reasoned.

"What, Zack? We've got him, don't we?" Zack was raining on her parade.

"Arya, they've had your statement the whole time. They ran surveillance on the Schaefer storefront before the murder and took these pictures. They had Blaine's picture the entire time. You gave them a surprisingly accurate description of the guy."

Zack held the surveillance photo and the composite drawing up together, side by side. "They've had this connection all this time and didn't share it. Why?

"Considering all of this, I don't think going down there and pointing out the obvious is going to make a damn bit of difference in how they proceed. They will not dismiss the charges. They will not admit they were wrong. Perhaps it's too embarrassing. With Ronald John running all over the country condemning Muslims and focusing on the Khan family, the government will not want to admit the terrorist, in this case, is the white guy."

"So, what do we do, smart guy?" Micah challenged.

"I don't know, maybe nothing," Zack cogitated. "Surprise them at trial with the photograph of Blaine and the composite drawing."

"We can't do that, Zack," Micah corrected. "You forget one thing."

"What's that, Micah?" Arya wondered.

"The cops don't know who Benjamin Blaine is. They don't know the guy in the picture is Blaine and they don't know he's the killer. Even if they do some research like our boy Reed, here, they won't find a current picture, right, Reed?"

"That's true," Reed agreed. "So, what are you driving at, boss?"

"We need more. Zack, I think we need an expert."

Zack intuitively knew where Micah was going and what he was thinking. "Micah, you are a fricking genius!" He would have utilized the other F-word, but Arya was in the room. "We need to take the old photo of Blaine to an age progression software specialist. Have him run the software on the young Blaine photograph. And I'm willing to bet the farm the software proves the young and old are both Blaine. We put the tech on the stand. He names that tune in one note, and Arya is sent home free as a jaybird. Bialy won't know what hit him until it's too late. Micah—I could kiss you!"

"Please don't, you're not my type," Micah quipped. "Does anyone know anybody in the age progression software field? We need a specialist's specialist. The guy everyone turns to when there are similar photos of the same person as a young man and as an old man. We need the best of the best."

Zack was intrigued. He hung on every word as Micah continued. "Reed, Matt, and I will ask around. We'll be discreet, Zack. Don't want to ask the wrong guy and tip off the other side, get my drift?" This was the Micah Love who solved and won cases. Zack felt fortunate to have Micah Love on Team Blake, and in this case, Team Arya.

"I read you loud and clear, Micah. Great work, you guys. Arya now has a fighting chance at freedom, and she has this terrific team to thank."

"Thank you, all of you," Arya cried. "This is the first time I've felt hopeful since this whole nightmare began."

"We couldn't let them convict an innocent woman, Arya. Not a nice, wonderful lady like you," Micah spoke for his crew. He raised his plastic cup of cranberry juice. "A toast," he offered. Everyone raised a plastic cup of whatever they were drinking. "To the innocence of Arya Khan. May she stay innocent until she finds the man of her dreams," Micah toasted.

"Micah!" Arya gasped.

"Sorry, Arya. I couldn't help myself." The men snickered. Arya blushed. They all laughed. Prudish Arya was willing to excuse almost anything at that moment. She finally had something to smile about.

Chapter Thirty-One

The following Saturday, Zack Blake and his two stepsons, Kenny and Jake Tracey, were in the backyard of Zack's Bloomfield Hills estate, tossing a baseball around in a triangle formation. Zack would toss to Kenny, Kenny to Jake, Jake back to Zack, and so on, in turn. The backyard was a teenager's dream. There was a pool with a large deck and cabana, a mini basketball court, and an expansive fenced-in lawn area almost half the size of a football field. The boys had many friends, and constant sporting activities were going on in the Blake-Tracey backyard. Today, however, Zack was happily alone with the two boys who were quickly becoming like sons to him.

Zack signaled to the boys he'd had enough. The boys continued a two-way game of catch. Zack walked over to a pool lounge chair, placed his baseball mitt on the ground, and lay across the lounge. He closed his eyes, enjoying the warmth of the late spring sun on his face. Zack had a busy life, and relaxing moments like this one were few and far between. He reflected upon his recent good fortune, the success of the Tracey case, his practice, his beautiful new wife, and an instant family with two terrific sons. He thought about the Khan family and, in his mind, began to make comparisons between the Khan's family situation and his own.

The Tracey family faced a deep emotional crisis. The institution in which this devoutly religious family placed its faith and trust had betrayed Jennifer and the boys in a most heinous manner. With Zack's help, they emerged better and stronger than they were before the incident. Zack was hopeful he could accomplish a similar miracle for the Khan family. *The situation is vastly different, isn't it?* Yet, Zack could not help noticing similarities, especially the fact both families were victims of atrocities tied to religion. As Zack pondered other similarities, he drifted off to sleep.

He awoke with a start when Kenny and Jake jumped on the lounge and shouted, "Wake up, lazy!" Zack shot up into a sitting position and pushed the two boys off the lounge and onto the brick paver deck. The boys were laughing hysterically.

"Very funny, you two. You could give an old man a coronary doing that. I'm up. I'm up! I wasn't sleeping, anyway—I was just resting my eyes," Zack joked.

"Sure, Zack, sure," Jake rolled his eyes.

"Does someone who is resting his eyes snore like a pig?" Kenny imitated Zack's loud snoring, and they all cracked up with laughter. *There was a time, not too long ago, when these boys were incapable of laughter. Their recuperative processes are remarkable.*

"Okay, okay, maybe I did doze off for a second or two. What of it?" Zack conceded.

"Nothing, Zack, nothing at all. It is just hard to concentrate on our game with all those pig sounding noises going on in the background," Kenny joked.

"You guys are a laugh riot," Zack scowled. "Hey, sit down for a second, would you? I've been really busy with this Dearborn case, so we haven't had a chance to talk for a while. How's everything going? School good?"

"Everything's fine, Zack. We're kind of famous again if you know what I mean." Kenny became somber and serious, gazing at the ground.

"How do you mean?" Zack queried, knowing what the 'again' reference was, but not sure what was currently making them 'famous.' The boys' status as plaintiffs in a multi-million-dollar lawsuit against the church was a hot topic at their respective schools back in the day.

"Everybody's asking us about your case. Why are you representing Muslim terrorists?" Jake advised.

"How long has this been going on? Why didn't you tell me?" Zack demanded. This was the last thing the boys needed as they continued their remarkable recovery from sexual abuse and its aftermath.

"No big deal, Zack. We can handle it," Kenny blustered. "But Zack, why are you handling this case? Wouldn't it make more sense for someone from Arya Khan's own community to handle it?"

"No, Kenny, it wouldn't. This is what I do. More than that, this is who I *am*. When I see injustice, I am compelled to seek justice. When I see a wrong, I try to right it. Before your mother came to me with your situation, I was pretty much lost. These days, I have the means and the power to take the cases I want to take and fight the battles that need fighting. This is one of those battles. Because Arya Khan is a Muslim doesn't mean she's a terrorist. The one does not necessarily follow the other. You guys get that, don't you?" Zack was concerned the boys were starting to believe some of the poison emanating from their 'friends.'

"I guess so," Kenny grunted. Apparently, he wasn't convinced.

"Compare this situation to Father Gerry. He was a predator, a child molester, right?"

"Right," the boys grumbled, in unison, *duh*.

"That didn't make Father Bill Stern a bad guy, did it?" Zack suggested.

"No, Father Bill is a great guy," Jake chirped. He *loved* Father Bill. Both boys did. Father Bill was now Bishop William Stern, a member of the Interfaith Council and a friend to Rabbi Joey and Baqir Ghaffari, imam of the Mosque of America in Dearborn.

"While some terrorists today happen to be Muslim, not all Muslims are terrorists, just like not all priests are child molesters. The vast majority of Muslims are decent, hardworking people. Some are very religious, others not religious at all. They are just like Christians, Jews, or any other religion. They are what they are. They observe their religion and customs the way they want to. A small number of misguided Muslims decide to hate and adopt a terrorist ideology or align with a terrorist group. You can't fault an entire religion or race of people for that, can you? In fact, the largest segment of jihadist terror *victims* is other Muslims," Zack advised.

"I guess we never thought of it that way," Kenny admitted, glancing over at Jake, who nodded in agreement.

"I guess your friends weren't thinking at all," Zack snapped, with more anger than he intended.

"Sorry, Zack, we didn't mean to piss you off," Jake conceded.

"No, no, Jake, I'm sorry! I didn't mean to snap at you," Zack apologized. "This case and how good people, who happen to be Muslim, are viewed because of things going on in the Middle East, piss me off. You guys could never piss me off! Arya Khan, my client, is the sweetest young lady—you guys would really like her. Yet, many people have judged her guilty simply because she is of Muslim faith. They even ignore the fact the guy who died was a white supremacist, racist, Islamophobic bigot."

"What's a 'white supremacist'? Jake inquired.

Zack smiled at Jake's innocence. *If we could all see racial or religious differences from the eyes of a child.* "The guy who was killed, Keith Blackwell, is a member of a group of people who hate anyone who is not white and Christian. White Supremacists believe white Christians are superior to those of other races and religions, and they believe they should control society. Many advocate the destruction of all those who are not white and Christian."

"So, if Arya killed this guy, he deserved it?" Jake posited.

"No, Jake. That's not what I am suggesting at all. I am convinced Arya is innocent. Someone is setting her up. *In this case*, this Blackwell guy and the people who set Arya up are the bad guys. Jihadi terrorists are terrible people. While Arya Khan and her parents are Muslims, they are not bad people. Have you read about Timothy McVey in school?"

"The Oklahoma bomber guy?" Kenny boasted with pride that he knew the answer.

"Yeah, the Oklahoma bomber guy. He was a Christian. Does the fact he was a Christian and a terrorist make all Christians terrorists?" Zack queried.

"Of course not," Kenny agreed as if the question was ridiculous.

"Of course not," Zack mimicked. "So why then, if a terrorist is Muslim, are we so quick to assume all Muslims are terrorists?" Zack challenged.

"You're right, Zack. We all do that, don't we? I'm glad we had this talk. I am going to straighten out a lot of people when I get back to school," Kenny promised.

"Yeah, me too," mimicked Jake, something he used to do with 'Kennyisms,' often when they were younger.

Jennifer opened the patio door and announced lunch was ready.

"Coming Mom," shouted the boys, rising from the lounge. "Thanks for the explanation, Zack—we appreciate it."

"No problem, boys—last one in the house is a rotten egg!" Zack yelped, as he took off for the kitchen patio door. Laughing and screaming, the boys took off running behind him, quickly overtook him, and beat him to the door.

As Zack reached the door, the boys laughed. With nose lifted, Jake sniffed at the air. "It suddenly smells like rotten eggs over here." The three laughed and walked, arm in arm, into the house.

Chapter Thirty-Two

The following day, Bishop William Stern stepped up to the podium of Our Lady of the Lakes Church in Farmington Hills, Michigan, addressing his congregation and honored guests. He declared this particular Sunday to be "Interfaith Embracement Day" and invited people of many different faiths. In attendance, for example, were Rabbi Joseph Norman and Imam Baqir Ghaffari and other religious leaders from the interfaith council. Zachary Blake, Jennifer Tracey, and her boys were also in attendance. Bishop Stern paused for a moment and looked out into the congregation, nodding and establishing a connection with many members and guests. Finally, he began to speak.

"Brothers and sisters, fellow congregants, neighbors, friends, and honored guests. Today is Interfaith Embracement Day. We encourage everyone to learn all they can about other ways to pray and worship the Lord. We encourage everyone to respect those who choose not to pray, even those who choose not to believe in a higher being. We must be tolerant and respectful to our fellow human beings, regardless of their color or creed, beliefs, sex or national origin, or how or whom they choose to love.

"We have many honored guests in attendance; there are too many to name. I have invited one to deliver today's sermon. Rabbi Joseph Norman has been my friend for many years. He will speak to you today about religious and cultural tolerance. I have the distinct honor and privilege to serve on the Southeastern Lower Michigan Interfaith Council with him and other dignitaries in attendance today. You may stay for a luncheon we have prepared in their honor, and you will have an opportunity to meet and greet every single one of them if you choose to do so. I encourage a vigorous exchange.

"Also in attendance is Imam Baqir Ghaffari, imam of the Mosque of America in Dearborn, Interfaith Council member, and another good friend of mine. You may recognize his name and the name of his mosque. Both have been victims of a recent firebombing that caused significant damage to the mosque and injuries to its congregants. This cowardly act was senseless. This and other similar occurrences are born out of fear of religion many do not understand or appreciate.

"The person or persons who committed the mosque bombing are no better than the extremists they accuse Muslims of being.

If a Christian or Jew commits an act of terror, do we consistently blame the Christian or Jewish religions? We do not, of course, yet we seem to have no problem making that extraordinary link when the terrorists are Muslim.

"Many Muslims, Imam Ghaffari among them, have been victims of jihadi terrorism. Terrorism knows no religious boundary. Despite being a recent terror victim, Imam Ghaffari will be staying for lunch and will be available to answer questions. If I can persuade him to, perhaps he would be willing to give us a mini-seminar on Muslim customs and practices.

"For now, though, I return to our guest speaker this afternoon. Rabbi Joey, as his friends and colleagues know him, is the chief Rabbi of Congregation Shaarey Yisro'el, which, in English, means Gates of Israel. To Jewish people, the synagogue is truly the gateway to the Promised Land, and, as we all know from our scriptures, the Jews are God's Chosen People.

As I speak, however, Jewish cemeteries are being desecrated in this country. Bomb threats are being called into synagogues and Jewish community centers all across the country. Anti-Semitism is on the rise." Members of the congregation shuffled, uncomfortably, in their seats. Heads turned from side to side, and a buzz of voices filled the room. Bishop Stern waited quietly before continuing.

"We Christians represent the world's majority religion. It is our responsibility to embrace minority religions, and learn about them and the people who worship in a slightly different way than we do. We need to stand up to intolerance, bigotry, and hatred. If someone shouts words of hate, we must speak louder words of love. If someone is intolerant, we must patiently demonstrate how to be tolerant. If someone lashes out in anger, we must reach out in friendship.

"I am not necessarily referring to confrontation. If we see someone being harassed or bullied due to race, religion, or for any reason, confronting the bully might make the situation worse. Perhaps we can approach the harasser and the harassed with a changed subject. How about this weather? How can anyone deny climate change? Or, can the current Tigers make one more pennant run? Or, how about this one: Can our Detroit Lions become this year's Chicago Cubs?" A congregation full of long-suffering Detroit Lions football fans laughed long and hard at this one.

When the laughter and murmuring subsided, Bishop Stern continued. "I know. I know. I feel your pain. It's impossible to believe, but folks have been praying for the Cubs for more than 100 years and look what happened. Keep praying, folks. You never know." Bill smiled. The congregation chuckled.

"More importantly, however, the mention of the Lions and their misfortunes diffuses a dangerous situation and lets the bullying victim know he or she is not alone, okay?" The congregation nodded and mumbled assent to the suggestion. "Both Rabbi Joey and Imam Ghaffari have certainly seen their share of hate. Please show both of them some real Christian fellowship and make them feel welcome. Rabbi Joey, please address our congregation."

Rabbi Joseph Norman stepped up to the podium and embraced Father Bill. As Bill did, earlier, he paused and studied the congregation, nodding acknowledgment of certain dignitaries and friends, including Zachary Blake and the Tracey family.

"Thank you, Father Bill, for that stirring introduction. We are, indeed, living in troubled times, and I'm not speaking only of the Detroit Lions." This comment prompted more chuckles over the pathetic failures of Detroit's professional football team. "All of us have free choice. We can choose to hate or love. We can choose to embrace or fisticuffs. We can choose education or ignorance, tolerance, or intolerance.

"While the news reports acts of religious and racial intolerance, religious and ethnic *tolerance* is a rapidly growing social movement, a real *phenomenon* in this country. We live in a pluralistic society where there are billions of practicing

Christians and Muslims, Hundreds of millions of Hindus and Buddhists, and millions of Jews. And, while it may surprise you, we live in a world where there are over 150 million Atheists. We live in a world of religious pluralism. Therefore, isn't it common sense we embrace the simple concept of trying to get along with each other?

"Why should we hate or trash someone because of his or her faith? After all, religion, regardless of how it is practiced or who is practicing it, is supposed to be a good thing, right? One of its main purposes is to help us comprehend the difference between right and wrong. It also provides its practitioners with lessons on how to cope with the difficulties and tragedies of life. It helps people cope when life throws a curveball. Peace and fellowship are central themes. Do unto another, as you would have he or she do onto you, right?" The congregation murmured and nodded its assent.

"However, religion is often invoked to justify hate. The Israeli-Palestinian conflict, ethnic cleansing in Bosnia, Nazi Germany, Russian pogroms, the Armenian genocide, and Chaldeans being chased out of Iraq are but a few examples of hatred and bigotry related to or grounded in religion. Religion can just as easily be used as a force for evil rather than a force for good. Since we know this to be true, doesn't this present us with opportunity? Shouldn't we seize the moment to be more tolerant of each other's beliefs, so hatred is not victorious in this moral battle?

"This lesson is most important in a country like the United States. You see, my friends, here in the good old USA, we are blessed to have a larger variety of religions and cultures when compared to most other countries in the world. We speak different languages, worship different gods, or none at all. We appreciate different things. We are unique in our many differences. Thus, I ask all of you this question: Should we have a common religion? Wouldn't that solve many of our problems?" People looked at each other, confused. Was he *serious*? A buzz of dissenting voices could be heard in the crowd. Rabbi Joey quickly quieted the crowd with his next remark.

"The answers, of course, are 'no' and 'no.' We are far too different and have multiple views and opinions about religion. In America, one of our precious freedoms, guaranteed by the 1st Amendment of the Constitution, is the freedom of religious choice. We can choose who we love, where we live, and who we vote for or support politically. We can choose to educate ourselves or to go to the school of hard knocks. Why shouldn't we be able to choose how and who we worship? I believe in God, but I cannot be so arrogant as to assume my way of worship is the right way or the only way. Does anyone in this room believe He really cares how we worship Him?" Many in attendance began shrugging their shoulders or shaking their heads from side to side. The rabbi continued.

"My young son, Oliver, likes to recite the following limerick: Roses are red. Violets are bluish. If it weren't for Jesus, we'd all be Jewish."

The congregation laughed out loud. As the laughter subsided, Rabbi Joey continued. "While my son's observation is not entirely correct, it *is* true Christian faith is rooted in Old Testament principles. Yet, many New Testament scholars believe the only way a person purges himself of sin is by accepting Jesus Christ as his lord and savior. The New Testament suggests that even Jesus preached this concept. So, I ask you this. How could Jesus be so embracing and loving but, at the same time, be so intolerant of other's beliefs? Is Jesus the only way to God, as John 1:1, 14 suggests?

"If you are honest with yourselves, doesn't this concept strike you as an excuse for Christian intolerance or judgmental behavior toward other religions? Could it not be used, by way of example, to justify the anti-Semitic behavior of a devout bigot? At its core, Christianity calls upon its worshippers to live in peace, love, and harmony with others. Jesus did not preach hatred or bigotry. At the end of the day, all religions teach us, in one way or another, to love friends and enemies alike, and you cannot do that in an atmosphere of condemnation, hatred, and intolerance. Timothy 1:5 says, 'the goal of our instruction is love from a pure heart and a good conscience and a sincere faith.'

"The dictionary defines 'tolerance' as a 'fair, objective, and permissive attitude toward those whose opinions, beliefs, practices, racial or ethnic origins differ from one's own; freedom from bigotry.' Most violence in the world results from man's inability or stubborn refusal to respect someone else's contrary opinion. But honest differences of opinion are an essential part of day-to-day life. Whether we agree or disagree with someone else's opinion or conviction, isn't it our responsibility to try to understand and accept his or her point of view or to be forbearing or civil about our differences? Tolerance is a quality that enables us to function together. It allows positive relationships.

"Please do not misunderstand. I am not telling you how to believe. I am not telling you to embrace Judaism any more than I would want you to tell me to embrace Christianity. What I am asking of you is for you to be tolerant, understanding, loving, and accepting of both similarities and differences. Being different makes all of us more interesting and gives us each something to learn about another.

"If you have been intolerant, unkind or hurtful, you can ask God's forgiveness, but wouldn't it be better if you seek forgiveness and understanding from the victim or victims of your intolerance or hurtfulness? Demonstrate you genuinely care for them in some tangible way. Take steps to learn what floats their boat. You may find your similarities outweigh your differences. We must learn to celebrate, not fight over, our differences. A pluralistic society requires no less, and the world will be a vastly better place if we can find a way to embrace this simple truth. What's the bottom line? Regardless of religious, cultural, ethnic, or other differences, we need each other. Thank you, and God bless you."

After the sermon, lunch was served. Many congregation members were gathered around Imam Ghaffari, looking to learn more about Islam, or asking what they could do to help rebuild the mosque. Perhaps some closed minds were being opened. Zack, Jennifer, Jake, and Kenny were seated with Father Bill and Rabbi Joey and other council members.

"Guys," Zack addressed his luncheon companions. "You remember my Rabbi, Rabbi Joey, right?"

"Sure, hi Rabbi," Jake chirped.

"Did you listen to my sermon, boys?" Rabbi Joey inquired.

"What do you mean? Jake was confused. "You mean your speech?"

"Yes, Jake. When a member of the clergy gives a congregational speech, it's usually called a sermon," Rabbi Joey explained.

"I didn't know that," Jake confessed.

"Sure you did, squirt. You just forgot," Kenny defended his brother.

"So, what did you guys think?"

"I think you're right," Kenny opined. "People don't like each other anymore, for a lot of reasons. Everybody is fighting with everybody else. And if someone is not the same religion or the same color as you are, you can use it as an excuse to dislike that person. Is that what you mean?"

"Kenny, that is exactly what Rabbi Joey means. Your analysis is spot on. Now, wouldn't it be a better idea to try to understand someone else's religion or opinion rather than using either as an excuse to dislike or fight with that person?" Bishop Stern proposed.

"Your stepfather, my friend Zack, is Jewish. He belongs to the synagogue where I serve as Rabbi. Do you think he's different? If so, is that difference a reason to dislike him?" Rabbi Joey challenged.

"Of course not," Kenny scoffed, without hesitation. He's Zack. He's like our dad. He's wonderful to our mom and to us." *Smart kid,* Zack smiled, looking over at Jennifer beaming.

"What about Imam Ghaffari over there? He's a Muslim. Is that a reason to dislike him?" Father Bill asserted.

"I didn't argue *I* couldn't like him; I argued *other* people might use his religion as an excuse to dislike him," Kenny corrected.

"Do you agree it's a better idea to get to know someone and learn about his or her ways before judging? What do you think, Jake?" Father Bill turned to Jake.

Jake was surprised. He was listening to the conversation and was delighted his brother was in the hot seat. Suddenly, the question was directed at him, not his brother. He paused to deliberate.

"My school has some Jewish people, some Japanese people, some Black people, and some Arab people. Once you get to know them, they are really no different than you and me," Jake declared. "Just like Zack!"

"Exactly, Jake. That was the major point of the sermon," Joey explained.

"There's a lot of peer pressure in school," Jennifer chimed in. "Some kids are less tolerant than others. Some kids are being taught the prejudices of their parents. They come to school and put pressure on others to exclude this person or that one."

"That's true, Jennifer. And it is tough not to follow in your parent's footsteps. After all, most of us follow the rules we follow or the religious teachings we follow because it is the way our parents have raised us," the rabbi advised.

He looked at Jake, then at Kenny. "Boys, your mom is right about peer pressure. I'm sure you guys have experienced that. But God gave us free will. Just because parents or friends choose to hate doesn't mean we don't have the capacity or free will to love. Do you see what I mean? And look what hate has done to Imam Ghaffari over there. What did he or any of his congregational members do to deserve the firebombing of their mosque?" Rabbi Joey inquired, nodding in Ghaffari's direction.

"Nothing," Jake and Kenny concluded, in unison.

"Well, that settles that," Zack chuckled. "Maybe there is hope for the rest of the world. But, when our people elect a guy like Ronald John as president, the notion of tolerance and unity seems a bit of a pipe dream."

"But we can't lose faith, can we? We can't give up. Jake and Kenny can see through the smoke and mirrors, why not the rest of the country? Why not the rest of the world?" Father Bill proposed.

"Almost every war has been fought over cultural or religious differences. The present situation overseas, the current cultural divide in America, both are related to those types of differences. I don't see things changing any time soon. And RonJohn makes the whole thing worse. He is the most divisive leader we have ever had," Zack opined.

"I agree we live in challenging times, but that doesn't mean we quit, does it? The important question is—are we up to the challenge? We need to get into the trenches and fight for civility, don't you think? If we give up the fight, this new president and his ilk win," Father Bill argued.

"He did win. He's president. That's the problem!" Jake grumbled. *Out of the mouth of babes . . .* thought Jennifer. *I love that boy!*

"He sure did, Jake, and to many, he is a problem. To others, he is a blessing. Again, the opinions of this president reflect some of the differences we have been talking about. But, if you are one who believes Ronald John is part of the problem, remember, he is president for four years, not for life. We have the power to hold him accountable for his actions. We can vote him out of office if we don't like his policies or his behavior. We can force our congressmen, senators, or judges to apply pressure to control him. In the Tracey family, it begins with you guys. Maybe it spreads to other families and other young people all across the country. When you see a wrong, try to right it. We can be a better country if people of goodwill ban together to do what's right," Rabbi Joey averred.

"How do we start?" Kenny questioned.

"One person at a time, Kenny. One person at a time," Zack declared, thinking of *his* one person, a sweet Muslim person named Arya Khan. "And one more thing," Zack continued, straight-faced.

"What's that, Zack?" Father Bill wondered.

"Can we say an interfaith prayer for the Detroit Lions?"

The table erupted in laughter as Baqir Ghaffari approached. After hearing a brief explanation for the laughter, Ghaffari offered a gesture of prayer for the Lions, which provoked additional laughter. The imam was then invited to join the group. Everyone scooted around to make room for another chair for him. Zack, the three clergymen, and the Tracey family, a very diverse group of people, continued their very uplifting conversation. Change was, indeed, possible, *one person at a time.*

Chapter Thirty-Three

Two weeks before trial in *People v. Arya Khan*, Dearborn Police task force members met for the first time in quite a while. The purpose of the meeting was to coordinate various segments of the investigation, prepare a final presentation of the evidence for Lawrence Bialy and his trial team, and determine whether the team could expect any surprises at trial. Present at the meeting were the senior members of the task force, Jack Dylan, Asher Granger, Shaheed Ali, and Noah Thompson. Also present was Eric Burns, several of the officers who responded to the 9-1-1 call and caught Arya with the murder weapon, and some of the officers who were involved in running surveillance on Blackwell and the Schaefer storefront. Jack called the meeting to order.

"Thanks for coming, everyone. I just wanted to go over everything. We have two weeks to go, and I want no surprises. Has Bialy briefed those of you who responded to the 9-1-1 call?"

Dylan was all business, determined to put a murderer behind bars. Shaheed squirmed slightly, unnoticeable to his colleagues. Today would be the day he disclosed his side investigation. He would accept the consequences and let the chips fall where they may.

"Yes, sir. We've been briefed and debriefed. We're ready to go. There isn't much to it. We all saw the same thing. When we got to the scene, the murderer was hovered over the body, covered in blood, and holding the murder weapon. I've never seen such an open-and-shut case in all of my years in law enforcement," a senior officer opined with confidence.

"You can stop after 'weapon.' Leave the 'open-and-shut' shit out," Jack scolded. This was serious stuff, and he had zero tolerance for flippancy.

"Sorry, boss. I get it. It won't happen in court. Just the facts." He resisted the impulse to deadpan the *Dragnet* line. He did not dare piss Dylan off twice in two minutes. Dylan moved on. "Surveillance?" He turned to the surveillance team.

"Not much to report, sir. Ms. Khan has been a model citizen. She has not left her house unless it is to go somewhere with her attorney or to religious services, wherever they happen to be held because of the bombing. They are moving them from place to place, depending on what's available. The community has been very accommodating, which is nice. She's had no visitors other than the attorney, Love, the investigator, or family members." The officer was a quick study from the other guy's mistake. He offered no bullshit or levity.

"Okay, thank you. Where are we on forensics?" Ash Granger rose and motioned for Eric Burns to join him at a lectern set up in front of a small white film screen. A laptop and projector were also set up. Eric glanced at Shaheed, who motioned with a slight nod and eye movement, encouraging Eric to comply. Eric joined Ash at the podium. Ash noticed the silent communication between Eric and Shaheed but did not understand.

"Forensics is solid, Jack," Ash advised, still wondering about the silent communiqué between Ali and Burns. "The perp was caught hovering over the victim's body. The victim's blood spatter is all over the perp's clothing. We've got the murder weapon, which is consistent with the victim's wounds. The perp's fingerprints are all over the murder weapon, inside the house, in the vestibule, hallway, and in the kitchen and linen closet." Eric worked the laptop, making sure the slides matched each segment of Ash's presentation.

"Linen closet?" Jack inquired.

"We believe she went in there to get towels," Ash advised.

"Why would she need towels?" Jack queried. In the back of his mind, this was one more inconsistency of many that made him a nervous wreck about this case.

"Who knows? Maybe she wanted to clean herself off. There were several bloodstained towels found on the porch."

"Do we have a tape of the 9-1-1 call?" The tape was another inconsistency keeping him awake at night.

"Yes, voice recognition confirms the voice belongs to Arya Khan."

"And our working theory is she made the call to disguise her guilt?"

"That's affirmative, sir. It seems quite obvious; pretty devious woman if you ask me."

"Anything else, Lieutenant?"

"Yes, sir. Footprints matching the perp's ran along the front lawn from left to right as you face the house. Given where we found Ms. Khan's car, the footprints are consistent with her exiting the car, running across the grass on a diagonal from the car to the porch, ascending onto the porch with the knife, and standing in wait for the victim to come out of the house."

"Is that it?" Dylan glared at Granger.

"That is the nutshell version, Jack," Granger deadpanned. He and Eric sat down.

"Next. Shaheed? You took the detailed statement of the accused before Blake shut us down. I know she offered 'alternative facts.' Are we going to have any problems there?" The question was an innocent one, and Jack assumed he knew the answer. He had no idea what was coming, nor was he prepared to hear it. To the total surprise of Ash Granger, Shaheed summoned Eric Burns to the lectern.

"Eric and I returned to the crime scene recently to evaluate Arya Khan's 'alternative facts' as you call them, Jack," Shaheed deliberately paced his presentation.

"Excellent idea," Jack agreed. "Make sure all bases are covered. That is sound police work, gentlemen." Jack approved—so far.

"Well . . . we reprocessed the scene. Actually, that's not correct. We *expanded* the scene and processed areas of the property and surrounding property that the original techs, because of Arya Khan's obvious trajectory, didn't process. Understand?" Shaheed continued.

"Yes, I think so," Jack hesitated. "Why would you do that, Shaheed?"

"Because she told an alternate story and because the defense has access to the crime scene, too. I didn't want to leave any stones unturned. If there was something the defense could surprise us with at trial, I felt it would be better if we got out in front of it."

"Are you telling me you found something that might derail our case?" Jack tensed.

"Not exactly. We found things that make Arya's story . . . shall we say . . . more believable?" Shaheed suggested.

"How so?" Jack fidgeted, curious but afraid of the answer.

"We found footprints in the bushes to the right of the porch."

"We? What the fuck?" Granger grunted.

"Eric and I—as I mentioned earlier, we visited the scene together," Shaheed looked Ash straight in the eye. Eric looked to the ground and returned to the computer and projector.

Jack noticed the temperature rising between the three men and broke in to defuse the tension. "So, footprints in the bushes—Arya Khan's?"

"No, I'm afraid not," Shaheed remarked. "Eric?" He motioned for Eric to continue.

"Well, s-sir," Eric stammered, addressing Dylan and ignoring Granger. "The footprints belong to a man."

"A man?" Jack gasped.

"Yes, sir." He continued to address Dylan as though he were the only person in the room.

"Go on," Jack pressed.

"He's a man. Approximately six feet tall—weighs about 200 pounds. Based on his gait, I'd estimate him to be 70 or older. He wore Wolverine Floorhand steel-toed work boots. He chews tobacco. We found DNA evidence, but no match to anyone in the system, sir." Eric nervously eyed Ash, then Dylan, and down at his own shoes.

"So, you guys are telling me, two weeks before trial, someone else was at the crime scene, and Arya Khan was telling the truth?" Jack sputtered. "Why wasn't I told about this earlier?" He was pissed. His eyes moved back and forth from Eric to Shaheed.

"First question, first," Shaheed interrupted, bailing out Eric. "No, Jack, we're not telling you that. We don't know when this man was present at the scene. It may have been days or weeks before the murder. There hasn't been any rain in the area. Those prints could have been left by a deliveryman, a gardener, by who knows who." Shaheed explained.

"And the second question?" Jack fumed.

"Uh, what was the second question, again?"

"Why am I, the guy in charge, only finding out about this now?" Jack folded his arms across his chest.

"Because we just finished processing the information and didn't want to present it until it bore fruit, Jack. I didn't think to follow up on Arya's version until last week. I requested Eric's assistance." The explanation sounded reasonable when Shaheed laid it all out.

"I don't believe this shit!" Jack charged.

"Jack, calm down," Shaheed pleaded.

"Calm down? Calm down? You bring me this shit right before trial, and you ask me to calm down?" Jack shrieked.

"No one else, including you, thought to do it. The more I thought about Arya's story, the more I believed it was a bad idea to turn a crime scene over to the defense, whose job is to offer an alternative theory of the crime, without checking it out ourselves. I'm glad I did it. I'd do it again. Would you prefer to be blindsided at trial?" Shaheed argued. He made a solid case for the side investigation. Jack tapped his chin, debating what to say next.

"That's fine," Jack finally declared. "But, that doesn't explain why you kept it to yourself."

"That's true, but it makes no difference. We didn't have the results until recently. This meeting was set. We wanted to get all of our findings into a report so we could present them at this meeting. Any delay was a matter of hours and days, not weeks. We're still behind the eight ball. I'm sure the defense, with their investigative personnel, has the same evidence. And they can't say these prints were left on the day of the murder, either," Shaheed reasoned. Jack continued to simmer.

"Uh, Shaheed, uh, that's not completely true—" Eric interrupted.

"Oh shit!" Jack started to boil again. "What is it, Eric?" he growled.

"Well, Jack, there's more."

"More what?" Jack was growing impatient with Eric's hesitancy.

"More evidence, sir. More footprints and tobacco in more places."

"Tobacco? More places?" Jack sat up straight. His eyes shifted back and forth from Eric to Shaheed. "What more places? What the fuck are you talking about?" Jack raged. Shaheed avoided eye contact. He'd forgotten about the other evidence when he made his argument for mercy.

"Well, sir, we found footprints from this guy and tobacco in other places in the bushes, at the next-door neighbor's house, in the house behind the next-door neighbor's, and we also found evidence of a motorcycle that apparently parked around the block and started up, leaving an oil stain in the street."

Jack could not believe his ears. Would he have a coronary on the spot? "Let me get this straight. You guys found these prints and other evidence of this guy in all these places, and you think he might be the fucking gardener? Are you fucking kidding me with this shit?"

"All we're saying, Jack, is someone else was there. We don't know when. We don't know who." Shaheed was failing to lessen the impact.

"And, in your opinion, the defense knows all about this, right?" Jack surmised.

"That must be our working assumption. Their whole defense is soddit, right?" Ash chimed in.

"Maybe she didn't do it," Jack conceded. He paused, considered these alternative facts, and started to boil all over again.

"Wait, wait just a goddamned minute! We have already complied with discovery, and this shit wasn't in the evidence dump. We're going to get accused of withholding this shit! What a fucking nightmare!" Jack returned to coronary mode.

"Not true, Jack," Ash rationalized. "This evidence was processed after the dump. Dump the whole thing again. They'll have to review the entire package to find the new stuff. Maybe that will reduce the amount of time they have to do anything with it.

"As Shaheed indicated, the defense already knows about this. Dump the evidence. Perhaps we temper the disclosure with 'unknown person or persons at unknown times and dates' or some such shit. Shaheed is right. It *is* better we know about this now rather than in the middle of the trial. I'll have to take the bullet with Bialy unless someone else wants to volunteer."

Everyone looked in a different direction, some at the floor, some at the ceiling, but none looked at Jack.

"Very funny, guys," Jack rolled his eyes and smiled for the first time. "Anything else? Noah? I forgot to ask you for your report, although I think I can be forgiven, no?"

"I forgive you, boss."

"Have you got anything?"

"Actually, I do, boss." The men had been murmuring over the shocking new evidence but stopped when it was apparent they were about to hear more.

"Whaddaya got, Noah?" Jack locked eyes with the computer nerd.

"I ran some of the surveillance photographs through our facial recognition software system—"

"Oh, shit, here we go," Jack erupted, fury and panic rising anew.

"No, nothing really out of the ordinary, but no one except Keith Blackwell is linked in cyberspace to the USA 1 Pure site. So, I asked myself, 'self, who are these guys, and why are they standing in front of USA 1 Pure, Blackwell's storefront?'"

"Good question. So, who are they, and why are they standing there?" Jack demanded.

"When I first ran the software, none of them came back to anybody in the system. If you notice, all of these guys are kind of old. You guys ever hear of age progression software?"

Each man looked at another around the room. The consensus among the group was that everyone was familiar with the software. It evaluates a photograph of someone at their current age or younger and predicts, based on a variety of external and environmental factors, what the person in the picture would look like at an advanced age.

"Well, I decided to create an algorithm to essentially reverse the process," Noah explained.

"You mean to make an older person younger? You can do that?" Ash marveled.

"Exactly," Noah boasted, pleased someone understood his thought process. "It is part art, part science, and part technology. The process is called forensic compositing. It is typically used to find missing children by taking an old photograph of a child from the time he or she went missing, running it through the software, and producing a composite photograph of what the child would look like today. That process is called age progression."

"Go on," encouraged Jack.

"So, I thought, if you can take a photo, run it through software and advance the age, why not reverse the process?"

"What do you mean, Noah? How does that apply in this case?" Eric was fascinated by the technology.

"Well, I began to think, what if we look at these pictures of old men who are not in the system, and could also get a look at what they looked like when they were younger? If we could figure out a way to do that, we could then compare their younger-looking selves with mug shots from long ago and see if there is a match," Noah explained. The entire group was riveted on him.

"Makes sense. Were you able to do this with these photographs?" Shaheed pressed.

"I did some research and reverse-engineered the software, creating what I call age *re*gression, essentially the reverse of age progression, and presto! Meet Benjamin Blaine and Samuel Ransom. I got two hits in the system. Both are white supremacists. Both were arrested and plead guilty to malicious mischief and malicious destruction of property back in the late '50s and early '60s during the civil rights movement. And what were the crimes they were initially accused of, you ask?"

"I ask," Jack grunted.

"Firebombing a black church," Noah blurted.

"You're kidding!" exclaimed Shaheed.

"I kid you not."

"So, what . . . what does all this mean? We think these guys were involved in the mosque bombing?" Jack shuddered. *Was Blackwell innocent too?*

"Well, Jack, DNA establishes Blackwell bombed the mosque, right, fellas?" He glanced at Shaheed, Ash, and Eric, all of whom nodded assent. Noah continued. "But that doesn't mean these guys—and maybe the others in the picture—weren't involved."

"Okay, so what does this have to do with the murder of Keith Blackwell?" Jack demanded.

"What if these guys were in this together? What if they were planning something big, bigger than the mosque?"

"That's a stretch," Ash suggested.

"Go on . . ." Jack prompted, fixed on Noah Thompson.

"What if Blackwell decided to go rogue and bombed the mosque without consulting the older, experienced guys, the 'daddy,' and the 'uncles?'" Noah postulated.

"The old guys would be upset." The scenario was coming into focus for Jack Dylan.

Noah continued. "They would be pissed as hell. Mad enough to kill him? I don't know. While they only have malicious destruction on their record, does anyone in this room think these guys, under the right circumstances, are not capable of murder?"

"Let me see that composite," Jack demanded. Someone handed him a photograph of Blaine as a young man. "No, not that one, the other one. The one Arya Khan gave the sketch artist." Everyone started pawing at the evidence.

"Here it is." Shaheed located and presented the rendering.

"Now, let's compare it to the photo in front of Schaefer." Jack searched the table for the photo as he spoke.

"Here's that one," Eric located the photograph and handed it to Jack.

"Well, I will be fucking damned!" Jack sputtered, staring, back and forth, at the two photos.

"It's Blaine! It's Benjamin Fucking Blaine!"

"Yes, it is," remarked Shaheed and Eric in unison.

"So, who is Benjamin Blaine?" Granger wondered.

"He's a white supremacist. There is limited public information available, but I hit pay dirt on the dark web. He is the head guy for an organization called TCC." Noah held up the photograph. "See the logos on their leather? TCC stands for 'The Conservative Council.'"

"Never heard of them," Asher asserted, unconvinced. "Who are they?"

"Think Ku Klux Klan on steroids, boys. These guys go way back, back into the late 1800s and early 1900s. They were linked to multiple lynchings, church bombings, and rapes. You name it, these guys have done it. Blaine has been linked to the group since the '50s, but it is much more on the DL now than it was when racism, anti-Semitism, and general asshole-ism was more in style," Noah lectured.

"DL?" Shaheed inquired.

"Down low, not as public as it once was. They are an underground group. They seek publicity through the back channels, on the dark web only." Noah suppressed a snicker at Shaheed's naiveté.

"So, what does the dark web say about TCC today?" Jack demanded.

"They are huge supporters of Ronald John and his anti-Muslim, anti-immigration policies. They are equal opportunity . . . haters, that is. They hate anyone who isn't white and Christian. They used to focus on Jews and blacks, but their principal target today?"

"Let me guess," offered Shaheed. "Muslims?"

"Ding, ding, ding, ding, ding! Give that man the grand prize!" Noah shouted. "More like Islamic terrorists, as far as TCC is concerned. Every Muslim is a terrorist. Every mosque is a terrorist front. Every immigrant from a Muslim country is a threat. They are running the president's playbook on steroids!"

"Bombing a mosque would be right up their alley, then," Jack concluded.

"Yes, it is absolutely up their alley. But, as we discussed earlier, not a single member of TCC has ever been caught or charged, much less convicted, of any type of terrorist activity. Members have been linked to multiple acts of firebombing, murder, lynching, beating, terrorizing, you name it. But no one with ties to TCC has ever been formally charged or convicted of a single crime.

"The amount of evidence found at the mosque, the way the firebombing was so easily linked to Blackwell, tells me this was not a TCC-planned event. I think Blackwell did this on his own to impress Blaine and his crew. However, he fucked it up and became an embarrassment to Blaine and a huge liability Blaine had to get rid of," Noah hypothesized.

"So, what do we do with all this? Do we all agree Blaine is more likely to have done this than Arya? She's been telling us the truth the whole fucking time, but no one would listen to her!" Jack was pissed, primarily with himself.

"It looks that way, Jack," Shaheed agreed.

"This is great police work, gentlemen. A little late in the investigation, but this is terrific fucking work! I'm proud of you. Now, what do we do with all of this stuff?"

"We have to set up a meeting with Zack Blake and let him know what we have," Shaheed recommended, relieved to be back on the team.

"Right, but the physical evidence doesn't specifically point at these other guys on the Blackwell murder, now does it?" Jack suggested. "It still points to Arya Khan."

"It points to her, Jack, but she didn't do it," Shaheed argued. "The Muslim didn't kill anyone this time, Jack. Muslims were victims, this time." He tried not to sound bitter. "Our mosque was bombed. Our community members were threatened with deportation, and one of our own has been framed for a murder she didn't commit. And . . . *we* are the terrorists?"

Shaheed eyed Jack, who paced around, his mind elsewhere. Shaheed wasn't sure Jack heard a word of his mini tirade. "What are you thinking, Jack?"

"Arya Khan has developed a bit of a relationship with you, Shaheed, hasn't she?" Jack charged, still pacing, still brainstorming.

"I don't know if I would call it a relationship," Shaheed deflected. "I guess it is fair to say she trusts me more than she trusts you guys."

"Exactly!" Jack shouted, louder than intended.

"Calm down, Jack. We're right here, in front of you. I'll ask again—what do you have in mind, Jack?"

"Do you think you could set up a meeting between her and me? Obviously, her attorney would have to be present. He and I hit it off pretty well, and that investigator, what's his name?" Jack continued to pace and cogitate.

"Love, sir. Micah Love," Eric advised.

"That's right, Love! That's the guy. He'd have to be involved, too. And, of course, Bialy would have to sign off . . ." Jack's behavior was odd, as if he was the only person in the room.

"Jack, what is it? She could still be guilty, you know. Do you think you could share what's on your mind with the rest of us?" Granger was uneasy, rising out of his seat.

"Yeah, yeah, sorry," Jack paused, still dazed, still thinking, still pacing, still 'elsewhere.'

"Jack!" Shaheed clapped his hands together rapidly, snapping Jack out of it.

"Arya Khan is very likely an innocent woman. We are officers of the law and of the court—" Jack stopped in mid-thought.

"Right," Shaheed concurred. "And . . ." His hand was motioning Jack to complete his thought while Ash Granger sat down in a huff.

Jack stopped pacing, sat down, and addressed his fellow police officers. "Okay, guys. Here's what I have in mind . . ."

Chapter Thirty-Four

Marshall Mann walked into the courtroom of the US Immigration and Naturalization Service in the McNamara Federal Building on Michigan Avenue in downtown Detroit. Zachary Blake, Hamid, Riah, and many of their children accompanied him into the courtroom waiting area. There wasn't a seat to be had. President John's executive order affected and irritated a significant number of people.

Fortunately, those people who were represented by counsel were handled first. Because Marshall was a regular in the court, he knew how to manipulate the system and shorten the wait time. Despite the presence of at least fifty people awaiting some form of justice from the court, Hamid and Riah's case was called into the courtroom within 20 minutes.

The two lawyers and their clients walked into the courtroom. It was empty but for the clerk and the court reporter. The judge had not taken the bench. Everyone was seated—Hamid, Riah, and Marshall at the party's table and Zack and the children in spectator seats. The clerk called the case, and the judge appeared from a door behind the high bench.

"All rise; Immigration and Naturalization Administrative Court is now in session. The Honorable George T. Farhad presiding."

Is he Muslim? Zack wondered. Judge Farhad called the case and commenced the proceedings.

"This the deportation hearing of Hamid and Riah Khan. The petition indicates the defendants are from Yemen, which has been declared by our president to be a country that sponsors terrorism and harbors terrorists. By executive order of the president, all people who immigrated into the United States from Yemen and other select countries are subject to deportation. Mr. Mann, I understand we have some stipulations. Is that correct?"

"It is, Your Honor," Mann stated, with appropriate courtroom demeanor.

"Please state your name for the record, Mr. Mann, and introduce your clients as well," the judge ordered.

"My name is Marshall Mann, Your Honor. I represent Hamid and Riah Khan, seated to my left. Also present are attorney Zachary Blake and my clients' children."

"Welcome to all," the judge exclaimed. "Please carry on, Mr. Mann."

"Thank you, Your Honor. Preliminarily, for the record, Hamid and Riah Khan are naturalized citizens of the United States. They have never been in trouble with the law, not even a traffic ticket. They pay taxes, respect law enforcement, and love their adopted country. This proceeding violates their constitutional rights and should be dismissed on constitutional grounds."

"Mr. Mann, are you suggesting President John lacks the authority to issue an executive order related to this area of the law?"

"No, Your Honor, I am not. President John has the authority to issue executive orders, but those orders must be constitutional. President John's executive order must meet certain constitutional requirements before it can be effective. In this case, the order is overbroad and describes prospective dangers only. There is no rational basis for linking terror to particular countries or to all people who emigrate from those countries. Even if such a link could be made, the government must show these defendants are in some way dangerous to the public, and such a showing cannot be made in this case." Mann was describing in a few sentences the fatal flaw of the *global* John policy, not only as it related to the Khans but to *all* Muslim people.

"Let's get a little housekeeping out of the way," the judge declared. He had the court clerk swear in the Khans and then began to question them. What were their names and ages, and how long did they reside in the United States? What did they understand their legal status as immigrants to be? Did they arrive with legal status? Were they citizens? If so, for how long?

He inquired about their marriage, their health, and their health care. He queried them about their siblings and extended family, as well as their children, and whether any were school-aged. He also wondered about their education and employment history, both in the United States and abroad.

He apologized for the next set of questions and then proceeded to inquire about their criminal and civil litigation history, explaining he needed to make a proper record. Did they have any history of drug use, drug sales, or drug rehabilitation? Were they ever disciplined at work or in school? Did they serve in the military service or perform other types of public service? He was pleased to discover both Mr. and Mrs. Khan were volunteers at the mosque and at the local hospital.

Finally, he quizzed them about potential deportation. If they were deported, would they have any problems in their country? Would they be able to find employment? Healthcare? Did they have any family still in the old country? Were they afraid to return? The Khans testified they lived in the United States for too long to return to Yemen. They had no close family ties to the country, and considering the current political climate, their US citizenship would be in danger. Yemen was a poor country. The prospects for employment, especially for people who were forced to return from the United States after an extended stay, were slim to none.

Judge Farhad moved on to citizenship. Where were they born? Did they have any relatives who were US-born? "Of course we do, Your Honor. All of our children were born here." He wondered if they were naturalized citizens and when the answer was yes, he launched into a series of follow-up questions about their status and, again, the possibility of criminal records. Were they ever charged with public intoxication, drunk driving, crimes involving dishonesty? The answers were all, "No, Your Honor."

The government's case consisted of broad generalizations about terrorist threats emanating from the countries cited in the executive order. A terror 'expert' was called to the stand to testify about the clear and imminent dangers presented by allowing free access to our country to people from the affected countries.

On cross-examination, Mann got the so-called expert to admit that American citizens, Muslim or not, were responsible for the vast majority of terrorist acts that occurred within our borders. Further, people from countries not on the list carried out 9/11 and other attacks on our country. Mann demanded to know why these other countries were excluded. The man could not answer, except to say, "it's not my list" and "I serve at the pleasure of the president." Mann called President John's business interests in other countries a possible reason for their absence from the list. The witness claimed no knowledge of that. Mann then named Saudi Arabia, by way of example, as the home of the majority of the 9/11-suicide squad. The witness had to agree with what everyone in the room knew was true. Mann's cross-examination of this expert was brilliant.

Mann argued Hamid and Riah Khan were citizens of this country and were naturalized decades before. They were hardworking, decent, honest, law-abiding *American* citizens. He argued the removal proceeding was unlawful and unconstitutional because of their citizenship status and their long history of leading a lawful, positive, and exemplary life since arriving from Yemen. He cited their family ties. All their children were U.S. citizens, born in the U.S.A. He cited their job and community histories, their years of paying federal and state income taxes in the United States, and the hardship that would fall upon their children if their parents were suddenly deported. America was their children's country, the only country they have ever known. Mann referred to them as "citizens of these United States."

In the event the judge felt compelled to honor the president's unlawful executive order, Mann had an alternative to removal— asylum. Americans were not well-liked in Yemen. Hamid and Riah were American citizens, and both previously renounced their Yemeni citizenship. The deadline for seeking asylum had long since passed. However, Mann argued, the couple's circumstances substantially changed when Ronald John became President of the United States.

Finally, Mann argued the order could not affect the Khans and removal proceedings must be canceled. They were citizens. They resided in the country for over ten years and were people of exemplary moral character for more than the prescribed time in this country. It would be an exceptional and extremely unusual hardship to their American-born children if they were deported.

Mann was an expert in the field of immigration law. He knew what words to use to create a record. He knew hardship to the deportees was not relevant, but "exceptional and extremely unusual" hardship to US-born children was the showing necessary to cancel removal and suspend deportation. Mann wanted to give the judge every possible legal remedy available to avoid John's order.

Following Mann's arguments at the close of the Khans' testimony, Mann called the Khan children to the stand to testify about the shining example their parents were in their lives. The adult children were devoutly religious and community-oriented. All of Hamid and Riah's adult children attended and graduated from college with exceptional academic credentials. The younger children were following their older siblings' examples, as their parents were excellent teachers of how to succeed in America and how to live an exemplary life. Tearing parents away from their children at this stage in their development would amount to cruel and exceptional and extremely unusual treatment and hardship, which certainly met the legal standard for canceling the removal and suspending the deportation.

Zachary Blake sat in the gallery and listened. He was mesmerized by the presentation, and extremely impressed with Mann's immigration expertise and courtroom skills. He was grateful to have him on the team. Immigration law was not in his scope of practice. He never had much need for the specialty, nor were its mandates and nuances of interest to him until he met Arya Khan.

Given the mood of the country and President John's passion for bigotry, this was a field of law that was about to explode. Zack would have to talk with Marshall to see if he would be interested in giving up solo practice for a cushy office and partnership in the Blake firm, heading up its new immigration department.

When the testimony and closing statements were completed, the judge thanked everyone, advised he would issue an opinion in a few weeks, and closed the record.

The attorneys and the family walked back through the waiting area, where the remaining masses awaited justice. Zack studied the room. Would the judiciary protect them from the man in the Oval Office? What would happen to those who could not afford attorneys? What resources were available to them? Were there free clinics that specialized in these cases? Legal aid? He promised himself he would locate these resources and donate thousands, hundreds of thousands—millions even—to combat institutionalized bigotry.

Hamid and Riah embraced, first together and then with their children. *What a beautiful family*, Zack admired. He turned to Marshall Mann.

"So, my friend. As I told Riah and Hamid, I don't know much about immigration law, but that looked like a pretty solid ass-kicking in there." He forgot about the younger children and immediately put his hand over his mouth in mock apology. Everyone chuckled, especially the children, who rarely heard such salty language. Even Hamid and Riah laughed. The mood became more serious as Marshall began to answer the question.

"Zack, Hamid, Riah, kids: If these were normal times, I could tell you, with absolute certainty, these proceedings are unconstitutional and will be dismissed or withdrawn. But these are not normal times. For the first time in my lifetime, we have a president who I consider openly bigoted. I'm not saying others haven't been bigots. I'm sure some have been. But those who came before Ronald John were smart enough to keep their prejudices to themselves. They certainly didn't act them out against any particular race or religion. Unfortunately, this is not the case in Ronald John's America.

"Now, the good news is the government of this great country has three branches for a reason. The judicial branch of government, Judge Farhad, for example, rules independent of the president, as a check and balance to the abuse of power. A judge is responsible only to the rules of court, the law, and the Constitution. He is obligated to follow the law, not any illegal or unconstitutional mandate, even if it comes from the President of the United States. Politically, Farhad is an appointee of a former president. I don't know his political ideology firsthand, but I have known him for a long time. I have been in his courtroom many times. He treats people with dignity and respect. He is firm but fair. He has never mistreated a single one of my clients, nor have I ever had to appeal one of his rulings. In this case, I do not see how he could, in good conscience, follow the law, obey the Constitution, and enforce this executive order at the same time. So, I think we are going to be fine and, hopefully, Judge Farhad's ruling will have a far-reaching effect, far beyond its impact on this family, this case, and this city."

"Amen to that," Zack cheered. "I sure hope you're right. This case is a travesty. It should never have been brought before a judge."

"Thank you, thank you, *thank you*, Mr. Mann," offered a delighted Riah. "From the bottom of our hearts."

"You are very welcome," Marshall acknowledged. "Hang in there; we should have a ruling soon. I'm not usually cocky about these things, but I don't think you have much to worry about. Even if Judge Farhad surprises and rules for the government, the 6th Circuit will never sustain his ruling. Trust me on that."

"Thanks again, Mr. Mann," a buoyant Hamid remarked.

"Please call me Marshall, folks—all my friends do."

"Marshall, nice work in there. I was really impressed," Zack praised. "Would you please give me a call sometime this week? I have something I would like to discuss with you."

Marshall raised an eyebrow at the compliment. "Sure, Zack, no problem. Gotta run." He started trotting off to the east, then turned and faced Zack and the Khans while trotting backward. "I'll let you know as soon as I hear anything!" he yelled before he turned and continued east at a faster pace.

The Khan family turned to Zack. Arya spoke for them. "What do *you* think, Zack?"

"What he said," Zack offered, lamely pointing east, the direction Marshall Mann headed. "He's the expert."

"Our problems are far from over," Hamid cautioned. "Now, we can concentrate one hundred percent on Arya's case."

"Arya, there have been some developments I have meant to tell you about," Zack announced.

"Oh?" Riah waited.

"Is there somewhere around here where we can talk?" Zack scanned their surroundings.

"Dearborn is only 15 minutes away, Zack. Lunch?" Hamid suggested. "I'm buying. How do you feel about Middle Eastern?"

"Love it," Zack smiled, rubbing his belly. "Lead the way. Mezza?"

Chapter Thirty-Five

While Zack and the Khan family were enjoying a traditional Mediterranean feast at the Mezza Restaurant on Oakwood Boulevard in Dearborn, Benjamin Blaine was meeting with senior members of TCC at a secret location. He was pissed.

"Goddammit! That fucking Blackwell really screwed the pooch!" he ranted.

"Calm down, Ben. Tell us; what's going on?" a terrified member inquired.

"According to my source at Dearborn PD, there are now some in the department who think Arya Khan is innocent, and 'elements in the white supremacist movement' killed Blackwell to silence him."

"Shit! I can understand now why you're pissed. But Blackwell is dead, and there ain't a fucking thing we can do about the past. Where's this coming from? Who in the department feels this way?"

"I have no fucking clue," Blaine blustered. "But we've got to close this up and make the camel jockey bitch look guilty as hell."

"How in hell are you gonna do that?" a rookie exclaimed.

Asshole would ask the obvious question. "I don't know—I'm still working it out. Who was friendly with Blackwell?" Blaine inquired.

"Stevens was the one who spoke for him at the termination meeting. Why?"

"Perhaps we can set the bitch up for another 'anti-white' killing," Blaine contemplated.

"What do you have in mind?" A member smiled and rubbed his hands together. Apparently, he didn't like Stevens very much.

"Still working it out," Blaine stared into space, wheels spinning in his devious mind.

The men looked from one to the other. They were a group that always had two things in common: white supremacy and loyalty to Benjamin Blaine. But, was he getting too old? Senile?

This was not torching a building or even killing a few scumbags who happened to be inside when the bomb went off. This was a second, planned, cold-blooded, first-degree murder. If things continued this way, someone was going to go down for these murders. Silently, all of them, to a man, hoped that 'someone' was Blaine.

Benjamin Blaine was anything but senile. He sat hunched forward in his chair, both elbows on the conference table. He was tapping his chin with the index finger of his right hand, deep concentration on his face. As he pondered his next move, his face relaxed and slowly turned into a look of revelation. He broke into a broad smile.

Everyone was staring at him. Finally, his number-two spoke up. "What's up, Ben?"

"Uh-huh . . . uh-huh . . . yep . . . it might work," Blaine murmured, more to himself than the others. "I got myself an idea, fellas. Tell me what you think about this . . ."

***

Two days later, at 10:00 a.m., the phone rang in Arya Khan's apartment.

"Hello?" Arya chirped.

"Arya Khan?" whispered an ominous caller.

"Speaking," Arya confirmed.

"I have information about the murder of Keith Blackwell. This information will get you off the hook for the murder and identify the real murderer. Would you like to hear it?"

"Who is this?" Arya demanded.

"A friend. Do you want to hear the information or not?" The caller's voice dripped in mystery.

Arya paused, nervous. *This guy might get impatient and hang up*, she feared. "Of course I do."

"Meet me tomorrow night at the Arab American National Museum, 8:30 p.m. sharp. There's a conference called the 2nd Triennial Conference on Arab American Studies, and it lasts until 10:00 p.m. I'll be watching you. If I don't feel safe, I will not approach you. So, come alone."

"I won't do that," she protested.

"Then you won't get the information," the caller warned.

"I need some time to think." She struggled with the thought of meeting some unknown person alone, in the dark. *But what if he really has something that would set me free?*

"We're out of time," the caller determined. "I'm in danger, making this call. I need to hang up and get out of here."

"Who are you?"

"All will become clear when we meet," the caller promised, his tone softened.

"Okay, I'll meet you," she consented.

"Good, you won't be sorry. And remember, come alone," he warned.

Arya heard an audible *click*. The phone beeped twice and disconnected. *What am I doing? I must be crazy! But what if the offer is sincere? What if he can help? What should I do?*

Chapter Thirty-Six

Shortly after Arya received her mysterious phone call, Jack Dylan and members of the mosque bombing task force met with Zachary Blake, Micah Love, and their investigative team. Asher Granger did not attend because he was required to appear in court on another matter. Lawrence Bialy represented the prosecution's legal team. Bialy had been briefed and was not happy. Significant human and financial resources were expended on the Arya Khan case, and the city and county had nothing to show for it. They could not and would not bring the case to trial. This was the place and time to face the music, eat some well-deserved shit, and lay everyone's cards on the table.

Dylan was not sure what Zack and Micah uncovered, but it didn't matter. Dylan was an officer of the law. The truth was all that mattered. Putting a guilty person behind bars was the objective. Arya Khan was not guilty. Begrudgingly, Bialy felt the same way.

"Zack, Micah, it is my understanding you guys processed the west side of the Blackwell property for verification of Ms. Khan's alternate perpetrator theory, am I correct?"

Micah and Zack looked at each other, deciding who would speak. Micah responded with a head nod to Zack to proceed.

"Yes, Jack, that is correct," Zack affirmed. "And, you know what else?"

Dylan knew what was coming and, while he didn't like taking the bullet for one of his subordinates, he saw little benefit to outing Shaheed or Eric for keeping him in the dark. Either way, he looked like an idiot who could not control his men. "Yeah, Zack, I kinda do know what else," he conceded.

Zack continued as if Dylan didn't respond. "We found evidence someone else's tech had already processed the alternate scene and probably came up with the same conclusions we did," Zack charged.

"I figured that was what you were gonna say, Blake, but you gotta understand—"

Zack cut him off mid-sentence. "I don't 'gotta' understand anything, Jack. And furthermore, I don't give a shit. I just want to hear you say what you probably came here to say: You found evidence to support Arya's theory of an alternate suspect. You have determined this suspect is the killer of Keith Blackwell, and you are going to drop all charges against Arya Khan." Zack folded his arms and awaited Jack's response with a smug expression on his face.

"Not quite ready to do that, Blake. But we are ready to postpone the trial and suspend prosecution pending further investigation," Dylan offered.

"Well then, let's go to trial instead. And I will proffer my evidence and further demonstrate to the court you've had the same evidence all this time and failed to turn it over. And then I'll make fools out of Larry, you, and the entire Dearborn Police Department and crime lab. How does that sound?" Zack threatened.

"Zack, you have to listen to reason. I must know what you know. We need your assistance and your client's, too. I want to put this bastard and his entire organization away for the rest of their natural lives. But, to do so, we have to take some calculated risks. Even if we fully exonerate Arya, which we're willing to do, we don't have a slam dunk against the murderer, and certainly not against his co-conspirators. All we have is a boot print, some tobacco, a photograph, and the eyewitness testimony of a person who was charged with the same crime and has a powerful motive to lie. Hell, we don't even know where he is or how to find him."

Zack was starting to grasp Dylan's dilemma. "I'm listening, Jack. No promises, but I'm listening," Zack conceded.

"Good, that's a start. Now, will someone tell me if your investigation has produced a particular suspect?" Dylan inquired.

Zack nodded to Micah, who nodded, in turn, to Reed Spencer and Matt Jordan. Jordan and Spencer looked at each other comically, deciding silently who would speak first. Reed nudged Matt.

"We processed the scene . . ." Matt began, "and we found the things you mentioned. They were leftovers from your crime scene, but there was enough to go on to get a profile."

Shaheed and Eric looked at each other and shifted uncomfortably, immediately breaking eye contact. Matt continued.

"We found tobacco and footprints on three neighborhood properties, including Blackwell's, and we found evidence of a motorcycle, parked around the block. We determined, from footprint analysis and the tobacco, the alternate suspect was a tobacco-chewing man, 70 years old or older." Matt stopped at that point and turned to Reed, who continued the narrative.

"We were not granted access to the crime scene until later in the investigation—"

"That's because you focused on my client from the beginning, refused to listen to her story, and figured, what the fuck, she's a Muslim. She must be guilty," Zack charged.

"That's not fair, Zack. She was caught on the porch with the murder weap—"

"Forget it, Jack, let's move forward, not backward." Blake cut Dylan off and invited Spencer to continue. Blake apologized for the interruption.

"As I was saying," Reed continued. "We tended to believe Ms. Khan, but we were not able to identify anyone until we processed the scene. We had this new evidence the guy was big and over 70 years old. I remembered we had a photo and a composite, and the composite had some similarity to the photo. We could not get a facial rec from the photo or the composite, so I ran a reverse aging process in the computer and came up with a hit on a Benjamin Blaine, a white supremacist with a conviction over 30 years ago. I was able to match the reverse-aged photo with an old mug shot."

Noah Thompson marveled at the impressive piece of computer-assisted investigative work. He and Reed came to the same conclusion and the same suspect utilizing entirely different technology.

Zack turned to Jack Dylan. "So, Jack. Did you guys come to the same conclusion?"

"We did," Jack admitted. "We used a slightly different method in getting there, but Blaine is the guy. I'm certain of it."

"So, release Arya and go arrest Blaine, dammit!" Zack demanded.

"It isn't that simple. We do not have concrete evidence that it was Blaine. We only have Arya's eyewitness testimony, and she has a motive to lie. The rest is circumstantial. There is no DNA, and multiple 70-and-older men on that porch."

"What's her motive to lie?" Reed wondered aloud.

"She's pissed, Reed. His buddy bombed her mosque. She killed the guy and is now trying to frame the 70-year-old dude," Zack explained.

"So, what do we do about it?" Micah spoke for the first time.

"We have to draw these guys out," Dylan schemed.

"And how do you propose we do that?" Zack queried.

"I'm glad you asked me that question, Dylan began. "I've got more to tell you, much more. This might be dangerous, but I don't see many options if we want to capture everyone involved. Here's what I've got in mind . . ."

Chapter Thirty-Seven

The Arab American National Museum was located on Michigan Avenue in Dearborn. It is the first and only museum of its kind in the United States, devoted to Arab-American history and culture. The museum's self-proclaimed function is demonstrating how "Arab Americans have enriched the economic, political, and cultural landscape of American life."

The museum opened its doors in 2005. It is an affiliate of the Smithsonian, and endeavors to shed light on the shared experiences of various Arab ethnic groups to further demonstrate ethnic diversity in the United States. The multi-story museum houses three permanent exhibits related to the arrival of Arab immigrants, their experiences while living here, and the impact they have made on the American way of life.

Temporary exhibits are very popular and last about a month or so. They deal with topics such as the arts, parallel paths of different ethnic groups, Arab life in Dearborn, anti-Arab propaganda and cartoons, music, civil rights, and assimilation.

Arya Khan searched online to check the museum's schedule for the day, and, sure enough, there was a conference on Arab American Studies, a subject she was quite knowledgeable about. The conference began at 5:00 p.m. and ran until 10:00 p.m. She checked her watch. It was 4:30 p.m. She showered and dressed and was out the door by 5:30 p.m. She took the Michigan Avenue bus to the museum and arrived at 6:15 p.m. The place was packed.

Arya strolled around, admiring the exhibits and stopping at various exhibitor tables of interest to her. She chatted quite easily with the numerous vendors, especially those representing Yemeni cultures and interests. She stopped at the bookstore and purchased some tee shirts for her younger brothers and a book on Yemeni immigration to America for her parents. She was excited to present it to them and to tell them about the conference. She also hoped to tell them she was much closer to helping the police capture the man who murdered Keith Blackwell.

As she walked around and soaked in the atmosphere, she almost forgot why she'd attended and completely lost track of time. She glanced at her watch. It was 7:35. She looked around the room from her location on the second floor. She walked to the railing and looked down at the exhibition room below. There was no sign of her contact, but she was comforted by the presence of so many people.

She turned away from the railing to find a familiar face staring at her from about ten to twelve feet away. *How do I know him?* The man started toward her. She noticed he had one free hand and one hand buried in the pocket of his sports jacket. *I know him from somewhere!* She could not remember as he strolled toward her.

***

Ash Granger walked up to Arya Khan and reminded her how she knew him. Initially, she relaxed, pleased a police officer was nearby in case things went sour. Then she remembered the caller's warning: "Come alone." She needed to get rid of Granger without arousing his suspicions. After all, it was now 7:40 p.m. The caller could be watching her right now.

"Lieutenant Granger, it's really nice to see you, but I have to go. I am meeting someone," she advised, hastily scanning her floor and the floor below.

"I know you are, Ms. Khan."

"Excuse me?" she gasped.

"I know you're meeting someone," he repeated.

"And how would you know, Lieutenant?"

"Because your meeting is with me," he indicated, looking around the room.

"You?"

"Yes, ma'am."

"I don't understand, Lieutenant. I mean, don't get me wrong, I am happy you've developed a suspect and believe my story. But couldn't this have been handled on the phone? In fact, wouldn't it be more appropriate for you to be taking this information to my attorney?" Arya wondered

"Well, I could have, but it wouldn't have been as much fun as this is going to be," he quipped.

"I, I don't understand, Lieutenant. What on earth are you talking about?"

"Ms. Khan, come with me. This way, please." He pointed to an exit door on the back wall of the hall.

"No! You're scaring me now. I'm not going anywhere with you until you tell me what's going on!" She became panicked.

Asher Granger pulled out a remote-control device. "If you don't follow me out that door right now, I am going to blow this place up. All of these people will either die or suffer serious injuries. How would you like that?"

"Lieutenant, what is going on? Why are you doing this?" She pulled out her phone. "I'm calling 9-1-1."

Asher held up the remote. A red light was flashing. Granger had his finger on a button.

"Put down the phone, Ms. Khan. You don't want to test me. And you certainly don't want to make me push this button!"

"Okay, okay, I'll put it down," she conceded.

"Hand the phone over, right now," Granger demanded.

Arya did what she was told.

"Now, the door." He motioned with the remote toward the door.

The two began walking, side by side.

"Careful steps, Ms. Khan. I have a gun in the other pocket," he warned.

As they continued to walk, Asher Granger noticed a man lurking in the darkness. *Security?* He scanned the room and noticed a couple of museum patrons glancing his way, lips moving. The situation was suddenly clear to him.

"You know, Ms. Khan? Perhaps we should call 9-1-1 after all."

Granger pulled out his phone. He was quickly connected to the recipient.

"Emergency 9-1-1. Where are you calling from, please, and what is the nature of your emergency?"

"Yes, I'd like to report a bomb, scheduled to go off in a half-hour, at the Arab American National Museum in Dearborn," Ash Granger reported, his demeanor calm.

"Sir, please stay on the line," encouraged an anxious operator. "I am notifying the proper authorities now. May I have your—"

Asher terminated the call in mid-sentence. The couple continued to walk toward the exit. Suddenly, all hell broke loose. Alarms began to blare. A recorded announcement, its volume much louder than necessary, ordered people to evacuate. People panicked and started running into and over each other. The person who was lurking in the corner was immediately blockaded by a stampede of people. The suspicious patrons Asher observed were no longer visible.

Asher and Arya continued through the exit door. Arya wasn't moving fast enough for Asher, so he dragged her hard enough to pull her off her feet until she got the message to pick up the pace. They, and others who followed in terror, ran down a flight of stairs and out a side emergency exit. Asher again yanked Arya along to increase speed. A short distance away, at the curb, sat a black-paneled van. Behind the wheel of the van was Benjamin Blaine. TCC members occupied the front passenger seat and several rear seats. The two seats immediately inside the sliding vehicle door were reserved for Ash Granger and Arya Khan. Granger dragged Arya toward the door with his back to the vehicle. He arrived at the opening, backed into the vehicle, and yanked Arya Khan inside. Arya screamed. A TCC member slammed the door, and the van took off into the night.

Chapter Thirty-Eight

Jack Dylan raced down the stairs leading from the exit at the back wall. He heard a scream. He looked out the window and saw Arya Khan being dragged into a black van by Ash Granger. The van door slammed and was gone before he could react.

"We lost her! What the fuck happened?" he screamed into his earpiece.

"That smug asshole called in a bomb threat, and all hell broke loose," tech support advised.

"What a mess. What am I going to tell Arya's parents? What am I going to tell Blake? What about the Muslim community? If we don't do something, and fast, this whole case is going to blow up in our faces!" Jack roared.

"Calm down, Jack. We planned for this. She's wired, remember?"

He had indeed failed to recall that extra layer of protection. There was a tracking and listening device on her. In the building mayhem and the subsequent panic of losing Arya to these maniacs—and his friend, the traitor—he'd forgotten.

"Who's got the comm?" Jack inquired, back in command mode.

"I do, sir," Noah Thompson chirped into Jack's earpiece.

"Great!" Jack was relieved Noah was in charge. "What's happening?"

"Traveling west on Michigan. No conversation yet. Wait! I'm picking up some chatter now."

***

The van traveled west on Michigan, heading to Wayne Road in Westland. Once on Wayne, they would head south to TCC's warehouse on Eureka Road in Romulus. Protest signs, chains, motorcycles, flashbangs, knives, an assortment of guns and automatic weapons, and bomb-making materials were stored there.

216 Betrayal of Justice

"Do we have anyone at the museum?" Blaine questioned, looking at his passengers through the rearview.

"Yes," Asher assured him.

"Call them. Find out what's going on over there," Blaine commanded.

"Right away, Ben," Asher promised.

A Dearborn police lieutenant was taking orders from and was on a first-name basis with a white supremacist terrorist. Arya was dumbfounded.

Asher made the call, requested an update, listened for a while, and hung up the phone.

"Things are calming down, and the bomb squad is searching the place. What do you want to do?"

"Detonate. We need a diversion."

"You sure about that?" Asher hesitated.

"Absolutely. This op went about as south as an op can go. Instead of painting Ms. Camel Jockey here as the bomber, accidentally killing herself in the explosion, we have to improvise a Plan B. Threatening to blow the place may have gotten you the fuck out of there, but it completely blew your cover and jeopardized our entire operation." Blaine was quite displeased, and the target of his displeasure was Asher Granger.

"That's bullshit, Ben. My cover was blown long before I ever walked into that place. The museum was crawling with undercover cops! If I hadn't called in the threat, I would never have gotten out of there."

"What went wrong?"

Blaine is clueless. "Little Miss Camel Jockey alerted the cops, Ben. Isn't it obvious?"

Arya tried to ignore the incessant conversation. She felt helpless in the moving van. She was surrounded by hostiles, with her hijab tied around her eyes and her hands tied behind her back.

She recalled her conversation with Zack and Dylan and the sting Jack wanted to run on Ash Granger and TCC boys. Arya immediately and willingly agreed, just as Dylan knew she would. Zachary Blake thought Arya was nuts and threatened to call her parents. In the end, he decided she was an adult, capable of making her own decisions.

Arya hoped her well-concealed tracking device and earpiece were still transmitting her location. She prayed for some instruction to transmit into her earpiece. *Why haven't they searched me? Is the wire recording their conversation? They've admitted everything!* Arya wasn't sure whether these men were sober, drunk, high, or stoned, but they sure liked to talk about their escapades.

Blaine enjoyed himself and loved to brag, laughing it up with Asher Granger and his good ol' boy band of bigots. The boys blabbed on and on about what an idiot Blackwell was. He wasn't a coward. The website and anti-Muslim rant were things of beauty. The mosque thing was careless and stupid. Blackwell was nuts to do that solo, but it took balls. He was so careless he had to be eliminated. They were all deliriously happy to have planned and implemented his demise.

Blaine bragged about killing Blackwell and his good fortune in Arya's sudden appearance at the perfect moment. He wished he'd been more careful at the crime scene, but after Arya was disposed of, there was, in his opinion, insufficient evidence to place him at the crime scene. *An old guy with steel-toed boots? Yes. Benjamin Blaine? No.*

Asher Granger also let off some steam. He was happy to be in the presence of like-minded people who cared deeply for the future of this country. He was sick of working in law enforcement, sick of the way the system spit the vermin he arrested right back out onto the street. He was convinced blacks committed most of Dearborn's crime but was disgusted by the preferential treatment given to the Muslim population in Dearborn. Every cop in the precinct feared terrorist retaliation if Muslim feathers were ruffled. And, he reasoned, Muslim crime in Dearborn was way up. The camel jockeys were catching up to the niggers, as he so crudely put it.

He turned to Arya and gave her a tongue-lashing. Everyone in the van enjoyed a good laugh over his tirade. He scolded her for 9/11 and for other terrorist acts as if she perpetrated these acts herself. He told her he was proud of the Arya he invented, the

Arya who would be left behind when the bomb went off, and the evidence was discovered. He was sorry the plan went awry because he wanted her body to be found in the rubble. He wanted her to be held responsible for the mosque bombing, the Blackwell murder, and the museum bombing. Obviously, that would not happen now. Her corpse, scattered in pieces, would not be discovered at the bomb site.

But maybe they could still pull something off. They'd have to find a permanent means of disposal. Her body couldn't be found. Perhaps someone would scatter some pieces of her over at the museum wreckage tomorrow or the next day. Arya quivered at the thought. Her ponderings were interrupted when Blaine began screaming at Lieutenant Granger.

"You promised this was *handled*, Granger! What a fuckin' mess!"

"It *is* handled, Ben. We still have the girl. We still have the device, and it is still a long-range motherfucker. I say we detonate before the bomb squad can locate it," Granger suggested.

"Great idea, Lieutenant," Blaine cried, saluting to the rearview mirror. "I couldn't agree more. Hit the motherfucker!"

Ash held the detonator. He looked back at Michigan Avenue, toward the eastern horizon. He ordered Arya to turn around and watch. When she refused, he grabbed her chin violently and turned her face to the east. He pressed the activator, and the eastern sky exploded with a blast and a bright fireball. TCC struck again. Asher Granger bombed the Arab American Museum. Arya Khan broke into tears.

***

Jack Dylan grabbed his cell phone and pressed some numbers. "Get the fuck out of the building! I repeat! Get the fuck out of there. Clear the squad! Detonation is imminent!"

"Come again, boss?" Someone responded.

"There's a bomb! Get out! Get out!"

If someone answered, Jack couldn't know it, as a fierce explosion detonated in his earpiece. A bomb exploded at the Arab American Museum.

Chapter Thirty-Nine

Devastation, chaos, and confusion reigned at the Arab American Museum. The east wing was demolished and on fire. Fortunately, trucks from three different suburban fire departments were deployed at the time of the initial bomb alert and were already present on the scene when detonation occurred. These brave men and women were in the process of getting the fire under control.

Police completely evacuated the museum when the initial bomb threat was called in. Only minor injuries occurred from people knocking others over or stepping on someone in the fight to evacuate. The bomb squad was searching in the west wing of the building. Except for some flying debris striking a member or two, there were no serious injuries.

The building took a hit, but good fortune blessed its potential recovery. Damage to the beautiful and pricey exhibits was minor. The book and novelty store received the brunt of the damage. The store was destroyed and on fire. Novelties and books could be replaced. Precious exhibits and artifacts could not. All in all, the impact of the bomb was minimal. If TCC wanted to make a major statement to the Arab and Muslim communities, the group failed.

Jack Dylan was on the phone with members of his department on the scene, as well as those in charge of locating the bomb and evacuating the building. He was pleased to discover the injuries were minor and the building damage inconsequential. The community would come together and rebuild a bigger, better, and stronger museum. Dearborn law enforcement officials would do everything in their power to prevent anything like this from ever happening again. Jack would see to it.

For now, however, he had to let those handling the museum devastation do their jobs. His primary focus was to keep track of the van and bring Arya Khan home, unharmed. Bringing

Benjamin Blaine, TCC, and that asshole traitor Asher Granger to justice would be the icing on the cake.

***

The van continued west on Michigan at a high rate of speed. Blaine saw the museum explosion in his rearview mirror.

"Did you see that fucking explosion? Woo-hee! What a blast!" cried Blaine. He was a happy man, continually checking his rearview. He saw Ash Granger staring at a terrified Arya Khan. Blaine suddenly wondered whether she was wired. *Stupid, stupid, stupid! Everybody talks too fuckin' much and does too fuckin' little. If it weren't for me, where would these assholes be?*

"Did anyone search the little bitch?" Blaine accused, giving his passengers the stink-eye in the rearview.

"Great minds think alike," Granger chirped. "Was just about to do that." He was going to enjoy this.

"Ms. Khan," he faced her and smirked. "I need you to remove your hijab and your outer garments."

"What?" Arya quivered.

"You heard me, darlin'," he ordered.

"I will do no such thing," she protested.

"Shall I have Abner here do it for you?" Abner's eyes lit up. He rubbed his hands together and smacked his lips.

"Why is this necessary?" she pleaded.

"To see if you're wired."

"If I am and I give you the wire, may I keep my clothes on?" she capitulated.

Asher looked at Blaine's eyes in the mirror. He nodded.

"Given all the talk in this van before any of you fuckin' idiots thought to search her, it hardly matters anyway," Blaine moaned.

"Well, aren't you the lucky young lady? The boss says if you give it up, you can keep the clothes."

"No one here wants to see your camel ass anyway," declared one of the back seat boys.

"I do," Abner gyrated.

"Keep your shorts on, Abner. We've got more important business to attend to," Blaine admonished.

***

Jack, Noah, and the rest of the team monitored the conversation until the moment the transmission was terminated. The wire went dead, as expected, but the boisterous and boastful admissions of TCC were recorded.

"Does she still have the earpiece?" a desperate Jack inquired.

"Checking on that now, sir," Noah advised. "The tracking device on her hem is still working. The earpiece is working, as well, sir. She can still hear us, but we can't hear her. We can still track their location."

"That's good news. Hopefully, they don't follow through with the threat to undress her," Shaheed gulped.

"I don't care if they undress her, Shaheed. If we don't get to her quickly, they're going to kill her," Jack snarled. "Where are they now, Noah?"

"Heading south on Wayne Road, sir, toward the airport."

"Farmland and . . . warehouses . . . warehouses! They're taking her to a warehouse of some kind. Can we get a map of the area? Perhaps a satellite feed? Any more chatter? Any fucking thing will do!"

Chapter Forty

The previous day, the intercom buzzed at Zachary Blake's desk. He picked up the receiver.

"Yes, Kristen?"

"Arya Khan for you on line one," Kristen chirped.

"I'll take it."

"Here it comes." The call was automatically transferred to Zack.

"Zachary Blake."

"Zack, it's Arya." She sounded upset, panic-stricken, maybe. She needed Zack's advice.

"Arya? What's wrong?"

"I just received a strange phone call . . ." Arya related the details of the call she received earlier that morning. The worried lawyer convinced Arya to allow him to contact Jack Dylan. She finally assented, and Zack terminated the call. He immediately placed an emergency call to Jack Dylan, who picked up on the first ring.

"Jack, it's Zack Blake," Zack advised.

"Zack, I was just going to call you. We've got to talk," Jack advised.

"We sure do," snapped Zack.

"You first. What's going on? What's wrong?"

Zack told him the sum and substance of Arya's mysterious telephone call. Jack listened without interruption. Zack's story seemed to validate Dylan's own thoughts and suspicions. When Zack completed his narrative, he demanded Dylan's assessment of the situation.

"Zack, we have evaluated all of the evidence. We have even re-processed the crime scene to validate Arya Khan's story. We now believe her to be innocent of the murder of Keith Blackwell."

"Great! I'll draft a dismissal for Bialy to sign and tell Arya there is no reason to meet with this guy tomorrow." Zack was relieved.

"I can't do that, Zack. Can we talk face-to-face? I'll come to you, okay?" he pleaded.

Zack hesitated. *What the fuck? What could be so important that he'd want to meet me here?* Zack was intrigued by the offer. He wanted Arya exonerated, and if a clandestine meeting with Dylan was the way to get that accomplished, he was willing to do it, despite his suspicions.

"Okay, Jack. How about I meet you somewhere off 696 near I-94? That'll save time. When would you like to do it?"

"Right now," Jack urged.

"There's a National Coney Island on Gratiot near I-94 in Roseville. Half-hour?"

"Half-hour works for me. Thanks, Zack. You won't be sorry. This is some big shit," Dylan promised.

Forty-five minutes later, Dylan and Blake sat across from each other at National Coney Island. A bored server came to take their drink orders. Both ordered Diet Pepsi.

"Coke, okay?"

"Fine, fine." Dylan shooed her away.

"Talk to me, Jack. What the fuck is going on?" Zack demanded, annoyed at the secret agent shit.

"Zack, I don't know how to tell you this, but we have a mole in our Department."

"You don't say!"

"The call Arya Khan received this morning came from that mole. We've been attempting to monitor his activities and his phone conversations, but he's been extremely cautious. Today was one of our few breaks."

"Who the fuck is it?"

"Lieutenant Asher Granger."

"Granger? Shit!" Zack spurted. "How long have you known?"

"We've known something wasn't quite right for a while now. It wasn't everything and every time. His behavior wasn't consistently bad. We tried to figure out whether there was some sort of a pattern. Shaheed Ali came to me on a different issue and wondered whether I thought Ash had a problem with Muslims. I decided to pay attention, and I determined when Ash investigated

Muslim suspects, the files were papered to death, and conviction rates and charge severity were always high. But when Muslim *victims* reported a crime, those investigations were half-assed, files were thin, and prosecution was minimal. Most of the cases were dismissed. I had my pattern."

"So, arrest the two-faced asshole! What do you want from me?" Zack huffed.

The server returned with the Diet Cokes and offered to take their orders. The two men returned to the plastic-covered menus again. Zack ordered a Coney Special.

"What's a Coney Special?" Dylan wondered.

"A Coney Island hot dog smothered in loose hamburger, mustard, chili, and onions," Zack advised. The server smiled at his spot-on description.

"I'll have one of those, too," Dylan decided. "Sounds good."

"The best garbage in this area of the city," Zack counseled. "Not quite as good as Lafayette or American, downtown, but damned good. Continue your story, Dylan."

"We want to take down everyone, Blake—Blaine and the whole kit and caboodle. We want all of his co-conspirators, too. Otherwise, it's worthless. Recently, we picked up some chatter on our surveillance of Granger. He was talking to Benjamin Blaine," Dylan confided.

"How do you know that?"

"Because he addressed him by name. The conversation involved a plot to blow up a prominent Arab site and blame the bombing on Arya Khan."

"Holy shit! What would be her motive for blowing up an Arab site?"

"She would make it look like white supremacists did it to take the pressure off her and put it on TCC."

"TCC?"

"Blaine's organization."

"Go on." Zack prodded.

"Ash apparently told Blaine your defense was going to be that Blaine killed Blackwell. Blaine wants Arya convicted of the Blackwell thing. He's concerned a Muslim might be believed in

this 'politically correct world' over a white Christian, especially
if her attorney can demonstrate bigotry.

"So, Blaine and Ash concoct this plot to blow up the Arab
American Museum in Dearborn and blame Arya for it. The idea
is she's so evil she'd blow up her own people to disguise her
prior crimes. If Blaine's plan works, Arya dies in the explosion.

"Detailed plans of the museum, bomb-making material and
instructions are planted in her apartment, along with a fake
manifesto confessing to the crime. She dies in the explosion. The
police investigate, search her house, and find incriminating
evidence postmortem. Who's to contest this evidence?"

"Jesus Christ, Jack! What are we going to do about it?"

"I have an idea, but you're not going to like it. I want you to
keep an open mind, okay?" Zack didn't like it already but
promised to listen.

"I want to put Arya Khan in play—" Jack began.

"*WHAT?*" Zack shouted. Heads turned in the restaurant.

"Quiet, Zack!" Dylan hunched over the table and put his
head down, scanning for busybody restaurant patrons. "Just shut
up and listen for a second. As I told you, the person who set up
the meeting is Ash Granger. He may be a bigot and a piece of
shit, but I don't think he'd hurt Arya. I'd like to wire Arya, have
her attend the meeting, and see whether we can get Ash to say
something incriminating."

"She won't be able to do that knowing Ash is dirty," Zack
presumed. "She's got a terrible poker face. She can't lie worth a
shit."

"So, we don't tell her. Let her attend the meeting. Ash walks
up to her and reminds her of who he is. She tells him she's
meeting someone, and he says, 'I know; you're meeting me.'"

"What does that accomplish, Jack? It's a bullshit plan.
What's she do after she realizes he's dirty and we didn't tell
her?"

"Maybe he tries something. We can arrest him on the spot,
no harm—no foul for Arya. Maybe he mentions a hideout, a
plan, something about Blaine and his organization. Who knows?
It may be our only opportunity to catch these guys."

Zack shook his head vigorously from side to side. "No, no, no, no, no! It's too dangerous. I can't let her do it."

The food arrived. The men were engaged in a hostile argument, with vigorous hand gestures and loud voice levels. The server was afraid to approach them.

"Here we go," she called from a distance. Gestures and voices took a break. The food was served, and the men started to eat.

"She has the tether, and she'll be wired . . ." Jack began, his mouth full of food. "She'll have a cell phone and an earpiece, both traceable to wherever they're going. If they catch one, we'll have the others."

"No, Jack. This isn't safe, dammit. These guys are dangerous, and they hate Muslims." Zack took a bite and devoured almost a third of the sandwich.

"Isn't that for Arya to decide?" Jack softened.

"No! What does she know about this kind of danger? She's led a pretty sheltered life up to this point," Zack pointed out.

"Yeah, you're right, of course. What does she know about the dangers of conducting her own investigation or the dangers of following a firebomber and witnessing his murder? It's not dangerous to get locked up and become a defendant in a murder trial, is it? Yeah, you're right, Blake. She's a real crime virgin, this one," Dylan mocked. "Real sheltered life."

"Okay, I see your point. We can ask her. If she asks my opinion, I am going to be honest with her and tell her I think this is a fucked-up plan. Got it?"

"I got it, Zack. But in the end, you'll let her do what she wants to do, right?"

"Yes, Jack, yes," Zack conceded, exasperated. "Whatever she wants to do."

Both men took a deep breath, devoured what was left of their specials, and gulped down their Diet Cokes. Zack called the indifferent server over. He ordered two more Diet Cokes and two more Coney specials. The men continued to chat, continued to plan. As he listened to Dylan, Blake could not stop thinking about Arya Khan and how ill-equipped she was for this kind of operation. The more Dylan talked, the more dubious Blake

became. They consumed three Diet Cokes and three Coney
Specials . . . to Zack, this felt like the last supper.

Chapter Forty-One

As Jack Dylan and Zachary Blake were wrapping things up at National Coney Island, the President of the United States was engaged in a heated conversation with his Attorney General.

Much to the chagrin of his cabinet and his executive and administrative staff members, President John was addicted to internet 'news' and constantly browsed the World Wide Web for stories about him or issues important to him. There was no more important story than the judiciary's handling of his policies relating to Muslims and Muslim immigration. President John was particularly fixated on reports of a particular deportation hearing about to be conducted in the Michigan courtroom of Immigration Judge George Farhad. He wanted to discuss the case and the judge with his Attorney General, and he summoned Parley to the White House. Parley tried to mask his disgust.

"What do we know about this case, Parley?" RonJohn demanded.

"Well, sir . . . in the short time that I had to prepare for this meeting, not much. This is the first I am hearing about it," Parley explained.

"What the fuck?" John exclaimed. "You're the Attorney General, aren't you? This is a legal matter, isn't it? Aren't you supposed to know what's going on in our federal court system?"

Parley was stunned. Was this president really this clueless? Did he really believe the Attorney General knew about every case in every federal courtroom in the country? Did he realize how vast the system actually was? Immigration was only one small part of the system, and immigration courts all over the country heard thousands, if not millions of cases per day.

"Sir, I ask with all due respect. Are you serious? There are millions of cases in thousands of courtrooms all over the country. They are within the purview of the judicial branch of government. My job is to oversee the justice department, not to monitor cases in every courtroom in America."

"Dammit, Parley!" The president screeched, spitting maniacally. "Your job is to handle my legal agenda, and there is no more important issue on that agenda than the issue of Muslim immigration! Is that clear?"

"Crystal clear, sir," Parley hung his head.

"This case is about parents who have raised a murderer in our country. This is a perfect example of the homegrown terrorist problem we have in this country, and I want to get every homegrown terrorist and every parent who raised one out of America. Do you get my drift, Parley?" The president was rabid.

"I get your drift, sir," Parley sighed.

"I want you to get me as much detail on this case as you can. Do you know the attorneys? Do you know the judge? Farhad is his name. Who the fuck is he? Does that sound like a Muslim name to you? It sure does to me! Is he a Democrat or a Republican? Will he talk to us? Can we reason with him?" The president paced back and forth, head down, plotting.

Parley gazed at him, nonplussed. "Mr. President—are you asking me, a member of the executive branch, to 'talk to'"— Parley hand-signed quotation marks—"a sitting judge about a case he's currently adjudicating, in an effort to sway his view of the case?"

"I'm suggesting a simple conversation, Parley. 'Hi, Judge. Parley here. How's it going?' What's wrong with that? It's not like I'm interfering with an FBI investigation or something."

"Nothing is wrong with that, the way you phrased it, sir," Parley conceded. "Sometimes, though, it is the *appearance* of impropriety that gets one in trouble, sir." Parley attempted, in vain, to extract the president from the brink.

"Excellent. Have a conversation with him. Find out what the case is about and what he intends to do with it. Let him know I'm interested and I'm watching. Let him know I'll be making appointments to federal benches, courts of appeal, even the Supreme Court. Let him know these things, got it, Parley?" The president winked and smiled at the Attorney General.

"I've got it, sir," a disillusioned Parley acknowledged.

"And I want you to stay on top of situations like this, okay, Geoffrey? These issues are at the center of my campaign. I have

to keep my promises to the American people. We cannot let
these people lawlessly roam around our country harming our
citizens. This is a *murder* for Christ's sake!" The president
continued to pace and wave his arms.

"I've got it, sir," Parley uttered, wishing he were somewhere,
anywhere than in the Oval Office with this man. "Anything else,
sir?"

The president waved him off with his left hand. "That'll do
for now, Parley. Carry on. And make me proud, dammit!"

***

The following afternoon, Attorney General Geoffrey Parley
picked up his office telephone. He directed the justice
department operator to connect him with the Detroit office of
Immigration and Naturalization Appeals. A second operator
answered, and Parley requested a direct connection to Judge
George T. Farhad. After listening to some mellow music for a
few minutes, the line clicked, and Judge Farhad came on.

"This is Judge George Farhad; how may I help you?"

"Judge Farhad? Geoffrey Parley here," Parley pontificated.

"Mr. Attorney General," a surprised and deferential Farhad
responded. "It is, indeed, an honor to hear from you. To what do
I owe this pleasure?"

"I'd like to talk with you about a case if you please, Judge
Farhad."

"Past, present, or future, Mr. Attorney General?" In an
instant, Judge Farhad regretted his enthusiasm.

"Call me, Geoff. Please," Parley suggested.

Farhad was skeptical but continued to be respectful.
"Certainly, Geoff, and you may call me George. Is this a past
case, current case, or something coming across my desk
shortly?"

"It is a current case, George—" Farhad cut him off.

"With all due respect to you and your office, Geoff, that's an
easy one. I cannot discuss current cases with anyone outside of
this office."

"I understand, George, but POTUS has a vested interest in seeing his policies and his executive orders implemented, and you have a case he's been following. This case will test those policies and orders, and it's of vital importance to the president that the case is decided per his policies and orders."

"Once again, with all due respect to you, your office, the president, and his office, I cannot and will not discuss a current case with the executive branch or anyone else outside of this office," Farhad repeated.

"How about if I talk and you listen, then?" Parley knew he was negotiating from weakness.

"I'm listening, no harm in that."

"The case is a deportation case; Hamid and Riah Khan. Do you remember them?"

"I do," Farhad conceded. *Where is he going with this?*

"Did you know their daughter is on trial for murder?"

"I read the papers, sir. What does that have to do with me or with my case?"

"The president is looking to remove foreign undesirables from this country so we can better protect our citizens. A family with a murder indictment pending is a poster child for these efforts. Dealing with these people harshly, convicting the daughter, and deporting the parents who fostered her evil depravity, would provide a wonderful beginning for the president's 'Make America Pure' initiatives."

"As I indicated, I will not discuss this case with you or the president."

"I understand your position, but please understand mine. The president wants this case decided soon and will generously reward people who assist him in promoting his vision for America."

"I understand," Farhad trembled, dropping his chin and shaking his head from side to side.

"Many federal judicial positions are opening during this administration's tenure. We have our eyes on you. You may be in line for a huge promotion."

"I understand," Farhad continued to shake his head. He could think of nothing else to say.

"The president is counting on you, George," Parley encouraged.

"I understand, sir," Farhad whispered. "Please give the president my regards."

"I will, George, nice talking with you."

"And you as well, sir. Goodbye."

"Goodbye, George."

Judge Farhad heard an audible *click* and hung up the receiver. He walked into his private bathroom and looked in the mirror. He saw a man in shock, his head still turning from side to side, his jaw-dropping slightly. *The President of the United States just offered me a bribe to decide a case in a way that promotes his agenda. He conveyed that bribe through the Attorney General of the United States. Who do you report something like this to?*

He remembered the case well. This was Marshall Mann's case. The executive order was clearly overboard, and these people were American citizens. Moreover, they were terrific people who lived the American dream—their children were born and raised in America. They deserved to live here and call themselves Americans, even if they were born elsewhere. Their daughter was in trouble, true, but what did that have to do with them?

This wasn't even a close case. Of *course,* they would not be deported. Apparently, Judge Farhad and his brethren would be very busy for the next four years. Men like Ronald John and Geoffrey Parley would not relent. Farhad was extremely thankful the framers of the Constitution had the wisdom and foresight to create an independent judiciary. He would stand up for what was right and just. Neither the Attorney General nor the President of the United States could bully him into disrespecting a citizen or violating their constitutional rights.

He washed his face, rubbed his temples, and looked in the mirror again. He stepped out of the bathroom and sat down in a recliner his wife purchased for him to celebrate his appointment to the federal bench. He peered out his window down to Fort Street and the lights of downtown Detroit beyond. A tear trickled down the side of his face. *What is happening to my country?*

What a sad time for America. He hung his head and pondered what was coming next.

Chapter Forty-Two

Jack Dylan and his anti-terrorism team pulled up a map of Michigan Avenue to Wayne Road through Romulus and toward the airport. There were numerous warehouses in the Wayne-Eureka corridor and, of course, Detroit Metropolitan Airport in Romulus. Jack doubted they were going to the airport. The current climate in America was not conducive for a bunch of redneck bigots to be dragging a Muslim lady through security. They were heading for a warehouse of some sort. *Hopefully, these scumbags are content with discovering the wire and won't re-search her and discover the earpiece or tracker.*

The map wasn't helpful. There were too many warehouses and commercial properties in the area. He'd have to go after them with all he had at his disposal. Dylan already requisitioned a SWAT truck and a Special Response Team (SRT). The vehicle was gassed and ready. The team awaited instructions. Jack jumped in the passenger seat and instructed the driver to head west on Michigan Avenue.

The vehicle was a Lenco Bearcat built on a Ford F-550 Super Duty chassis. *Bearcat* was an acronym for Ballistic Engineered Armored Response Counter Attack Truck. This one had a v10 Triton gasoline engine and six-speed automatic transmission commercial truck chassis. The vehicle had half-inch-thick steel armored bodywork with .50 caliber-rated ballistic glass windows. It was capable of multiple hits, had blast-resistant floors, gun ports, and a rotating roof hatch. This one was also equipped with a battering ram, spotlights, and a thermal camera. It featured extras like protection against high yield explosives, a tear gas deployment nozzle, and a remotely operated weapons station.

It was one badass vehicle. Jack and his teams were going to wage the first, and what he hoped would be the final battle with TCC.

***

Benjamin Blaine came to realize Arya Khan was no longer a valuable asset. The Dearborn cops knew she didn't kill Blackwell and also knew who did. They even knew who blew up the museum. So, the way Blaine figured things, Arya was valuable for two things and two things only, bait or protection. Ben assumed if she was wired that she also was equipped with a tracking device. He really didn't care. He wanted the cops to follow him. He assumed the cops wanted to rescue her unharmed. *Don't they always want to rescue hostages unharmed, even if they're Muslim?*

Presuming his assumptions were correct, one strategy was to put her in harm's way and make the stupid cops choose to save her over catching him and his men. The other choice was to keep her with them at all times and use her as a human shield. The cops couldn't draw on them if she were in the way.

Blaine thought about asking for advice from his men, especially Ash Granger, who had once been so valuable. But he could no longer rely on these idiots. They and that asshole Blackwell fucked everything up. Blaine was their leader. He alone was wise enough to plot their way to freedom and, ultimately, carry out their mission to rid America of its scourge and pestilence. Besides, he decided what to do about the 'Arya Khan problem' long ago.

They pulled up to the warehouse. Blaine instructed Abner and Stevens to grab the girl and bring her inside. He had a germ of an idea and was pleased he hadn't dealt with Stevens earlier, as intended. Stevens was his specialist in all things related to computers, and his idea required Stevens' expertise.

Inside the warehouse was a large desk with a Dell computer monitor on the top and a Dell CPU underneath. The warehouse was primarily a weapons and explosives stash. Blaine instructed Stevens to grab some rope and tie Arya to the old executive chair that sat behind the desk. Arya struggled, but her strength was no match for Stevens. Blaine instructed the others to retrieve all the weapons and explosives they could grab and get the stuff into the van, pronto.

Blaine walked over to the shelving unit that contained explosives and explosive devices, triggers and timers. He selected C-4 explosive putty, a timer, and a detonator, smaller, but similar to what was used to bomb the Arab American Museum. He instructed Stevens to grab a toolbox and remove the back cover of the CPU. He asked Stevens which components in the CPU would heat up enough so that when they came into contact with a C-4 explosive, the explosive would become hot enough to detonate. Without going into technical detail, Stevens powered up the CPU and hooked the C-4 to what he referred to as a "hot spot." The detonator was a long-range remote, similar to the museum remote.

The men finished loading the van. The small group was now heavily armed. Stevens and Blaine completed their work on the computer, and Blaine placed Arya behind the desk, picked up the CPU, grabbed more rope, and tied the CPU to Arya's lap. He placed a telephone on the desk next to the monitor, wrote a number down on a sticky note, and attached the note to the phone. He smiled at the trembling Arya, blew her a kiss, and backed out of the warehouse.

A minute later, the van was a mile away in a wooded area. Blaine watched the warehouse with long-range binoculars and waited.

***

Ten minutes later, the Bearcat pulled up to the warehouse. Dylan could not understand why the tracker showed the truck stopped for equal periods at two separate locations. Was this some sort of elaborate trick or diversion? They knew where the tracker was. They decided to investigate this warehouse location first.

Jack and his men exited their vehicles and surrounded the warehouse. They thought about ramming the doors with the Bearcat but were fearful of explosive devices. Jack inserted a scope under the garage door and gyrated it around the inside of the warehouse. He viewed the inside of the door and discovered it was not rigged to explode. That was the good news. The bad news was that further inspection revealed Arya Khan was sitting behind a desk, with a CPU on her lap, gagged and bound to a chair.

Jack called for the Bearcat driver to bulldoze the door. He climbed into the driver's seat, revved it up, and drove it right through the steel door. It might as well have been Jell-O. Jack walked through what was left of the door and up to Arya Khan. She was shaking and trying to verbally communicate through her gag. Jack removed the gag and noticed a phone and a note.

With gag removed, Arya screamed there was a bomb in the computer. Bomb specialists were non-existent because all of them stayed at the museum. Jack turned off the CPU and told Arya to remain very still while he looked around for a screwdriver. He ignored the note and the phone number because he decided that was the first thing Blaine wanted him to do. Dylan wanted to cross him up if he could.

Jack found the screwdriver and slowly unscrewed the cover of the CPU. He loosened the rope so he could pry it and look inside. He immediately saw the C-4 putty and saw it was not hooked to the outside cover. He continued to ignore the telephone. Suddenly, the phone rang.

***

Benjamin Blaine had long-range, night vision binoculars, but could not see as well as he would have liked from the distance separating him from the warehouse. He thought about getting back into the van and getting closer, but he did not wish to chance it. They needed some distance. He wanted maximum casualties but could not confirm whether anyone entered the warehouse. That was what the phone would confirm. No cop could resist an invitation or temptation to make the call, as instructed, and as soon as a cop placed the call, *BOOM!* The bitch and several cops would die a horrible death. Were they there? *Pick up the phone and make the call!*

Blaine couldn't wait any longer. He was as anxious as he thought the cops would be. He dialed the warehouse. The phone rang and rang. No one picked up the receiver. *Should I blow it anyway? At least the camel bitch dies.* No, he decided. He wanted it all. He wanted the cops to feel his wrath, especially that asshole Dylan, the Muslim lover. He was hopeful his Muslim buddy cop, the guy who was such a pain in Granger's ass, was there, too.

***

Jack removed the outside cover of the CPU and immediately telephoned the leader of the Dearborn Police bomb squad, still at the museum site. Stu Edishinski, bomb squad leader, answered on the first ring.

"Stu? Jack. I've got a problem," Jack advised, distracted, studying the bomb.

"Whaddaya got, Jack?" Stu queried.

"I don't know bombs as well as you do, but this looks like C-4. It's connected to the guts of a PC computer. I don't think we have much time."

"What is the substance?"

"Putty"

"How big?"

"A little bigger than a golf ball, a racquetball, maybe?"

"Shouldn't be a big deal. Walk in the park."

"Easy for you to say, Stu." *Give me a fucking break!*

"Where are you?" Stu requested.

"At a warehouse in Romulus."

"What's around you?"

"Nothing, really."

"Then throw the fucking thing as far as you can and get the hell out of there!" Stu yelled, animated for the first time.

Now, there's a real technical solution! Why didn't I think of that? Jack would have been amused if he wasn't so panic-stricken. He untied the computer from around Arya's body and yanked it away from her lap. He shoved her with his foot sending her rolling fast across the cement floor toward the garage door, still tied to the desk chair. At the door, a SWAT team member grabbed a screaming Arya, chair and all, and raced out of the warehouse.

Jack ran in the opposite direction, holding the computer to his chest. He spotted and then ran out of a rear exit door. Once outside, he scanned his surroundings for a convenient disposal site. The bomb could detonate at any second. He saw a dumpster about 20 yards from the building, ran up to it, tossed the computer inside, and shut the lid. Then, he ran back into the building. The phone was ringing. He picked it up and bellowed: "Hello!"

"Bye-bye, asshole," Benjamin Blaine laughed. "Give the camel bitch a kiss goodbye for me." This was the last thing Jack remembered before an explosion claimed his consciousness.

***

Benjamin Blaine heard the explosion and saw smoke and flames rise in the sky about a mile east of his location. The bitch and the cop were dead. Perhaps others were too. Those who weren't dead would have all sorts of other problems to deal with. They wouldn't have the time or energy to chase ol' Benjamin Blaine. It was time for Blaine and his TCC brothers to hightail it out of there.

The men high fived each other and enjoyed a big laugh at the expense of Arya and the Dearborn PD. Ash Granger was unusually jovial. They entered the van and took off south, then east, and hooked up with I-275 South. They took I-275 South to I-75, I-75 South through Monroe, and across the Ohio border into Toledo. TCC operatives owned a small farm on the outskirts, near the Ohio Turnpike. The men could hide out there for as long as necessary. They could *hold* out there, as well. They were armed to the teeth.

Chapter Forty-Three

Arya and the rest of Jack's men reached the Bearcat seconds before the blast. Everyone inside was protected by the strength in the construction of this dynamic law enforcement vehicle. Arya was shaken, but otherwise fine. The SWAT leader instructed one of his men to untie her. The leader, Chad Lynch, jumped out of the vehicle and surveyed his surroundings. All of the vehicle occupants felt an impact, light compared to the effects that must have occurred outside the vehicle. However, if the warehouse suffered damage, it would be to the rear of the building, because the front of the building was intact.

Suddenly, Chad noticed smoke and flames shooting out from behind the building. He ran around to the back and found the entire back wall of the warehouse engulfed in flames, with a destroyed dumpster entangled in the hot mess. No one was going to get in or out of the building through the back.

Many questions were going through Chad's mind. Did Jack dispose of the bomb before it went off? If so, was he able to get to safety? *Where the fuck is he?* Chad ran back to the front and through the garage door. The warehouse wasn't huge, and Chad could see the fire raging near the back door, pushing its way across the cement floor and along the sidewalls. The whole place would soon be in flames. Where was Jack?

Toward the center of the floor stood a wooden desk with a toppled monitor on top. Suddenly, the desk moved slightly. Out from the well, a dazed, confused, and obviously injured Jack Dylan emerged. His nose was bleeding, and his face was riddled with small cuts, bruises, and scratches. When he turned back one hundred eighty-degrees to survey the damage, Chad noticed Dylan's back was completely covered in soot and debris. He now staggered around like a drunk exiting his favorite establishment. Chad ran to him, lifted him off his feet and carried him out the front garage door. Sirens were heard in the distance as emergency vehicles responded to yet another explosion and fire orchestrated by Benjamin Blaine and TCC.

Chad brought Jack to the Bearcat and ordered the driver to put distance between them and the burning warehouse, in case of a subsequent detonation. They drove to the entrance of the industrial park, stopped the Bearcat, and waited for the fire trucks and EMS to arrive. Chad lifted Jack out of the vehicle, stood him on his feet, and began dusting soot and debris off his clothing. His face was covered in a film of soot and dust, and he coughed violently.

Fire trucks and EMS arrived. Jack was stripped to his underwear, hosed and toweled off, then given water, oxygen, and surgical scrubs to wear. Within a half-hour, he was a new man. He thanked Chad for helping him—"*I was just doing my job, sir*"—and then sought out Shaheed. He needed to know how Arya was doing.

"She's fine, Jack. She's been asking about you. She says you saved her life. How about that?" Shaheed smiled, relieved his friend, colleague, and mentor was all right.

"Thank God she's alright. If something happened to her after the way we treated her, I would never forgive myself. Where is she?"

"She's quite shaken up, Jack, but physically, she's fine. She's in the Bearcat."

Jack's smile quickly went south and turned into a grimace. "I'm glad she's doing well, Shaheed, but I'm pissed we let those bastards get away. They could be anywhere by now. This bomb was nothing more than a huge distraction and it worked. Goddammit!"

"Jack, well, not so fast. I'll let Arya tell you the news."

"What news?"

"Come on over to the Bearcat, man."

The doors opened, and Arya Khan stepped out of the vehicle and wrapped her arms around Jack Dylan.

"Jack, oh, Jack, I'm so glad you weren't hurt!" she cried, tears running down her face. "Thank you for saving my life! Thank you for your bravery and your kindness. Thank you so very much."

"Arya, sweet lady. I'm so sorry for the way we treated you. And I'm so happy you weren't hurt. I should have believed you

when you told me your story. I wanted to believe you. I knew in
my heart you weren't capable of such a brutal crime, even when
I first met you and treated you like a criminal. Still, I let my own
prejudice and bigotry get in the way. Can you ever find it in your
heart to forgive me?" The near-death experience had a profound
effect on Jack Dylan.

"You saved my life. Of course, I forgive you! I wouldn't be
standing here now if it weren't for you. That bomb could have
gone off at any time, but you put your own life on the line, ran
into the building, and saved my life. I've witnessed a lot of bad
things and some good things in my life, but I have never seen
anyone act so brave and so selfless, ever. I will never forget this,
Jack. Never!"

"Just doing my job, Arya. In your case, it's about time I did
my damn job," a guilt-stricken Jack confessed.

"Cut yourself some slack, man. You weren't the only one
who thought she was guilty," Shaheed opined.

"Arya, you should thank Shaheed, not me. He's the one who
believed in you. Shaheed and Eric proved your innocence. Thank
them, not me."

"I already did. I know what they did, and I will be forever
grateful to them as well. I guess there is more than one way to
save someone's life."

"Jack, I almost forgot. Remember, I told you Arya has
something to tell you?" Shaheed snickered.

"I do?" Arya pondered.

"Yes, Arya." He nodded in Jack's direction. "Tell him."

"Tell him what?" Whatever Shaheed was trying to get her to
say, Arya wasn't grasping it.

"Tell him about your hem." He continued to look at Arya and
nod toward Jack, encouraging her to tell him something.
Suddenly the lights went on for Arya.

"Oh! The hem! The tracker! Is that what you're referring to?"

Shaheed continued to glare at her and nodded in Jack's
direction. She looked at Jack and paused, milking the moment.

"Well, Jack, remember that tracking device we hid in my
hem?"

"Of course, I remember. I'm the one who had it placed there. What about it?"

"Well . . . You see, Jack . . . when we were getting out of the van, I was worried they'd search me again. So I took the tracker out of the hem and placed it in the well between the seat and the door. No one saw me do it, and no one can see the device."

"Wait! Are you telling me we still have surveillance on these guys?" a jubilant Jack Dylan exclaimed.

"That's exactly what she's telling you, Jack," Shaheed advised.

"And we know where they are right this instant?"

"We do." Shaheed enjoyed the moment. "Well, at least we know where their vehicle is." He corrected himself.

"They could dump the vehicle at any time, Shaheed," warned Jack, springing into action. "Get additional squad cars over here. We'll need more men. We'll take the Bearcat and the SWAT team and some others. Let's go get these bastards—oops, sorry, Arya."

"Don't mind me, Jack. Nothing I haven't heard before. I have brothers. Besides, I agree. Go get the bastards!" Arya blushed. Everyone was staring at her.

"Where are they, by the way, Shaheed?" Jack queried.

"Just crossed the Ohio border headed to Toledo."

"Notify the Ohio State Police and the Toledo Police, but make sure they know these guys might have an arsenal and should be considered heavily armed and extremely dangerous. Ask them, as a courtesy, not to engage until we get there. Okay? Just establish location and surveillance. Since they've crossed state lines, perhaps we should also notify the FBI. Tell them we are in hot pursuit and to lay low, for now. We've got this. If they're inclined to disagree, ask them to lay off, pretty please with sugar on top. This is our collar."

"You got it, boss. What about our young lady?" Shaheed glanced at Arya.

"Get her into a squad car and take her home," Jack commanded. He turned to Arya. "Are you sure you're all right? I can have someone take you to a hospital and have you checked out."

"I'm fine, Jack. Now, go get those bastards!" She smiled, winked, turned, and climbed into a squad car.

Chapter Forty-Four

Benjamin Blaine called ahead, and several men from the Ohio chapter of TCC were there to greet him and his men. Blaine briefed the Ohio men on the group's recent activities and indicated they needed a place to lay low for a while. The owner was a middle-aged man named Ernest, a scruffy man who wore soiled overalls and smelled like manure. Blaine and his men were certainly not the cleanest people in the world, but Ernest was a man in pressing need of a shower.

Ernest walked Blaine and his men over to a large barn. According to Ernest, its purpose was for situations like this one. TCC members from all over the country needed to be able to count upon one another. To Blaine's surprise, the inside of the rectangular barn was beautiful. It was well appointed and heated. Moreover, there were multiple beds lined up along the sides of each long wall.

A couple of couches and love seats sat in the middle, with a large-screen projection television system hanging from the ceiling and projecting to a theatre-sized screen hanging on the back wall. There were three small bathrooms with a sink and shower in each, positioned in three separate corners of the barn. Best of all, a large shelf against the back wall contained multiple firearms and automatic weapons to add to the Michigan TCC's already impressive arsenal.

Ernest told them to help themselves to whatever they needed. His wife and daughters were warned in advance that Michigan TCC was coming. In honor of the visit, the ladies were preparing a terrific spread for all to eat. After all, nourishment and strength were needed for the days and weeks ahead. Tonight was for freshening up, eating like pigs, relaxing, enjoying each other's company and camaraderie, and preparing for whatever would come tomorrow.

***

Reinforcements arrived, and Dylan and his men were on the move. Toledo Police and Ohio State Police were cordial and cooperative and agreed to let Jack and his men take the lead. Noah tracked the van and advised it stopped, apparently for the night, at a rural location just north of the Ohio Turnpike on the outskirts of Toledo. The exact location was identified as a farm, owned by Ernest and Paula Cronin. Ohio police checked Ernest's record and found multiple arrests and convictions for illegal gun ownership and marijuana possession and distribution. His multi-faceted rap sheet also indicated his connection with various underground white supremacist organizations. Obviously, this was the right place. Multiple Ohio law enforcement agencies kept tabs on the situation, maintained long-range surveillance on the property, and were awaiting instructions.

As Jack and his men drove over the Ohio border, a cavalcade of cops following behind him, he received an update from surveillance. Blaine and his men were, indeed, at the farm. The van was parked outside of a large barn, which appeared to be operating as barracks. The farm was actually located in Oregon, Ohio, slightly northeast of where I-75 intersects with I-80, the Ohio Turnpike. The land was flat, and the farm was somewhat isolated, giving occupants a clear view of police and government-owned vehicles coming up the road.

Ten minutes after crossing into Ohio, a similar Ohio SWAT vehicle and several cruisers joined the Michigan Bearcat caravan. For Jack and his men, this mission was a battle between law enforcement and lawlessness. The cops enforce the law—the citizens obey the law and respect each other in the process. Racism, bigotry, and religious fundamentalism were the enemies here. People of all races, creeds, colors, religions, and ethnicities deserved to live in peace, wherever they wished to, including in the city of Dearborn.

For Benjamin Blaine, the battle was about whom the country belonged to. Jews, Blacks, Arabs, Muslims, Japanese, Chinese, and their ilk had no place in his or Ron John's 'pure America.' America was settled by and belonged to white Christians. Ronald John was a man who fully grasped and embraced Blaine's concept of a 'pure America,' and John now ran the federal government. It was up to Blaine and other like-minded men to teach various state governments what President John already knew and preached. In Blaine's mind, the government needed to be taught where freedom ended and tyranny began.

Shortly after midnight, under cover of darkness, a mighty two-state police force assembled at the entrance to the farm. They were completely unexpected because Blaine was unaware Arya Khan hid a tracking device inside his van. He believed the farm represented a temporary safe haven. Had Blaine and Cronin been paying attention, though, they would have seen the dust being kicked up by the many vehicles trudging down the country road.

Jack and the others weighed their options. Was it possible for members of the SWAT team to sneak up to the barn and plant incendiary or explosive devices? Was this the outcome they wanted? Could they talk TCC members into surrendering? Was it their obligation as law enforcement officials to try to resolve this peaceably? Or did they owe it to public safety to end this chase by any means available? What were the rules of engagement here? The men, despite their years of experience, were in uncharted territory.

Jack and his Ohio counterpart, Peter Willis, decided upon two main objectives: first, to persuade all TCC members present in the barn and in the farmhouse to surrender without violence and second, to establish an exterior perimeter close enough to the two structures to prevent anyone from escaping. However, they were unsure of how many men were inside the two structures. Furthermore, they assumed TCC members were heavily armed with weapons that included automatic and semi-automatic machine guns, ample ammunition, bombs and bomb-making material, and a demonstrated willingness to use any and all weaponry at their disposal.

Still, Jack and Peter's primary objective was to convince TCC operatives to surrender without injury or loss of life. They ordered all officers to withhold fire unless fired upon, or their fellow officers' lives were in danger. However, while hoping for a negotiated settlement, Jack and Peter were undoubtedly not counting on a peaceful solution.

In the dead of night, members of both police forces and
SWAT teams established the required perimeter. No one was
escaping from the Cronin property without the use of force. The
strategy used in other successful standoffs around the country
would be to slowly tighten the perimeter. If the crisis didn't
quickly resolve, they'd begin to limit or deny necessities like
food, water, and electricity to the occupants.

As dawn approached, with the perimeter firmly established,
Jack Dylan prepared to notify Benjamin Blaine and his men they
were under siege.

***

Benjamin Blaine opened his eyes for the first time in six
hours. As his eyes adjusted to the dim light of dawn creeping
through the barn's small window, he listened to the sounds of
silence. Soundless peace was nice for a change. He hoisted
himself up into a sitting position, wondering what kind of day it
was. The sun started to peek into the windows, but Blaine
wanted a better look. He rose, walked over to the barn door, and
opened it. A police megaphone abruptly and obstreperously
interrupted Blaine's short-lived peaceful silence.

"Benjamin Blaine! This is Detective Lieutenant Jack Dylan
of the Dearborn Police Department. We have the barn and the
farmhouse completely surrounded. We know there are several
people inside with you and that you have multiple weapons. We
do not want to see anyone hurt or killed. We need everyone to
come out, now, unarmed, with hands raised, and we promise not
to fire a single shot!"

A startled Blaine rushed back into the barn, closing and
locking the door. His men, woken by the loud megaphone, were
scurrying about and grabbing weapons.

Asher Granger rushed up to Blaine. "Ben, if Dylan says
we're surrounded, you can believe him. He wouldn't have made
an announcement if he wasn't prepared in advance."

"Shit! I gotta think," the panic-stricken Blaine rambled. "I
figured they'd come after us, but I sure as hell didn't think it

would happen this quickly. What the fuck do we do? Anyone got any suggestions?"

The others gathered around. An eerie silence resulted as Dylan's team awaited an answer while Blaine's group contemplated what their response would be.

"I say we shoot it out with the motherfuckers," Abner blustered. "I ain't afraid to die."

Granger rolled his eyes. He dragged a stool to a front-facing window and looked out. The show of force Jack Dylan amassed was impressive, to say the least. Granger's peripheral vision was limited by the small size of the window, but there were men lined up, armed to the hilt, as far as his eyes could see. He suggested others check the views from all available windows. All reported the same. Multiple men, an impressive array of weapons, and two Bearcat-type SWAT vehicles. The sound of an approaching helicopter was heard in the distance.

"Ash Granger!" Jack's voice boomed again through the megaphone. "Ash, you fucking traitor! You've seen these types of situations. You know how they go and what can happen if bravado and stupidity prevail. Please tell Blaine and the others to end this, now!"

"Fuck you, Dylan!" yelled the still defiant Blaine. "Come and get us!"

"Ash!" Dylan's voice boomed again. "Tell 'em, Ash. You know this is over. Be the voice of reason here. We don't want any bloodshed!"

Ash Granger looked into the eyes of an angry, defiant Benjamin Blaine. The other men were gathered, awaiting sage advice from their fearless leader.

"Ben, I know you don't want to hear this, but I've got to tell you anyway. I've worked side by side with this guy for many years. He's an excellent cop, a careful cop. He would not have gotten on that megaphone if he didn't have all his ducks in a row," Granger reported.

"So?" Blaine snarled.

"So . . . we are surrounded." Ash warned. "If we don't surrender, Jack will tighten the screws. Water will be cut off. Electricity and gas will be cut off. He'll limit and then terminate our food supply. This is a fight we can't win, no matter how many weapons we have. The only questions remaining are these: Do we surrender peaceably and live? When should we do that? Can we negotiate any sort of deal? Or do we fight and die? How many cops can we take with us?"

As Blaine considered these options, his thoughts were interrupted by some commotion outside. A fully equipped Sikorsky Black Hawk Helicopter was landing in the clearing between the farmhouse and the barn. The landing of the powerful helicopter was more than enough for Ernest and Paula Cronin to exit their farmhouse, accompanied by their two daughters. All had hands raised in the air.

"We surrender!" Cronin shouted over the roar of the helicopter landing. "The farmhouse is yours. There is no one else inside!"

The family was taken into custody, and the farmhouse perimeter was narrowed considerably. A robot, retrieved from the Bearcat, was sent into the house to determine whether it was occupied or booby-trapped. The place was clean, and police and paramilitary personnel descended to remove any and all weapons from the premises.

Ash Granger watched the entire surrender and farmhouse occupation unfold and reported the events to Blaine.

"So much for loyal and steadfast support from brothers and sisters all over the country," Ash mocked.

"What the fuck were they supposed to do?" reasoned Blaine. "Most of the weapons are in this barn."

"True, I guess," Ash conceded. "They did the right thing; they did what we should do, Ben."

"Fuck that shit," an increasingly obstinate Benjamin Blaine grumbled. "How many cops you think we can kill before we go down, Granger?"

"No idea, Ben. We're surrounded. They have heavy explosives, two Bearcats, and a Black Hawk capable of leveling this place in one fell swoop. They have the superior manpower, superior weaponry, barricades, and protections we don't have. Can we kill or injure a few of them? Sure. Is it worth losing our lives over? It seems to me this should be something we all decide, don't you think?" Asher pressed. He was willing to spend the rest of his life in prison—even though he knew the ramifications, him being a cop—but he did not want to die.

"How about you go out there, talk to your buddy Dylan, and discuss terms?" Blaine floated, suddenly in the mood to negotiate.

"I can do that, Ben," Ash assented. He grabbed a bed sheet off one of the cots, tore it in half, and started waving it in the center of the barn. "This will do as a white flag," he declared. He walked to the front door of the barn and opened it, waving the white flag, the internationally recognized sign for a truce, ceasefire, or request for negotiation. Or, as Ash was thinking, *please don't shoot!*

"Hold your fire, men!" Dylan ordered into the megaphone. He and Asher started moving toward one another.

"Hey, Jack," Asher hesitated.

"Granger," Jack groused. "What can I do for you?"

"Blaine wants me to discuss terms for our surrender."

"Simple, you all come out, unarmed, arms raised, peaceably, and you all get to live in prison for the rest of your worthless, miserable, traitorous lives. The traitorous part applies only to you, asshole," Jack goaded.

"Noted, Jack," Ash grunted, immune to Jack's scorn. "Can we negotiate charges, sentences, places of incarceration?"

"You know I don't have that kind of authority, not that I would recommend any type of fucking leniency for racist murderers anyway," Jack sneered.

"Come on, Jack. I've worked with you for a long time. You want to tell me you give a shit about Muslims?" Ash challenged.

"I haven't always been the bastion of civil rights for Muslims in Dearborn, but Arya and you fuckers have helped me see the light. Besides, whoever I am and whoever I was, I would never betray my comrades in the Dearborn Police Department, and I would never associate myself with people who would kill people because of their race or religion. So don't even try to suggest you and I are somehow the same," Jack scoffed.

"Get off your fucking soapbox, Jack. How do we resolve this?"

"You get your guys to surrender, come out unarmed, hands up, and you all go to prison. That's the deal. Take it or leave it, Granger."

"I'll tell Blaine," promised Asher. "See ya, Jack."

"Not if I see you first, Granger," Jack warned.

Asher Granger turned back and walked toward the barn. Suddenly, he turned back toward Jack Dylan and raised his arms.

"I surrender, Jack!" Ash screamed. He started jogging toward Dylan with his hands raised. A shot rang out. Everyone ducked for cover. Granger pitched forward and fell face-first into the white flag bed sheet he was holding. The white sheet slowly began to turn red.

"Asshole!" Benjamin Blaine yelled from inside the barn. "I knew he couldn't be trusted."

"Let me recover his body, Blaine! Don't shoot!" cried Jack.

"Leave that prick lying in the dirt," Blaine shouted. "I'll let you know when—or if—you can retrieve his stinking corpse."

"Surrender, Blaine! We don't want anyone else hurt. Are there any women or children in there with you?" Dylan requested.

"That's for me to know and for you to find out!" Blaine hissed.

Jack discussed the issue of women and children with the Cronin's, and both indicated Mrs. Cronin and her daughters were the only woman and children on the premises. Jack was convinced they were telling the truth. Silence prevailed once again as seconds, then minutes, ticked by.

Jack interrupted the silence as he had at dawn, with a megaphone blast. "What's it going to be, Blaine?" There was no answer. Both sides hunkered down in silence to plot their next moves.

Chapter Forty-Five

An hour expired with little activity. Jack ordered the water and electricity turned off in the barn. Paula Cronin advised the vast majority of food supplies were in the farmhouse. The only food in the barn was leftovers that some of the men took with them from the prior night's feast. That supply would not last very long.

Jack ordered the complete sequester of the property—no one in, no one out, except police and military personnel. So, he was surprised to hear the sound of another helicopter hovering over the farm, perpendicular to the barn. He looked up to see who and what it was. A circle seven logo and '7 Action News' was written across the side of the helicopter and a camera was shooting out the side facing the barn. The helicopter descended slowly and landed near the farmhouse on the side where the Black Hawk landed. A cameraman and a woman exited the helicopter while the blades were still spinning. The woman was holding a microphone. Both began walking toward the police line. The man held a camera and pointed it at the woman as she backpedaled toward the line. Her lips were moving, but no one could hear her over the roar of the helicopter blades.

"What the fuck?" Jack shouted. "Get those people out of the line of fire!"

A group of military personnel ran over to the duo, grabbed both rather violently, and dragged them to a spot behind the barricades. The helicopter blades were slowing, and the noise was subsiding.

"Did you idiots not get the memo?" An angry Jack Dylan approached the two news people. "This is a restricted area. You could have been killed! What the fuck were you thinking?" He addressed the woman. He turned to the cameraman and noticed his tirade was being filmed. He slapped at the camera, unsuccessfully attempting to knock it out of the cameraman's hand. The cameraman proficiently backed away.

"Hey," the woman protested. "That's an expensive piece of equipment!"

"Then tell him to shut it the hell off, or I'll do it for him. And I don't give a shit how expensive it is," Jack seethed. The woman ran the side of her hand across her neck to advise the cameraman to "cut it" or end the shoot. The cameraman did as he was told and lowered the video camera.

"We have heavily armed white supremacists holed up in that barn and you land a fucking helicopter right in the middle of the battle zone? What the fuck is the matter with you? Who are you?" Dylan ranted.

"I apologize. Thanks for rescuing us," the woman smirked. "The pilot miscalculated. We meant to land behind the barricade, not in front. I'm really sorry." Her remorse seemed genuine, and Dylan eased off.

"Fine, fine, but why are you here? This place is restricted."

"We didn't hear that. We picked up a report of the standoff on the police scanner, and we jumped in the helicopter to cover the story. I'm Heather Tallow, by the way."

"Lieutenant Jack Dylan, Dearborn Police, in charge of this operation. I need you to get back into your helicopter and get the hell out of here. Now that we have been properly introduced, I can say get the hell out of here, pretty please?"

"Can we continue to report if we stay out of your way?"

Their conversation was interrupted by a call from the barn.

"Hey, Dylan! Is that a reporter?" Blaine wondered.

"What about it?" Dylan snapped.

"I'd like to be interviewed. If you let me talk to her, I'll give up peacefully."

"Oh my God, Dylan! Let me do it! Please!" Heather pleaded.

"Not a chance in hell," Jack ranted. "The minute you go in there, he's got a female hostage. Are you crazy?"

"What a story, Jack! I could get an Emmy for this!" Heather urged.

"Heather, this man is crazy and desperate. You cannot and will not go anywhere near that barn. Gentlemen . . ." He turned to the military escort team that rescued Heather and her cameraman . . . "Instruct the helicopter pilot to lift off and land behind the perimeter somewhere. Then, escort Heather and her cameraman to the helicopter and watch them take off. If they do not leave the area within two minutes, you have orders to shoot them down. Am I clear?"

"Crystal, sir," the squad commander affirmed with an obscure wink of the eye.

"You've got to be kidding, Jack! Give a girl a break," Heather implored.

"Get them out of here, now!" Jack ordered.

The squad commander turned to the news people as his men surrounded them. "Let's go. I'd prefer to do this voluntarily." The two had no choice. Heather looked at Jack with an exaggerated lower lip pout and promptly extended her middle finger.

"It was lovely meeting you, too, Heather. Be sure to call me for an interview, if I live through this. Now, if you two don't start moving, right now, I will confiscate the camera, and you will have nothing to show for your little adventure. Would you like that?" Jack teased.

When Heather realized Jack was going to let her keep the footage she shot and provide an after-the-crisis interview, she realized it was the best she was going to get. She was the only reporter on the scene. *Will this be enough for my Emmy?* However, like most reporters, male or female, she had balls.

"Jack, I have your word on the post-standoff interview?"

A frustrated Dylan blurted, "Yes, yes, now get the fuck out of here before I arrest the both of you."

The helicopter took off, as ordered, and the two news people were escorted away. Blaine watched them leave through his small window on the world.

"I guess that's a 'no' on the interview, right, Jack?" He cackled.

"Sure, Blaine. I was going to send two innocent hostages in there to listen to your white nationalist, racist, anti-everything garbage. What do you take me for? Now, are you ready to surrender peacefully, or do I have to come in and get you? I am running out of patience," Jack deadpanned.

"We'll keep you posted, Jack. Keep your pants on," Blaine jeered. Silence again descended on the farm.

Chapter Forty-Six

As dusk approached on the first day of the standoff, Jack Dylan decided to take a calculated gamble and turn the electricity back on. As darkness fell on the farm, a member of the SWAT team was sent to shoot a high-powered camera through a small hole in the side of the barn. The risk was the operative might be seen, and, worst-case scenario shot or killed. Everyone agreed the move was risky but necessary.

As night fell, the operative quietly and undetected approached the barn and planted the camera. *God, these guys are good!* Jack marveled. As the agent signaled thumbs up, Jack cut the lights again, prompting confusion inside the barn.

"What the fuck, Jack?" Blaine protested.

"Sorry, Ben," Jack snickered into the megaphone. "Electric company error."

Dylan and his massive police force now had eyes on everything happening inside the barn. It was essential to know how many men inside, how many were armed, what type of firearms and explosives were inside, and if there were any hostages. This information was critical before implementing their plan of attack.

***

At midnight, Jack ordered the plan into effect. Five SWAT team members, under cover of darkness, converged on the barn door and inserted steel rods into the door handles, locking the supremacists inside. A second team wearing gas masks was in charge of pumping a "sleep agent" through the barn's exhaust ventilation system. A long, high-pressure hose was carried to the roof and inserted into the attic exhaust air outlet. The odorless gas was quickly processed through the tube. Because all the windows were closed, the gas quickly filled the one-room structure. It wouldn't be long before the occupants were fast asleep.

This particular formula had been time-tested, used to defuse other similar type situations, and Jack was confident it would be effective to bring a successful conclusion to this one. However, he also had considerable concerns. A similar agent was used to diffuse a hostage situation in 2002 at a Moscow theater. In that incident, 50 or so Chechen rebels stormed a theatre during a sold-out live performance and took 700 people hostage. One hundred twenty-nine hostages died during the rescue attempt, many from respiratory arrest.

Fifteen minutes later, Jack gave the order to breach the door, and he and several operatives entered. Immediately, Benjamin Blaine and five of his men leaped to their feet and started shooting with rapid-fire automatic and semi-automatic weapons. Several men, including Jack Dylan, were shot. However, Blaine's men were quickly neutralized by reinforcements who followed the original breach team into the barn.

As Peter Willis approached Jack Dylan, he saw blood oozing from Jacks' left leg and right arm. Blaine was also badly wounded, shot in the stomach. The total body count was 6 white supremacists, including Ash Granger, and 3 SWAT team members who died as heroes. The remaining supremacists were handcuffed and arrested. The loss of the lives of three SWAT members was devastating, but considering the firepower both sides possessed and were clearly willing to use, law enforcement deemed the mission successful.

Chapter Forty-Seven

Jack Dylan was hospitalized in Toledo for a week. Upon his return to Dearborn, the chief of police ordered Jack to go home and stay there until he completely recuperated. Dylan promised to do so, but planned a couple of side trips first—he attended two Wayne County Circuit Court hearings in front of the Honorable David Grinder. Before the first hearing, he shook hands with Zachary Blake and Larry Bialy. Then, he stood, face-to-face, tears in his eyes, with the diminutive Arya Khan. Jack smiled at Arya through his tears.

"I can't tell you enough times how sorry I am for what we put you and your family through," the guilt-ridden police lieutenant confessed.

"Jack, sweet Jack. I've told you 100 times. You saved my life. I will never forget your bravery and your kindness. It was Blaine and Blackwell and the men who hate for the sake of hating. *They* are responsible. Please don't apologize for doing your job."

The court clerk interrupted their conversation. "All rise," he ordered. "Circuit Court for the County of Wayne is now in session. The Honorable David Grinder presiding." Grinder entered through the door of his chambers and assumed the bench.

"This is the case of the *People v. Arya Khan*. I understand the People have a motion. Is that correct, Mr. Bialy?"

"It is, Your Honor," Bialy acknowledged.

"And what is your motion, Mr. Bialy?"

"Your Honor, the People move for the dismissal of all charges against Ms. Khan. New evidence has come to light proving another person is guilty of the crimes of which Ms. Khan was accused," Bialy explained.

"I see. Mr. Blake, I presume the defendant has no objection?" Grinder winked at Zack and smiled.

"None whatsoever, Your Honor." Zack grinned and turned to Arya.

"Ms. Khan . . ." started Judge Grinder. "I hereby grant the People's motion and dismiss the charges against you, with prejudice. Bond is discharged, and I order all bail money returned to the bondsman forthwith. On behalf of the Wayne County Circuit Court, I apologize to you and your family for all you have been through. You are free to go. Good luck to you." Judge Grinder ordered.

The judge addressed his clerk of court. "I understand there's a second matter in front of me this morning?"

"There is, Your Honor," the clerk declared.

"The clerk will call the case," Grinder commanded.

"Calling the case of the *People v. Benjamin Blaine!*"

"Are the parties here on Blaine?" the judge inquired, looking around. A door on the side of the courtroom opened and a court officer emerged pushing Blaine in a wheelchair. A young attorney rose from the back of the courtroom and approached the bench.

"Your Honor, Scott Lewis, public defender, representing the defendant."

"Welcome to my courtroom, Mr. Lewis. First time?"

"Yes, Your Honor," Lewis nodded.

"Have you had a chance to review the charges, Mr. Lewis?"

"I have Your Honor."

"Is everything in order, Mr. Lewis?"

"It appears to be, Your Honor, thank you."

"Appears to be?" Judge Grinder demanded, annoyed.

"It is, Your Honor," Lewis corrected.

"The defendant has been charged with 13 counts of murder in the first degree. How does the defendant plead, Mr. Lewis?"

"The defendant pleads not guilty on all counts, Your Honor."

"Is that so, Mr. Blaine?" He muttered with disdain.

"You bet, Judgie. I want this case moved. I can't get a fair trial in this shit county." Blaine babbled.

"Watch your language, Mr. Blaine. Show some respect for the Court, or I'll find you in contempt," Judge Grinder warned. "For the record, you are requesting what is known as a change in venue. Your attorney will file at your request, I'm sure."

"I have nothing but contempt for the court, Judge. And this little pussy couldn't represent a jaywalker. I want a real lawyer," Blaine snarled.

"You may have any lawyer you are willing to pay for, Mr. Blaine. Mr. Lewis is court-appointed because you appear to have no assets. By the way, you are in contempt of court. The fine is $250. You will remain in custody until it is paid," Judge Grinder ruled. The contempt ruling was meaningless. Blaine was staying in prison, without bail, on the murder charge. The judge turned to Lawrence Bialy. "People on bail, Mr. Bialy?"

"The defendant is a predator, murderer, racist, Islamophobe, white supremacist, Your Honor. He's responsible for at least 13 murders and probably more. He's been incarcerated in the past. He crossed state lines to avoid an arrest. The People move bail be denied," Bialy requested.

"Mr. Lewis?" inquired the judge.

"Your Honor, Mr. Blaine is innocent until *proven* guilty. Ms. Khan was accused of the same crime. Your Honor granted *her* bail. We ask for the same courtesy for Mr. Blaine," Lewis argued.

"Mr. Lewis, Ms. Khan was accused of one murder and had never been in trouble before. Mr. Blaine stands accused of at least 13 murders and has a checkered past, to say the least. Furthermore, Mr. Blaine fled the police and crossed state lines while fleeing and eluding. Bail is denied. The two situations couldn't be more different." Grinder pounded his gavel and shouted. "Next case!"

The court officer grabbed the handles of Blaine's wheelchair and turned to wheel him out of the courtroom. As the side door opened for Blaine to leave, a line of defendants awaited arraignment in Judge Grinder's court. Each was charged with 13 counts of murder—they were the men arrested while sleeping during the assault on the barn. As participants and co-conspirators of Blaine's, the felony murder statute made them as guilty as Blaine.

Blaine screamed. "Remember Waco! Remember Ruby Ridge! Remember the Alamo, Attica!" The men in the hallway cheered him on, yelling and clapping.

"Get him out of here, Officer. Bailiff, have these men brought in immediately. All of them are in contempt of court!" Grinder shouted.

Bialy turned to Zack and Arya. "It looks like I'm going to be a while. I echo Judge Grinder's statement. I'm sorry about all of this. Please accept my sincere apology."

"You did your job when Arya was charged, and when presented with the evidence of her innocence, you did your job a second time. You have nothing to apologize for," Zack reassured him, turning to Arya.

"Ditto," Arya concurred, a broad smile on her face.

"Good luck to you, Arya Khan," Bialy smiled.

"Thank you, Mr. Bialy. I hope I never see you again," she laughed.

"Amen," Bialy agreed.

Zack and Arya turned to walk out of the courtroom. They pushed the swinging doors separating the parties from the spectators. Arya's jubilant parents stood just outside the doors, and, as usual, both were crying. This time was different, though. This time, Hamid and Riah Khan were crying tears of joy. Completely forgotten in the joyous moment was the fact the Khan family had one more battle to fight. A decision on Hamid and Riah's deportation was expected soon.

Chapter Forty-Eight

On a beautiful early summer day, a large contingent of the Detroit Metropolitan Law Enforcement community assembled to pay tribute to the men who investigated the bombing of the Mosque of America, the murder of Keith Blackwell, and various acts of terrorism committed against the American Muslim community. Several injured officers received Purple Hearts. Family members of fallen SWAT team officers watched as their loved ones, who gave their lives to protect the safety of the area's citizens, posthumously received the Law Enforcement Medal of Honor. The Dearborn chief of police gave an introductory speech. He praised Lieutenant Jack Dylan and the anti-terrorism task force for their tremendous work. Not only did they solve the initial crime, but they also solved multiple crimes that followed and hunted down those responsible for all of the murder and mayhem.

"Ladies and gentlemen. I'm proud to stand here on this beautiful summer day. I'm proud to be surrounded by heroes and, in some cases, families of fallen heroes. I mention the families because they support our heroes in ways many of us could never understand. Every time an officer of the law leaves home and says goodbye to his family, in the back of its mind, the family knows this might be the final goodbye. As you've heard today, for three families in attendance today, their loved ones made the ultimate sacrifice.

"President Barack Obama once said 'perfect valor is doing without witnesses what you would do if the whole world were watching.' The president spoke these words on May 16, 2016, when bestowing Medals of Valor upon thirteen police officers from all over the United States, who were wounded or killed while protecting the citizens of their respective communities. The men who gave their lives for the cause of justice, and the man I am about to introduce, do not do this job to receive recognition for their many accomplishments.

"For the three families of slain heroes, they would prefer their loved ones received no medals and no recognition. They would prefer to live in a society where we love and respect one another and celebrate our diversity, rather than to fight or to kill because of our differences. The same is true for our Medal of Valor recipient.

"Lieutenant Jack Dylan of the Dearborn Police Department would gladly spend this day having a cup of coffee or a beer with his fallen friends and colleagues. He would prefer to address a crowd to advise his community is safe, crime has ended, and murder and mayhem are non-existent. Instead, he is here today to salute and mourn fallen comrades, thank and salute injured ones, and thank and honor the families of those comrades who made the ultimate sacrifice to keep all of us safe. If Jack had his way, he would be having that beer, and none of us would be here today.

"But we are here, because Jack Dylan, and many others being honored here today, recently spent a few crucial weeks protecting the lives of people they have never met. Jack and the others would tell you, hey, it's no big deal. It's what we're paid to do. It's what we do each and every day. But all of us thankful citizens know otherwise, don't we? We know it *is* a big deal. We know these men and women risk their lives every day to keep us safe. Unfortunately, some gave their lives to that cause. Many are mothers, fathers, sons, and daughters. Others are colleagues, brothers, sisters, or friends. They're always on the job, always on guard, on duty, honoring their oath to protect and serve.

"This case presents a prime example. A bomb explodes in a place of worship, a place where peaceful, religious people assemble to pray. The men we honor today hunt down the perpetrator and discover other crimes and a vast conspiracy to commit more crimes. The brave men we honor today hunt these criminals down and bring them to justice. Jack Dylan is seriously injured, and three of his comrades are killed, when Jack leads a group of men into battle against dangerous terrorists brandishing automatic and semi-automatic weapons.

"Now, Jack would say this day was no different than any other, the two gunshot wounds he suffered, the surgeries, subsequent hospitalization, and recuperation were all part of the job. He would tell you his sacrifice was less than the sacrifice of others.

"Most of us spend our lives not thinking about the Jack Dylan's of the world. We go about our business, eat breakfast, lunch, dinner, and go on outings with our families. We travel to sporting events, to work, to school, and we feel safe doing so because people we don't know are working under our radar, keeping us safe. All of these unseen, unknown, under-appreciated law enforcement officers deserve the Medal of Valor. They place the public safety ahead of their own safety, loving their neighbors more than themselves.

"Lieutenant Jack Dylan is a man who embodies sacrifice, a man who leads by example. In this instance, he was the first man through the door. Whether he likes it or not, whether he wants it or not, it's important the community honors his sacrifice and expresses its gratitude. So, Jack, on behalf of the Dearborn Police Department, the greater Detroit law enforcement community, and the citizens of Southeastern Lower Michigan, it is my pleasure to present to you with this Medal of Valor. Ladies and gentlemen, Lieutenant Jack Dylan."

Jack Dylan stepped up to the podium so the police chief could place the medal around his neck. As Jack approached the lectern, the audience applauded and cheered.

"Ladies and gentlemen, I will be brief. The chief is quite correct. None of us feel medals are necessary to honor us for performing our jobs. Most of us do our jobs well every single day, without ever receiving an acknowledgment, honor, or award. Since you have decided to honor *me*, however, I have to thank some people who made this day possible.

"First, I want to thank our amazing chief of police for his kind words, and the brilliant example he sets for all who have the privilege of serving under him. If you look up the word *leadership* in Webster's, you will find his picture. Secondly, I'd like to thank all brave men and women who wear the various uniforms of our branches of service and keep us safe. Third, I'd like to thank those courageous officers who serve with me, especially the members of the task force the chief created for this mission. Fourth, I'd like to thank and acknowledge all of the brave men who followed me into a very dangerous situation, those who were injured, and those who, by the grace of God, were not. I especially thank those who made the ultimate sacrifice. Your brothers in blue will never forget you.

"Finally, I'd like to acknowledge and thank a civilian whose courage and quiet dignity in the face of tremendous adversity helped us crack the case. In the process, this woman made me a better man and a better police officer. I ask her to rise and be acknowledged. Ladies and gentlemen, Ms. Arya Khan."

Arya rose to thunderous applause and quickly sat back down. Jack stepped down from the podium, walked over to Arya, and took her hand. He gently pulled her up to a standing position so she could acknowledge the cheers of an appreciative law enforcement crowd. Hamid and Riah Khan were seated next to her, beaming with pride. Zachary Blake and his family, seated next to Hamid and Riah, cheered loudly. This was a proud day for law enforcement in Metropolitan Detroit.

Chapter Forty-Nine

Police actions and procedures that result in the deaths of officers or civilians are typically subject to administrative review. The Toledo Farm Standoff, as the case became known, was no exception.

The Dearborn chief of police, the Department of Internal Affairs, and the commander of SWAT conducted a joint review. All were team leaders with vast experience, excellent tactical skills, and were on the cutting edge of strategic planning and training. Many in attendance had prior military experience. The chief was given the responsibility of publishing their findings:

"In light of recent events in Dearborn and Toledo, and the study of the so-called Toledo Farm Standoff, it is imperative for the law enforcement community, and especially our first responders, to take a look at traditional response methods and new, unique methods available to us, in an effort to increase safety and reduce loss of life.

"In the Toledo Farm Standoff, the perpetrators possessed a substantial cache of firearms and explosives and exhibited a willingness to use them before the breach of the barn. They demonstrated a 'throw caution to the wind' mentality and had no problem engaging with and causing harm to police officers or citizens. We were fortunate the conclusion of this event occurred in a rural setting where there were virtually no innocent civilians. Either way, our first responders were the front line of defense.

"First responders do not have the luxury of awaiting FBI Delta force or hostage rescue teams. Some such incidents may not even allow notifying and summoning local SWAT teams, although that was not the case here. Since terrorist elements will typically engage in these standoff type situations with a plan of attack already in place, this administrative review body believes the appropriate response for situations like this is to engage the perpetrators as early as possible.

"Police command actions, in this case, prevented the perpetrators from engaging law enforcement in a more public forum, the wisdom of which prevented the possibility of hostages and mass casualties. If not for the swift actions of team leaders in the case at issue, the supremacists would undoubtedly have wired explosive devices, set traps, and put innocent civilians in harm's way. Further, while this event may not be case in point, future leaders must guard against situations where perpetrators are willing to sacrifice their own lives in furtherance of their cause or to kill as many first responders as possible.

"Many local law enforcement agencies remain insufficiently trained in controlling the activities of terrorists, especially those terrorists who put their cause ahead of their own safety. Local law enforcement agencies will need to be trained as first response options. Charging into a situation like Toledo, after devising strategies to minimize casualties, is a vital police function, one well worth the cost and risk when we consider the terrorist may be suicidal and may be interested only in how many officers and innocents he can take with him. Fast action is necessary because time is on the side of the criminal.

"The terrorists cannot be given time or means to communicate with potential co-conspirators or control elements of the situation, as this will only result in grave consequences. Limiting time and space, closing the perimeter, and forcing a retreat into a smaller defensive area were keys to resolving this crisis with minimal casualties. Fast response and quick, decisive action limited both time and space available to the terrorists in question.

"Keeping the lines of communication open, developing a rapport with the terrorists, and attempting to learn their motives and intent were also keys to the swift and relatively safe resolution of this crisis. Prompt control of the perimeter, strategic use of communication, and clandestine planting of an optical device inside the terrorist location were vital to resolution.

"While not applicable in this case, it is essential to find out as much about the surrounding area as is available. Intelligence gathering is vital. This will limit the possibility of outside interference or assistance to the terrorist elements, and also will limit the possibility of stray civilians entering the hot zone. Here, there was a failure to secure airspace, and a civilian helicopter was permitted to enter the hot zone and land. Quick action by team leaders prevented this incident from resulting in tragedy, but in future cases, airspace must be secured.

"Finally, the use of a sleep agent played a vital role in capturing or killing the perpetrators. The strategic thinking of command leadership in introducing this agent through the barn's ventilation system was ingenious. Studying environmental conditions to assure maximum efficiency and minimal casualties were essential. Unfortunately, a few terrorists remained, and for yet unknown reasons were immune to the effects of the sleep agent. This resulted in an unexpected loss of life. However, traditional methods would most likely have resulted in many more casualties. Going forward, it is imperative to further study the use of these types of agents and their effectiveness in certain situations and environmental conditions.

"In summary, this body commends those in charge of this operation. Their steady and sensible decisions and the devices used to end the standoff led to minimal loss of life. Well done!"

Chapter Fifty

The private line rang in Judge George Farhad's chambers. The judge, distracted because he was reviewing a brief, picked up the phone without looking up from his reading.

"George Farhad, here. May I help you?"

"Hello George, Geoffrey here. How are you today?" Geoffrey Parley was unusually cheerful.

"I'm fine, Geoffrey. What can I do for you?" *Ugh! What does he want now?*

"The president is wondering when we can expect a decision in the Khan case, and whether we can have an advance look at what the decision might be. Have you considered our little discussion?" Parley queried.

"I haven't thought about it at all, to be quite honest. As I told you, I will decide the case on its merits, based upon the Constitution, not because of pressure asserted by you or by the White House," Farhad maintained. "Your behavior is highly inappropriate."

"No pressure, George, more like a friendly request on this end."

"Well, these constant calls and reminders *feel* like pressure. I promised to take your 'request' under advisement."

"Very well, as long as you know the president's feelings. This case is important to him and to the country."

"I know how important it is to him. I'm just not certain he is on the same footing as the country," Farhad scoffed.

"We strongly believe the two are aligned. The country is with us in this endeavor. It is one of the issues that resulted in his election."

"I don't disagree, I guess. But, because something is popular doesn't make it constitutional."

"An attorney general must make unpopular decisions. I understand where you're coming from, George. However, we have extensively briefed this issue. May I send you the brief?"

"I can't stop you," Farhad conceded.

"Good man, George. Expect a fax within the next ten minutes. When can we expect the decision?"

"Within the next few days. It's first on my list."

"Thank you, George. The president thanks you as well," Parley deferred.

"You're welcome, Geoffrey. Have a good day."

"You do the same, George. Goodbye."

"Goodbye, Geoffrey." George Farhad waited until he heard the dial tone. *Why do I feel like taking a shower every time I finish talking to that man?*

***

"I'll see if Mr. Blake is in. May I ask who's calling?" Kristen, Zack's receptionist, answered a call to his office.

"This is attorney Marshall Mann. I have important news for him," Mann advised with a touch of urgency in his tone.

"Hold, please." A few seconds of elevator-type music and the phone clicked.

"Marshall? What's up?" Zachary Blake came on the line.

"Judge Farhad has made a decision, Zack. Because of its importance, he wants to read it to the parties from the bench."

"Is that unusual?" Zack wondered.

"Very," Marshall assured. "I've never had a judge do this before."

Zack paused, speculating on the meaning of the moment. "In my experience, Marshall, this means the decision is very bad or very good. Do you agree?"

"I totally agree with you, Zack."

"I presume Judge Farhad wants the Khans to be there?"

"He does."

"When?"

"Day after tomorrow, 10:00 a.m."

"I'll make sure they're present and accounted for. May I appear? May Arya?"

"Yes, to both. I'd like the whole *mishpacha* there, if possible," Marshall joked, using the Hebrew word for "family."

"What's Islamic for family, Marshall?" Zack wondered.

"Hell if I know," Marshall chuckled. "Look it up. Gotta go. See you in two days."

"Marshall!" yelled Zack, concerned Marshall had disconnected.

"Yeah, Zack?"

"What do you think?"

"About what?"

"What do you think the judge is going to do?" *This is like pulling teeth. I hate lawyers!*

"I know what he should do and what the George Farhad I know would do," Mann cautioned.

"What's that?"

"The attempt to oust naturalized citizens because of the criminal behavior of their child is unconstitutional. This is especially so since Arya has been cleared of all charges."

"So, what's the problem?"

"I don't know what political pressure is being applied, positive or negative," Marshall posited.

"Positive or negative?" Zack was confused. "Maybe I'm naïve, but I don't get your drift."

"Would you agree our president is ethically challenged?"

"Absolutely," Zack blurted.

"Do you think he's capable of bribing a judge?"

"I don't know."

"Do you think Farhad is someone who would accept a bribe?"

"No, absolutely not."

"Do you think John is capable of scandalizing or otherwise hurting a judge?"

"I get your drift, positive or negative. Do you really think a POTUS would do either of those things, even RonJohn?"

"I'm sorry to say I do," Marshall moped.

"I'm sorry to say I agree with you," Zack conceded.

"Judge Farhad has always been a fair judge, principled," Marshall was willing the statement to be true.

"Let's hope his allegiance is to the Constitution and US citizens and not to RonJohn."

"Let's hope. I really have to run, Zack. I'll see you soon."

"Bye, Marsh."

"Bye, Zack."

***

Zack Blake hung up the phone and immediately called Hamid and Riah Khan. Arya picked up the line. *"As-salamu Alaykum,"* she chirped.

"Wa Alaikum As Salaam," Zack beamed.

"Very good, Zack!" Arya cried. "What's up?"

"Are your parents there?"

"No, they're out. I'm kind of watching the little ones who my parents and no one else thinks need watching, if you know what I mean," she joked.

"We've heard from the court. Judge Farhad wants to read his decision in the courtroom the morning after tomorrow," explained Zack.

"Oh, Zack, that is exciting, isn't it?" The idea the decision could be anything but positive did not dawn on this incredible woman.

"If the decision is in our favor, Arya," Zack warned, the voice of impending doom.

"And if it's not?" Arya wondered.

"Not the end of the world—we appeal. Either way, they are not leaving the country any time soon."

"At least there is movement, right?" she offered, always with the positive spin.

"Yes, Arya, movement," Zack rolled his eyes and chuckled. "You'll tell them the news?"

"I will, Zack. Thanks."

"Oh! And Arya, please bring the whole *'aa'ila.*"

"You looked up the word for family? Nice! I'm proud of you!"

"Thank you, my dear. I'm proud of me, too," Zack boasted. "I'll see you guys in a couple of days."

"We'll be there. And Zack?"

"Yes, Arya?"

"From the bottom of my heart, thanks for everything you have done for my family!"

"You're welcome, from the bottom of mine. See you soon."

Chapter Fifty-One

Judge Farhad's courtroom had never been as crowded as it was on the day he was to read his opinion in the case of the *United States of America v. Hamid and Riah Khan*. The crowd was overwhelmingly Muslim. Men in the gallery wore suits, while the women wore burkas and hijabs. People were talking to each other. The courtroom was abuzz with anticipation. Instead of the usual one or two, *four* court officers stood in the back at the entrance to the courtroom. Members of the press, cameramen, and local and national news cameras lined the back wall. A door opened at the front, just to the right of the bench, and the clerk and stenographer entered and took their appointed seats. The crowd hushed, and an audible buzzer sounded. The clerk rose.

"All rise, Immigration and Naturalization Court is now in session, The Honorable George Farhad presiding!" the clerk shouted. Farhad entered from a similar door on the opposite side of the bench, climbed a couple of stairs, and assumed the bench.

"Please be seated," he requested. "I have called a special session of the Court to issue my opinion in the case of *United States v. Hamid and Riah Khan*. Let me first acknowledge the presence of the parties and their attorneys. Thank you for being here on short notice.

"For the record, I note the large gathering in my courtroom today, as well as a large contingent of the local and national press corps. You are my guests, and I expect you to maintain the dignity and decorum expected in a United States federal courtroom. While the decision is being read, I expect all in attendance to remain quiet and civil.

"This Court is cognizant of the local and national importance of this case. The conclusions of the court are based upon sound applications of fact and the law, and not upon any outside political or public pressure. The role of any judge in a legal dispute is to listen to the facts and apply the law in a fair and just manner to all parties. This is what I've tried to do in this case. Thank you in advance for your anticipated cooperation."

Judge Farhad paused. He peered over his reading glasses and glared out into the gallery. He appeared to scan each and every face in the crowd. Finally, he commanded, "The clerk will call the next case."

The clerk rose. "Calling the case of *United States v. Hamid and Riah Khan!*"

"This is a case of national importance . . ." Farhad began, glasses perched at the end of his nose. He looked down, reading through them in earnest.

"On the one hand, we have a presidential executive order, 14822, entitled 'Protecting Our Nation from Foreign-Born Terrorists.' Our newly elected president sees a 'very serious threat to the security of our nation' and believes he has broad powers, under the Immigration and Nationality Act, to remedy foreign threats to national security and to limit or stop foreigners from entering or staying in the United States.

"On the other hand, we have the rights of foreign-born people, legally in this country, citizens or not, to be allowed to live peaceably, seek education, work, marry, have children, pray, pay taxes, and contribute to our economy, and the great multi-cultural experiment we call America.

"At issue in this proceeding is whether the president, under his aforementioned powers created under the Act, has the right to deport naturalized US citizens because of these national security concerns.

"To rule on the government's petition, the Court must consider several factors, including whether the government has shown a likelihood to succeed on the merits in the 6th Circuit Court of Appeals, the degree of hardship to either party caused by a grant or denial of the petition, the impact of the decision upon other foreign-born citizens or non-citizens legally present in the country, and the public safety and public interest in approving or denying the petition. The Court assesses these factors even though this is a case of first impression. The executive order is new, and, to the Court's knowledge, this is the first test of its validity and constitutionality. As such, the Court is mindful that there are untested, sensitive, and important concerns on both sides of this issue.

"By way of background, the president issued Executive Order 14822 citing terrorist attacks that took place in New York City on September 11, 2001, the San Bernardino, California, attacks of December 2, 2015, and the Orlando Nightclub shootings of June 12, 2016, among others. He argues these three events give him 'emergency' authority to act for the national public safety.

"The government argues the United States must ensure those entering or already admitted into this country do not bear hostile attitudes toward the United States and its founding principles. The government further argues deteriorating conditions in the countries affected by the order due to war, strife, disaster, or civil unrest increase the likelihood foreign-born terrorists will use any means possible to enter the United States or recruit foreign-born citizens or foreign-born people who are already here, whether legally or illegally.

"The executive order in question makes numerous changes to the status quo, which are already a matter of record and will not be mentioned here today. The impact of the order was immediately felt all over the country—indeed, all over the world. People received deportation orders. Visas were canceled, preventing thousands of travelers from boarding airplanes bound for the United States or causing a denial of entry upon arrival.

"At issue here is the deportation petition of two naturalized citizens. For grounds, the government indicates a particular family member of defendants was charged with a serious criminal act and, therefore, subjected responsible family members, regardless of current status, to deportation by virtue of the order.

"The defendants argue the order violates the 1st and 5th Amendments of the Constitution, the INA, the Religious Freedom Restoration Act, and the Administrative Procedures Act. They further argue this order was not intended to protect the public from terrorist attacks but was instead intended to remove and ban all Muslims from the United States, a promise our new president made on the campaign trail. As such, say the defendants, the executive order is overboard, illegal and unconstitutional, and the government's petition must be denied. Oral argument was heard. Both sides filed briefs, as did other interested parties, filing *amicus curiae*. This brings us to today's hearing and my ruling.

"The petitioner has standing because of its assertion the public safety is in danger, and quieting this danger requires emergency action. The defendants must show legal and constitutional violations, as well as particularized hardships caused by application of the order to their personal status and situation. Since it could be argued we live in dangerous times, this Court will acknowledge, in certain applications of this order, standing to protect the public at large has been established.

"The defendants, by virtue of their long-standing status as naturalized citizens, the fact their family members are United States-born citizens, and the order means uprooting their lives and separating them from family, including underage children, have made a showing the order would cause irreparable harm. Thus, as previously stated, the Court must weigh these competing interests, the law, and the Constitution as they apply to this case.

"The government argues the president has 'unreviewable authority' to alter the status of any immigrant or citizen, legal or illegal, and as such, is immune from judicial control. The Court feels compelled to dispel this notion here and now. Although our system has long given deference to the various political branches on issues of national security and immigration, no court, including our Supreme Court, has ever held our courts lack authority to review executive actions in those areas to assure compliance with the United States Constitution.

"To the contrary, the Supreme Court has consistently rejected the notion the executive or legislative branches have unreviewable authority over issues relating to immigration. There is no precedent to support this claimed unreviewability, which is contrary to the fundamentals of our system of separation of powers. In our system, it is the role, no, the *duty* of the judiciary to interpret our laws and the constitutionality of those laws. Sometimes that duty requires the resolution of litigation challenging the constitutional authority of the other two branches. This Court strongly believes this is such a case.

"This is still true, even when the proposed presidential action raises concerns about national security. While this Court may owe deference to presidential policy on immigration and national security, it cannot be questioned the federal judiciary has the authority to adjudicate constitutional challenges to executive action.

"Applying this analysis to the facts of this case, this Court concludes the government has failed to meet its required constitutional request. The hardship to the defendants, coupled with the government's complete failure to link these defendants to *any* type of terrorist activity, the sponsorship of or even the *hint* of advocacy for terrorist activity, is fatal to the government's case. There are no public safety or national security concerns in adjudicating the status of peace-loving, law-abiding *citizens* of these United States, whether born here or born in foreign lands.

"This Court also rules 14822 violates the 1st and 5th Amendments as they relate to religious discrimination. The 5th Amendment prohibits the government from depriving individuals of "life, liberty, or property, without due process of law." This Court is not persuaded executive orders expelling foreign-born citizens of this country or aliens legally present here pass the 5th Amendment's stated test. The Court further notes, contrary to the government's argument, the 5th Amendment Due Process clause applies to all 'persons' within the United States, including aliens. In this case, the Court does not reach that issue because the defendants are United States *citizens.*

"The 1st Amendment prohibits any "law respecting an establishment of religion." A law that has a non-secular, religious purpose violates the 1st Amendment. In this case, the president limited all actions executively ordered in 14822 to citizens of certain Muslim countries. His verbiage targets and specifically addresses *Muslims*, and his public speech has referenced a '*Muslim* purge' and a '*Muslim* ban.' Official action targeting religious conduct for distinct treatment is unconstitutional.

"The government argues combating terrorism is an urgent objective of the highest order. This Court agrees with the government and the president. However, the government is required to establish a two-prong approach when attempting to implement policies intended to achieve the stated objective. First, there must be a terrorist threat. Second, the person or persons the government is targeting must be shown to be responsible for that threat. In other words, the government must demonstrate it is applying its primary objective to people who are actually a threat to national security.

"In the Court's opinion, as we apply the standard to *this case only*, the government has failed on both counts, especially the second one. Furthermore, the government has failed to demonstrate any irreparable injury whatsoever will result to the public if these citizens are not deported. In fact, even giving the government the benefit of the doubt, its stated reason for the deportation petition, the parents' breeding of a dangerous person, is now moot, because the child in question has been cleared of all charges. The mention of three separate terrorist acts committed in this country is specious at best, and the parties hereto have no relation whatsoever to those incidents or anyone involved in them. Their link, if any, is that their religion is Islam. That link alone violates the 1st Amendment.

"Obviously, our government cannot immunize this country from a terrorist attack. There is no certainty a terrorist won't slip into the country despite legitimate and constitutional screening processes. The countries subject to 14822 are countries of concern, ones where there have been terror-related issues. However, our president seems to believe being born in a country listed in 14822 brands you a terrorist. With no evidence whatsoever, the president believes ISIS has now infiltrated the consciousness of foreign-born citizens from the 14822 countries, and they are more likely to engage in terrorism. There is not only no evidence to support this belief, but it is also rank speculation.

"All states in this union receive federal aid under the Refugee Act provided aliens are accepted without regard to race, religion, nationality, sex, or political opinion. As far as this Court knows, the state of Michigan has not refused to accept this federal aid.

As such, the state of Michigan may not reject or deport foreign-born citizens or aliens of other status based upon the criteria prohibited in the Act. Fabricated fear that immigrants from the subject countries will breed terrorists, or worse, create a potential for terrorism, is not an appropriate standard for review of status.

"The government further alleges certain Yemeni refugees are, in fact, terrorists posing as refugees. However, the government makes this blanket allegation with no support, and further, fails to demonstrate any one of these Yemeni refugees has *ever* committed an act of terrorism in the United States. In fact, while the order refers to certain terrorist incidents, those incidents were committed, in some cases, by people who came here from countries not on 14822's list.

"Imagine what the public outcry would be if the president stated he didn't wish Blacks or Jews to settle in the United States, not because they're Jewish or black, but because he is afraid of them. Since his motivation is fear, not race or religion, he is not discriminating. That rationale, as fictional President Andrew Shepard declared in the movie *The American President*, would make him the 'President of Fantasyland.'"

The gallery broke out into spontaneous laughter and applause at Farhad's 'Fantasyland' comment. The judge pounded his gavel and demanded order in the court. The clerk and court officers began to circulate through the gallery in an attempt to maintain decorum. The people were on the edges of their seats with anticipation. The judge continued reading his opinion.

"In conclusion, for all the reasons set forth in this opinion, and based on precedents and statutes cited in the written version of this opinion, President John's Executive Order #14822 is hereby declared unconstitutional, the request for the relief sought is denied, and the Petition for an Order of Deportation against Hamid and Riah Khan is hereby dismissed."

The gallery again erupted in cheers and applause. The judge repeatedly pounded his gavel and shouted for order. He was not finished. Court officers escorted people out of the courtroom. The judge pounded the gavel and threatened further evictions. The crowd began to calm, but a permanent buzz filled the crowded courtroom. Judge Farhad concluded his remarks.

"This Court offers its deepest apologies to the Khans and their family members. The president's vision of America is not the America my grandparents immigrated to. It is not the America Hamid and Riah Khan immigrated to. We are better than this. I will sign an order, Mr. Mann, do you have an order?"

"I just happen to have one handy, Your Honor. May I approach?" Marshall Mann reveled.

"You may."

Mann approached the bench, and the judge executed the order. Mann turned to his clients, Zack Blake, Arya Khan, and the rest of the gallery, as he hoisted the signed order into the air for all to see.

"The Constitution lives!" he exclaimed.

The gallery again stood and cheered, shrieking and applauding. Judge Farhad pounded his gavel and shouted: "Order in the court!" but to no avail. He lifted his gavel to hammer again, stopped himself, smiled, and quietly eyed the stenographer. She gazed back at him, grinning, straining to hear his words. He mouthed the words, "Court is in recess," smiled, and left the bench.

Reporters clamored for interviews with the lawyers and the Khans. Photographers began to take pictures of the courtroom, the lawyers, and the participants. Pandemonium erupted in an ordinarily sedate and solemn federal courtroom. The four officers opened the courtroom doors and started ushering the press and the camera people out. Then they went to work on the spectators and the parties. Court was in session in other courtrooms in the building, and the officers were attempting, with limited success, to restore order and keep noise to a minimum.

Doors began to open in other courtrooms on the same floor. People spilled into the hallway, trying to determine what all the excitement was about, then joined in, whether they understood what they celebrated or not.

Officers in other courtrooms began to bar exit from other courtrooms in an effort at crowd control. All officers were talking on walkie-talkies, communicating crowd status with each other. Elevators to the ground floor were consistently filled to capacity, and people waited nearly an hour to finally exit onto Fort Street.

When the Khans, their family, and their attorneys finally exited the building, press, news, television, radio, and social media reporters were waiting for them. Reporters hurled a barrage of questions. Family members and attorneys patiently stood their ground, took questions, and did their best to answer all questions.

"Mr. and Mrs. Khan! Congratulations! How do you feel at this moment? You have made history here today!" shouted one reporter.

"We are elated!" a happy Hamid Khan retorted. "I want to thank my family, my lovely wife, and especially my daughter Arya, for their sacrifices to this important cause. We did not seek this publicity. We are simple people who have led simple lives until American-born terrorists bombed our mosque, killed the bomber, and then, like the cowards they are, tried to set our daughter up as the perpetrator.

"We thank Judge George Farhad for his well-reasoned opinion and our attorneys, Marshall Mann and Zachary Blake, for believing in us and for their brilliant advocacy. We also wish to thank the Dearborn Police, especially Lieutenants Jack Dylan and Shaheed Ali, for working hard to rectify a travesty in justice, and for hunting down the perpetrators of terror against our community."

"Mr. Mann!" shouted another reporter. "Were you surprised by the judge's ruling?"

"Surprised? No, not really. Judge Farhad is a constitutional scholar, has always been a fair jurist, and we were quite confident he would be fair in this case. Still, from a purely political perspective, his decision was courageous.

"These are strange times in our country, and there is significant political pressure being applied to our judiciary by people in powerful positions. We have three branches of government in this country for a reason. Judge Farhad alluded to that important fact in his decision. This is a constitutional *democracy*, not a dictatorship. Unchecked power, even if well-intentioned, is the reason the geniuses that founded our democracy set it up the way they did. On behalf of the Khan family and my colleague and friend Zachary Blake, who brought me into this case, thank you, Judge Farhad, for your commitment to the Constitution."

"Arya! Arya Khan!" shouted another. "How are you doing? Has life returned to normal for you since your ordeal?"

Arya hesitated. She did not expect the question. "I'm fine," she gushed. "Thanks to all these wonderful people." She nodded at the attorneys and her parents. "I'm doing well. I have a ways to go, but everything in time."

The questions continued for an hour or so, and the family and attorneys very patiently answered all questions directed at them. This was discussed before making the trip downtown. Marshall and Zack wanted to put a sense of family in front of the American people, human faces, and human voices to the Muslim side of senseless terror and tragedy. After all, Muslims are the ethnic group most targeted by those we refer to as 'terrorists.'

After the attorneys and clients vacated the scene, "talking head" attorneys, former federal judges, national security experts, current and former legislators, court watchers, and constitutional scholars were interviewed. All, regardless of party affiliation, praised the decision and the judge's bravery in the face of significant political pressure. Detroit and Dearborn were in the national spotlight, and those now basking in the limelight declared Southeastern Lower Michigan to be a shining example of democracy at its best.

Chapter Fifty-Two

Three days after Judge Farhad's decision was issued in the Khan case, the judge's private line rang in his chambers. He'd been expecting and dreading this call.

"Judge George Farhad, how may I help you?"

"Hello, George, Geoffrey here. Will you hold for the president?"

"Uh, yes, I will." Farhad was shocked the president himself wanted to speak with him. He waited patiently until the line clicked.

"Farhad?" the president blustered.

"Yes, Mr. President?" Farhad attempted to be deferential.

"Ronald John, here," the president huffed, as if Farhad didn't know who was on the line.

Farhad repeated, "Yes, Mr. President?" Farhad began to tremble with pent-up anger and frustration. That this man was President of the United States made Farhad's blood boil.

"I know Parley's been talking with you. I wanted to discuss your recent decision if you don't mind."

"I don't mind at all, sir. The opinion speaks for itself, though," Farhad contended, cognizant of the power of the man on the other end of the line.

"It sure does," the president retorted. "I'm wondering if you would be willing to revisit the decision, call for a rehearing or something. National security is at stake, after all."

"There is no precedent for that kind of thing, Mr. President. Besides, I have made it clear that, in my opinion, there are no national security issues in play in this case."

"George . . . May I call you George? You may call me Ron."

"You may certainly call me George, Mr. President," Farhad deferred.

"George, if you don't do something and do it quickly, I am going to have to embarrass you in the 6th Circuit Court of Appeals," the president threatened.

"With all due respect, Mr. President, I don't think you have a prayer of overturning my decision. In fact, in the interests of our nation, its governing principals, and out of respect for the office of the president, I encourage you to let this go or risk further embarrassing our country, yourself, and your office. Executive Order 14822 is blatantly unconstitutional, and you have no chance of overturning my ruling." Farhad lectured the president. All pretense of respect was dropped.

"We'll see about that, Farhad. I heard you were an arrogant son of a bitch, but I had no idea how arrogant," RonJohn roared.

"I'm sorry you feel that way, sir. I am hanging up now, sir. You may be president, but I am a federal judge, and my power, like yours, emanates from the Constitution. That blessed document created three separate branches of government to protect our citizens from the likes of you, Mr. President. Goodbye and good luck, sir. I have a lot of work to do."

"I am going to crush you, Farhad! You will rue the day you tried to cross me," President John exploded.

"Again, sir, I am sorry you feel that way. This decision was based on the facts and the application of the law to the facts. It was in no way meant to cross you or disrespect you."

"'President of Fantasyland' is not disrespect?" the president bristled.

"An unfortunate quote, Mr. President. Originally, I regretted using it. I almost deleted it. After this conversation, I'm pleased I didn't. Whether I respect you or disrespect you is beside the point. The decision was an easy one, constitutionally sound, and I do not regret it one bit."

"You will live to regret it, Farhad," the president threatened.

"Time will tell, Mr. President. I believe it is you who will live to regret attempting to deport lawfully constituted citizens of the United States from our great country. Hopefully, other federal judges will rule in kind and not bend to your will or to your special brand of intimidation."

"I look forward to proving you wrong and making a fool out of you, Farhad."

"I shall look forward to the making of a fool, sir," Farhad quipped. He was tired of this nonsense, president or not. "Goodbye, sir."

The phone clicked in George Farhad's ear. The president had hung up. *No hello, no goodbye, just fuck you,* Judge George Farhad reflected. *What a dick!*

Epilogue

Several months later, the trial of Benjamin Blaine and several co-conspirators and perpetrators began in Wayne County Circuit Court. Judge David Grinder maintained jurisdiction. Lawrence Bialy was the prosecutor.

The case was already solid, with eyewitness testimony given by various police officers, Arya Khan, and other witnesses. Arya's testimony was highly anticipated by the press and the public and provided the most interesting moments of the trial. Lawrence Bialy astutely guided her through direct examination:

"Ms. Khan, how was it you happened to be at the scene of the crime on the day in question?" Bialy interrogated, setting the table, so to speak.

"I was quite concerned the Dearborn Police were not going to vigorously pursue the mosque bomber or bombers. I was concerned about anti-Muslim bias. I went to visit with Lieutenant Ali. That's him, over there." She smiled and pointed to Shaheed Ali, who smiled back. Arya continued:

"I wanted his assurance those responsible for desecrating our holy place were being aggressively pursued, and the police were confident in solving the crime."

"Please continue," Bialy prodded, reluctant to lead the witness.

"He assured me the case was solvable, and there was an active investigation with several warm leads. He got a phone call and left his desk for a few minutes. I . . . uh . . . I . . ." Arya stammered and hung her head, reluctant to continue.

"You what, Ms. Khan?" Bialy pressed.

"Well . . . I . . . saw a document on Lieutenant Ali's desk. I looked around; no one was watching me. I decided to look at the document," she admitted, embarrassed.

"And what, if anything, did you do next?"

"I looked at the document. The police had a suspect. His picture was there, along with his name and two addresses."

"And then?"

"I decided to follow the suspect, a man named Keith Blackwell. I found him at an address on Schaefer, one of the addresses on the document. Subsequently, I followed him to his home on Orchard." Her voice was becoming less tentative, gaining strength as she continued.

"When he got home, his front door was already open. He looked around the neighborhood like, 'what's going on, here?' Then, he went into the house. While he was inside, an older man came from behind the house and climbed on the porch, waiting for Mr. Blackwell."

"What did this man look like?" Bialy coaxed, slowly taking her through the nightmare.

"He was older, perhaps late 70s, early 80s. He wore an old leather jacket with a distinctive logo on it, worn jeans, and a diamond stud earring in one ear. He had tattoos. I specifically noticed a swastika tattoo on his neck. He had scraggly, long, unkempt hair and a flowing white/grey beard."

"Do you see the man in the courtroom today, Ms. Khan?"

"He's cleaned up a bit, but that's him, over there." She pointed at Benjamin Blaine, sitting at the defense table, glaring at Arya Khan. Suddenly, Blaine jumped up from his seat and advanced, malevolently, at Arya Khan.

"You lying camel jockey, fucking bitch! I'm gonna fucking kill you!" He screamed. Court officers stepped in, grabbed the old biker, and restrained him. As he sat down, chained to a chair and to the defense table, he warned, "Sleep with one eye open, camel baby. We're coming for you."

Judge Grinder admonished Blaine that further outbursts would result in his removal from his own trial. A short recess was taken, and court continued after a 10-minute break.

"You've identified the defendant, Benjamin Blaine, as the man on the porch, Ms. Khan. What, if anything, happened next?" Bialy prompted. Bialy continually inserted the words "if anything" into his questions to avoid the assumption that something had, indeed, happened. An assumption of activity would make the question leading and improper.

"Mr. Blaine had a huge knife in his hand. I wanted to do something . . . get out of the car . . . scream . . . but I was, I'm not sure how to describe the feeling, paralyzed, with shock and fear. Before I could do or say anything, Mr. Blackwell came out of the house and Mr. Blaine came from his left side and plunged the knife into his stomach. Mr. Blaine jumped off the porch and ran away the way he'd come. Mr. Blackwell slumped against the house and fell down onto the porch landing. It was horrible!" Arya buried her head in her hands. A court officer handed her a tissue. She wiped her eyes and nose and composed herself. Bialy waited patiently until she was ready to continue.

"And, so we're clear, Ms. Khan, is the person who stabbed Mr. Blackwell sitting in the courtroom today?"

"He is, that's him over there." Arya confidently and defiantly pointed at Benjamin Blaine.

"Bitch!" Blaine shrieked. He tried to rise, shaking his chains violently. "Fucking camel jockey whore! I'll get you for this!" He bounced his chair up and down.

"Court officers! Remove the defendant from my courtroom. He is in contempt!" Judge Grinder ordered, pounding his gavel.

"You want to see contempt? I'll show you contempt! No fucking kike will judge me!" Blaine screamed, as officers picked up his chair and carried him, yelling, kicking and jostling, chains rattling, out of the courtroom.

Judge Grinder ordered another short recess. When court continued, the court-appointed defense attorney registered an objection to resuming the trial with this jury, as if Blaine's outburst never happened. He demanded a mistrial and argued the defendant could not get a fair trial in front of this jury after his violent, anti-Islam, anti-Semitic rant. The judge almost laughed out loud as he denied the motion.

"By the standard you propose, sir, every defendant would rant and rave in front of the jury and blurt out racial and ethnic slurs in a rather transparent attempt to obtain a mistrial. Your client chose to behave this way in front of the jury. This Court will not reward him for his own abhorrent behavior. Motion for a mistrial is denied."

The judge brought the jury back into the courtroom and apologized for the defendant's behavior and for the delay in proceedings. He further explained the trial would continue without the defendant present. Judge Grinder admonished the jury, not to ignore the defendant's outburst—that was impossible—but to disregard it as evidence, the defendant committed the charged crime. Blaine's courtroom antics, however offensive, did not excuse the prosecutor's burden to prove him and his co-defendants guilty beyond a reasonable doubt.

Arya completed her spirited testimony. The young defense attorney conducted a vigorous and discomforting, cross-examination, but Arya stood her ground. One poignant moment in Arya's testimony exemplified the defense attorney's frustration during cross-examination. The strategy was to demonstrate the witness was biased against the defendants. The argument could have been effective with someone other than Arya Khan.

But in *this* case and *this* witness, the strategy backfired. The defense attorney attempted to suggest Arya hated Benjamin Blaine and the other defendants because they were white supremacists and anti-Muslim bigots. Arya whimsically acknowledged the attorney correctly labeled Blaine and his colleagues as bigots. However, she did not, nor should the jury, hold prejudice against them for their views. Arya further reminded the youthful lawyer she tried to save the life of Keith Blackwell, another member of Blaine's group.

Making the case airtight were the plea bargains entered into by the Cronin's and numerous TCC members who found consciences when facing life in prison without the possibility of parole. Their testimony sealed the deal, and, after a 4-week trial, all defendants were convicted on every count. A week later, Judge Grinder issued maximum sentences to every defendant who did not enter a pre-trial plea. There were automatic appeal rights, but for all practical purposes, the convictions and sentences ended TCC Michigan and placed all of its members in prison for life.

***

There were also interesting developments in another legal matter involving the Khan family. President John appealed Judge Farhad's decision. The president called a press conference and lambasted Farhad as a radical Muslim sympathizer, and vowed justice would prevail in the 6th Circuit Court of Appeals. National Security concerns, argued the president, trumped the 1st and 5th Amendments and gave the president "unbridled power." Attorney Geoffrey Parley handled oral argument in the 6th Circuit.

The three-judge panel consisting of two Republican appointees and one Democratic appointee directed pointed questions at the Attorney General, questioned his understanding of the Constitution, and essentially invited him to revisit his constitutional law class in law school. Shortly after oral argument, the panel issued a unanimous opinion affirming Judge Farhad's decision and going out of its way to criticize the administration's policies relating to Muslim immigrants and Muslim immigration.

The panel also singled out the president for scathing criticism, describing him as an "Islamophobic megalomaniac" in the opinion. If the appeal was filed for the purpose of embarrassing Judge Farhad, it had the opposite effect. Farhad was hailed as a constitutional hero, and the president was exposed to ridicule not seen in Washington since the days of Nixon and Watergate.

President John, never one to take a hint, appealed the decision to the United States Supreme Court. He announced the appeal at another of his infamous and threatening press conferences. In this one, he threatened to expose the bias and abuse of power demonstrated by the 6th Circuit panel. He challenged the Supreme Court, inviting the justices to "grow a set." The Supreme Court denied leave to appeal, ending the case of *United States v. Khan*. The Supreme Court's decision to deny leave prompted another celebration in Dearborn.

***

After the Court of Appeals and the Supreme Court's public denunciation of President John's deportation policies, the president's approval ratings took a sharp nosedive. He never regained the popularity or mainstream populace support that swept him into office. Numerous legislators attempted impeachment proceedings, but his political power was severely weakened. He became a relative non-factor in Washington. Politicians on both sides of the aisle decided their re-election prospects were more important than the president's, and they chose to get off his bandwagon. A bipartisan decision was made to permit Ronald John to ride out his presidency, but it was a foregone conclusion he would not win re-election.

***

The Dearborn-based Mosque of America was rebuilt with the help of the multi-cultural community and national contributions. Its grand re-opening was, coincidentally, exactly one year from the date of the dismissal of all charges against Arya Khan. A gala event marked its re-opening, and religious leaders of all faiths, from all over the country, were in attendance.

The guests of honor were Imam Baqir Ghaffari, Arya, Hamid and Riah Khan, Marshall Mann, Zachary Blake, and various members of the Dearborn Police Department, especially members of the mosque task force. Rabbi Joey and other members of the Interfaith Council were also in attendance. Imam Ghaffari publicly addressed and praised the generous offers of their own houses of worship as temporary sanctuaries for Muslim worship while the Dearborn mosque was rebuilt. Another special tribute and prayer were delivered to the fallen SWAT team members whose families were in attendance to witness this shining example of multi-cultural unity their loved ones died to protect and defend.

Arya's date for the event was Shaheed Ali. The two had been seeing each other for eight months. All who knew them could tell they were falling in love. The grand re-opening event was a smashing success and a soothing coming together for a once broken, healing community.

When the event was over, friends and family embraced with broad smiles and tears of joy. Arya and Shaheed decided to walk home, alone, together. They stopped along a promenade, holding hands, kissing, and gazing into each other's eyes. It was a beautiful early summer evening. Endless stars and a bright full moon lit up the sky. A horrible year in which faith was tested and justice was betrayed transitioned into a new year, one filled with the joyful and tangible rebirth of love, justice, faith, and, as Allah willed it, *salaam.* Peace.

END

Thank you for reading, and I sincerely hope you enjoyed *Betrayal of Justice*. As an independently published author, I rely on you, the reader, to spread the word. So, if you enjoyed this book, please tell your friends and family, and I would appreciate a brief review on Amazon. Thanks again.

Mark

Join Zachary Blake on his next journey into justice in Betrayal in Blue. Please continue for an excerpt. You can also buy it now from Amazon.

Betrayal in Blue

ATTENTION FREEDOM BROTHERS:
BVI A.M. DB / SARIN CAMEL-COP OP
DARK WEB ONLY
—SUPREME WHITE KNIGHT

Noah Thompson rushed into the office of Captain Jack Dylan and handed him the message, direct from a search of the dark web.

"Sarin in Dearborn? Are you shitting me?" Jack pounded his desk; his morning coffee spilled all over the burglary file he had been studying. Coffee was everywhere, flowing across the desk and dripping onto the floor. Jack didn't notice; he was staring at the two-sentence message.

"What do we know, Noah?"

"We don't have any details, Jack," Noah advised. Thompson was Dearborn PD's technology guru. "What you see is all we have. We've decided that DB, together with 'camel-cop,' means that Dearborn, cops, and Muslims are the principal targets; this is probably some sort of revenge plot for the Blaine situation."

"We can't take this lightly, Noah. We need to gather the team immediately."

***

The men around the table became quiet as they absorbed the news. They were an elite unit of Dearborn Michigan police officers, a task force that had achieved some notoriety for bringing down a group of white supremacists after one member had bombed the local mosque and an Islamic museum. In the process, the task force exonerated and rescued Arya Khan, a young Muslim woman falsely accused of murdering the mosque bomber and who had, later, been held hostage by these homegrown terrorists.

Their leader was Benjamin Blaine, head of the "The Conservative Council" and an icon/exemplar for numerous, similar groups. After their capture, trials, and various plea bargains, Blaine and seventeen others were now serving multiple life sentences in a Michigan prison.

"What do we know about Sarin gas? How is it released? What kind of damage does it cause?" Jack Dylan's mind was racing as he addressed his elite group of cops.

"According to my limited internet research, Sarin was developed by the Germans in 1938. No surprise there, I guess," Noah snorted.

"Go on . . ."

"It has been associated with acts of terror in the past, as you probably know. There was the Japan subway attack in 1995, twelve deaths, fifty injuries, and five thousand afflicted with temporary blindness of some sort."

"Keep going, Noah," prompted Shaheed Ali, Jack Dylan's right-hand man. Shaheed was lieutenant on the task force and its only Muslim. He and Arya Khan had become "an item" following her rescue. Their relationship was the talk of the task force. Shaheed refused to provide the level of prurient detail that his nosy and obnoxious colleagues were interested in, which caused them to be more curious and more obnoxious. Such was life in the brotherhood in blue.

"It was used more recently in Syria last April, where more than ninety civilians were killed by the Syrian air force rockets of Bashar al-Assad. United Nations weapons inspectors have confirmed this incident. This stuff is lethal, guys. Sarin is a clear, colorless, tasteless liquid; exposure to as little as a couple of drops of it in liquid form might cause death. It is extremely volatile, turns to gas at room temperature, and can penetrate the skin. It attacks the nervous system, over-stimulating nerves that control muscle and gland functions. Sarin is almost thirty times deadlier than cyanide, if you can believe that.

"A victim might inhale or ingest it or might be exposed to it through skin or eye contact. It can remain on an affected person's clothing for thirty minutes or so, which will not only expose that person but all the people he or she comes in contact with for that period." Noah stopped and surveyed the room. His colleagues were digesting the information, in stunned disbelief.

"What happens to someone who is exposed?" Shaheed wondered.

"The victim will first experience a runny nose, chest tightness, and eye problems. After those initial symptoms, the person becomes nauseous and begins to drool as he or she loses muscle control in the mouth and throat. The next progression is full-fledged vomiting, loss of body functions, perhaps twitching, shaking, and jerking. Finally, the victim chokes, convulses, and dies from asphyxiation. The whole thing is over within minutes of exposure," Noah grumbled.

Jack rose and began to pace around the room, thinking, indifferent to the presence of the others, virtually ignoring them, muttering to himself. He was a distinguished-looking middle-aged man who was graying at the temples. Being a no-nonsense cop, he took this threat very seriously. Because of Arya Khan, Shaheed Ali, and the events of last year, Jack had become a better cop, someone more aware of racism and bigotry in his community, and someone who the citizens well respected. Suddenly, he stopped pacing and sat down at the head of the table, eyeballing his colleagues.

"These internet ramblings are obviously not enough to do anything with at the moment." Turning to Noah, he ordered, "Noah, you and your team continue to monitor all internet activity. We need more detail. Shaheed, I want you to investigate all white supremacist or nationalist groups in the area. I know the activity among such groups has been increasing over the past year. Look for which groups are most active in the Detroit Metropolitan area and which have close ties with Blaine and The Conservative Council. We are still recovering from the last incident. We have to stop this plot if that's what it is; we have to stop it cold before it gains any traction."

"Got it, boss," Shaheed acknowledged.

"And by the way, Shaheed, get together with Noah and investigate whether or not the threat may be foreign rather than domestic. Sarin may have been invented in Germany, but its recent use has been limited to Middle Eastern countries and

Islamic terrorists. The noise on the web could be a smokescreen for all we know. Better to be safe than sorry."

"Understood."

Jack turned from his men and gazed out onto Michigan Avenue. It was a dreary spring day. The nasty weather mirrored how he was feeling after hearing the news of another potential terrorist attack in his beloved city.

The leaves on the trees were in bloom. Dark clouds still blanketed the sky; a storm had only just passed. Jack could hear an occasional angry horn as drivers weaved in and out of stop-and-go traffic.

Commuters with their morning cups of coffee hurried along the sidewalks and streets of the city. The enveloping fog was eerie, like a tightening vice, given the possibility of a Sarin gas attack in Dearborn proper. Was the fog a sign of evil about to descend on the city? Jack was startled out of his intense, trancelike state by Shaheed Ali.

"Boss? Jack? Earth to Jack?" Shaheed jested.

Jack shook himself back into the meeting and immediately turned to Andy Toller, a new cop on the task force. His primary talent was research and operational planning. Andy had replaced Asher Granger, once a good cop and a trusted friend. Granger, it turned out, was more invested in the white nationalist agenda than being a loyal officer of the law. Ultimately, Benjamin Blaine had killed him after Asher attempted to betray Blaine.

"Andy," Jack continued, "I need you to get me everything you can on a black-market distribution of chemicals. If someone wanted to smuggle Sarin gas into the city, how would they do it? Where are the obvious and less obvious points of entry? How would they weaponize it? Talk to narcotics officers in all local police departments. Talk to undercover operatives and snitches. I want to get a handle on the situation before making any decisions involving the Feds and Homeland Security. Got it?" Jack was determined, all business.

"Got it, boss. Glad to be here; glad to be of service," Andy confirmed, pleased to be seeing some action and excited to prove himself to Jack and the others.

"Anybody have anything to add?" Jack inquired, looking around the room. Silence.

"Then let's get to work. Sarin...shit! We must stop these guys...again."

The men nodded, stone-faced. Was it really déjà vu all over again?

The Zachary Blake Legal Thriller Series

Betrayal of Faith (Book 1)
Betrayal of Justice (Book 2)
Betrayal in Blue (Book 3)
Betrayal in Black (Book 4)
Betrayal High (Book 5)
Supreme Betrayal (Book 6)

About the Author

Mark M. Bello is an attorney and award-winning legal thriller author. After handling high profile legal cases for 42 years, Mark now treats readers to a front-row seat in the courtroom. His ripped from the headlines Zachary Blake Legal Thrillers are inspired by actual cases or Bello's take on current legal or sociopolitical issues. Mark lives in Michigan with his wife, Tobye. They have four children and 8 grandchildren.

Connect with Mark

Website: https://www.markmbello.com
Email: info@markmbello.com
Facebook: MarkMBelloBooks
Twitter: @MarkMBelloBooks
YouTube: Mark Bello
Goodreads: Mark M. Bello

Subscribe to our mailing list and receive notices of book giveaways and other surprises.

To request a speaking engagement, interview, or appearance, please email info@markmbello.com.

Made in the USA
Monee, IL
25 February 2022

91838742R00177